ALSO BY DAN POPE

In the Cherry Tree

HOUSEBREAKING

A Novel

DAN POPE

SIMON & SCHUSTER

New York London Toronto Sydney New Delhi

Simon & Schuster
1230 Avenue of the Americas
New York, NY 10020

First Simon & Schuster hardcover edition May 2015

SIMON & SCHUSTER and colophon are registered trademarks of Simon & Schuster, Inc.

For information about special discounts for bulk purchases, please contact Simon & Schuster Special Sales at 1-866-506-1949 or business@simonandschuster.com.

The Simon & Schuster Speakers Bureau can bring authors to your live event. For more information or to book an event contact the Simon & Schuster Speakers Bureau at 1-866-248-3049 or visit our website at www.simonspeakers.com.

Manufactured in the United States of America

1   3   5   7   9   10   8   6   4   2

Library of Congress Cataloging-in-Publication Data

Pope, Dan, 1961–
  Housebreaking : a novel / Dan Pope. — First Simon & Schuster hardcover edition.
     pages ; cm
  1. Domestic fiction. I. Title.
  PS3616.O65H68 2015
  813'.6—dc23
                    2014040481

ISBN 978-1-4767-4590-9
ISBN 978-1-4767-4592-3 (ebook)

In memory of Donald Pope

Contents

It was a splendid summer morning and it seemed as if nothing could go wrong.

—John Cheever, "The Common Day"

Prologue

The first day of summer, 2007

AUDREY MARTIN-MURRAY hadn't been back to Wintonbury since she'd graduated from the Goodwin Academy, twenty-five years earlier. In the town center, she recognized only two shops from her prep school days, the hardware store with creaky wooden floors and the stationery shop, where she'd once bought a leather wallet for a boyfriend. All the other storefronts had been transformed into boutiques and restaurants, coffee shops and art galleries, the provinces of the wealthy.

"It's a terrific downtown," her husband said, turning at an intersection.

"I went to high school in this town, remember?"

"They didn't have Crate & Barrel back then. They didn't have Starbucks. All your favorites."

Favorites? Starbucks coffee gave her stomach pains and she hadn't been inside a Crate & Barrel in her life, but she didn't want to argue. Andrew liked arguing; it pleased him, and the more pleasant he became, the more annoyed she got. His good humor was a sort of rebuke to her. *You can be happy*, it said. *Just move to a different place.*

They were looking at houses. Andrew had circled the listings in the real estate flyer, numbering them in his neat hand. He hadn't bothered with anything on the south side of town, which was less wealthy. The north side had one of the best public high schools in the state, known for its music department and high test scores. Emily would have an excellent

1

shot at the Ivy League coming out of a place like Wall High, as Andrew pointed out. "It's ranked higher than most prep schools in the state," he said, "including your beloved Goodwin. That's a thirty-thousand-dollar savings right there."

Audrey restrained herself from mentioning that they'd be taking Emily out of Denton, one of the best schools in the country, for this lark of his. She felt out of sorts. It was barely 9:00 A.M. and she hadn't had breakfast yet. Andrew liked an early start. He'd programmed the open-house addresses into the car's GPS. Her husband was organized, if nothing else. They'd already toured a six-thousand-square-foot architectural eyesore that smelled of glue and drywall, part of a new development called Stonecutter's Crossing. A bulldozer sat on the adjacent lot, cleared down to dirt. "Excellent amenities," Andrew had said during the tour.

"Take a left at the next intersection," announced the GPS device in a fussy voice.

"Is that it?"

There was a Realtor's sign at the edge of the road, festooned with balloons: OPEN HOUSE TODAY.

He consulted his map. "No," he said. "Not on my list."

Audrey wouldn't have programmed the GPS, wouldn't have consulted a real estate flyer, and definitely wouldn't have started out so damn early. She would have just driven into town and followed the roads. *Too much control*, as her drama professor used to say, *is the antithesis of invention.*

Andrew slowed as they approached the property, an old one-story farmhouse at the base of a street that rose toward the mountain in the distance. The house was L-shaped, the clapboard painted barn red with wooden shutters. There was a stone well in the front yard and a weather-beaten split-rail fence around the property, collapsed in a few places. The grass was wildly overgrown, and as they got closer she could see paint peeling and ivy crawling over the windowpanes.

"The Hufnagle house, built in 1807," she said, reading the plaque on the side of the house. "Let's take a look."

"It's not—"

"Forget your stupid list."

"Fine."

He turned in to the gray-pebble driveway. The house seemed out of place in the manically manicured neighborhood, with the lawn overgrown and strewn with a few stray newspapers. Insects hissed loudly in the brush. A rabbit sprang up from the tall grass and ran toward the trees beyond the backyard.

"Nobody's lived here for a long time," she said.

"Probably for good reason. You'd think they could at least mow the lawn for an open house."

They got out of the car and followed the brick walkway to the entrance. The Realtor appeared, a middle-aged woman with dyed blond hair, wearing a pencil skirt. She met them on the stoop, crying, "Early birds get the worm!"

The "Hufnagle" had once been the only house for miles, she told them. On the kitchen table she laid out an early-nineteenth-century town map, framed in glass, and pointed it out: "Hufnagle Farm." The interior hadn't been renovated in fifty years: 1960s refrigerator and stove, worn linoleum, fuse box in the basement. There were only two bathrooms, both relics with claw-foot tubs. The ceilings were crossed with dark oak beams. The Realtor offered coffee and blueberry muffins. She explained that a recluse—an old woman who painted landscapes—had lived alone in the house her entire life. The hardwood floors of her studio were splotched with dabs of color, like a Jackson Pollock. "A pity, those planks," Andrew muttered. After the old woman died, her heirs battled over the estate, and the house fell into disrepair.

"You've got ants," said Andrew cheerfully, gesturing toward some sawdust along the baseboards.

"It's a corner lot," said the Realtor. "Historical register."

"Needs work. Real work, not just a paint job. New roof, new kitchen. I'm surprised they'd put it on the market looking this bad."

"It's a fixer-upper, that's for sure," said the woman, trying to sound chipper.

When they left, the Realtor waved like a beauty queen from the stoop, squeezing out a phony smile.

Back in the car, Audrey said, "Did you see those beams? You can't find wood like that anymore."

Andrew pulled out his handwritten list. "It's cramped."

"No," she said. "It's perfect."

When he didn't answer she grabbed the paper from his hand, balled it up, and tossed it into the backseat. "That's the one I want."

"It's too small, Audrey. It's barely two thousand square feet."

"Would you rather live in that Tyvek McMansion?"

"Yes, I would."

"Well, I won't."

He sniffed, an expression of disapproval, which she considered one of his more irritating habits. "We'd have to do the whole thing over," he said. "You want to do all that work? Deal with contractors? They're all thieves and drug fiends."

"You can pay people for that."

"Let's look at a few more, at least."

A reasonable suggestion, of course, but he wasn't just offering alternatives. She knew him too well. He would wear her down, try to change her mind. "No, Andrew. This move is your brainchild. You're pulling Emily out of school without even thinking—"

"That school's been nothing but trouble for her. You said so yourself. We should've gotten her out of there last year—"

"I'm not looking at any more houses."

He glanced at the information sheet and disclosure forms the Realtor had passed them. "It's not exactly a bargain. And you're talking another hundred grand in renovations."

She glanced out the window. "What does it matter?"

He sighed. "Do me a favor. Stop saying that. You say that all the time. You've got a master's in English literature, you've read more novels than Alex Trebek—"

"Alex Trebek?"

"The *Jeopardy!* guy."

"I know who he is. What makes you think he reads novels?"

"First name that came into my head." He started the car. "You really want this house?"

"Yes."

"Fine. We'll buy it. Happy now?"

She had to stop herself from repeating the words: *What does it matter?* Jobs, houses. Before, when there had been a future, these were primary concerns. The accident had changed that. Everything had changed overnight, their personal 9/11. There was before and then after. Nothing could be the same, although Andrew liked to pretend otherwise.

She noticed the street name on the sign as they backed out of the driveway: Apple Hill Road. Andrew opened his mouth to speak, but the computer voice drowned him out: "You are going the wrong way. Take the next legal U-turn and proceed in the opposite direction."

As they drove off, Audrey glanced up the street at all the white houses and green lawns, the children's toys lying unattended in driveways. Pretty in a sculpted sort of way, but mildly sad. It was an illusion, one that promised happiness indefinitely. But the whole thing could collapse at any moment.

Part One

THE MANDELBAUMS

The last day of summer, 2007

THE NIGHT his wife kicked him out, Benjamin Mandelbaum took the dog and a bag of clothes and drove to his father's house in Wintonbury. It was 10:00 P.M. on a Saturday, the suburban street as quiet as a graveyard. He got out of his car and felt the wind rise, stirring the leaves of the apple tree he'd climbed as a boy. He took the spare key from under the flowerpot and let the dog in ahead of him. The house smelled like mothballs and stale cologne, an old man's lair.

A few minutes later Leonard appeared in his bathrobe at the top of the stairs. "Who's there?"

"It's me, Dad."

"Benjamin? What's going on?"

Yukon rushed up the stairs and sniffed at a stain on Leonard's robe. Benjamin realized that, in all the commotion, he had forgotten to feed the dog its dinner. "I'll be staying over, if that's okay."

"That's fine. That's fine." His father had a habit of saying things twice. "Where's Judy?"

"She's home."

His father's eyes were bloodshot, his face puffy from sleep.

"Go back to bed," said Benjamin. "We'll talk tomorrow."

"There's some tuna salad in the fridge."

In the kitchen, Benjamin filled a bowl with water while the dog went from room to room, inspecting. The refrigerator was practically empty: the bowl of dry tuna, a few brown eggs, mustard and ketchup on the side shelves, lemons and wilted lettuce in the crisper. His father had lost weight since Mom's death, and now Benjamin could see why. In the cold-cuts drawer he found an unopened can of corn. In the freezer, among the frozen vegetables and meats, he found something even odder: a pack of Marlboros with only two cigarettes left. His father didn't smoke. Had he started now, at eighty-four? And why keep them in the freezer?

After Myra's funeral, Benjamin and his sister had tried to convince their father to sell the house and move into a retirement community. They thought it would be good for him: Leonard had always been a social creature; part of his job at the car dealership was going to restaurants and functions, handing out his business card. But Leonard wouldn't hear of it. He kept up the house as if Myra were still alive. It became a shrine of sorts: her clothes still hanging in the closet, her prescription bottles in the medicine cabinet, framed photographs of her in every room. His sole occupation was maintaining everything as she had liked it. He hired landscapers, gardeners, and handymen. It all made Benjamin wonder if he would end up the same way: old, alone, going to bed early, living with the ghosts of his past.

He went into the den and stood before the wet bar. His father always had a fine selection of single malt—not Benjamin's intoxicant of choice, but he'd left his stash of pot in the glove compartment. He poured a Glenlivet and added two ice cubes. His father had excellent taste in the good things—liquor, clothes, shoes. The old man had style, even if he now wore his pants cinched over his navel, shuffling around the house in his slippers. Benjamin eased onto the sofa and found himself exhaling after each sip of scotch, happy to be home.

Home. The word gave him some comfort. Sure, Leonard was eighty-four. But his father would take care of him, even if Benjamin didn't need taking care of. He felt a luxurious heat rising from the liquor, and for the first time in a while he felt like he could breathe easily. Judy's presence had weighed on him for so long. He'd been held accountable for nearly every moment; his cell phone rang ten times a day, a phantom chaperone. Where was he? Did he remember to pick up the dry cleaning? Her prescription? He sighed. Years ago, he'd found it endearing that she wanted their lives so intertwined.

Yukon came into the den and stood before him, panting. "Lie down," Benjamin said. "We're not going anywhere." The dog obeyed, but was up again after a few minutes, padding out to the kitchen, roaming the first floor. Benjamin intended to walk the dog—their nightly ritual—but he dozed off after his third glass of scotch, and Yukon lay in the doorway, head between his paws, watching him. The dog slept, but not deeply. He whimpered throughout the night, unaccustomed to this strange house and its old man's smell.

Outside on the front lawn, a mob of deer nibbled at the arborvitae, silent as ghosts, watchful as criminals. Somewhere deep in the woods, an owl warbled.

THE NEXT MORNING Leonard Mandelbaum came downstairs to find his son snoring on the couch, his hair covering his face. He had a fine head of curly black hair, Benjamin did. Leonard stood for a moment, admiring his son, who looked childlike curled in sleep, his hands tucked under his chin. Leonard saw Benjamin regularly at the office, but it had been a long time since he'd been able to watch his son sleep. Leonard noticed the bottle of scotch and the empty glass on the coffee table. Benjamin had been a beer drinker ever since high school, when his pals would come to the house to play Ping-Pong in the basement. To take up the hard liquor meant something was bothering him. More trouble with Judy, no doubt. It was a shame that they argued so often. Leonard had always liked Judy. She'd helped out with Myra during her illness, staying up nights when the late nurse didn't show. You could always depend on Judy. A fine, sturdy woman. A good mother to the children. And she'd converted too, mainly to please him and Myra. How many gals would do that for their in-laws?

Leonard went into the kitchen to start the coffee and opened the *Hartford Courant* to the obituaries. Each day, it seemed, he knew one of the deceased, usually someone who'd bought a car from him. Leonard Mandelbaum never forgot the name of a good customer.

Today it was Manny Silverman. Above the obituary was a thumb-size photo taken in the 1950s, around the time Leonard had put Manny into his first DeVille. *In lieu of flowers donations may be made to the Dana-Farber Cancer Institute.* Cancer, then. Poor Manny. Leonard had sold him another five Cadillacs over the next fifty years, most recently a top-of-the-line XLR. That had been when? Last year? No, longer than that. He recalled telling Myra about it—dapper old Manny in his seersucker suit, zooming off the lot in a seventy-thousand-dollar convertible.

Leonard went into the front hallway and sat at the mahogany desk, where he made his phone calls and wrote his personal notes and letters to the editor. When his grandchildren visited they treated his black rotary phone like some Ice Age fossil. Fingering the dial, David had once asked, *Does this actually work, Grandpa?*

Leonard took a sheet of his personal stationery from the desk drawer and wrote, *In Memory of Manny Silverman.* He checked the date on his calendar—September 23, 2007—and wrote a hundred-dollar check to the Dana-Farber Cancer Institute. On another sheet of paper, he composed a letter to the editors of the *Wintonbury Gazette.*

Manny Silverman, who died recently, served this community for more than forty years as a dentist of great skill. He filled two pages with remembrances, then concluded: *When we lose a man like Manny Silverman, we lose a small part of the qualities that he stood for: integrity, wisdom, professionalism. We will miss you, Manny.*

He addressed the envelopes, pasted on the stamps, and brought them to the front porch. He checked his watch: not yet 8 A.M. As he put the letters in the mailbox, Benjamin's dog appeared in the doorway, tail slashing.

"Stay," said Leonard, trying to conjure the dog's name. "Stay right there." The dog wanted to go outside and run around, like all dogs, but he was well trained and would not disobey. Benjamin always trained his pets well. So many dogs and cats had come and gone, Leonard could not remember this animal's name. "Good boy," he said. "That's a good boy. Now go sit."

Benjamin would be up soon, and hungry. His son liked raspberry Danish from the Crown Market. He complained that he couldn't find anything as good in Granby. Leonard picked up his keys and his wallet, got into his Escalade, and accelerated out of the driveway.

At the bottom of the street he noticed a few pickup trucks parked outside Eleanor Hufnagle's place, with workmen milling around the yard. The farmhouse had been unoccupied for years, ever since Eleanor collapsed at her ironing board and the postman found her four days later.

The woman had lived to ninety-nine alone in that house. He had one of her oil paintings hanging in his den. *Loss of a great artist,* Leonard had written, then, to the *Wintonbury Gazette.*

At the supermarket, he clipped the curb pulling into the handicap space. His physician had gotten him the permit for his arthritic knees. All those years of running—on the track team at City College, in boot camp in the Navy, then later on the tennis courts at Tumble Brook Country Club—had taken their toll. *You're rubbing bone on bone*, the doctor had told him, and that was exactly what it felt like these mornings, worse in wintertime.

At this hour he had his pick at the bakery. Most days the challah went before noon, no matter how many times he complained to the manager about the shortage. He often had to go without challah or marbled rye if he got there late. And Benjamin was absolutely correct about the quality of the baked goods. You'd have to go to New York City to find a better challah. He picked out a couple of loaves, a few Danish, and a coffee cake. Orange juice, he remembered, which Benjamin drank like water. He examined the cartons in the cooler, feeling the chill of the refrigeration. Was it Tropicana or Minute Maid that Benjamin liked? Pulp or no pulp? There were so many different brands now, so many choices. Reaching for one of the cartons, he lost his grip on the challah, and it fell, followed by the marbled rye. "Dammit," he hissed.

"Let me help you, Mr. Mandelbaum."

Leonard turned to see a middle-aged man, dressed in sweat clothes and a baseball cap like a high school kid. He gathered Leonard's items from the floor and rose to his full height. "It's Dick Funkhouser," he said, smiling.

Leonard took his hand. "I knew your father. A wizard with a nine iron. How's your mother? I haven't seen her at the club lately." Terri Funkhouser, originally from Newark; she'd never lost the accent. Myra hadn't liked her. Said she smelled like cheap perfume.

"She's not a member anymore. Ever since Dad passed."

"I'm sorry to hear that."

The man carried Leonard's goods to the checkout line and placed them on the conveyor belt. Leonard began fishing in his wallet for some cash.

"She doesn't get out of the house very often," said Dick Funkhouser.

"She always speaks fondly of you." He produced a pen and scribbled something onto a scrap of paper. Leonard pulled his reading glasses out of his breast pocket and examined the note: a phone number.

"She'd love to have dinner or see a show. You should call her."

Leonard tucked the slip of paper into his pocket. Why would he call Terri Funkhouser? He hardly knew her. The woman hadn't been a regular presence at the country club or synagogue. Dick Senior had once complained that his wife would rather stay home with a bottle of sherry than go to the Met. *She has low tastes*, he had confided.

"Are you a member of the club?" asked Leonard.

"I'm not much of an athlete," said Dick Funkhouser.

"I see." Leonard remembered now. The son had resigned from the club following the scandal at Funkhouser's Dry Cleaning. After Dick Senior died, the son had ruined the business on bad loans, second mortgages, tax evasions. A shame, that sort of financial mismanagement. Dick Senior had put his life into dry cleaning.

"Let me take the groceries out to your car."

Leonard shook his head. "I'm fine. I'm fine."

Back at the house, he carried the brown bags up the front steps. Benjamin met him at the door. He looked puffy-eyed but otherwise his same boyish self, curly-haired, fit, more handsome than his dad ever was. The girls had always gone wild for Benjamin, as far back as junior high school. Fonzie, some of the gals called him then, on account of the resemblance.

"I've got Danish," he told his son.

AFTER BREAKFAST a car horn blared from the street. Benjamin looked out the kitchen window and saw the familiar red pickup truck pull into the driveway; MARIANI LANDSCAPING, read the faded letters on the side. Two men got out, slamming the doors.

"Who's that?" said Leonard, peering over Benjamin's shoulder.

"No one."

"Are those Judy's brothers? Why are they honking the horn? It's a Sunday morning, for goodness' sake."

"I'll take care of it."

Benjamin went out the front door in his socks. "What's up, guys?"

Anthony, the youngest of the three brothers, glanced at him and went around to the back of the truck and pulled down the tailgate. There was a third brother, currently under house arrest on a DUI charge. In the winter they did snowplowing, and sometimes Lou worked maintenance for a guitar factory in New Hartford.

Anthony pulled a set of golf clubs from the bed of the truck and dumped the bag onto the lawn. A couple of yellow Titleists rolled out of the bag toward his dad's Japanese maple.

"Here's all your shit. Special delivery."

The truck smelled of gasoline and grass clippings. Benjamin peered into the back, seeing a jumble of clothes, luggage, skis, books, DVDs, Rollerblades. Actually, those were his son's Rollerblades. Judy must have gotten confused in her frenzy. He could picture her rifling through the closets in the basement and attic, plucking his possessions from the wreckage of their marriage. How exhilarated she must have felt, purifying herself of him. She'd always liked throwing things out. He noticed random clutter as well. Board games. A black-and-white TV with a broken antenna. Even some of her old clothes. He recognized a French maid's costume, a Valentine's gift from years ago. The brothers tossed it all onto the lawn, a showering of his worldly possessions, old and new. His *Matrix* trilogy hit the grass, and one of the DVDs slipped out of its case and rolled toward the street.

So this was payback.

He had played nice with the brothers all these years, sharing beers at family gatherings, listening to their inane opinions about Bill Clinton and George W. Bush, their crass jokes. He shouldn't have tried so hard. They'd turned against him openly ten years ago, after the blowout with Judy over the Dutch au pair. But they'd never liked him. They were Italians; he was a Jew, and their sister had converted to marry him. Sometimes they'd even called him that to his face as a sort of joke: "the Jew."

Anthony was wearing his usual ripped jeans and T-shirt. He had a closely cropped head with a long, thin string of hair growing from the nape of his neck, like a rat's tail. He was the talker in the family; the other two rarely said a word.

"Twenty years you jerked my sister around," he said.

"You've never been married," said Benjamin. "You don't know what you're talking about."

"No?" He flicked away his cigarette and pulled a pile of clothes on hangers out of the bed of the truck and tossed them onto the driveway. Benjamin noticed his navy blue Brioni on the top of the pile, his best suit. He'd worn it to weddings and parties, never to work. On sale it had cost him eight hundred bucks.

"You ruined her life," said Anthony, stepping close to Benjamin. "That's what she told me this morning. Her exact words."

Benjamin held his gaze, feeling vulnerable in his socks. Both brothers were wearing heavy boots flecked with cut grass. "Yeah, well. She had some things to say about you over the years, believe me."

"Fuck you," said Anthony.

Lou quickly stepped between them. "Cut the high school stuff." He shoved his brother back. "Look," he said to Benjamin. "You got no reason to go back to the house. This is all your junk right here. Judy doesn't want to see you anymore."

"That's the way it's going to be," said Anthony. "Got it?"

Benjamin didn't answer.

The brothers got into the truck and backed out, running over his suit.

Leonard joined Benjamin in the driveway, squinting into the sun. "A shame, throwing around private belongings like garbagemen. You should tell Judy what they did."

Benjamin picked up his suit. There was a tire tread on the front lapel. Maybe the dry cleaner could get it out.

"Judy sent them."

"Not Judy. She wouldn't do that."

"Well, she did."

"She'll cool off. She's a fine woman. A good mother."

Maybe she would cool off, but Benjamin doubted it. *Temper, temper*, he used to lecture, like a schoolmarm, whenever she lost it and started yelling at some slowpoke driver or snippy salesclerk. Maybe she hadn't told her brothers to trash his stuff, but she certainly had packed it up and told them to take it away. Take *him* out of her life.

Benjamin gathered the rest of his clothes, his hands trembling with adrenaline. He was conscious of Franky DiLorenzo, watching from his front lawn next door, a water hose in his hand. Benjamin rubbed the tears from his eyes. It always happened when he felt angry or threatened, ever since he was a child, this sudden welling. He never cried when he was sad, not even when his mother died—not at her funeral, not even the night before her death when she'd told him in a moment of lucidity, *You're my love, Benjamin. You always were.*

A car pulled up on the street. A man in shorts and a Hawaiian shirt got out and strolled up the driveway, pursing his lips. "How much for the skis?" he said.

"What?"

"The skis. What are you asking?"

Leonard and Benjamin stood staring at the man.

"This a tag sale, isn't it?" the man asked.

Benjamin sighed. "Sure." He hadn't gone skiing for five or six years, not since the kids rebelled against weekends in the woods near Okemo with nothing to do, so far from their friends. "Twenty bucks."

The man scratched the back of his neck. "Would you take ten?"

THAT AFTERNOON was the first day of autumn, technically, but it felt more like mid-July, the sky an endless canvas of pale blue, the temperature well into the eighties. After a few trips up and down the stairs, Benjamin felt the sweat dripping down his face and back.

"That's a lousy delivery job."

Benjamin looked up to see Franky DiLorenzo coming across the lawn. Benjamin forced a laugh. "I'll say."

They shook hands. In the silence that followed he became aware of Franky DiLorenzo eyeing his wrinkled slacks and button-down shirt, which he'd worn to work the day before. "A bit of trouble on the home front," Benjamin explained. "I'll be sticking around for a while."

Franky's eyes flashed with interest. "I'm sorry to hear that."

"Part of life, I guess."

Franky DiLorenzo was wearing a T-shirt, shorts, and flip-flops. He wore this same garb into November, sometimes December. He was horseshoe-bald, a bit stooped in the shoulders, and thin as a marathoner, yet he seemed impervious to the elements and he never tired of physical labor. He'd worked as a mechanic for thirty years at a garage in town. Now he spent his days in his yard, mowing, trimming, repairing. He also did chores for Leonard and Betty Amato and other elderly people in the neighborhood—taking out their garbage, fixing what needed to be fixed—and he refused to accept any payment in return. Benjamin considered him a godsend, the way he helped out his father.

"Did you see what's going on at the Hufnagle place?"

"No." Benjamin looked toward the bottom of the street, shading his eyes. He saw a couple of trucks parked in front of the old farmhouse.

"It finally sold," said Franky. "Court-ordered, I heard."

"That house has been empty for a long time."

"Five years almost," Franky said and nodded. "A lawyer bought it, a guy named Andrew Murray. He's about forty-five. He gutted the place—kitchen, bathrooms, wooden floors, central air. A hundred grand in upgrades, minimum."

"Is he going to flip it?"

"No, they just moved in. I met him and his wife a few weeks ago in the yard. She goes by her own name, Audrey Martin. A real pretty lady. They mentioned a seventeen-year-old daughter, but I haven't seen her yet."

"Audrey Martin?" It had been many years, but the name clicked instantly.

"Do you know her?"

"I went to high school with an Audrey Martin. She was in the class ahead of me at Goodwin."

Franky shrugged. "It might be her. She's about your age. They're moving up here from Greenwich. He took a job at a firm in Hartford."

"You're amazing, Franky. Nothing gets by you."

Franky smiled. "Well, I like to keep an eye on the neighborhood, with all the break-ins lately."

"What break-ins?"

"I told your dad, but I guess he forgot to mention it. Somebody's been smashing car windows, stealing things out of garages and toolsheds."

"When did this happen?"

Franky DiLorenzo leaned in close and lowered his voice. "The trouble started last year, about the same time this family moved into a ranch on Lostwood Drive. They're from Texas. The mother's divorced with two teenage boys on her hands. The oldest is seventeen. Billy Stacks. That's the punk. He assaulted some girl in Texas when he was fourteen, I heard. Too young to do jail time. You'll see him riding around the neighborhood on a motor scooter. He's got a shaved head, tattoos all over his arms, wears his pants down below his waist. I got my eye on that kid."

"You think he's the one causing trouble?"

"I can't prove it, but I got my suspicions."

Franky loved conversation, and with time on his hands, he was in no hurry to get back to watering his lawn. He was nearly fifty years old, retired early. He lived in a bedroom above the garage in his mother's house, had lived there his entire life, a room Benjamin had never entered. All the kids Benjamin had known growing up—Mike Cosgrove, Diana Estabrook, Tony Papadakis, Timmy and Albert Amato—had moved away long ago; only Franky DiLorenzo remained, the mainstay, the keeper of the vineyard. Benjamin found it ironic that Franky would be concerned about this neighborhood troublemaker because, in his teen years, Franky himself had been the local delinquent, driving hot rods around town and raising hell at the bowling alley. But after Franky's sister went off to college (rarely to be seen again) and his dad died, Franky had evolved, instantly, as far as Benjamin could recall, into the person they all knew—Franky the dependable, the squire of Apple Hill Road. He went back and forth to work at the garage, year after year. There had been girlfriends, but Franky had never married. Every night he and his mother had sat down to dinner, all those years, and when she died, a decade ago, Franky had remained alone in the house, unchanged, unchangeable.

"How's Len?" asked Franky.

"Same." Benjamin didn't mention the unopened can of corn in the fridge or the pack of cigarettes in the freezer. Sure, Leonard was eighty-four, but he was still living on his own, taking care of himself. He got along fine. "Thanks for everything you've done for him lately."

Franky waved away any credit. "I'm happy to help," he said. "If he needs anything, you just let me know."

"That means a lot to me."

They shook hands, as if finalizing a contract.

BY LATE AFTERNOON Benjamin had hauled the last of his belongings up to his bedroom. Although he'd moved out of his parents' house after high school, his mother and father had never encroached upon his childhood territory; they'd left the bedroom as it had always been—same furniture, same turntable and eight-track player on the desk, same posters thumbtacked to the wall (Elton John in six-inch platform shoes; Farrah Fawcett in her red one-piece). In the past, whenever he came back to visit, it had always pleased him to step into this time capsule, but now, unpacking his clothes and folding them into the dresser and closet, he felt unsettled and anxious. What was he doing back in his single bed, surrounded by these totems of his teenage self?—the baseball cards and field day trophies, the blue ribbons from forty-yard dashes he didn't remember running, the stamp albums, LPs, and textbooks he hadn't touched since high school.

From the bookshelf he pulled down one of his high school yearbooks. The Goodwin Academy was a prep school located on the grounds of a nineteenth-century estate in the woods along the rise of Avon Mountain, less than a mile away. There were seventy-five students in his graduating class, most of them boarders. Benjamin had been one of a handful of day students. Every afternoon he'd taken the bus home after sports period, feeling left out of the rituals and shenanigans that took place in the woods and dorm rooms during the evenings. He had been popular and athletic, a standout on the soccer and lacrosse teams, but he remembered Goodwin primarily as a place of loneliness and longing and missing out.

He turned to the page he was looking for: Audrey Martin's senior photo. She had been one of the senior prefects, the editor of the school newspaper, and cocaptain of the gymnastics team. Her senior photo displayed her sparkly blue eyes and auburn hair, but she had been most revered for an attribute the photographer hadn't captured: the best ass at Goodwin, full, round, and deep, but not wide. From the front, you would not suspect. But when she turned in profile, her bottom bulged into a perfect C. Often the guys would stand outside the gym, gawking as she did splits and backflips in her blue leotard.

He couldn't claim they had been friends in high school. She probably had never noticed him, a pimply underclassman. She'd regularly passed him in the hallway without saying hello. He'd never spoken more than two sentences to her, but along with every male in his class he had admired her from afar all those years of high school, had lain awake at night thinking about her smile, her ass, imagining silly scenarios to gain her affection—saving her from thugs in a dark alleyway, or rescuing her from drowning. Back then, he'd studied the pretty senior girls as if they were exam questions. He used to make lists: who had the best legs (Gretchen Peters), best hair (Diana Castenda), best boobs (a tie, Wendy Brewster and Wendy Yelton). The two Wendys had been inseparable, one blond, one dark-haired, often walking arm in arm, hugging or leaning against each other; you could practically hear the boys groan when the two ran up and down the soccer field. Their particular shapes, and the shapes of the other girls of his school, remained fixed in Benjamin's consciousness like graven images, as clear in memory as if they were standing in the room with him now, his first exemplars of the contours of womanhood, and he'd lusted after them with a teenage ferocity, wholly disproportionate to anything the girls had done to inspire it, driven close to madness by a whiff of their shampoo or the sway of their hips.

Benjamin had dated only one girl in high school, a day student like himself. Their romance had lasted a few months during his senior spring. She was a tall, green-eyed sophomore named Maureen O'Geary who favored gray corduroy pants. At night Benjamin would pick her up in his father's Cadillac at her house in Farmington and they would drive to the public library to study. Afterward they would park at the mall or behind the town hall until eleven, her curfew; she had only one rule during these make-out sessions—that her corduroys remain buttoned. Despite his best efforts he'd never succeeded in violating this decree, although after three months those gray cords were loose around the waist. She'd broken up with him suddenly and vehemently for reasons he didn't understand, and afterward she refused to speak to him.

From downstairs came the sound of his father clanging pots and pans. The old man was making dinner. Benjamin checked his watch: not yet 5:00 P.M. Leonard was getting to be an early diner in his old age. Although he wasn't hungry yet, Benjamin put away the yearbook and went down to the table. Leonard had made hamburgers, mashed potatoes, and peas.

For dessert he served coffee cake. "You want another piece?"

"Sure. I'll get it."

"No. You did enough today, carrying all that stuff." His father got up from the table and shuffled to the counter, his slippers scratching against the linoleum. "It's a fine coffee cake. Look how it crumbles."

Benjamin asked, "Have you started smoking, Dad?"

"No. Never. I never smoked a cigarette in my life. You know that."

"I noticed a pack in the freezer."

"Your mother's," he said without lifting his head. "Her last pack."

Of course, Benjamin thought. He should have guessed. His father wasn't getting senile, just more sentimental. This fact made Benjamin feel even worse about the information he had to impart.

"I have some bad news, Dad. Judy and I are getting a divorce."

"She asked for a divorce? Judy did?"

"Yes."

"And you can't work it out like before?"

"I don't think so. Not this time."

Leonard exhaled, nodding slowly. "Have you told the kids?"

"No." Benjamin had been putting off that task all day, dreading the inevitable, like a schoolboy before the first day of classes. He knew what would happen. Sarah would cry. David would take the news stoically, with barely a word.

"And this is final? This is your mutual decision?"

Benjamin nodded.

"I'll give Brendan McGowan a call. He's the best. You'll need the best."

McGowan had been his father's lawyer since the sixties, when Leonard had first opened Mandelbaum Motors. "You need to act quickly on something like this," said Leonard. "Freeze bank accounts. Put liens on property. There's no going back once you take that step."

Benjamin paused, feeling the weight of the decision. Once lawyers got involved, things became permanent. But this had been building for a while, he knew. The way Judy had ranted, she would never take him back anyway. "Yeah, okay," he told his father. "Maybe you're right."

His father went off toward the front hallway, and a moment later Benjamin heard him dialing the rotary phone. Calling his lawyer already. That had always been his nature, to look out for his family above himself. At each whir of the rotary dial, Benjamin felt the weight of his own failure.

You're just not equipped, Judy had screamed at him during their blowout the night before. She'd found a hotel receipt in his pants while doing the laundry. *You're never going to change, Benjamin.* Ironically, this time he was blameless. He'd gotten drunk at an early business dinner in New Haven and had checked into the hotel across the street for five or six hours to sober up, before making the long drive back to Granby. She called him a liar. She said she didn't believe a word of it. She said he was back to his old ways. She accused him of lacking some basic gene inherent in good husbands like Leonard. She said she was done. Finished with him. He raised his voice, calling her paranoid, and so on, the same long annoying rigmarole, the same petty complaints.

They first met in 1983. She had been hired as a secretary at Mandelbaum Motors, her first job out of high school: Judy Mariani, eighteen years old, in her short denim skirt, answering the phone at the front desk, tapping away at an IBM Selectric with her long, painted nails. She was tall, nearly his height, with a wealth of black hair, teased up to the height of eighties fashion. She was large in the chest and the behind, sticking out in both directions like the Vargas girls in his father's *Esquire*. She had big, soft brown eyes. He didn't know, then, what he was getting into—the extent of her ambition, the plan she had for her life and the role she needed him to play. She'd grown up in a two-family house east of the river, her three brothers living in the same bedroom, the whole family sharing a single bathroom, and she wanted something different for herself, something closer to the beautiful lives she saw on *Dallas* and *Dynasty.*

He was twenty-two when they married, she two years younger. He loved her with a sort of mania. He couldn't get enough of her, her beautiful body, open to him. He found her seventh- and eighth-grade diaries and read them with fascination. He wanted to know everything: her first kiss, her first boyfriend, her first love. It was like pulling teeth, but he extracted from her a detailed history of her sexual life, and with that knowledge came jealousy. How could it bother him? she asked. Things that happened before he even knew her? She'd had a few boyfriends, so what? He couldn't explain it, but it bothered him. It obsessed and enraged him. Which was odd, because he'd never been a jealous person and he was not jealous of the *present* Judy, his wife, Judy. He trusted her completely; he didn't even mind when other men admired her in public, as long as they weren't rude; he was proud to be seen with her. But the past Judy—that was another story.

What really burned him, and what Judy couldn't dismiss as ridiculous, was her final boyfriend, an East Hartford fireman named Robert. The *overlap* burned him. That's what Judy called it. He called it *betrayal*. At the start she had wavered between him and the fireman, going on dates with them on different nights. Without explanation she would disappear for a weekend. Later she would admit that, yes, she had been with Robert—at his house or away at some country inn in Massachusetts. Benjamin once found a photograph of the man in her wallet, a mustachioed guy in his thirties. It upset him to the point that he couldn't say the other's name; instead he said it backwards: Trebor. *Were you with Trebor? Is that why you didn't call me?* He would drive by the fireman's house in the middle of the night, sometimes spying Judy's secondhand Volvo in the driveway. This went on for two or three months. It wrenched Benjamin's heart, a pain wholly beyond anything he'd experienced during his teenage crushes, something close to unbearable. He would drink a six-pack to numb himself, just to be able to get to sleep. Then came his triumph over Trebor: Judy standing beside him at their wedding, him stomping on the glass in celebration. She belonged to him now.

As the years passed, they settled into their routines. He worked at the dealership. She stayed home. The kids came a year apart. They had their television shows. He had his beer, she her wine. When the kids left for college, a silence came between them. She nursed a list of complaints, which seemed to intensify over the years: He lied to her; he made her feel insecure; he watched porno movies after she went to bed; he disliked her family; he didn't listen to her; he was passive-aggressive; he chastised her for spending money even though she rarely bought anything but necessary household items. In Benjamin's view they fought about nothing; when there was no reason to be unhappy, they found a reason. *I'm missing something*, he thought. *I'm living someone else's life.*

Maybe she was right; maybe he just wasn't equipped to be a happy husband, or maybe he hadn't tried hard enough. Judy, to be sure, was not an easy woman to get along with, with her temper, her longing for nice things, her compulsion to be someone altogether different from her mother. Or maybe they had simply started out too young, with too much responsibility too soon. Still, the end felt wrong to him: wrong and too sudden, and for a nonreason; he was innocent; he hadn't done a thing. But the result was the same: his marriage finished, his family broken.

At least this hadn't happened while the kids were still living at home. David was a junior at the University of Tampa, quick and wiry, like his dad. Sarah was a sophomore at BU. They hadn't had to witness the last couple of months of wordless dinners and door slammings, and they'd avoided the final drama of Judy screaming her head off in the driveway in her black panties and T-shirt, the same clothes she'd been wearing when she found the hotel receipt: "I never want to see your face again! Go! Get out!" She could keep the house in Granby—the Vulcan range and Sub-

Zero refrigerator, all the Pottery Barn and Restoration Hardware furniture she'd stuffed into the place, the Williams-Sonoma kitchen gadgets, all of it—but not his dog. Yukon was the only thing he wanted from that house. She'd need a sheriff to get that dog away from him.

Benjamin went into the den and poured a scotch to stiffen his resolve. He would call David first, he decided. He might even put Sarah off until tomorrow. She was eighteen, as pretty as her mother, the same thick black hair, the same deep brown eyes. A beautiful girl. She'd always had boyfriends; they'd been coming around since she was in the seventh grade. He didn't want to ruin her night. But before he finished adding ice cubes to his scotch, his cell phone was ringing. Speak of the devil.

"Daddy, is it true?" She was crying, her voice shaking. So Judy had already told them. At that moment Benjamin could *see* his daughter, her eyeliner running, her face contorted. Sarah hadn't called him Daddy in years. Now it was Dad or Ben. Sometimes David called him Benji to be funny.

"Everything's going to be okay, honey."

"No, everything is *not* okay. Don't tell me it's going to be okay."

Nothing was settled, they still might work it out, he told her weakly, not even convincing himself. What else could he offer his daughter but assurances? And if his wife did go through with it, as he knew she would, what then? Well, so be it, Benjamin decided. Look on the bright side. He would get his freedom, a chance to be himself again. Judy would find someone else; she was forty-two, fit and beautiful as always. But for Sarah and David, there would be no benefit; they would carry the rupture with them, their childhoods abruptly reconfigured, their sense of security shattered.

"We're still a family. Nothing will change. You'll see, honey." But he wasn't even sure she could hear him over her own sobs. His daughter had always come to him for consolation, not Judy. When playmates betrayed her, when boyfriends didn't return her phone calls, he'd always been the one to calm her fears and heartbreak.

As his daughter cried, he refilled his glass.

A WEEK LATER a state marshal knocked at the front door. "Benjamin Mandelbaum?"

"Yes."

He handed over some papers. "You've been served," the man said.

He phoned her that night and at least ten times over the coming weeks, but she refused to answer. He told her answering machine:

It's all a mistake, Judy. I didn't cheat on you.

And:

Look, I know we have issues, but we should at least get the facts straight.

And:

Come on, Judy. Pick up the phone. We don't need lawyers. We can be reasonable about this. We can go to a mediator. Lawyer bills are gong to cost us both a fortune. Let's talk about this.

Talk he did, until her machine beeped and cut him off. Instead of calling back, she sent legal letters by certified mail. He even received a letter about Yukon, seeking return of the dog: *Defendant has removed the family animal without permission to a new and unknown environment, causing emotional distress to Spouse,* her lawyer had written.

That was the nature of divorce, he realized after a month of such frustration: You didn't get to talk to your wife anymore. You didn't get to justify or rationalize or talk your way out of trouble. You got served, and then the lawyers did the talking for you.

LEONARD MANDELBAUM usually said the same thing whenever his son asked for advice about some problem: *Always go with the best.* Leonard had learned that lesson from his own father, a haberdasher: *You can never go wrong with the best.* This was the credo he lived by. Back in the sixties, when Leonard opened the dealership with his life savings and loans from the bank, the best meant Cadillac. He had the sole franchise in East Hartford. If you wanted a Cadillac, you came to Mandelbaum Motors. Customers drove off the lot happy, and they were happy when they came back for oil changes and tire rotations—happy because Cadillacs worked; when you got behind the wheel and turned the key, the car started.

Over the years Leonard had many opportunities to expand. He could have acquired the Jaguar franchise in the early seventies, but he'd passed without giving it a second thought. Why? Because Jaguars broke down, because Jaguars meant trouble, and trouble cars—Saabs ("sob stories," Leonard called them), Mercedes, BMWs—meant unhappy customers.

Back then European cars were trouble, Japanese cars were junk. It had all changed since then, of course, and when it did, Leonard had branched out.

Mandelbaum Motors didn't *sell*. That was Leonard's other rule of business. *Never use the hard sell*. Customers didn't trust car salesmen who chased them around the showroom, barking like carnival hucksters. Leonard purposefully kept the lot understaffed; he didn't want his boys charging out the door with their hands out whenever some poor sap drove onto the premises. Just the opposite. You had difficulties finding a salesman at Mandelbaum Motors. You had to wait until someone had a moment to hand out a brochure, hop in for a test drive, quote you a price. Because Leonard Mandelbaum was no pitchman. You came into his office, he gave you his best price, you signed the papers, or not.

For thirty-odd years Leonard had been the first to arrive on the lot every morning, newspaper in hand. Days off didn't sit well with him. He'd find himself restless and fidgety, even at the country club sitting by the swimming pool with Myra and the kids. "Go already," Myra would tell him. "You're making everyone crazy." So he would drive out to East Hartford, get behind his desk, work the phone.

This went on into his golden years, even after Benjamin had taken the reins. His son knew the business from the ground up; he'd started in the car wash when he was thirteen. College hadn't appealed to Benjamin. After two years in Pennsylvania he'd dropped out. His grades were so-so, even in economics classes, and Benjamin had always excelled in mathematics; his heart just wasn't in it. He started full-time when he was twenty, and he'd married Judy a couple of years later. And ever since, father and son had worked side by side, through the difficult eighties, the roaring nineties. Afternoons they would lunch at Shelly's Deli down the block, then return to their offices across the hall from each other. With his door open, Leonard could see Benjamin, feet up on his desk, fingers flying on the computer. Benjamin worked magic on that computer, bringing in out-of-state customers; once he even sold a fleet of Eldorados to Arabia.

But it all ended when Myra got ill. Leonard nursed her himself and left the house only when she insisted. "Get out of my sight, Leonard," she would say. "Stop hanging over me like a vulture." Four years she battled the cancer, holding on long past the time any doctor thought possible. Six months to a year, they'd given her. But they didn't know Myra Mandelbaum. A stubborn woman, his wife. When it was over, finally, when she called it quits, the fight was gone from Leonard too. He hadn't considered the possibility of outliving her. It had been a sticking point back when he'd courted her, their ten-year age difference. Her parents hadn't liked the idea of her marrying an *old man*—he was thirty-seven at the time; they didn't want Myra being left to fend for herself in her old age. They needn't have worried. Leonard had planned well: life insurance, disability insurance, stocks and bonds. All that was irrelevant now. He'd cashed in the insurance policies and transferred the securities to Benjamin and Sissi. He hadn't planned to survive Myra, and after she was gone he didn't know what to do with himself.

In time, he returned to the lot. But five years had passed and almost everything had changed. His first day back, he wandered the showroom, bewildered, looking for his office, which had been relocated when Benjamin renovated the building. His own familiar secretary had retired; new employees roamed the aisles, watching him with curiosity those first few days. Was he a customer? Someone's uncle? There were new makes and models, new technology. But the biggest change was within Leonard himself: He had lost the desire to sell. What was the point? Benjamin had everything under control; the business was making more money than ever. His son assured him that they needed him—untrue, of course—but Leonard found it difficult to summon the energy to get dressed every morning and make the long drive across the river. To please his son, he came into the office on Friday afternoons, mostly just to have lunch with Benjamin like old times. But he didn't sell, and people asked for him less and less. He'd outlived his customers, and the ones who were still breathing had no need for cars in their nursing homes and retirement communities. Leonard was a museum piece, like the 1955 red Coupe DeVille they kept in the front showroom. In some ways it was a relief not to be needed.

So he was surprised to find three pink Post-its on his desk waiting for him one Friday afternoon that October. Leonard got out his reading glasses, examined the notes one by one. They all said the same thing:

Dick Funkhouser called.

* * *

WHEN THE WAITRESS delivered the bottle of wine, Leonard examined the label with his glasses perched halfway down his nose. A red wine from Orvieto. The waitress filled a glass and passed it across the table to Terri Funkhouser. Leonard waited for her to take a sip. She gulped. "Well?" he said. "Do you like it?"

She shrugged. "What's not to like? It's a forty-dollar bottle of wine. Of course I like it. Do you expect me to send it back?"

Terri Funkhouser was husky-voiced, a lifelong smoker like Myra. Her dyed blond hair was pompadoured high above her head; gold baubles dangled from her ears. *A handful,* Dick Senior used to call her. Leonard was never sure if he meant her ample figure, her disposition, or both.

The restaurant was called the First and Last Tavern, and Leonard thought that apropos: This would be his first and last evening with Terri Funkhouser. The whole thing had been a trick. Dick Junior had tricked him. When Leonard had returned his calls earlier that day, Dick Junior had proposed a dinner meeting to discuss buying a new car for his mother. *I'm off to sell a Cadillac,* he'd told Benjamin proudly. ("Drive safely, Dad, okay? Your night vision's not so great these days.") But when Leonard arrived at the Funkhouser house to pick them up, Dick Junior claimed an emergency and begged off, saying, *You can get Mom home okay, right?*

"What kind of car are you interested in?" asked Leonard.

Terri Funkhouser reached into the breadbasket and picked through the rolls. "They're cold," she said. She ripped one in half and took a bite. "I'm not interested in cars. That's Dickie's idea. He thinks I should have a new one, something with an air bag. He doesn't trust the Cutlass anymore. He says I drive like a blind person."

"What year is the Cutlass?"

"You're asking me dates? You expect me to know the make and model?"

"They stopped making them in the nineties."

She shrugged. "I'm used to it."

"You have to keep up with the times. You can never be too safe."

Her nails were long, painted a bright red. "Who can afford a new car?"

"New, used. You'd be surprised at the deals you can get these days. Dick Junior wants the best for you."

"Forget it, Leonard. Dickie's a dreamer. He can't afford a lawn mower, let alone a new car, and neither can I. Let's not talk about cars anymore."

"Fine. That's fine."

"Dickie's been after me to call you for a month. He thinks we should be friends." She emptied her wineglass and held it toward him. Leonard refilled the glass, which was smeared around the rim with lipstick.

"He wants you to be happy."

She laughed, a short raspy sound. "He wants me off his hands." Again, she gulped the wine, dripping some out of the side of her mouth, and quickly lapped it with her tongue. "He wants me out of my house so he can sell it and take the money and go to Florida with his shiksa."

"He's a good boy," said Leonard, trying to calm her. Her voice traveled; a couple at the next table turned their way. When Leonard had parked outside the restaurant, she'd grabbed his arm to steady herself as they walked toward the entrance. A bit tipsy already, he'd thought then. "He means well, I'm sure."

"You think it's a good idea we become friends? You like that idea, Leonard Mandelbaum, do you?"

"Most of my friends are dead."

"You're an old man, Leonard."

"Eighty-four."

"You outlived them. Myra, Dick Senior. Everyone."

"I always liked Dick Senior."

"Oh, Dick was a prince. A real prince." She offered her wineglass. "To Dick Funkhouser, wherever he may be." Leonard clinked her glass with his own, and she drank off a few ounces. "I need a real drink. Order me one."

When the waitress arrived with their dinner, Leonard told her, "A sidecar for the lady and a scotch on the rocks for me."

"How did you know?" She had her head down, sawing her chicken cutlet with a serrated knife.

"You always asked for it at parties."

"It's been thirty years since I've been to a party at your house."

"Part of my job. I never forget a drink or the name of a spouse. People like to be remembered."

"What a salesman. You and your Cadillacs."

"Staci and Gary. Your grandkids."

"For God's sake, don't you forget anything?"

"Seems like all I do is forget these days, or try to."

"Don't be maudlin." She wore a white sweater with gold sequins, and Leonard noticed a fresh splotch of spaghetti sauce on her chest. The woman had a healthy appetite. Half the cutlet was gone already. Her plump fingers worked diligently, cutting and forking the meat into her bright red mouth. "Dick Senior was a maudlin man. He cried during television commercials. Tears streaming down his face during an Alpo ad."

"I always liked Dick Senior."

"You said that already, Leonard. Please stop saying things twice."

"Fine," he said. "Fine."

"Dick Senior got me pregnant on a cot in his dry-cleaning shop. I came in to pick up a blouse for my mother and I ended up in the back room with my skirt up. I was married at seventeen. I didn't even finish high school. Did you know that?"

"Did I know what?"

"The man was twenty years older and hung like a horse. I never knew men could be small until I found out the hard way. No pun intended."

Leonard glanced at the neighboring tables to see if anyone could hear her. "Keep your voice down."

"Am I embarrassing you?"

"I might know someone here."

"All your friends are dead, Leonard. You said so yourself. Who's going to care if you're seen cavorting with a drunken woman? Who's left to notice?"

"Eat your shells," he said.

"Fine. I'll eat my shells. You talk. I'll eat."

"I didn't know Dick was that much older."

"You mean you didn't know I was so young. You mean I look older."

"No, no. You look fine."

"I don't look fine, Len. I'm a wreck. I'm sixty-nine years old and I can't afford a car and my son feels he has to pimp me out to an old devil like you."

This made Leonard smile. He was enjoying himself, he realized, in spite of the commotion she was causing, in spite of the spectacle of her spilling gravy onto her sweater. She was a disaster, but in her presence he *did* feel somewhat devilish—the way she'd hung on his arm when they'd entered the restaurant, the movement of her large hips and breasts. The woman was lively conversation, you had to give it to her. You never knew what might come out of her mouth next.

"You don't look a day over sixty," he said.

"Sixty-*nine*," she stressed. "That's a dirty number, you know."

"A what?"

"A dirty number. 'My favorite number,' Dick Senior used to say."

Leonard's face must have betrayed his bewilderment.

"Never mind, Len," she said, patting his hand. "You play your cards right, maybe I'll show you sometime." She winked lasciviously. Something sexual, then. He would ask Benjamin or one of the salesmen. They knew all the dirty jokes.

"You do have those little blue pills, Len? All the old men have them these days."

His Halcion were blue. He couldn't sleep without them, ever since Myra died. Alone in the big bed, the sheets drawn tightly. She'd always run hot, Myra had. *Better than an electric blanket*, he used to say. "Sure," he said. "I can't get to sleep without them."

Terri snorted so loudly that he flinched; a small piece of food projected out of her mouth and landed in his salad. "*Viagra*, Len," she blurted. "I'm talking about Viagra. For your you-know-what. For your putz. Not for sleeping."

"For God's sake, Terri. They'll throw us out."

And indeed, he looked up to see the waiter approaching, looking stern. But the man was only delivering their cocktails. Leonard bit into his meatball; he'd barely touched his dinner.

"Go to your doctor," she said. "They give them out like vitamins these days." She forked the final piece of chicken into her mouth and began wiping up the sauce with a roll. "More bread, Len," she rasped.

Myra too used to get boisterous in restaurants. Once she'd asked the maître d' at Scoler's to dance, and when he politely declined, she called him fancy pants. *You'd dance with me if I were a man, wouldn't you, fancy pants?*

"To little blue pills," Terri Funkhouser was saying, her sidecar raised. She drank it down in a few swigs. But that was her final toast. The sidecar finished her. She became quiet, then unresponsive. Finally she announced that she felt sick. "Take me home, Leonard."

He and the maître d', a heavyset Italian man, got her out to the Cadillac, Leonard holding on to one arm, feeling the fleshy weight of her against him. They managed to strap her into the passenger seat. On the drive back to her house, her mouth fell open and she began snoring. In the close confines of the car Leonard began to feel light-headed from the scent of her; he opened the driver's-side window to get some air; her perfume, as Myra had always said, could stop a bull.

When Leonard pulled into her driveway and honked the horn, Dick Junior came out immediately, striding purposefully toward the passenger side, as if he'd been expecting them.

THE NEXT MORNING Leonard got the photo albums out of the den closet. He was looking for a picture he'd taken of Terri Funkhouser, many years ago. He could summon the image in his mind: young Terri standing ramrod straight, chest thrust forward, a cocktail glass in her hand. One of his grandkids, combing through the photo albums, had once said, *Who's the pretty lady in the red dress?*

As Leonard searched, Benjamin suddenly bounded down the hallway, calling out, "I'll be right back." Where are you going, he wanted to ask, but the door had already closed behind his son. Leonard smiled. That was Benjamin, always in a hurry. He talked fast, typed fast, drove fast. It was nice having his son back in the house, despite the marital concerns. They had dinner together most evenings and TV time afterward in the den. Benjamin even watched television *fast*, flipping through the channels in a blur.

Leonard turned past the countless photographs of dogs and cats, the pets that had kept Benjamin and Sissi happy in their youth. The two of them had taken the photos with their Instamatic cameras. "Take pictures of *people*," he'd lectured his children, but they hadn't listened. One of the albums had a psychedelic purple plastic cover with a typewritten title page: *Winter Sojourn by Benjamin Steven Mandelbaum*. This was his son's junior high photography project, an album of black-and-white pictures of clouds and trees in winter. His son had developed these pictures himself in the darkroom he'd jury-rigged in the basement, with his potions and trays and red safelight. Leonard could detect, even now, a lingering whiff of the chemical solutions. Photography had been a phase of Benjamin's, like his interest in baseball cards and the electric guitar, hobbies that got boxed up once he turned sixteen, when he discovered beer and girls.

As he thumbed through the albums, Leonard lingered over pictures of Myra, so vivid in her prime: Myra in her tennis whites at the club, racket in hand; Myra on the beach in Sarasota, reclining on a lounge chair; Myra in ski pants at the foot of the mountain in Stowe, leaning on her ski poles.

He pulled another stack of photo albums from the bottom shelf, breathing heavily, pushing aside board games and poker chips, coughing on the dust. He opened their honeymoon album, covered in white leather: *Bermuda, Summer of 1959*. He'd taken these pictures with his Hasselblad 1600f with its eighty-millimeter lens, a camera he'd bought in Paris a few years after the war. The photographs were three-inch squares. The negatives, nearly as big, were contained in an envelope, taped to the back cover of the album. Leonard had always been well organized with his hobbies.

There was Myra, twenty-seven years old in a white bathing suit outside the cottage they'd rented on the grounds of the Black Angus Hotel, posing Hollywood-style, one hand behind her head, hip cocked. Every night they dined at the same small corner table in the hotel restaurant. "We'll have the roast beef and Yorkshire pudding," she would tell the waiter. "We're hungry people."

His beautiful Myra, so young, so full of life. How proud he'd been, walking arm in arm with her through the hotel dining room. "You're a lucky man," the waiter had confided to him one night. Lucky, indeed. Leonard could see the joy in his face in the final photo in the honeymoon album, slightly out of focus: Leonard grinning, his eyes narrowed to slits against the sun. He had the woman of his dreams, with a lifetime ahead of them.

His eyes watered. The loss was nearly unbearable. How could he express it in words? When his neighbor Betty Amato called to check on him, when she asked how he was doing, he would always say the same thing: *Not very well without Myra. Not very well at all.* He missed her every hour, every day. *I know, Leonard,* Betty would say, *I miss her too. I miss her so much.* That would start him crying again, and Betty would say, *But you can't dwell on it. You have to move on or you'll make yourself sick with grief.* Move on? How could he tell her that there was no possibility of moving on? That there was nothing left for him, no life without Myra? She couldn't understand. Neither could Benjamin or Sissi. For them, life was about looking ahead, about what would happen next.

There was one final photo album. Leonard flipped absentmindedly through the pages, and there it was, the shot of Terri Funkhouser. He'd almost forgotten he was looking for it. In the picture, she was posed exactly as he'd remembered—standing tall and proud in a flashy red dress, cocktail glass in hand—but she was younger than he'd thought (barely into her twenties, by the look of her), and Leonard had forgotten the other person in the photograph, with her arm curled around Terri Funkhouser's waist: Myra herself, wearing a short black cocktail dress and pearls. How young they seemed, the two women staring into the lens, unsmiling. He removed the photograph from its cellophane sheath and turned it over: *Summer solstice party 1963,* Myra had written on the back.

Leonard carried the photograph to his desk in the hallway and dialed Terri Funkhouser's number. Benjamin had gone outside; Leonard could see him through the front window, standing on the lawn, talking to some woman—the new neighbor, he guessed, who'd moved into Eleanor Hufnagle's house. Just as well, Leonard figured. He wouldn't need to keep his voice down. He hadn't told Benjamin about his outing with Terri Funkhouser. Benjamin might find it disloyal of him, calling another woman. But Leonard only wanted to tell her about the photograph and offer to send her a copy. It would be a quick phone call, before his son came back inside.

She answered immediately.

"I've got a picture of you," he said.

"Not from last night, I hope."

"From 1963. It's you and Myra at a cocktail party on the patio in my backyard. You're wearing a red dress."

"Dick bought that dress for me at Saks. I told him it made me look like a streetwalker, but he insisted."

"Myra has her arm around your waist."

"Myra was lovely. I always envied her those almond eyes and her figure—so trim, not falling out everywhere like you-know-who. You had the pick of the litter, Len."

"I did. I did." This started him crying again, though he tried to hide it by clearing his throat.

"Don't get weepy on me. I told you last night, I can't stand that sort of thing."

"I'm surprised you can remember last night."

"Of course I remember. Did you do what I asked? Did you call your doctor?"

"My doctor?"

"*Viagra*, Len. The little blue pills."

"For goodness' sake, Terri. You're not serious."

"Of course I'm serious. It'll be a nice change for you. Don't underestimate the benefits of a good lay. You'll feel twenty years younger."

"Don't talk like that. Dickie will hear you."

"Dickie's out with his shiksa. And he wouldn't care anyway. He wants us to be friends, remember. This whole thing was his idea."

"You and Myra." He sighed, holding the photograph a few inches from his face. He'd left his reading glasses in the den. Somehow it made him feel closer to Myra, seeing her together with Terri. "The two of you. You look like movie stars. I'll show it to you."

"When?"

"Soon. Soon."

"Get the pills first. But you have to be able to do five push-ups."

"Push-ups? What are you talking about?"

"The doctors won't give you the pills if they're worried about your heart. They don't want you jumping into bed and having a coronary, which is what happens sometimes with old devils like yourself. So they'll ask you to do five push-ups before they'll write a prescription."

"That's nonsense."

"Trust me, Len. I've been through this before. You did push-ups in the Army, right?"

"Navy."

"Then it'll be no problem for you."

She fumbled the phone, and a moment later the line went dead. Leonard shook his head. Barely past noon and she was drunk again. The way she talked, she had to be drunk. Or maybe just teasing. Didn't she know that he hadn't been with a woman for twenty years? And a woman other than Myra for how long—fifty years?

He went back to the den and slid the picture of Myra and Terri Funk-houser into its cellophane holder. Then he gathered the photo albums, got to his hands and knees, and stacked them on the bottom shelf in the closet. He sat on the rug, resting for a few moments.

Five push-ups! Could she possibly be serious? He hadn't done push-ups since his Navy days, but back then they'd performed marathon sessions, one hundred at a time, more. Leonard was fit. A bit hunched, the years weighing on his back, but not overweight; he'd never been overweight, never smoked, never drank as much as the others—Terri Funkhouser, Myra, Bob Amato; they'd poured it down like water. He had always been the one to drive them home. He'd played golf every Sunday at the country club during the season, competing in tournaments well into his sixties, until at last he'd torn his rotator cuff to shreds slicing a three wood.

Leonard stretched out on the rug. Good thing Benjamin couldn't see him now. How could he explain these gymnastics? He took a deep breath and pushed himself off the floor.

"One," he said aloud. "Two. Three—"

He felt it coming, a welling up, like a storm rising.

He never reached five.

SOME MINUTES EARLIER, sitting at the kitchen table with the newspaper, Benjamin had glanced up to see the dog through the kitchen window—an odd sight in suburbia: a malamute trotting up the street without leash, without master.

He'd seen the dog before, tied to a tree outside the old farmhouse, roaming the lawn on a thirty-foot line: *her* dog.

Immediately, he jumped to his feet. Like any good salesman, Benjamin Mandelbaum knew when to seize an opportunity. He grabbed a turkey leg out of the refrigerator, picked Yukon's old leash off the hook by the kitchen door, and hurried outside.

He whistled. The dog turned toward him, both ears raised. When Benjamin tossed the turkey leg onto the lawn, the dog ambled over to inspect the offering, and Benjamin reached out and snapped the latch onto its collar.

Gotcha.

FOR THE PAST MONTH, since he'd moved back into his father's house, Benjamin had kept a sort of vigil. Each morning on his way to work he would linger at the stop sign at the bottom of the street to inspect the farmhouse. Most days there would be a workman's truck or van parked in the driveway, sometimes a whole fleet—plumbers, landscapers, carpenters, painters. On his way home, he would examine what they'd accomplished during the day. The row of tall pines along Mountain Road was cleared, the logs and stumps cut up and removed, the brush fed into a wood chipper. A fresh coat of paint was applied, the house a soft gray, the shutters barn red. The split-rail fence rose up from where it had fallen.

Finally, a couple of weeks ago, he'd gotten his first glimpse of her, walking her dog up the street. He'd squinted. There was the red hair, down to her shoulders. Yes, it was her, it was *his* Audrey Martin, he knew in the first instant. That night he'd pulled out the yearbook again. In addition to her senior picture, there were three other shots of Audrey Martin: a candid of her lying on a blanket on the senior green; the group photo of the gymnastics team with her kneeling in the front row; and the cast picture from the spring musical, with Audrey dressed in leather pants as Sandy in *Grease*, wearing too much makeup. He wondered where her life had taken her since Goodwin, and how she had ended up living on his childhood street. They had expected so much of her; she had everything—talent, beauty, intelligence, athletic grace. (Not to mention that fine ass.)

He closed the yearbook, distracted. A Pavlovian reaction of sorts had occurred, almost against his wishes, the same thrill that had seized him every June in high school on the day they handed out the new yearbooks, smelling of ink and glossy paper. He had a hard-on. Did the other boys do as he did, race home and flip from one page to the next, gorging on images of Wendy Brewster and Wendy Yelton, the girls' soccer team photo? Back then, it had offered more excitement than *Playboy* or *Penthouse*, the intimacy of knowing the girls in the photos, even if they weren't naked on a hay bale. He'd turned on his laptop and lowered the volume so as not to wake his father in the next room. He hadn't had sex in more than a month, the longest period of abstinence of his adult life. Maybe *abstinence* was the wrong word—did abstinence include jerking off every other night, a forty-four-year-old man tiptoeing downstairs to do the laundry so his father wouldn't find his soiled boxer briefs? It was pathetic, he knew. Likewise, this infatuation with Audrey Martin. She was someone's wife now, his high school dream girl long gone.

So far being single wasn't what Benjamin had expected. Since Judy kicked him out, he hadn't gone on a single date. His social life amounted to a stop at Starbucks on his way home from work, where he'd smile at the young woman who handed over his decaf latte. "Would you like your receipt, sir?" To her, he was another middle-aged man, an automaton in a blue suit. Once in a while the pretty barista would come out from behind the counter to sweep the floor or refill the condiments, wearing low-cut jeans under her green apron, a black thong peeking out. The vision caused a hollow in his gut, a desperate longing as sharp as an ulcer. Was this pain going to last indefinitely? Would he be a seventy-year-old codger, alone and unhappy? How could he meet someone new in this town? No matter where he looked, his attentions were inappropriate. He lived in a town populated by married people and their minor children. The trio of schoolgirls studying at the big table in their uniform of blue jeans and Uggs: They were younger than his daughter. The woman with the Coach bag, waiting impatiently in line: Her ring finger sported a hefty diamond.

During all the years of his marriage it had seemed that single women were everywhere, in stores, restaurants, on the streets. Where had they gone, all those possibilities? At the dealership, an accountant came into the office twice a week to do the books. She was in her late thirties, her hair pulled back, usually dressed in a skirt and a silky blouse. Her arrival in the morning—the click of her heels on the tile floor of the show-room—caused a sort of primordial explosion in his brain, obliterating the possibility of higher thought. But she was off-limits, like the secretaries and saleswomen. He'd learned that lesson ten years earlier, when one of the senior salesmen got the company involved in a sexual harassment lawsuit, costing their insurance carrier a $200,000 settlement. (The fool had been obsessed with one of the female mechanics. He'd left obscene notes in her locker and messages on her home answering machine for six months.) Two hundred thousand dollars! The figure had sent Leonard into paroxysms. "She had to sue? She couldn't say to him, 'Go fly a kite'?"

During his marriage, Benjamin had engaged in two affairs, and both times Judy had caught him. The first was Annika, nineteen and free-spirited, the Dutch au pair. She'd arrived at their doorstep, barely proficient in English, impossibly beautiful. This had been Judy's idea, hiring an au pair, something she thought rich people did. One afternoon she walked in on the two of them in the guest room, smoking pot naked, with a Swedish pop song that was big that summer playing on the tape player. (Later, whenever the band's sole hit played on the radio, Judy skewered him with an "Oh listen, they're playing your song.") She sent the girl back to the agency and relegated Benjamin to the very same guest room for the next six months. A trial basis, she called it, contingent on his attendance at couples' therapy twice a week. He went along with it—six months of regret and desperation, anxiety and self-recrimination—until he finally won Judy's forgiveness. Deep down, he saw the fault as partly hers, for her betrayal with the fireman, although he hadn't justified his actions that way to Judy. Still, he'd had his mulligan with the au pair; and so they were even.

But a few years later, he met Rachel Rosenberg, and it happened again. She was his daughter's ninth-grade Spanish teacher. He met her at the annual parent-teacher get-together. She was freshly divorced, with a rose tattooed on her right shoulder blade, and she never wore panties, not around him at least. In their Cancún hotel room she drank tequila from the bottle and danced to flamenco music. "I used to buy into all that AA crap," she told him, "before I decided to lighten up." He couldn't stop, even after Judy found out, even after she threatened to take the kids and go. Eventually Rachel herself called it off. She refused to see him. "Recess is over," she told him. "I need a serious man in my life." The next year she moved to Boca Raton with a bank president.

It had been love, he'd thought, stupidly. But Rachel had discarded him like an old newspaper. And he had not even missed her. He found himself relieved to be free from her craziness and self-absorption and drunken drama. This time, Judy let him come back with a simple dictum: *That was your last chance. Next time, it's over.* He agreed, elated to win her reprieve. What a fool he had been, to risk his marriage, and for what? His two extramarital affairs had been about sex. Sex, alone. He knew that, in retrospect. He'd had a couple of drunken one-night flings during his four semesters at college, but Judy had been his first real sexual partner, and he had married her. He'd had to get that urge out of his system. After Rachel, he vowed never to cheat again, and he hadn't, no matter what Judy suspected. In the seven years since Rachel Rosenberg he'd been as chaste as Jimmy Carter, lusting in his heart but nothing more than that.

Still, he and Judy grew apart. A phantom unease entered into their marriage during that time of fidelity, a slow-growing silence, which got worse after the kids left for college. That silence had done more damage to his marriage than any affair.

So now, here he was, single: This was what he'd contemplated over the past few years like some tropical vacation, a release from marital servitude, a return to the world of women. Long ago, the summer after his first year of college, Benjamin had rented a cottage on Martha's Vineyard with some buddies. They would sit on the front porch, the raucous five of them, calling out to the girls who passed by on their way to the public beach. Often a few of the girls would come up on the porch, have a beer from the cooler, join them for a swim or meet them later at the bars. That's how he'd always imagined being single would be: a procession of women in the summer sun.

Now, sitting on the front stoop with the leash in his hand, Benjamin waited for Audrey Martin to appear. Her malamute lay on its stomach, picking away at the turkey bone. She would show up before long, he figured. If she didn't come looking, he would deliver the dog to her. He would play dumb. *You look familiar*, he would say. *Did you go to Goodwin by any chance?*

FIFTEEN MINUTES LATER she appeared, alone, calling out, "Sheba." When she saw the dog, she came striding across his lawn. "You found her," she said. That same sparkly smile, only slightly dimmed by the twenty-five years in between. She took the leash from him. "You're a lifesaver."

"Actually, I'm a car salesman. Benjamin," he said, extending his hand.

"Audrey."

Audrey. A thrill went through him at the sound of her name, even though he'd known it was her. He shook her hand—soft skin, wedding ring, no watch or other jewelry. Her face showed no recognition. She didn't remember him.

"Do you live nearby?" he asked, playing his part.

"We just moved into the house at the bottom of the street, my husband, daughter, and me."

"Ah, the new neighbors. You're doing a terrific job with the renovations."

"Thanks."

There was a pause, and she patted her dog, looking down. Before she could try to get away, he went into his act, affecting an expression of concentration. "Hey, you look really familiar. Did you go to Goodwin by any chance?"

Her mouth fell open. "How on earth did you know that?"

"Your name is Audrey Martin, right?"

"Wow. You've got a good memory. What was your name again?"

He told her.

She narrowed her eyes. "I'm sorry, I don't remember you. Did we have the same homeroom?"

"No. I was a year beneath you, a lowly underclassman with a serious crush. But that's not very original. All the guys had crushes on you."

She blushed, he was pleased to notice. "Hardly," she said.

"Well, it's true."

"How long have you lived here?" she asked.

"I don't. This is my dad's house. I'm visiting, sort of."

"Sort of?"

"Well, I'm waiting."

She laughed. "Waiting for what? The rapture?"

"For my divorce to become final." He hadn't planned to volunteer that information, but her question had thrown him off-balance. "There's a ninety-day waiting period," he informed her. "I've got—let's see, what is this, October twentieth?"

"Yep."

"A little more than two months to go."

"Is that all it takes?"

"Ninety days to freedom, yes."

"Lucky you," she said with a mysterious smile.

Benjamin had no idea how to answer that. "What happened after Goodwin?" he asked, trying to keep the conversation going. "Give me the CliffsNotes version."

"I was a drama major at Wesleyan," she said. "Then grad school at Yale, English literature."

"I never finished college," he said. "I didn't like it all that much."

"You must think I'm a terrible snob," she said, "giving you my résumé like that."

"Not at all," he said, happy to throw her off-balance. "You were never snobby, it was one of the things we all liked about you. Not like Skippy Brooks and Ginny Hunter and that gang."

"Skippy was actually really nice."

They talked about former classmates, teachers and class reunions. (She hadn't gone to any.) He settled into his easy salesman's style, feeling the awkwardness fade—she had thrown him with that "Lucky you" response. What was she trying to tell him? That her marriage was in trouble? That she wanted out? He rattled off all the gossip he could recall from the last issue of the *Goodwin Alumni News*. "Do you remember Mr. Dorfman?" he heard himself saying. Their old gym teacher had won the state lottery. "Three million dollars, but he kept his job at the school. He works for a dollar a year now."

"You really keep up," she said, patting her dog. She told him that Gretchen Peters had moved to Paris and married a famous artist, but otherwise she hadn't kept in touch with anyone.

They reached a lull. He took a deep breath, not wanting to force the conversation further. He'd made contact. He'd gotten her attention. That was enough for now.

In the silence that followed, she pulled a leash out of her pocket. "Here, let me," said Benjamin. He bent down to unsnap his old leash from the dog's collar. His head was level with her waist, just inches away, so close he could smell the fresh-laundry scent of her jeans. The clasp was stuck. As he fiddled with it, he felt her fingers graze the nape of his neck. He lowered his head, and she ran her fingers through his hair. Her touch surprised him, shocked him, but at the same time felt completely natural, so soothing that he wondered if he were imagining it.

"You have beautiful hair," she said.

"Thanks," he said, without looking up.

At last he detached the clasp and stood.

"Thanks for rescuing her." She smiled, snapping on her leash.

"Glad to help."

He watched her as she walked away. The dog turned back to look at him, but Audrey didn't.

HE WENT INTO the kitchen through the garage door. Yukon jumped up and rushed to sniff at his legs, then ran to his water bowl, lapping furiously—a good sound, that hectic splashing and the pushing of the bowl across the linoleum. Sometimes Yukon would plant his foot inside the bowl to keep it steady, a sight that always made Benjamin smile. A moment later the dog padded out of the room.

Benjamin could still feel her touch on his neck. Yes, she was married, but there were always consequences in getting involved, he had learned; it was the cost of personal interaction. Like the cost of doing business: unavoidable. In the past he'd fallen into entanglements without really meaning to. With Judy, he hadn't expected anything more than a few dates. With Rachel Rosenberg, he'd expected a single night, not a full-fledged affair. The bill always came at the end—often in some wholly unexpected form—but that was no reason not to play.

His thoughts were interrupted by Yukon, whining and whimpering from the hallway. "Hey," he yelled. "Stop that!" He expected the dog to come running toward him, but instead the whining intensified. Annoyed, Benjamin went down the hall, to where Yukon stood in the den doorway. He pushed past the dog and looked into the room. For a moment he didn't comprehend what he was seeing.

"Dad?"

His father was splayed facefirst on the rug.

"Dad, what are you doing?"

Leonard twitched. He seemed to be trying to speak, but only garbled sounds emerged, like those of a person choking. Benjamin bent beside him and rolled him onto his back. Leonard stared blindly at the ceiling, his tongue rolling.

The dog barked, and the noise roused Benjamin. He rushed to the kitchen, grabbed the wall phone, and dialed 911.

"I need an ambulance," he yelled. "Something's wrong with my father."

AT ST. FRANCIS HOSPITAL, Benjamin waited for two hours in the emergency room for the doctor to return. He was a middle-aged Indian man, barely five feet tall, with shiny black hair slicked across his forehead.

"Shall we have a word outside?"

Benjamin followed the doctor into the hallway. The intercom blared. An orderly pushed a cart loaded with dinner trays. Benjamin had not eaten all day, but the smell of the food made his stomach knot tighter.

An old lady was sitting in a wheelchair against the wall, her legs spotted with dark bruises.

"We moved your father into the intensive care unit," the doctor said. "He's stable but his condition remains serious. He's had a stroke. A blood vessel to the brain was blocked by a clot. When this happens, that part of the brain cannot get oxygen and begins to die."

From one of the emergency room cubicles came the cries of an old man. *Help me,* he yelled. *Please someone help me.* The man had been screaming for most of the afternoon, and at first the screams had shocked Benjamin. But now the man's voice was dry and hoarse; no one seemed to notice.

"Shouldn't someone sedate that guy?" Benjamin said.

The doctor continued as if he had not spoken. "One way we treat the stroke is with drugs that break the clots. These drugs are most effective when administered within a three-hour window from the onset of symptoms. A very small percentage of stroke victims reach the hospital within that time. But your father is one of the lucky ones. You got him here quickly."

In the back of the ambulance, Benjamin had held Leonard's hand as the EMTs worked above him on the stretcher: the siren blaring, the sickening smell of diesel fumes, the bursts of amplified voices on the two-way radio. *It's okay, Dad,* he'd repeated, averting his gaze from his father's stricken, uncomprehending face. *Everything's going to be okay.* The same thing he'd told his daughter not so long ago, he realized now. Would these reassurances prove to be just as empty? He pushed away the thought, trying to concentrate on the doctor's words.

"He has a partial paralysis on the right side. This means that the left side of his brain was damaged. And his speech has been affected."

"Will he be able to talk again?"

The doctor consulted the chart. "We're giving him Coumadin to prevent further clotting. Many stroke victims are able to regain capabilities, but of course we can't be certain. Your father is how old?"

"Eighty-four."

The doctor nodded. "A lot depends on his will to improve. The rehabilitation process can be taxing."

"How long will he have to stay in the hospital?"

"One week, at the very least. If all goes well, at that point we can transfer him to a rehabilitation clinic."

"May I see him now?"

"Of course."

From the hallway Benjamin heard the old man start up again, screaming for help, and then just screaming. Benjamin took the elevator to the ICU. In the room, the bright fluorescent light spilled across his father's pale and blotched face. Leonard lay on his back with tubes coming out of his nose and arms. His feet, protruding from the blankets, were sheathed in hospital stockings, like women's nylons. "That's to prevent clotting," the nurse told him. Benjamin stood by the hospital bed, holding his father's hand.

THAT NIGHT he came home to a darkened house. He went from room to room turning on lamps, trying to dispel the sense of dread, while Yukon followed him, panting. Benjamin scooped some brown pellets from the bag of dog food into the bowl. He sat at the kitchen table watching Yukon gobble the food. Thirty seconds later the dog was finished.

He needed to talk to someone, but could think of no one to call. He certainly wasn't going to worry his kids about it yet, if he could help it. He'd already called his sister in San Diego, to give her the news. She had wanted to come on the next flight, but he told her to stay with her husband and kids. There was nothing she could do, he told her. They just had to wait to see how Leonard responded. And besides, he said, it was only a "minor stroke."

In truth, the doctor had said no such thing. Benjamin had wanted to put Sissi's mind at ease. But now who would reassure him? What if Leonard didn't get better? Or if he got worse? His father, his business partner, the one person he trusted above all others: What would he do without him?

As a child, Benjamin had always worried that Leonard might suddenly drop dead: a heart attack while driving his Cadillac or cooking hamburgers on the grill. He couldn't recall what prompted this fear. Leonard had always been healthy. But he had been older than most of the other fathers in the neighborhood. If Benjamin woke in the night he would listen to the sound of his father snoring in the next room, awaiting the next percussive outburst, fearing that it might not come. In the morning, at the breakfast table, he would imitate the snoring, making his mother and sister laugh. *That's not me,* Leonard would joke. *That's your mother. She snores like a stevedore.*

Feeling an onset of panic, Benjamin decided to call Judy to tell her the news. To his surprise, she answered: "What do you want?"

"You're answering?"

"I'm sick of you clogging up my machine."

He tried to ignore that. "I have something to tell you." He paused. "It's not good news."

"Nothing is good news where you're concerned. How dare you call this late?"

He felt himself falling into the familiar fighting stance. "You didn't have to pick up. You could have let it go to the machine, like usual."

"I should have. God, I can't stand the sound of your voice. It makes my skin crawl."

Benjamin took a deep breath, trying to stay calm. "Judy, we should be able to communicate. For the kids' sake, at least."

"They're better off without you. You're poison. I don't want you seeing them."

"What about Thanksgiving? The kids will be home—"

"Forget about Thanksgiving. I'm having a peaceful dinner with my children. You're not invited. You're no longer part of this family."

"Come on, Judy. Don't be a pain in the ass. This is hard enough—"

"Talk to my lawyer if you don't like it."

She hung up. "Damn," he hissed, angry with himself for getting drawn into a shouting match. Only Judy could get him going like that. When he redialed he got the answering machine; he heard his own voice announce: *This is the Mandelbaums. Please leave a message for Benjamin, Judy, David, or Sarah.*

"Very mature, Judy," he said after the beep. He considered going on, telling her about Leonard—but he hung up instead. She had always been fond of his father; the two had been close ever since she'd started working at Mandelbaum Motors, all those summers ago. No matter how nasty she was being, telling her about Leonard's stroke on the answering machine would be a lousy thing to do.

This is the Mandelbaums.

He felt the weight of what he'd lost. He'd had everything: a family, a home, and all the warmth that came with it—the pleasant chaos of the kitchen, Judy cooking pasta, David and Sarah making the salad, their friends coming and going, the house alive with the familiar presences. A full life. How had he let that slip away?

Benjamin went into the den and turned on the TV. Sometime later he drifted into a dream of a snowy field. He and Yukon were walking toward a line of trees. Something was rustling behind the branches. Was it a deer? A raccoon? Pine needles fell and the wind rose like a chorus of voices.

LEONARD MANDELBAUM woke to a rumbling outside the window. He felt numb all along the right side of his body. A tube was attached to his wrist. He wanted to remove it but found that he couldn't raise his hand. With great effort, he managed to move his fingers, hardly more than a twitch.

This was not his bed. He was not at home, but at that moment he could not remember where his home was. The rumbling clouded his mind. He could not summon the word for the sound—for when water fell from the sky. It happened during storms. The clouds opened up and the thing happened. It made you wet. Your clothes would get soaked if you stood outside. A simple word. But he could not find it, and searching for the word made his head throb.

He opened his mouth to speak, but the sounds that came forth made no sense, like a record played on slow speed. The effort at speech tired him immensely, and he let himself fall back into darkness, not sleep, not waking.

"WAKEY, WAKEY, LEN."

Some time had passed, he could not say how long. He blinked, trying to focus. A face was peering down at him, not three inches away: enormous features, a grotesque painted mouth. *Who are you?* he tried to say, but only a slurred syllable emerged.

"Don't strain yourself, Len. You just take it easy. That's why they got you in this dark room, to reduce stimulation."

He fell into the blackness, tumbling backward. Where was this place? He thought he heard Myra's voice, and then he was pulled away, someone tugging at his arm.

"You probably don't even know who I am. Your mind's all muddled right now. It's Terri. Do you remember? Think, Len. You've got to start using your noggin again."

He felt ashamed that he didn't know the woman. "I'm fine," he managed.

"I called the house looking for you and your son told me what happened. You must feel terrible, you poor man. I went through the same thing with Dick Senior. He had a stroke in 'ninety-nine. He was a clotter just like you. We were driving home from the China Palace and he started swerving all over the road, and the leftover chicken teriyaki fell into my lap. I called him an idiot. 'Look what you did to my suede skirt!' Then Dick stopped the car and put his forehead on the steering wheel and started foaming at the mouth. I got out of the car and lit a cigarette. I was in shock. There was a pay phone there and I dialed Dick Junior. 'Dickie,' I said, 'your father just dropped dead.' By the time the ambulance showed up Dick Senior was speaking in tongues. 'Ooga booga booga,' he was saying."

Someone knocked on the door. There was another visitor coming to see him. Leonard felt that he should stand to greet the person, but he could not move his legs.

"Come on in, honey. Don't be shy."

She was a tall woman dressed all in white, like a saint. "Time for your sponge bath, Mr. Mandelbaum."

Leonard was in motion, being turned onto his side. Something cold and wet was running down his back.

"Doesn't that feel nice, Len? What a lucky man you are, to have such a pretty gal sponge your bottom. You got the legs of a showgirl, honey. You ever dance?"

"Some ballet when I was a kid. But I was too tall to be any good."

"How tall is that?"

"Six feet."

"You hear that, Len? A regular model, this one. Where you from anyway?"

"Jamaica."

"I knew it the moment you walked in. That lovely skin, like cocoa."

The nurse pulled the sheet up to his chest.

"Say thank you to the pretty lady, Len."

Thank you, pretty lady.

"Look at his face. Look how hard he's trying. He's an old-fashioned gentleman. If he had his wits about him he'd be kissing your hand."

"He looks very distinguished."

"You hear that, Len. *Very distinguished.*"

"How long have you been married?"

"Oh, we're not married, hon. Just pals."

"Well, you make a lovely couple."

"Thanks, dear. What's that you're giving him now?"

"Stool softener. He should avoid bearing down, if possible. Try not to let him blow his nose, cough, or sneeze."

"You got another one of those stool softeners, honey? I could bring one home for my son's shiksa. She looks like she needs one. I'm joking. You run along. I'll make sure he stays relaxed. You got that, Len? No coughing, no sneezing."

A smell of something clean. Myra always used it in the kitchen. The word eluded him, but the scent lingered in his lungs. He heard a rhythmic beeping and the sound of a loudspeaker in the distance. Was he at the airport? Was he going on a trip?

"Dick Senior came home from the hospital as blind as a bat. For two months all he did was dribble and drool. Then one day he said, 'I can see. Terri, I can see.' He could barely hold his head up. One minute he'd be sitting there, next minute his chin was on his chest. The doctor wouldn't give him a cane, said if he started with one he'd be using it for the rest of his life. I tell you, that man had to learn how to walk again, how to use a fork—everything. He tried to comb his hair with a toothbrush. It would have been funny if it wasn't so pathetic. And Dick Senior was a proud man. They gave him exercises to work his mind, a stack of cards with pictures on them, even a first grader could do it. I showed him a picture of a refrigerator and a picture of a car and asked, 'Now, Dick, which one is the car?' and he got it wrong. 'No, Dick. That's a refrigerator.' So I asked again, and he got it wrong again. I'd give him a pencil and paper and say, 'Spell frog,' and he would write *fog*. One day he wanted to help with dinner. I told him to boil the water. A minute later, he was on fire. He lit his sweater on the burner and didn't even know it. He couldn't feel a thing in his right arm. I realized something was wrong when I smelled the burning wool. 'You're on fire, Dick,' I said and threw a glass of water on him.

"But each day he got a little better. He'd go out for a walk and pull his right leg along like it was a piece of wood. 'Come on, leg,' Dick would say. 'Keep up with me, you prick.' Then one morning he woke up, with tears streaming down his face, saying that his leg hurt. 'Let me get the heating pad,' I said. 'No, Terri. You don't understand. I can feel my leg again. *I can feel my leg.*' A few weeks later he was back on the golf course.

"This doesn't mean anything to you now, Len. You probably don't even know your own name. And you won't remember any of this later. You're like a newborn baby in your diaper. The important thing is not to worry. You just stay calm. Listen to old Terri. Everything's going to be just fine."

He felt a hand, stroking his hair.

"Oh look, Len. It's Oprah. Last week she had a show on sex addiction. One gal said she'd had relations with twenty-five men. Everyone oohed and aahed and clucked their tongues. I'm thinking, *Twenty-five? Is that all?* Shush, Len, stop that gibbering. Let's listen to Oprah."

BENJAMIN MET HER on Leonard's fifth day in the hospital. *A friend of your mom and dad from the old days*, she called herself. She'd phoned the house a couple of days earlier, asking for Leonard. Benjamin recognized her last name—the dry-cleaning franchise. Dick Funkhouser had been one of Leonard's cronies. (Benjamin remembered the dry-cleaning man from childhood. When his father would take him into the shop to pick up his weekly supply of starched white shirts, the man would come out from behind the counter and tousle Benjamin's hair and hand him stacks of shirt cardboards, which Benjamin liked to draw on.)

He didn't remember Terri, though. She said she'd reconnected with Leonard the week before, over dinner. "Did he try to sell you a Cadillac?" Benjamin asked, putting it together. "That was Dickie's idea. My son Dickie. He thinks I should have a new car. Fat chance." The woman didn't seem like Leonard's type—she wore enormous gold hoop earrings and exuded a powerful perfume—but Benjamin found her to be comforting, in a way. "He's much better today," she told him, patting his arm. "I was here yesterday too, and his color is coming back." Benjamin himself could discern no difference in Leonard's condition—his father lay there in a frozen-face stupor, unable to drink water, now and then barking out a few sudden, slurred syllables. "He's going to be fine," Terri reassured him.

After leaving the hospital Benjamin drove to Wintonbury Center for a slice of pizza. He sat alone at a windowseat, looking over sales figures on his laptop. Business was booming. With six days left in October, they'd already met the Cadillac sales goal, which would give them a bonus worth—he did the figures quickly—about seventy-five grand. Sure, he made his dealer holdback on every car they sold, but with overhead, that manufacturer bonus often meant the difference between the dealership being in the black for the month or being in the red. The bonus number changed every month—and if they fell just one car short the dealership got nothing—but his salesmen hadn't missed their numbers in a year. They'd even hit September, a rarity, because the first week of school was always lousy for sales in the suburbs.

He put away his laptop and called his son. No answer, as usual. He could picture David, as he'd seen him do so many times, fishing the phone out of his pocket, glancing at the number, and then putting the phone away until it rang itself out. David wasn't like Sarah. He didn't want to discuss the breakup; he wouldn't even let Benjamin raise the subject. "It's fine, Dad. Whatever" was the most David cared to comment on his parents' divorce. Benjamin didn't leave a message. This was another thing he'd learned about his son's phone etiquette; he never listened to messages, and apparently it wasn't good form to leave one, at least in David's social universe. The number appeared on the screen; that was all he needed to know.

Next, Benjamin called his sister and updated her on their father's condition, all the while gazing across the street at the Thursday-night crowd at Max Baxter's Fish Bar. Benjamin could see the well-dressed men and women through the plate-glass window, pressed together in the small bar area, everyone drinking and talking. He felt the urge to walk over for a cocktail and join the conversation. He wanted some company, even a drunken crowd—anything but another night in front of the television. But Yukon needed to go out; there was no way to avoid his responsibility to the dog.

When he got home he found a card in his mailbox.

Thanks for rescuing my dog.

Beneath her name she'd written her phone number. He went into the house—he'd forgotten to leave any lights on, again. It was a bad time to call, six-thirty on a weekday, dinnertime. Her husband would probably be home, maybe in the same room with her. But she didn't have to answer the phone, did she? She could simply let the call go to voice mail. He cleared his throat and dialed, and she answered immediately.

"This is Benjamin Mandelbaum," he stammered, feeling much like the high school version of himself. "I got your note."

"My thank-you note?"

"Yes." He paused. "Thank you for that."

She laughed. "You're not required to thank someone for a thank-you note."

"No?"

"No. It could go on and on."

"Like pi," he said.

"Exactly."

There was a silence. Finally he said, "I was just about to take the dog for his evening stroll, and I was wondering if you'd like to come along." He braced himself for her rejection, but she agreed without a pause, suggesting they meet at the bottom of the street in ten minutes.

He felt his pulse beginning to quicken. Even if dog walking was all it would amount to, that would be okay. He welcomed the company. Dog walks could be a lonesome business this time of year. Still, he couldn't help but wonder if she wanted more than companionship from him. He certainly hoped so.

He brushed his teeth, rolled on some deodorant, and changed into a pair of khakis. Five minutes later he was tugging Yukon down the street, breathing in the crisp night air. He found Audrey waiting by the mailbox, her malamute wagging its tail. Yukon leapt at the sight of the other dog, howling and straining at the leash. Then, getting close, he quieted and politely inspected the other dog's rear.

Audrey greeted him with a hug, surprising him with the press of her body. "Let's go down to the grammar school," she proposed. "Sheba likes to dig in the sandbox."

"Fine by me," he said.

They crossed the intersection, Audrey leading the way. He studied her backside, a reflex whenever any woman walked ahead of him. (Judy called this his "biological necessity." She would roll her eyes and tell him to stop ogling.)

"I'm glad you called," said Audrey. "I've been sitting alone in that house all day. My daughter has a ten o'clock curfew and she uses every minute of it."

"How old is she?"

"Seventeen."

"Mine was the same way at that age. Social butterfly."

"When we first moved here, she wouldn't leave the house. Now she won't come home. I guess I'm happy she's made some friends. I just wish I knew who they were."

He said, "This is Wintonbury, Audrey. She'd have to look pretty hard to find trouble in this town."

"If there's trouble, she'll find it. That's Emily. She would stay out all night if I let her."

Audrey smelled wonderful, some perfume that went directly to his groin. Had she put on the scent for his benefit? If so, it had worked. His cock strained against his pants, giving him an awkward gait. His laptop just didn't satisfy the desire. *Biological necessity*, indeed.

They turned up the path toward the grammar school. The dogs ran back and forth on their leashes between the rows of tall pines at the edge of the property, sniffing at the bases of the trees. Smoke from someone's fireplace rose into the night air. The grammar school was brightly lit, every classroom illuminated, although the parking lot was empty. Behind the building, the asphalt playground was grass-eaten and potholed, splattered with chalk marks. At the far end of the school property was the sandbox and, beside it, an ancient metal swing set and a new contraption made of large red plastic tubes that looked like an enormous caterpillar.

They stood side by side, both holding long leashes, as the dogs busied themselves, sniffing and searching for some unknowable spot. Like most salesmen, Benjamin felt uncomfortable with lapses in conversation. He wondered if Audrey were cold. Judy was always freezing; she'd turn the thermometer to seventy-five degrees during winter. She called him cold-blooded, like a lizard, which didn't even make sense.

"We can go back if you're cold," he suggested.

"No, this is fine."

"You sure?"

"There's no rush."

A sudden growling came from the dogs, and he turned to see Yukon trying to mount the malamute, bucking and grasping from behind. He yanked the leash and pulled Yukon away. "Sorry about that," he said. "He's fixed but still interested. I'm not sure why."

"You could say the same thing about my husband."

Benjamin laughed uncomfortably, not knowing what she meant, exactly. Married people were always mentioning their spouses without thinking, so maybe this was accidental. He often caught himself doing the same thing—*Judy this, Judy that.* Even at the end, when they could barely tolerate each other's company, he would hear himself dropping her name at the office, a symptom of living too long with the same person. He spouted her opinions, assumed her likes and dislikes. Now, separated for five weeks, he still caught himself using words like *sketchy* and *basically*—her words, which he didn't even like.

Benjamin decided to push the issue. "Aren't you getting along?"

"Andrew and I are way past not getting along. Something's up, ever since we moved to Wintonbury. He doesn't come home until eleven o'clock most nights. I hardly see him."

"Do you think he's having an affair?"

"No. I'm pretty sure Andrew's incapable of that sort of thing. But there's always a chance, I suppose."

Benjamin couldn't think of anything to say, so he just made a sympathetic "hmm."

After a moment Audrey went on. "I think he's making some sort of power play at the office. He's a partner at a big law firm. He worked out of their Stamford office for the past fifteen years, but moved us up here to take over the employment litigation division—Wait, is this boring?"

"No," said Benjamin. It wasn't boring in the least. He enjoyed hearing her speak and being close to her, and he especially enjoyed knowing she didn't get along with her husband, which opened up room for him. This woman had occupied a pedestal in his mind for so long, and yet he knew very little about her. "Do you think he's doing something illegal?"

"God, no. Not Andrew. He's too smart for that. But unethical, or borderline unethical—who knows."

"Well," said Benjamin, "he's a lawyer, right?"

She offered a forced smile—and he winced, telling himself, *She's Wesleyan, Yale, you douche bag. The car lot humor won't work on her. Up your game! She's smarter than you and everyone you know—*

"Andrew keeps mentioning one of his junior associates, without seeming to realize it. They play tennis together. I've heard him calling him and leaving messages—"

"And that's unusual?"

"For Andrew, yes. Most of the people who work for him, he can't even remember their names. He'll socialize with the other partners, but only if it's necessary. So, I think he's using this new associate to do his dirty work."

"I see . . ."

She turned to him, shrugging. "Sorry, this *is* boring. I don't want to talk about Andrew. I'm past that stage."

"First of all," he said, "you couldn't bore me if you tried. Second, what stage?"

This time, her smile seemed genuine. "The complaining stage," she explained. "Back in Cos Cob, that was the theme at book club, no matter what we read: Let's complain about our husbands!"

"What does that sound like?"

She affected an exasperated tone—and he remembered what a terrific actress she'd been in high school. "'He never asks about *my* day. All he does is talk about work. He leaves dishes in the sink as if I'm the maid. He forgets our anniversary. He forgets the kids' baseball games. He drinks too much, golfs too much, wants sex too often, or not often enough. His feet smell like rotten cheese.' That's the theme and variation. Our stinky, rotten husbands."

"And you're past that stage?"

"For the most part. Although it does feel good to vent now and then."

He said, "Did anyone ever tell you how terrific you were in *Guys and Dolls*—as Sarah Brown?"

"I can't believe you remember that. The character's name, even."

Of course he remembered the character's name; he'd read the photo caption not so long ago. The yearbook was still open on the desk in his room. "I'm good with names," he explained. "Trick of the trade."

"Right. Car salesman."

"Well, the book club ladies don't seem so strange. My wife certainly enjoyed venting. But to me, mostly."

"That's not venting. That's bitching."

"I suppose so."

"But now you're free, right?"

"Sixty days and counting." He gestured vaguely to the north, toward Granby and the turn-of-the-century Victorian she'd bought and renovated with their savings. "All that stuff she crammed into the house. I'm glad to be free of it." He felt himself playing the part of the carefree divorcé, but for the most part, he realized, it was true, at least in that moment.

"I envy you," she said. "But if I got rid of Andrew, who would cut the grass?"

He laughed. "That's exactly what my wife said. *Who's going to mow the lawn? Who's going to shovel the goddamn snow?*"

"I understand her perfectly."

He paused, pleased with the direction of the conversation. "So, which was your husband?"

She glanced at him, her brow creased. "Hmm?"

"Too often or not often enough?"

She sighed. "The latter, unquestionably. We haven't done anything in that department for a long time."

"How long?"

She turned to him with a half smile. "You're pretty direct, aren't you?"

"Have I mentioned, I'm a car salesman?"

"You don't look like one, if you don't mind me saying."

"What do I look like?"

She examined him with mock concentration, narrowing her eyes in a way he found endearing. "Rare book dealer."

He laughed. "Now you're making fun of me."

"Not in the least. You have a rumpled sort of eclecticism about you."

He laughed extravagantly, although uncertain what the word meant. Her *Wesleyan Yale* vocabulary. "Don't try to change the subject," he said, changing the subject away from thesaurus territory before he betrayed his ignorance.

"Fine, but you tell me first."

"Me?" He laughed. "That's easy. Five weeks. A day or two before Judy kicked me out. You?"

"A year and a half."

"Really? That long?"

"I can give you the exact date . . ." Her smile faded and she fell silent. The dogs seemed to register the lack of their voices, and both animals turned to look at them—tongues hanging out, panting. *Idling*, Benjamin called that, when the dog just stood there with a blank look on its face.

"Do you like wine?" she asked brightly. "I'd love a glass right now."

He glanced at his watch. "It's only seven-thirty. We could go somewhere." Stupid suggestion, he realized immediately. She was married; how could they go anywhere in a town as small as Wintonbury?

"I don't feel like going out," she said.

"I have a bottle at my place, if you prefer."

"Don't you live with your father?"

He didn't want to ruin the mood by telling her about Leonard's stroke, so he simply said, "He's away for a while."

"Is it a red?"

"It is."

"Now you know my weakness. Red wine."

He tugged on the leash, and the dog bounded away from the sandbox. They started back toward Apple Hill Road. He could hardly believe that she was coming to his house. To distract her, so she wouldn't change her mind, he babbled about people who lived in the houses they passed—as if this were all perfectly normal, something they'd done a hundred times before.

At his house, when he opened the front door, the dogs ran down the hallway with their leashes trailing after them. She opened her jacket, revealing a tight T-shirt with glittery red letters across the front.

"Have a seat in the den. I'll get the wine."

He didn't realize that his hands were trembling until he fumbled the corkscrew. It took him a minute to get the cork out of the bottle. He hoped the wine hadn't gone bad; he'd found it in a low kitchen cabinet, behind the garbage bags, the sale tag still pasted to the bottle ($8.99 SPECIAL!).

He handed her a glass, and she took a long sip, looking around at the framed family photos. It felt strange being alone with a woman in his dad's den, among his fusty old-man possessions. Benjamin tried not to think about Leonard now, drugged up in his hospital bed.

She examined his black-and-white high school graduation photo on the wall, an 8 x 12 shot of young Benjamin accepting his diploma from the Goodwin headmaster. She said, "Did you really have a crush on me back then?"

"Of course. You were the most beautiful girl in the entire school. I thought about kissing you all the time."

"Why didn't you tell me?"

"Tell you what? That I wanted to kiss you? I'm sure that would have gone over well."

"Do you still want to kiss me?" She finished her wine with a long drink, put the glass down on the coffee table, and turned toward him. "I'd like that."

He swallowed involuntarily. "Are you sure?"

"Quite."

He kissed her gently on the lips. When he pulled away, she put her hand behind his head and brought him back. As they embraced, he ran his hands over her arms, lightly grazing the sides of her breasts. After a few minutes, she leaned back and yelped in surprise and said, "What the heck?" She reached behind and pulled Leonard's hot-water bottle from between the couch cushions: a bright red bladder, still filled with water, like an organ. She said, "Maybe we should go to your bedroom."

"Right." His voice felt thick. "It's upstairs."

"That's where they usually are."

He led her by the hand, past the sleeping dogs and up the staircase. She went into the room ahead of him and looked around. "It smells like you in here."

"I hope that's a good thing." *Audrey Martin is in my bedroom.* This simple fact seemed to paralyze him. He grinned dumbly and followed her gaze around the room. "I've been meaning to change the decor."

"I like the Farrah poster. Very retro."

She saw the yearbook on the desk and flipped through a few pages. "Been catching up on your reading?"

"Only the parts that have to do with you."

"You really did have a crush on me, then?"

"Still do."

She closed the book and kissed him, more urgently now. She reached down and fumbled with his belt buckle. She got that open, then unbuttoned his khakis and eased them down, together with his boxer briefs.

His hard-on sprang out. She stroked him, her hands warm and soft. This snapped him out of his daze, and he bent to help her take off her jeans. His face was down at her thighs, and she ran her hand through his hair, just like she did that first day. He felt down her legs: smooth, freshly shaved. Maybe that's what she'd done in those minutes before they met with the dogs.

"Take off your shirt," he said.

She did what he asked, then unfastened her bra. Her breasts emerged, bigger than he would have imagined. The sudden nakedness of a stranger, so shocking. He felt calm and oddly removed, like an observer at a tennis match. He took her in his arms and they fell onto the bed.

TWO DAYS LATER, Leonard Mandelbaum came to. He found himself on a couch, watching TV. Benjamin was sitting next to him, eating potato chips from a bag.

"Where am I?" He had to concentrate on his words; they felt like cotton balls in his mouth.

Benjamin turned to him with a dawning smile. "Are you feeling okay, Dad?"

"I feel strange. Where am I?"

Benjamin told him the whole story: how he found him in the den, the ride to the hospital, the three days he'd spent in the ICU, oblivious. Leonard remembered his collapse, the eruption inside his head like a great wind blowing. But after that, there were only flashes—the expressionless faces of nurses, people coming into his room at night, someone screaming in the hallway, intercoms and alarms, and all that time, a feeling of shame for losing control, for not being able to think straight.

"Seven days," Leonard repeated. It could have been a long night, a month, a year. "What's the date today?"

"Saturday. The twenty-seventh of October."

Leonard got to his feet. He could barely feel his right leg. His whole right side was numb.

"Pins and needles," he gasped, grabbing his son's arm.

"The doctor wants you to walk as much as possible."

Leonard pointed toward the hallway and shuffled forward. "Okay then," he said, leaning on Benjamin. "Let's go."

* * *

WHEN THEY got back to his room, Leonard saw the woman sitting in the corner by the window, a ball of yarn bouncing at her feet as she clicked the needles.

Benjamin said, "Hi, Mrs. Funkhouser," and Leonard gestured at her and said, "It's Terri Funkhouser. From Newark."

She looked up at him above her bifocals. "Is that the Leonard Mandelbaum I used to know?"

"I'm fine," said Leonard. He eased into bed.

"Dad's feeling much better," said Benjamin. "We went up and down the hallway three times and took the elevator to the gift shop." He set the magazines on the table, and she examined them.

"*Newsweek. The New York Times.* You were always so well informed, Len. Would you like me to read to you?"

"You do your sewing."

"Not sewing. *Knitting.* Guess what I'm making."

Leonard squinted at the wool in her lap. "Blanket."

"Guess again."

"Carpet."

Benjamin adjusted the sheets, covering his father's legs. "A carpet, Dad? Why would you say that?"

"Joking," said Leonard, exhaling heavily. He felt a sudden physical exhaustion.

"It's a sweater for my favorite patient. *You.*"

Benjamin patted his arm. "I'm going to head home, Dad. Mrs. Funkhouser will keep you company. She's been coming to see you every day. You remember that, right?"

"I'm happy to visit. Gives me something to do with myself."

After Benjamin left, Leonard closed his eyes. But it would be rude to fall asleep with the woman visiting him. "I'm awake," he said.

"Go ahead, nap if you want. You got an hour before dinner. I'm happy to see you back to your old self. You're not all glazed over like before. The same thing happened with Dick Senior after his stroke. One afternoon he got out of his armchair, wiped the drool off his mouth, and said, 'Terri, where am I?'"

"Who's Terri?"

"What was that, Len? Say again."

He sighed and closed his eyes. The clicking of the knitting needles, like Morse code.

* * *

WHEN HE OPENED his eyes again, it was dark, the curtains were drawn. The TV flashed without sound. In the corner the woman was sprawled in the chair, head back, mouth open, her chest rising and falling. Her blouse had come untucked and he could see some of her stomach, pale and rippled, spilling over her hip. As he raised himself up in bed, Leonard grabbed at his right leg, yelping in pain. Terri Funkhouser stirred and picked her glasses off her chest, attached to a thin gold chain that went around her neck. "What's wrong, Len? You're not having another stroke, are you?"

"Cramps," said Leonard.

"That's the paralysis," she said, rising heavily from the chair. "A little rubdown will do you wonders."

She pulled the blankets away, exposing his legs in the tight hospital stockings. Her hands, warm and strong, gripped his right thigh and squeezed.

"Too hard."

"Don't be a baby, Len. We gotta get the blood flowing. You can't just lie in bed all the time like a cripple. You don't want to get bedsores. Dick Senior used to beg for massages. He would pay me by the hour, like a hooker. Said I had million-dollar hands."

Leonard pulled his gown over his groin, trying to cover the diaper and his hairless thighs. Myra had once complained that, as he'd gotten older, he'd grown as smooth as a baby while she'd gotten hairy.

"Don't be shy," Terri said. "You've got nothing down there I haven't seen before." Her hands moved toward his stomach, making him laugh involuntarily. "My son Dickie's been hell to get along with lately."

"Dickie's a good boy," Len managed.

"He never had a head for business, but after Dick Senior died, he just went to pot. He lost the dry-cleaner business on bum stocks, thousands and thousands of shares, and the whole thing went poof overnight, like throwing money into the wind. His wife left him when they foreclosed on their house. Now he's back living with me, a fifty-year-old man. He's got a shiksa girlfriend and they want to sell my house out from under me and take the money and go to Florida. I hear them scheming in the next room, as if I were already dead. They even had the house appraised. After all I've done for him, this is the way he treats me, my only son."

"Oww." Her hands were digging into his kidneys, making him wriggle.

"Dickie's dead broke, and that shiksa twists his head all around. 'Wouldn't you be happier in a nice little condo in Sarasota, Terri? It would be so much easier for you *at your age.*' This she says to my face. 'You're sitting on a gold mine. The Realtor told us it's worth four fifty, maybe more. Think of what you could do with all that money in Florida!' You can practically see the dollar signs in her eyes. Stefanie is her name. 'Stefanie with an *f,*' she likes to say, as if anyone cares. Voice like a chipmunk. How does that feel, Len? Good?"

"Stop." He tried to turn away, but she pushed him back, her hands gripping his ribs.

"Don't get me wrong. I don't like living in that big house all alone. I'm glad to have the company. And I like Florida as much as the next person, but who wants to live there all year round in some concrete tower built in the sand? Who wants to get pushed out by some shiksa with a boob job? Well, I shouldn't mention the boob job because she had a mastectomy due to cancer and I wouldn't wish that on anyone, so forget I said that. Dickie never knew how to handle the ladies, and this one has her claws into him deep and she's not going to let go. I never begrudged Dickie anything. I spoiled him rotten. I'd give him the deed to the house tomorrow if he asked. I just don't like *her* asking. What's wrong, Len?"

"Hurts."

"There. Done."

Her face appeared just inches above him, peering down through her spectacles. Leonard felt his lungs clog with her perfume, pungent and stupefying.

"Can't breathe," he said.

She tucked the blankets around him like a straitjacket. "Dickie met her at the post office. She runs some sort of half-assed business out of her apartment, selling calligraphy—personalized invitations, wedding announcements, that sort of crap. Every day she schleps her packages to the PO. No wonder she's got her meat hooks into poor Dickie. Anything looks good compared to that type of life."

She went back to her chair and picked up her knitting needles. Her voice went on, but he tuned out the words, feeling a calm come over him. Myra would do the same thing—talk and talk, the words turning into a sort of music. He closed his eyes and let the voice draw him into a comfortable oblivion.

* * *

ON THE DRIVE home from the hospital that night Benjamin couldn't stop thinking about her. Her taut body, that lovely ass, raised for him. A silly refrain had gone through his mind for the first few minutes—*I can't believe it. I can't believe I'm fucking Audrey Martin*—as if he were his sixteen-year-old self, amazed at his good fortune.

For the past two days he'd wanted to call her, but—she was married. Better to let her make the next move, he figured. But now he couldn't stop himself. He got out his cell and dialed. "I was just thinking about you," he told her.

"That's nice," she said.

Her voice sounded flat, so he tried to bring her out. The direct route, always the best. "I enjoyed our little adventure the other night," he said, "in case you couldn't tell."

"Me too," she offered.

He checked the time: a few minutes past 6:00 P.M. on a Saturday evening. "I've got another bottle of wine, if you're interested."

"Is that an invitation?"

"It is."

"Hmmm," she said, drawing out the word in a teasing tone, which made his heart race. Teasing was good. Teasing meant it wasn't a one-time thing. She said, finally, "May I bring the dog? She hasn't had her walk yet and she's getting excited."

"That makes two of us."

They arranged to meet at his house in a half hour.

At home, he changed into a pair of jeans and a fresh pair of boxer briefs. He piled some kindling and a few logs in the fireplace and lit the newspaper to get it going. What woman could resist a fire? He opened the bottle of wine and readied the glasses. He got a blanket from his father's closet. What else? Condoms, of course. The half hour passed, then another ten minutes. He paced from the den to the kitchen, Yukon following him. Every few minutes he pushed aside the drapes and peered out at the dark street. What was keeping her? Had she changed her mind? Had her husband gotten in the way?

Finally, the doorbell rang. When he opened the door, her malamute raced past him, the leash slipping from her hand. Yukon pounced, and both dogs charged into the kitchen and began barking.

"The rain started," said Audrey. "I'm soaked."

"Come into the den. Warm up."

She stood before the fireplace in sweatpants and a sweatshirt. She pulled off the hood and let her hair down, shaking it out.

"You look terrific," he said.

"You haven't seen what I'm wearing yet."

"I haven't?"

She shook her head. "Turn around."

He did as she asked, staring into the darkness in the backyard. In the window he followed her reflection. She shimmied out of her clothes and bent to retrieve something out of her bag. Outside the window, the bushes trembled in the night breeze.

"Okay," she said. "You can look."

He turned to her. She was wearing black mesh panties, a pair of high heels, nothing else.

"Well? What do you think?"

"I'm speechless," he said.

AFTERWARD his cell phone buzzed. He fished it out of his pants and checked the caller ID.

"It's my son," he explained. "I'll call him later."

He turned off the ringer. He felt bad, but David had picked a lousy time to return his calls. Benjamin had been trying to reach him for a few days. He wanted to talk to him about Thanksgiving, just a few weeks away. Maybe his son could convince Judy to allow him to come to the house for dinner. He had called Judy three or four times since their last talk, but she wouldn't answer or respond to his messages. He still hadn't told her about Leonard's stroke. But now that his dad looked so much better, it didn't seem as urgent.

He tried to sweep his wife out of his mind as he rubbed Audrey's back. They were naked, lying side by side on the rug, on top of Leonard's Hudson's Bay wool blanket. Her dark red hair fell across her shoulders.

"You're good at that," she said, her voice raspy. She cleared her throat. "Really good."

"Thanks." He grinned. He had to admit, he'd been on his game. He hadn't rushed it. He'd taken his time, the way Judy always told him to, particularly at the start. Audrey had a beautiful body. It was blissful to run his hands over her soft skin, her breasts, the insides of her thighs. She was forty-five, but she looked a decade younger, easily, and he saw only the high school girl of his past. After some time with her on top of him, he'd switched positions, fucking her from behind, squeezing and slapping and caressing her ass, the way he'd always wanted to. He'd picked up speed as he went along, and her voice had gone hoarse with her cries of pleasure.

"Have you done this before?" he asked.

"What, had sex in someone's father's den?"

He laughed. "You know what I mean."

"This is a first."

"I'm your first affair?"

"Yes, Benjamin."

"Why me?"

"Because you're irresistible. Now stop fishing for compliments and let me enjoy the glow."

He laughed. "So you weren't faking?"

"Very funny, mister."

After a minute or two, with the logs cracking and hissing, he grew uncomfortable with the silence. "So what are your plans for Thanksgiving?" he asked, making his salesman's small talk.

"We're staying put this year," she answered. "We usually go to Andrew's parents' house in Longmeadow, but they already canceled. His father's not feeling well, apparently. It would have been awkward anyway."

"Why? Your husband still acting weird?"

"There's that. But I've got other trouble now: my daughter. She's giving me the silent treatment."

"What happened?"

She sighed. "Yesterday she disappeared after school. She didn't even bother to call to say where she was. I waited up all night. She showed up in a taxi at six o'clock this morning, stoned out of her mind. This afternoon I found a stash of prescription pills in her closet. God knows where she gets them."

"What did you do?"

"I flushed the pills down the toilet. That's why she's mad at me, if you can believe it. I invaded her privacy, she says. I don't know what to do with her."

"Try grounding her. That always worked with mine. She hated being trapped in the house."

"What would she want with OxyContin?"

"We smoked grass. Nowadays kids like the designer stuff."

"I never should have let her go to school in New York City. She always had a wild streak and that certainly didn't help. All those years, all those lessons—and she gets away from home for ten minutes and forgets everything."

He shrugged. "They have to learn it for themselves. Otherwise, it's like doing their homework for them. It just doesn't sink in."

"How old is your son?"

"David? He's twenty."

"Tell me about him," she said, her gaze lost in the fire.

"He's a great kid. Athletic, smart. He looks a lot like me, actually. He and I haven't talked much lately either, ever since Judy and I announced the divorce. But that's normal for David. He's always been quiet. When something's bothering him, he keeps it bottled up."

She was silent.

"You're not falling asleep, are you?"

She shook her head. A moment later, he felt her body trembling.

"Is something wrong?"

The tears flowed down her cheeks.

"Hey. What is it?"

"I don't want to talk about it."

"Was it something I said?"

"It has nothing to do with you."

"What, then?"

Between sobs, she said, "Just leave it alone."

He raised up on his elbow. "No, tell me. I want to know."

He felt her body tense. Finally she said, "Something bad happened, a year and a half ago. I'm not over it. I'll never be over it."

"Were you . . . raped?"

She wiped her eyes. "No, nothing like that," she said, her voice changing. "Why would you think that?"

"I was just asking—"

"This isn't Twenty Questions, okay?" She exhaled derisively. "Jesus, Benjamin. *Were you raped?*"

She got up suddenly and began searching for her clothes.

"I'm sorry if I said the wrong thing."

She shook her head. "I told you, I don't want to talk about it. I can't talk about it. So please don't ask stupid questions. Don't try to find out—" She pulled on her sweatpants and stuffed her bra and underwear into the pockets. She whirled around, looking for her sweatshirt. "I was raped in college, if you must know. I know what that feels like, okay? And I wish—I *wish*—that was it. I'd take that any day. I would *pray* for that."

She called for her dog. The malamute appeared almost immediately, pulling the leash after her. "I'm happy to talk about that. I can tell you all about the senior guy who got me drunk and locked me in his dorm room. There's a story for you. Very original, right? We can have coffee and I'll tell you what it felt like."

She turned, and he said, "Audrey."

"What!"

"Don't go."

She stopped in the doorway, her back to him. She rubbed her brow for a few long seconds and finally turned. "It's past eight. I have to go. I have to get back to my family."

"Okay. I'm sorry."

"Don't be sorry. Being with you, fucking you, that's all I want, okay? That's what I want from you. I don't want a fucking therapist, okay? Are you good with that?"

"Yes. Fine."

"Fine then."

She went out the front door, the dog trailing her. After she left he stared at the fire in a sort of daze.

HIS SON called back later that night. Benjamin roused himself off the couch, where he'd fallen asleep. The fire had gone out; a few embers were glowing a faint pink.

Yukon raised his head off the rug and gave Benjamin a look that seemed to say, *Why are you disturbing me?* The dog was not accustomed to being awake so late at night, and neither was Benjamin. He shifted on the couch, wincing. His groin felt sore; he hadn't used those muscles in a while.

"Hi, David."

"Is something wrong?"

"No," Benjamin said. This didn't seem like the right time to tell him about Leonard's stroke. "Why do you ask?"

"You called so many times."

"You're not very easy to get ahold of." On the other end of the phone, Benjamin heard car horns, loud voices. "Where are you?"

"Heading back to the dorm."

This was his son's habit, when he did deign to call—to talk during his walk across campus between classes or, like now, after leaving some party late at night. Their conversations lasted the time it took David to reach his destination, usually no more than a few minutes.

"Has your mother mentioned anything about Thanksgiving?"

His son didn't answer. The silence went on for so long that Benjamin thought he'd lost the connection. "Are you there, David?"

"Look, I don't want to be referee between you and Mom anymore. I'd rather stay down here in the dorm over Thanksgiving if it's going to be like that. The weather's better anyway. I don't need this shit."

"Whoa. Where did that come from?" Benjamin had assumed his son had accepted his and Judy's separation with his usual apathy toward all things parental. *It's fine, Dad. Whatever.* "What's your mother been telling you?"

"God, Dad. Did you hear what I just said? I don't want to be the fucking Ping-Pong ball."

"Watch your language."

"Listen to me for a change and maybe I will."

"I'd like to see you kids over Thanksgiving, like a family."

"A family. That's a joke. We're not a family. You took care of that."

"*I* did? Did your mother say that? That I was the one who asked for a divorce? Well, that's a lie—"

"Will you stop already? Are you even halfway listening?"

His son slurred the last few words, and Benjamin realized he must be drunk. "Look, David. I know it must be rough on you and Sarah—"

"Yeah, thanks for thinking of us. That's really awesome of you."

"I'd like to talk to you about this stuff in person. You *are* coming home for Thanksgiving, right?"

"Yeah, sure. Can't wait."

"Good. We'll—" he began, but his son had hung up.

*   *   *

THE NEXT DAY Benjamin got up late. It was a cold, gray Sunday, a few days before Halloween. He felt sluggish, as if hungover. Perhaps he was—a sex hangover, all that ecstatic effort expended on Audrey Martin, and her sudden meltdown afterward. It didn't help waking to an empty house, with no sounds of life but the boiler growling in the basement. There had been a certain comfort in coming down to a warm kitchen, even if it was only his father, making toast and eggs.

True, Leonard had seemed more like himself yesterday. But he'd grown tired so quickly, his face assuming that stricken, baffled expression. Without his false teeth, his cheeks seemed sunken. Benjamin hadn't even realized his father had false teeth, not until he saw him lying in the hospital bed, this aged, toothless version of Leonard.

Cruel, how the body changed, failed, the inexorable march toward deterioration. He'd had a vision of his father in his mind for so long—his golden self, a man in his forties, tossing Benjamin footballs. How had he failed to notice his father's changing face? His mother was gone nearly two years now, and his father was going, it seemed. Benjamin himself had been lucky to avoid illness, to reach forty-four without a hitch. A few of his friends had already succumbed to cancer and other diseases in their prime, victims of some cruel cosmic crapshoot. Was that all he could expect of life, a falling away of everything that had once made up happiness? A slow decline? Putting loved ones in the ground, watching children drift away? The Greeks had a saying, Benjamin had learned from the History Channel: *Count no man happy until his death, for no one knows what the gods have in store for him.*

He headed out into the morning with Yukon, the hood of his sweatshirt pulled over his head. Somewhere on the next street, someone was bouncing a basketball in a driveway; there was the solitary sound of the ball and the occasional thud against the backboard. A wonderful, lonely sound. Otherwise the street was quiet, the houses still, a ghostly morning.

Back when he was young, there had been packs of boys and girls running around the neighborhood—playing kickball in summertime, touch football in autumn, sledding in winter. Then, an *only child* had been rare, a condition worthy of pity and suspicion. Now it seemed like almost all the kids who lived on Apple Hill Road were *only children*. What joy was there in shooting baskets by yourself?

Yukon veered on the Pearlmans' lawn, sniffing and marking their rhododendrons. Well, Benjamin still thought of the house as the Pearlmans', but the place had been bought and sold twice since they'd lived there. Benjamin knew none of the "new" families on the street: nameless couples glimpsed now and then in their driveways, unloading baby seats from the backs of vans or SUVs. A generation had passed since his boyhood, like an ocean liner making slow distance into the horizon.

The white-brick house at the top of the street had once been, some 150 years ago, the house of the orchard keeper, who oversaw the terraced rows of apple trees rising up the hillside toward the mountain beyond, green, lush in season, inviolate. The farmhouse at the bottom of the hill had been the only other dwelling, then, before the tractors came to plow and dig for the coming subdivision, sometime in the early 1950s. If Benjamin closed his eyes he could summon the street the way it had been in his youth.

From those days, only Betty Amato and Franky DiLorenzo remained. Everyone else had moved away or died. Betty Amato kept Benjamin up-to-date with the news of her kids. His old friend Timmy was a bachelor who taught literature at a community college in New Jersey. He'd published a thin collection of short stories, available in paperback only, which Benjamin had seen selling online for ten cents. Benjamin and Timmy had been inseparable as kids, but they'd gone to different high schools and grown apart. Now, for some reason, Benjamin always felt awkward around Timmy when he saw him over holidays, even if they only spoke for a moment. Odd, that awkwardness. He didn't know where it came from, because as kids, he and Timmy had spent nearly every day together, usually just the two of them, playing basketball in the driveway or listening to records in his room, as silent as monks.

He wondered what his old-time neighbors might say about him. How did Benjamin Mandelbaum appear to the local gossips? They would say that he'd screwed up his marriage, that he'd moved back home with his dad because he had no place else to go, that he was selling his father's Cadillacs, as they'd always known he would. Everyone had known how Benjamin Mandelbaum would turn out—everyone but himself. *Photographer*, he'd said in high school whenever anyone asked what he wanted to do with his life or, more embarrassingly, *deep-sea diver*, even though he'd only taken a single course one spring holiday in Florida. Deep-sea diver! How absurd that notion seemed to him now, when Mandelbaum Motors had been his destiny from the beginning. Was it foolish to fight against the course of his life, now that it was half-gone, to break from the inevitabilities he had come to accept as his own?

He headed back inside. All those images from his childhood were as clear in his mind as the afternoon sky, but they were nothing. Shades and specters, misremembered, half-forgotten. His youth was gone, the people who had meant everything to him then had been usurped, replaced, removed. He'd known this, of course; he'd kept track of the passing years, registering the comings and goings of the calendar, like anyone else. But somehow it hadn't sunk in. He'd made a mistake, he felt now, moving back into his childhood home, unearthing these memories. The past, like a grave, was better left undisturbed. Here he was, forty-four years old, back in the house where he'd grown up, alone on the spinning earth.

THE NEXT MORNING, while driving down his street, Benjamin saw Audrey Martin in her driveway, getting into her car. A girl stood by the passenger side with a backpack slung over her shoulder, waiting for Audrey to unlock the door. As he drove past, the girl turned and squinted at him. Then she raised her right hand and gave him the finger. Benjamin glanced away from her, shocked. Did she do that to every passing car?

The girl was beautiful, like her mother, but in a wholly different way: tall, dark hair, full in the chest. She was how old—seventeen? If he didn't know better, he would have guessed she was in college, or older still. She had large, dark eyes, a wildness in her expression.

At the stop sign, he glanced in the rearview mirror and saw her, still, hand raised, pointing her middle finger at him like a knife as he drove off.

THAT EVENING he stopped for dinner at Max Baxter's Fish Bar. He sat at the bar, eating a cheeseburger and watching football highlights: the New York Giants and some blue and red team he didn't recognize. At one time he could name every starting backfield in the NFL. Now he didn't even know who coached the Giants. The NFL had gone on without him, like everything else, although the old Giants players remained in his mind as vivid as the screen above the bar: Spider Lockhart, as nimble as a thief; Pete Athas, with his long hair flowing from the back of his helmet; Ron Johnson, exploding out of the backfield, knees pumping high; and most of all, Fran Tarkenton, scrambling away from lumbering defensive ends, changing directions as quick as a dog. Recently Benjamin had seen the man on a late-night infomercial hawking rug cleaner, the great Tarkenton, looking like a retired accountant.

Before long the bar started to fill up with the evening crowd—stylish women in their thirties or forties, traveling in packs of two or three, eyes scanning the room. Hair in supermarket shades of brown, red, and blond, streaked and straw-like. Was this the type of place Judy would come to now, in search of his replacement?

"Brian, dear," one of the women said to the bartender, "an appletini, please."

"Check, please," Benjamin said to the bartender.

He felt off-kilter, after the way Audrey had left that night. He didn't know if he was supposed to wait for her to summon him, or if she expected him to make the next move. On the way home he decided, *What the hell*, and got out his phone. He wanted to see her; he might as well tell her so.

She answered in a formal voice he hadn't heard before: "Hold on a second, please."

Was her husband sitting next to her, chomping a steak? Benjamin had never had an affair with a married woman, never had to worry about these things. But he was half-drunk and not overly concerned with discretion.

"Sorry about that," she said.

"Is this a bad time?"

"Sort of. I grounded my daughter, like you suggested. So now I have to deal with her. She's always been something of a spy. A watcher and a listener."

"Where are you?"

"In my bathroom."

He got out a cigarette and lit up, something he did only when he drank. Judy used to complain about the smell. She would throw out his cigarettes whenever she found a pack and make him shower and wash his clothes before getting into bed. "I want to see you," he said.

"After the other night, you still want to see me?"

"That was my fault. I said the wrong thing—"

"Let's not talk about that anymore, okay?"

"Yes. It's settled. Good."

"Good," she said.

He took a long drag on his cigarette. He said, "I believe I'm a little bit addicted to you, Audrey Martin."

"To having sex with me, you mean?"

"Yes," he agreed, although he hadn't meant that—not only that.

"Why do you always call me Audrey Martin?"

"Because that's your name."

"Most people just use the first."

"I'd never think of using only the first. Audrey Martin is a totality. A concept that existed before it was given a title."

"You sound like Michel Foucault tonight."

"Who's she?"

She laughed.

"What's so funny?"

"You are," she said. "So you want to see me?"

"Yes. How about tomorrow?"

"Tomorrow isn't possible."

"What about the day after?"

"That's Halloween," she said. "Little goblins everywhere. Maybe the day after that."

He had trouble sleeping, thinking about her. On Halloween, every time some kid rang the doorbell, he jumped, thinking it might be her.

The following morning at the dealership, he found it difficult to concentrate. *Pussy brain*, the salesmen called it. When you can think of nothing else. He phoned her in the afternoon to see if they were on. Yes, she said, they were.

At home he lit the fireplace and poured the wine and prowled the empty rooms. She was late again. Did she do this to torture him? Or had he scared her away? His understanding had always been that women wanted to be wanted, but if you wanted them too badly you became *creepy* or a *stalker*. (Judy's words, again.) You had to express the proper amount of desire, but not too much. A game for daters. At forty-four, he didn't know how to play, or rather, he couldn't be bothered. He didn't want to dance around; he'd thought he and Audrey were on the same page there.

But maybe, he figured, she wasn't toying with him. Maybe she was having problems getting out of the house. Finally, he couldn't wait any longer and called her.

"Where are you?"

"Getting ready."

"You always keep me waiting."

"We said eight."

"Did we? I thought seven." He checked the clock. It was a quarter of. "Come now."

"Patience . . ."

Ten minutes later the doorbell rang.

"Where's your dog?" he said.

In response she tugged him down the hallway by his belt buckle. Later, this was the night he would remember most clearly, the way she'd stepped out of her dress to reveal the fishnet stockings and garter belt. They started on the rug in front of the fireplace. He was aware of Yukon in the doorway, watching with his head cocked to one side, like a ruffian at the ballet. *Go away*, Benjamin gestured with his hand. Instead, the dog padded into the room and stood beside them, panting.

"Just what I always wanted," said Audrey. "A threesome."

AFTER, they stared at the flames, both of them naked and glistening with sweat. They sipped at the wine until it was gone.

"More?" he asked.

"I'm perfect," she said sleepily, snuggling back against him.

"I saw you and your daughter on my way to work the other day," he said.

"Where?"

"In your driveway. She sort of glared at me."

"The patented Emily look."

"Then she flipped me off."

Audrey laughed.

"What's funny about that?"

"It's so Emily."

"Why would she do that?"

"I have no idea. You can't explain Emily. She takes sudden likes or dis-likes to people and things. She doesn't like the word *lugubrious*, she told me once. She said it doesn't sound like what it means."

He forced a laugh. Then he realized he was feeling too good—his arm wrapped around her, his face buried in her hair—to play the phony. "Actually," he began, "I don't know what that means."

"*Lugubrious?* Oh, sorry. It means gloomy, but in an over-the-top way, like *Dark Shadows.*"

"I can't believe you remember *Dark Shadows.*"

"I saw it in reruns when I was a kid. I always loved the name Barnabas Collins."

"That other word, too, you called me."

"Hmm?"

"You said I was . . . *ecclesiastic?* No. Not that." He laughed at himself. "Something like that."

She turned and kissed him. "I think I said eclectic. Someone who knows a lot of different things."

"Compared to you, I know nothing."

She moved onto her elbows and stretched, a yoga-like movement. "You know how to make a woman feel good. That's something, believe me."

"Why wouldn't she like me?"

"Who?"

"Your daughter."

"Stop obsessing about that. It was your car, probably. She hates SUVs, because of the carbon footprint. With Hummers, she goes berserk. She even threw a tennis ball at one once."

"You drive an SUV."

"The mini-model."

The flames rose from the fire, the wood crackling. It made him sleepy and slow-witted. "Is she still giving you the silent treatment?"

"Yes. She's really good at holding a grudge. It's as quiet as a tomb in that house."

"She's a beautiful girl. That can complicate things. It certainly did for my daughter. Boys and all."

"Emily's always been complicated. This is just her latest phase," she said, finishing her stretch and settling onto her stomach.

He said, "Maybe it's normal, in a way. Kids don't consider us as anything but *parents*. We're these people who live with them and provide things for them—money, a place to sleep, stuff they want. They don't really think about us until something goes wrong."

"It was the opposite with Emily."

"What was?"

Audrey didn't answer.

He leaned over to admire her. "God, I love your ass. Did I ever tell you that?"

In this light she looked like a woman in her late twenties. Petite girls like Audrey had the advantage in the long run, he decided, over the bombshells, the showstoppers at sixteen. He'd seen one of the Wendys at the dealership some years ago when she came in to buy a station wagon, and even then, in her mid-thirties, she was overweight, her high school face barely recognizable amid the jowly cheeks and garish makeup.

He squeezed her thighs. "Do you work out?"

"Yoga," she said. "Years and years of yoga. Before that, aerobics, Pilates, Nautilus. Push-ups to start the day, crunches in front of the TV at night. The great accomplishment of my life. All my education and ambition, and here you have it."

"Hey, don't be sarcastic. You look amazing. You've got the body of a twenty-something. Plus, you're smarter than anyone I know. You're talented. You're—"

"Okay, enough," she said. "You'll give me a complex."

Complex, too, he almost added, but he figured he better stay away from her complexity, after the other night.

In the silence that followed he felt himself starting to doze. He heard her gather her clothes, felt her brush against his leg. He intended to get up and show her out, but the next thing he knew he was asleep, the dog curled up against him where Audrey had been.

LEONARD COULDN'T GET the remote control to work. He could change the channels, but there was no sound. Terri Funkhouser knew how to work the thing, but she hadn't come. She usually showed up after breakfast, but today lunch had come and gone and still no sign of her.

He pressed the buzzer for the nurse, as he'd done many times already, without luck. They came on their own time when they were good and ready, and they did their poking and prodding, taking his blood pressure, twisting and turning him. If he asked a question or made a complaint, they smiled at him as if he were a simpleton. Even the nice nurse, the heavyset gal with the curly red hair, even she didn't answer his questions. He could understand why, with all the senile folks wandering the halls, talking to themselves, but shouldn't they be able to tell the difference between *them* and him?

When the door opened, Leonard pushed himself up in bed. "Terri, where have you been?"

"I had some errands. Did you miss me?"

"Miss you? I've been buzzing for two hours."

She set her handbag on the table and placed a large shopping bag on the floor. "What's wrong? You're not ill, are you?" She put her hand to his forehead. "Cool as a cucumber."

"I can't get the TV to work." He held out the remote control. She took it, and a moment later the sound came blaring at full volume.

"You had the mute on, Len. This little button here."

"Oh."

"What else?"

"Something to drink."

"How about a ginger ale?"

He was too upset to answer. She ducked into the hallway and almost immediately returned with the nurse.

"He's all discombobulated today," Terri Funkhouser explained.

The nurse said, "Maybe you'd like your ginger ale in the community room, Mr. Mandelbaum."

"I'm fine right where I am."

"No, Len. That's a good idea. A little exercise will do you good."

The nurse winked at Terri Funkhouser and went away.

"What's that winking business?" said Leonard.

Terri Funkhouser shrugged. "Sometimes people wink." She bent and helped him with his slippers.

"If you're not here they treat me like an imbecile," he said, grasping her arm for support.

She picked up her handbag and shopping bag. "Well, you can't blame them. I just passed a fellow in the hall dancing with himself."

"He should be locked up."

"He *is* locked up, Len."

Leonard couldn't find the word for the way the hallway smelled—a common word, having to do with cleaning. Mr. Clean, Myra always used in the kitchen, with the bald man on the bottle with biceps like a gym coach. That smell—the clean smell—masked another smell, impossible to name but relating to rot and death and wasting away. *That* smell came from the rooms, from the patients themselves, something the orderlies couldn't wash away.

"It's all old people," he said.

"This is the geriatric wing. They put the young people in a different place."

"Must be costing a fortune."

"Medicare, Len. It's all taken care of. We talked about this already, remember?"

"Somebody's paying for it, I know that much. They'll want their money back sooner or later."

"Stop worrying. Here," she said, opening the door to the lounge, "let's go in here and sit down."

He stepped inside the room, and there came a burst of voices.

"Surprise!"

Too many faces all at once. Who were they? He struggled to understand. These were people he knew. There was Abe Fish coming toward him with his cane, wearing a black-and-white checkered blazer. He held out his hand. "Health, Leonard," he said. "What else is there? What else matters?"

Poor Abe Fish. He'd become obsessed with health matters ever since his son dropped dead of a brain aneurysm playing pickup basketball at the Jewish Community Center. Forty-one years old. Never sick a day in his life before then. Looked like Paul Newman.

"How are you feeling?"

"Fine. Fine."

"That's what's important. Getting back your sense of well-being."

Next came Paul Pomerantz, his eyes bulging behind thick glasses. He took Leonard's hand in both of his, pumping. "Congratulations," he yelled. Paul Pomerantz was hard of hearing, even with the device in his ear. "You made it! You turned the corner!"

"Thank you. I appreciate you coming to visit."

"What? What was that?"

"Thank you," Leonard repeated, turning to Paul's good ear. "Thank you very much."

"It's my pleasure!" At last he stopped pumping Leonard's arm. He was two years older than Leonard, but still as strong as a defensive end. Paul Pomerantz had played football for a year at Syracuse University before joining the Marines. A sergeant, he'd fought at Iwo Jima, Okinawa, all the big battles in the Pacific. At parties he used to lower his pants and show off the shrapnel in his buttocks.

"And look, Len, look at the lovely ladies."

Betty Amato had done her hair, curled and set, colored a bright orange. She and Myra used to go to the beauty salon every Friday afternoon. They'd sit with their heads in the dryers, side by side, reading movie magazines.

"You look wonderful, Leonard. A little rest has done you a world of good."

Betty Amato had become something of a worrywart ever since Bob died. Her husband had left a fifty-thousand-dollar MasterCard debt. Where the money went, God only knew. Bob Amato had always been a big spender, like most Italians. Leonard had hired Brendan McGowan to take care of Betty's legal problems. *Send her a bill for a hundred dollars,* he'd told McGowan, *and charge the rest to me.* McGowan had wiped away the credit card debt and got the house deeded over to her free and clear. A wizard, that McGowan. But Betty still agonized about creditors, still thought she was responsible.

"Don't worry, Betty."

"I'm not *worried,*" she said. "One look at you sets my mind at ease. They must feed you very well, you look so *vigorous.*"

Leonard assumed it was a birthday party. His birthday. But was that correct? Was it the right time of year for his birthday? Before he could decide, another woman came forward and wrapped her arms around him. "How are you, Leonard? How are you, really?"

It was his daughter-in-law, he realized. What was her name? *Barbara*, he wanted to say, but that was wrong.

"The kids asked me to give you this. They're away at college but they told me what to write." She handed him a bright pink envelope. Leonard opened it with a trembling hand. *Get well soon, Grandpa! We love you, Grandpa!*

"They're fine grandchildren," said Leonard, wiping away the tears.

"Cut that out," said Terri Funkhouser, slapping him on the back as if he had digestion trouble. "We're here to celebrate, not pout." She opened her arms wide. "The doctor gave you a release date. Do you hear me, Len? Do you understand? They're moving you to a rehab clinic tomorrow. You'll spend a few weeks there to get your strength back. And after that, home sweet home. You'll be back in your own bed in no time!"

"Home? Are you sure?"

"Of course I'm sure. Isn't that wonderful?"

The tears flowed, distorting his vision.

WHEN HE GOT to the hospital Benjamin found his father's room empty. Where was he? Was he . . . *gone?* When he asked the nurse, she grinned and directed him to the lounge at the end of the hall. "Go see for yourself," the woman told him.

He could hear voices as he approached, all talking at once. Standing outside the glass partition, he saw Terri Funkhouser and Betty Amato, seated across from two of his father's cronies from the country club. By the window, startlingly, stood Judy, a paper plate in her hand. She'd straightened her hair and trimmed it to shoulder length, which made her look younger. She had a casual way of standing—one hand on her hip, chest thrust forward—which always turned him on. He stopped short, unsure what to do, and at that moment, Judy looked up and saw him and gestured him into the room.

"There he is, the prodigal son," screeched Terri Funkhouser. "Don't you answer the phone, buster? I called ten times. Ring, ring, ring."

He frowned momentarily, then realized she meant his father's landline. There was no answering machine; his father didn't like them. *Too many buttons*, he said.

"Who's he?" yelled Paul Pomerantz.

"The son," Abe Fish blurted into the other man's ear.

Benjamin glanced at Judy. He'd lived with this woman for most of his life, but now he felt nervous being in the same room with her. He hadn't seen her since the night she'd thrown him out. There had been conference calls with lawyers and legal correspondence, but all the arguing, threats, and negotiations seemed pointless now, somehow. She had come to see Leonard. He didn't know how she'd found out about his father's stroke, but she had come to support him, as she always had in the past. Benjamin offered her a smile, but before Judy could react, Betty Amato patted his forearm and said, "Timothy and Albert are coming home for Christmas. Maybe you boys could go for pizza like old times. The boys were always so close," she explained to Mr. Pomerantz, who was leaning forward, straining to follow the conversation.

"Who?" the old man boomed.

"My Eldorado's got a rattle in the front end," announced Abe Fish. "Sounds like a baseball card in the spokes."

"Bring it into the shop, Mr. Fish. I'll make sure they fix it."

Mr. Pomerantz leaned forward and bellowed, "He turned the corner!" He shot his hand out like a salute, surprising Betty, who put her hand to her heart. "He's on the upswing!"

"Have some pie, handsome," said Terri, pushing a paper plate toward Benjamin. "Lemon meringue from the Crown Market. You too," she said to Judy. "You're so trim. I'd kill for a figure like yours. How do you do it?"

"I'm on the divorce diet," said Judy. "Stress and ice cream."

"I tried Atkins once," said Terri Funkhouser. "I like a steak as much as anyone, but who could eat meat ten times a day? And then they tell you it's no good for you. First it is, then it's not."

"Moderation," said Mr. Fish in a lowered voice, as if divulging a secret.

"Margarine?" yelled Mr. Pomerantz.

Betty Amato smiled helplessly. "The rest has done you wonders, Leonard. You've got such lovely color in your cheeks."

"That's the medication," said Terri Funkhouser. "The first week he was as red as a lobster."

"How's *your* health, young man?"

"Good, Mr. Fish," said Benjamin. He glanced at Judy and found her studying him with a calm, unhurried gaze. He couldn't tell what, exactly, but something had changed. She looked disinterested, as impassive as a judge. He couldn't remember the last time she'd looked at him like that. With Judy, there was anger and passion, delight and disgust, but rarely, if ever, indifference. It confused him.

"Because that's what's important. That's what matters. Look at your father."

They all turned toward Leonard, who said, "I'm fine. I'm fine."

"Take Manny Silverman," Mr. Fish continued. "Lovely wife. Fourteen grandchildren, one of them a judge. One day his neck puffs up like a pelican. Doctor says pancreatic cancer, you have three months to live."

"Poor Manny," said Leonard.

"Manny Silverman chased everything in a skirt," said Terri Funkhouser. "He gave me gas once for an abscessed molar and I had body pains for three days afterward. He was like an octopus with those hands."

"He certainly had a twinkle in his eye," said Betty Amato.

"The man was a pervert, plain and simple."

"I always liked Manny," said Leonard. "A fine dentist."

"The cancer spread through his body like wildfire," said Abe Fish. "They had to amputate both legs. Two weeks later he died. What's the point of amputating a man's legs who has two weeks to live?"

"I'd rather die than have no legs," said Terri Funkhouser.

"You say that now," said Mr. Fish, shrugging, "but when the time comes?"

"A lot of young men are coming home from Iraq without legs," said Betty Amato. "It's enough to break your heart."

"Lambs to the slaughter," said Judy. "But we voted for him. This great country of ours."

"I didn't vote for him," said Terri Funkhouser. "I haven't voted for thirty years, not since Jimmy Carter. They're all a bunch of charlatans."

"Joe Lieberman is a fine man. I've known him since high school," said Mr. Fish.

"He's Jewish, Abe, is why you like him," said Terri Funkhouser.

"Should I not like him because he's Jewish?"

"He's a millionaire," said Judy, "like everybody else in the Senate."

"Do you hold that against him? A man who made a success of himself?"

"I like this new fellow, Barack Obama," said Betty Amato.

"Back problems?" yelled Paul Pomeranz.

"Politics, schmolitics," said Terri Funkhouser. "We're here to celebrate Leonard's good news. Let's not argue."

"Who's arguing?" said Mr. Fish, holding up his enormous, liver-spotted hands. "This isn't arguing. This is intelligent discussion."

"What news?" said Benjamin.

"Haven't you heard? Your father got his walking papers. Tomorrow they're sending him to the rehab center."

"Really? They're letting you go, Dad?"

"Allegedly," said Leonard, frowning.

Benjamin excused himself and went down the hallway, looking for a doctor. There was no one at the nurses' station. He rang the bell, without result. A moment later he turned to see Judy approaching.

"How can they let him go? He can't even walk. Why didn't anyone tell me?"

"You know how it is with insurance companies," she said. "Anything to save a buck."

"Who's going to take care of him? I have to be at the dealership—"

"He's going to a rehab center. It's an inpatient facility."

"Yeah, but for how long?"

"A couple of weeks, probably. In the meantime, you hire a home aide. Remember that Polish woman I hired when my mother broke her hip? She'll bathe him, clean, cook. Everything."

He felt a rush of affection for Judy. She could always ease his anxiety. He'd nearly forgotten that. At night, when some worry kept him from sleep, she used to go down to the kitchen and make him an amaretto with milk.

"Right. Good idea." He smiled, but she stared back with that same impassive expression. "What's going on with you?"

She wrinkled her brow. "What do you mean?"

"You look, I don't know, unconcerned."

"Unconcerned? Why would you say that? I'm very concerned about Leonard."

"That's not what I meant."

"I came here because of your father, Benjamin."

"Right, right," he said quickly. He tried another approach. "Judy, about Thanksgiving—"

"I don't want to fight about that. You can come. It'll be good for the kids."

"Really?"

She sighed. "Seeing Leonard like this, it puts things into perspective. You know how much I respect your father. He's the man you could have been. Still could be, if you could ever get your shit together."

"Thanks, I guess."

"Why didn't you tell me? Is this your idea of payback? Keeping me out of the picture? You know how much I care for Leonard—"

He held up his hands defensively. "I tried, Judy, about ten times. It's not exactly easy getting you on the phone lately, you know."

"You could have tried a little harder."

"If you say so."

Judy smiled mysteriously. "So, how long has this little love affair been going on?"

"What affair?" He wondered how Judy could possibly know about Audrey. Had she followed him? Had she hired a private eye to investigate him? That was the kind of thing divorce lawyers did—

"Terri what's-her-name," Judy explained.

"Oh that," Benjamin said, breathing easier. "Pretty funny, eh?"

"She's not exactly Leonard's type, if you ask me."

"She grows on you. She visits every day, watches over him like a hawk."

"Well, there's something to be said for loyalty."

He looked down. The words stung, even if she hadn't meant to dig at him. *You're just not equipped, Benjamin.* Had he been a better man, she was saying, a man like his father, they would still be together. Leonard was loyal above all else. For him, there was family, friends, and his people (the Jews of the world). He would never betray those close to him or speak poorly of others, not even when he felt wronged.

"She called the house, looking for you," said Judy. "That's how I found out."

"Well, I'm glad she told you. Did you tell the kids?"

"No. I figured you would want to do that."

Benjamin nodded. "I'll tell them at Thanksgiving."

Judy looked at her watch. "I have to get going."

"Yeah. I should get back to the party."

"Don't you want to talk to the nurse?"

"No. You're right," said Benjamin. "I'll hire a Polish girl."

"Don't forget to ask for one over eighteen."

He frowned.

"I'm joking," said Judy quickly. "Don't make that face. You're too old for au pairs anyway."

"What face?"

"You look like the Italian soccer players when they hold their arms out after a penalty flag. *Why me?*"

She was right; he'd seen himself with that very look in photographs. She'd spent more time looking at him than anyone else. Who else knew him as well as Judy?

She went off toward the elevator. He waited for her to turn and wave. But the bell rang, the doors opened, and she was gone.

BENJAMIN HEADED HOME with the taste of lemon meringue pie on his lips. Turning in to his driveway, he noticed Franky DiLorenzo coming toward him, waving to get his attention.

Benjamin rolled down the window.

"Did you hear about Juniper Lane?"

"No," said Benjamin. "What happened?"

Franky DiLorenzo was what the salesmen called a space invader; he got very close to you in conversation. "Somebody broke into half the cars and garages on the street. Took everything that wasn't nailed down. They kicked in Syd Goldman's back door and set off his alarm."

"Did they catch him?"

Franky shook his head. "You gotta keep everything locked up around here, ever since that Stacks kid moved into the neighborhood."

"You really think he's the one?"

"I got no proof. But it doesn't take a genius to figure it out. I hope he tries something at my house. I really do."

"Thanks for letting me know."

"How's your dad?"

"Much better. They're moving him to a rehab place."

"That's good news."

A long silence followed with Franky DiLorenzo standing by the driver's door, his eyes passing over the front yard. What did he see with those intense dark eyes? Things Benjamin wouldn't notice—something out of place or needful of repair: a lack of mulch, a patch of uncut shrubs, a dog turd left by some negligent neighbor to stink and harden.

"Well—" said Benjamin, and at the same moment Franky said, "You said you went to high school with Audrey Martin?"

"Yes, the same."

Franky lowered his voice. "She came by with her dog when you weren't here."

"When was this?"

"A few hours ago."

"We're old friends," Benjamin blurted.

Franky nodded, but Benjamin suspected he wasn't convinced. Would Franky mention this tidbit to anyone? It made for good gossip, something Franky might find hard to resist. Franky's eyes were still on him, so Benjamin added, "I've been trying to patch things up with Judy."

Franky seemed satisfied. "Say hi to your dad for me."

"Will do," said Benjamin.

Benjamin pulled into his garage. He wondered if it was true: *Was* he trying to get back together with Judy? Was such a thing possible, even if he wanted to? Seeing her at the hospital had rekindled a desire for her, had alleviated a weight that had been creeping over him. In her presence he had felt his old sense of equilibrium. Yes, he'd fucked up his marriage with his *behaviors* (as their therapist had put it), which had caused *marital stressors*, so in theory he should be able to win her back with some *good behaviors*. But did he even want to? True, he missed his kids, his house, his life. But did he miss *Judy* or the idea of her—the idea of their family? If he wanted her back, he'd have to work. He wondered if he had the energy for all that. That, and he'd lose his freedom, and everything that came with it. Audrey Martin, for one.

Inside the house he picked up the phone.

"Are you free?"

THEY ARRANGED TO meet at Starbucks in Wintonbury Center.

He got there first and ordered a coffee and settled at one of the tables in the back. A minute later she came through the door. Benjamin folded the newspaper and pushed it aside. "You look incredible."

She wore a clingy tan dress and heels. "No panties, as requested."

He grinned. "I guess it's true, what they say: You don't meet nice girls in coffee shops."

Audrey took the chair beside him with a little sexy frown. "You don't think I'm a nice girl?"

"That's a line from a song," he explained. "Tom Waits."

"Oh."

A man wearing a Red Sox cap passed by their table, barking into his cell phone: "I don't need anyone to tell me that. I know that all by myself, amigo."

She rolled her eyes and said, "Hell is other people with cell phones."

"Another song lyric?"

"A line from a play, sort of."

"We know different stuff."

"You know the good things."

"Like what?"

"Manners, for one. You put down your newspaper when I came in. My husband hasn't done that for twenty years."

He smiled. "What else?"

"How to look at a woman."

"How do I look at you?"

"With a sort of reverence. Like I'm still eighteen, still perfect."

"You are perfect."

"Hardly." She moved closer to him. "If you had such a crush on me back then, why didn't you ask me out?"

"I couldn't muster the courage. But you talked to me on two different occasions."

"Seriously?"

He nodded. "I remember it like yesterday. The first time I was sitting on the stone wall behind the chapel, playing 'Hotel California' on my Gibson. It was springtime. You walked by and hesitated for a half second and said, 'That sounds really good.' I nearly fumbled my pick, I was so nervous."

"I always liked the Eagles. What about the other time?"

"Well, that's a sadder story," he said. "It was winter. I was waiting for my mom to pick me up in the courtyard after school, freezing my ass off. You came out of the entrance and looked around and asked me, 'Have you seen Hal Nance? Did he come out here?' You didn't have a coat on. You were crying and wiping your nose. I shook my head and asked, 'Is everything okay?' and you said, 'No, everything is definitely *not* okay.' Then you turned around and went back into the building."

"Hal Nance," she sighed. "He broke my heart so many times."

"All the girls liked him. Although I have no idea why. He seemed pretty obnoxious to me."

"But he looked so good in his lacrosse uniform. There's something about a man wearing short shorts and a funny helmet."

"I was always a baseball cap sort of guy."

"Could I have been any dumber? And there you were, right under my nose, playing your Gibson." She reached under the table and felt for his crotch. She rubbed until his cock got hard. "Should we go to your place?"

"Well, that's what I wanted to talk to you about," he said.

"Is your dad back?"

"No. But my next-door neighbor—"

"The skinny guy?"

"Yes, Franky DiLorenzo. He saw you come to the house—"

"He's always watching! Every time I step outside he waves to me." She glanced out the window at the people passing on the sidewalk. Wintonbury had a busy downtown, particularly during the early evening hours: couples going into restaurants, young professionals tromping from bar to bar, husbands and wives strolling with their kids, window-shoppers, the stray loner. "What did he say?"

"Nothing specific, but I think he suspects something's going on between us."

She searched his eyes. "Are you keeping something from me?"

"Of course not. I just thought you should know. This is a pretty small town. It might seem bigger than it really is."

"I see." She seemed lost in thought for a few moments. "Thanks for telling me. For looking out for me." She shrugged. "I suppose I should care, but I don't. I don't know anyone here. I haven't met a single soul besides you."

"What about your husband?"

"Andrew?" She laughed. "That's the last thing I'm concerned about."

"Past that stage?"

"Exactly." She smiled. "Where are we going?" she asked, rubbing his cock through his pants again. "A sleazy motel would be nice."

"Somewhere closer, I think. It's getting to be a bit urgent."

"I can tell," she said.

From the bathroom came the sound of the toilet flushing, then the door opening and the cell phone guy coming down the hall, his voice growing louder. "Tomorrow's no good," he said. "I got a two-thirty tomorrow."

After he passed, Audrey got up. "I'm going to the ladies'," she whispered into his ear. "Give me one minute."

She left, not looking back. He heard her go inside the bathroom. The coffee shop was crowded, every chair filled—the high school girls bunched together at their table, the servers at their stations, the customers lining up to order. Reggae music pulsed, bass-heavy and repetitious. No one seemed to be watching him.

He got up and went down the back hallway and took a sip of water at the fountain. When he knocked, she opened the door immediately and pulled him inside and locked the door behind. The bathroom was bright, smelling of ammonia. He opened his zipper and took out his cock, the head bulging.

"Bend over," he said.

She raised her dress and grabbed the handicap bar with both hands, her legs spread.

Halfway through someone rattled the door handle. She covered her mouth, trying to stifle a giggle.

"Shhh," whispered Benjamin.

A minute later there came a knock at the door.

Audrey called out, "Diarrhea. Sorry."

Whoever it was went away.

BACK AT their table, he said, "I really needed that."

"I could tell." She straightened her dress and wriggled a bit in her seat. "What's next," she asked. "Dunkin' Donuts?"

He could feel his face taking on a vacant after-sex expression. "Maybe a motel next time. What do you think?"

"Don't worry about me. Your place is fine. If you don't mind, that is."

"It's fine for now. But my dad will be coming back soon." Before the idea fully formed he said, "I could rent an apartment in town."

"Sure," she said. "Whatever works best for you."

He smiled, the thought growing on him. "And you could still bring the dog, of course. I'll find a place that allows pets."

Her eyes widened and she straightened in her chair, looking past him toward the street. "Oh, shit."

"What?" He turned to follow her gaze. "What's the matter?"

"I can't believe it."

"What? Tell me."

"Andrew just walked by."

Benjamin tensed. "Your husband? You're kidding, right?"

She laughed. "No."

"Did he see you?"

"No. He was with some guy I've never seen before."

"Maybe he followed you."

She shook her head. "He was at the office when I left home. He called to say he'd be working late." She started giggling again.

"Why are you laughing?"

"It just seems funny, him walking by, looking so serious. And you just fucked the daylights out of me. I'm still tingling all over."

"Seriously. Should we go?"

She scoffed. "We're fine. Even if he came in here and ordered a decaf, he wouldn't notice me."

"I doubt that."

"If he did notice, I'd tell him you're my vehicular adviser. But he's not coming in, so stop worrying. Even though you look kind of sexy with that furrow."

He sat back in his chair, his heart beginning to calm. "You're pretty terrific, Audrey Martin."

"So you tell me."

SHE CAME BACK to his house later that evening, so that he could make love to her properly, and he saw her the next night and the night after that and nearly every night over the next two weeks leading up to Thanksgiving. They dropped most of the formalities: the den, the fire, the red wine, the small talk. Instead, they went straight to his bedroom, undressing on the way up the stairs. Sometimes she would stay for only ten or fifteen minutes, leaving him naked and out of breath on his twin bed, the sound of her footsteps trailing down the stairs. Always, she brought the malamute. She rejected the motel idea. For now, it was easier for her, she said, to make the little detour up his driveway on her nightly walk. He enjoyed the secrecy and the anticipation. It came to seem almost routine—this stretch of days that would later seem so manic and vital and extraordinary to him— racing from work to the rehab center to home, taking a quick shower, turning off the exterior lights so no one could see her heading up the driveway, keeping a lookout for her from the front window. The moment she stepped onto the porch, he would swing open the door and pull her into his embrace, the same way she'd pulled him into the Starbucks restroom. He knew it couldn't go on like this. His father would be home soon, and he needed to make arrangements, but he couldn't seem to concentrate on anything outside of the moment, this *Audrey* moment. After making love, if they had time, he would run his hands over her—caressing, massaging, kneading; he loved the feel of her—but if he tried to tell her how much he cared for her, or direct the conversation away from the commonplace, she would stiffen and cut him off. And after her first meltdown, he didn't want to risk another by provoking her. Besides, it was enough having her beside him nearly every night, possessing her, even if only for a short time.

ON THANKSGIVING AFTERNOON he tied a big red bow around Yukon's neck and drove out to his old house in Granby. "Say hello to my date," he said, presenting Yukon. The dog jumped all over Judy, then searched the kitchen and den and raced up the stairs with one of his old rawhide dog bones in his chops.

Judy asked, "Did you play football with your old pals this morning?"

"Gosh, no. We quit that for good." It had been an annual tradition, he and a group of his high school buddies, getting together for a game of two-hand touch, rain or shine. Once it had been a crowded, heated, well-played affair. Over the years, the Thanksgiving-morning game had dwindled to a handful of diehards, some of whom brought along their teenage kids toward the end, along with their own tender hamstrings, delicate ankles, and bad backs. A couple of years ago, when one of the diehards ripped his Achilles tendon on the opening kickoff, they'd finally come to their senses and called off the game.

"I'm glad," said Judy. "You used to come home hobbling for a week."

"You don't forget much."

"I was your wife. I don't forget anything."

She led him through the house like a museum docent. Her three brothers were seated in the living room, Budweiser bottles in hand. Lou sat on the couch next to Chris, who had his feet up on the coffee table, without any ankle-bracelet gizmo, Benjamin noticed, his house arrest apparently served. They nodded at him, while Anthony toasted him from the love seat, with his arm around a peroxide blonde with a long, razor-thin nose. He introduced her as Linda, his latest girlfriend, apparently. Benjamin was surprised to see the brothers. In his excitement, he'd forgotten that Judy always invited them for holidays; sometimes they showed up, in part or in whole. This year they had come out in force, probably to give him a hard time, he figured.

Judy reappeared with a glass of wine and said, "Sit," depositing him in an overstuffed armchair he hadn't seen before. The living room—the whole house, in fact—was looking more and more like a Restoration Hardware showroom. He wondered what she'd done with his old furniture, like his leather reading chair. He loved that chair, and he guessed he'd never see it again. She'd always liked throwing things out, a sort of recreation for her.

"Linda and I just got back from New Smyrna," Anthony was saying. "The shark attack capital of America. The bastards like it warm and shallow. They'll tear you to pieces ten feet from shore. If not them, the jellyfish will get you. Best thing to do is stay out of the water."

Sharks, college football, asbestos removal—Anthony had inexhaustible expertise about every topic he introduced into conversation. The other brothers sat across from him, raising their Budweisers and nodding their agreement. On his way to the bathroom, Lou paused by Benjamin's chair. "Sorry for dropping off your gear like that," he mumbled. "Heat of the moment and all."

"It's forgotten," said Benjamin, taking the man's hand. He wondered if Judy had put him up to the apology. It certainly seemed that way, as the brothers were excellent at holding grudges. He'd never heard any of them admit to being sorry about anything. So, was Judy just ensuring that things went along smoothly? Or was she trying in some way to apologize herself, to signal that all was forgiven? He couldn't get a read on her as she rattled around the kitchen, refusing all offers of assistance.

When she came to refill his wineglass, she asked, "How's Leonard?"

"He's doing good. I stopped by the rehab center to see him a couple of hours ago. He and his lady friend were having turkey in the lounge."

Judy rolled her eyes. "You sure she's not a gold digger?"

"Just lonely, I think. Where are the kids?" He felt almost nervous to face them; he hadn't seen David or Sarah since the end of August—before the blowout.

"In their rooms. Go say hi."

At the top of the staircase, he glanced into his and Judy's old bedroom. The comforter was new, green and billowy. Judy's smell wafted into the hallway, and he felt his gut tighten with longing or nostalgia, probably a little of both.

He opened David's door and peeked in. His son was sitting at his computer, speaking into his cell phone. He looked up. "Not now, Dad."

Benjamin said, "Sorry," and backed out.

When he knocked on Sarah's door she called, "Come in!" But she too was talking on the phone, lying in bed with Yukon sprawled beside her. She held the phone away from her ear for a moment and said, "Is dinner ready yet, Daddy?"

"Not quite."

"Call me when it is, please."

He didn't know what he'd been expecting, exactly—forgiveness, anger, or some combination of both—but mostly he was ignored by Judy, her brothers, and his children. His son endured the meal as if it were a sentence to be served, bored and monosyllabic. He fiddled with his cell phone under the table, texting, paying no attention to Benjamin's instructions to put it away. He and Sarah seemed to perk up only when he related the story of Leonard's illness. Sarah wanted to go visit him *right now*, and David kept saying, "But he's okay, right?" When Benjamin assured them that Leonard was fine, that they could visit him over Christmas break, they both returned to their gadgets. Meanwhile Judy occupied herself with cooking, serving, and cleaning up, not standing still long enough to utter a full sentence.

As the brothers argued about the war in Iraq, Benjamin found himself wondering what Audrey Martin might be doing at this moment. Would she have finished with the meal already? Would she and her husband and daughter be sitting in the old farmhouse den, flipping stations? Or would each have retired to a separate room, separate laptop, separate screen? Either way, the vision seemed lonely, and he felt strangely glad to be sitting at this noisy table, back in his old home, the head of the family again. Well, he wanted it to be another family Thanksgiving, like nothing had changed, but everything felt off-kilter, his kids distracted, his wife aloof, his brothers-in-law overly polite. Even the dog acted like a stranger. "Come, boy," he said, but the dog backed away as if sensing a trap and sat next to the ex-con on the other side of the table.

During dessert, the kitchen phone rang and Judy rushed to answer. As they listened to her lowered voice in the next room, Anthony announced, "That would be the new one."

"New one?" said Benjamin, glancing up. "New what?"

"The new Jew, and this one's got more money than you even."

"What does he do?" Benjamin tried to keep his expression unchanged.

Anthony took a gulp of beer and wiped his lips before answering, evidently enjoying the moment: "Divorce lawyer."

So that was it. A boyfriend. This explained her lack of anger, her new tolerance of him.

After dessert, Judy produced a camera and said, "Okay, smile, everyone," but Anthony's girlfriend turned around.

"No fucking way," she said.

Benjamin realized it was the first time he'd heard her voice the entire night. He was surprised—first by her crudeness, and then because she looked like she'd spent hours in front of the mirror with her makeup. One of the brothers started to laugh, but it was clear by her expression that she wasn't kidding.

"You look great, babe," Anthony assured her, but she shook her head.

"They used to photograph me when I was a kid," she said. "I don't like it. I never liked it."

In the long silence that followed. Judy lowered the camera and said, "I'm sorry."

I'm sorry.

She said those same words to Benjamin an hour or two later when he was putting on his sports coat to leave. *For what?* he nearly asked. For tonight? For her brothers' boorishness? For his children's apathy toward him? Or for her own newfound happiness?

"Yeah," he mumbled. "Me too."

* * *

BACK AT his father's house he clicked the garage door remote, sending its ancient gears groaning. It hadn't worked properly for months, and he'd meant to call the repairman. He still had so many things to do to prepare for his father's return from the rehab center. He hadn't yet arranged for a home aide, or cleaned out the clutter from the guest room, where the aide would sleep; nor had he looked for an apartment in Wintonbury Center for himself.

The garage felt bare without Leonard's Cadillac. A few days earlier, Benjamin had taken the car to the dealership for maintenance—at least he'd gotten that task done—but the empty space, like the dark house, depressed him. Why couldn't he remember to leave on a light or two?

He released Yukon from the backseat, and the dog rushed past him, nose to the kitchen door, fur bristling. "Take it easy, boy," Benjamin said, thumping the dog's side. The visit had put Yukon out of sorts. All that attention—David and Sarah hugging and kissing him, feeding him turkey and potatoes under the table—was a rare indulgence.

As Benjamin opened the door, the dog raced ahead of him into the kitchen. The house was drafty and ice cold. He flipped the light switch and saw that the back door was wide open. His mind whirled. Had he left it open? No. He hadn't been in the backyard in a month, not since the last warm days of October.

Someone's home, he thought.

He had the odd sensation that he had entered the wrong house. The dog's bowl was overturned, water pooling across the linoleum floor. A half-empty beer bottle was perched atop the counter, one of his Coronas, but Benjamin hadn't left it there.

"Who's there?" he called out. His voice reverberated in the kitchen, sounding awkward and rehearsed.

Yukon inspected his upside-down bowl and licked the water off the floor. Then he ran from room to room, sniffing and whining. When he reappeared in the kitchen, he darted toward the back door, but Benjamin grabbed his collar before he could get away. "Stay here," he told Yukon, but the dog was too agitated to sit.

Benjamin examined the back door. The latch was torn from the wall, the wood splintered. He had been *robbed*. This fact didn't seem to register until he touched the broken door with his fingertips.

"Shit," he said aloud.

* * *

THE PATROL CAR roared into the driveway. The cop—a squat man with a crew cut—scribbled on his pad with his head lowered, listening to Benjamin. "Okay," he said. "Wait by the cruiser. I'm not going to call for backup because I'm pretty sure he's long gone by now. But stay here anyway, just in case." The man went around to the backyard, pointing a short black flashlight that emitted a bright beacon. A few minutes later he reappeared and went into the kitchen through the garage door. From the driveway, Benjamin watched the lights go on inside, room by room. He stood next to Yukon, starting to shiver in the cold night air.

Finally the cop opened the front door and gestured to Benjamin. "No sign of the perp," he said. "Did you see anyone?"

"No."

The officer scribbled in his well-worn pad. "All right," he said, tucking the pad into his jacket pocket. "Let's go through the house. See if we can figure out what he took."

The den and dining room had been ransacked: pulled-out and over-turned drawers, the empty silverware box on the rug, broken crystal figurines on the den floor.

"There's more upstairs," said the cop.

Benjamin's bedroom was untouched, as far as he could tell, but his dad's room had been trashed. His mother's jewelry box lay on the floor. Benjamin noticed a white duffel bag by the bedside, filled to bulging.

"That's not mine," said Benjamin, pointing.

"That's not your laundry bag?"

"No."

The cop hoisted the bag and emptied it onto the bedspread. Myra's jewelry tumbled out, as well as her silverware, and a pile of DVDs. "Do these items belong to you?"

"Yes."

"Do you notice anything missing?"

"I have no idea," said Benjamin.

The cop nodded. "If you do notice anything, just make a list, after you have a chance to go through the house. You can give me a call anytime," he said, passing over his card, "or ask for the detective if I'm not there."

"Okay."

While the cop looked out the window, shining his flashlight around the backyard, Benjamin wondered what would have happened if his father had been home. The robber might have frightened him into another stroke, and for what? A bunch of junk.

Benjamin followed the cop out the back door and across the yard, where the man pointed out muddy footprints. At the far end of the yard, the tracks led to the fence and off toward Juniper Lane. "He was on foot."

Benjamin told the cop what he'd heard from Franky DiLorenzo—that a kid with a police record had moved into the neighborhood. "Apparently he's some sort of delinquent."

The officer nodded, his expression blank. "But you didn't see anyone, is that correct?"

"Correct."

"And you don't know this individual personally?"

"Like I said, I heard it from my neighbor. He knows all the details. You should talk to him. He lives right next door," said Benjamin, nodding toward the house.

The cop scribbled a word or two on his pad, and Benjamin suffered an odd sense of guilt, as if he himself were under suspicion. Perhaps he was. Perhaps some homeowners staged robberies to collect insurance premiums. Was that why the police officer eyed him so coldly? Or was it just the way this man looked at the world after spending years listening to lies, seeing the domestic disturbances, the bloodstained rugs and rifled closets?

"Well, that's it, then," said the cop, opening the cruiser door.

"Aren't you going to take fingerprints?"

"I'll put a call out for an evidence tech. It's a good burglary. Looks like he ran off pretty quick. I'd bet he heard you drive in, or maybe something else spooked him."

"You'll call him now? The tech guy?"

"He's not on duty 24/7. He comes in at eight tomorrow morning. In the meantime, you've got some printable surfaces there. The beer bottle, jewelry boxes, glass figurines, the dresser drawers, the door. He'll want to print the POE—point of entry. Don't disturb those areas. But you can clean up the rest. He'll also want to check those muddy footprints."

"To make a mold?"

The cop laughed. "You've been watching too many cop shows. No, to photograph the footprint with a ruler next to it, to get an idea of shoe size. Then we can check your delinquent pal, get a look at his feet."

"So you're going to talk to my neighbor?"

The cop checked his watch. "It's a little late tonight. His house looks dark. But I'll have a chat with him tomorrow. And I'll canvas the neighborhood now, to see if anyone's out and about."

"I see," said Benjamin. "Well, thanks for all the help. I'll be expecting this tech guy tomorrow morning?"

"Yeah. He'll be here first thing."

After the cop left, Benjamin began cleaning up.

HE SLEPT POORLY, plagued by nightmares.

It was the day after Thanksgiving, "Black Friday," which meant a busy day at the dealership—they'd been gearing up for this sale for weeks. But he had to wait around for the tech cop. By 10:00 A.M. there was still no sign of him. Benjamin grabbed the bedside phone and called the number the cop had left him but got his voice mail. Then he called his secretary to tell her he wouldn't be coming in for a while.

After that, he dialed Judy. She answered, sounding tired: "I've been cleaning the kitchen all morning. You ever try scrubbing turkey grease? No, you haven't."

"Actually, I have. And it was a terrific meal."

"Isn't this your big sale day?"

"I didn't go in yet."

"Why not?"

"I had a lousy night."

She had that flat tone, again, unconcerned. Her new-boyfriend voice. It annoyed him. "Why didn't you tell me you were dating your divorce lawyer? Your brother had to tell me? And I'm not sure that's even kosher. Legally, I mean."

"You call at ten in the morning to interrogate me? I thought we'd gotten past—"

"Hey, take it easy. It surprised me, that's all. We're still married, technically. And ten o'clock's really not all that early."

She sighed. "I assumed you wouldn't want to know about my love life."

"We're grown-ups." He heard a commotion in the background—the dishes clattering in the sink. "We should be able to discuss things."

"In that case, yes, I'm seeing a man," she said. "He's not my divorce lawyer, but they work together. And yes, I'm sleeping with him."

He winced, imagining them together, the man's hairy back. "How old is he?"

"He's your age, maybe a little older."

"How much older?"

"Never mind. I can see where this is going."

"I simply asked the man's age."

"And next you'll want to know his name, his income, the size of his dick, and whether he's good in bed."

"Is he?"

She didn't respond.

"I just need a little time to get used to the idea of you sleeping with someone else," he said.

"Fine," she said. "Get used to it. I won't ask what you're up to. I can only imagine."

"I'm not up to anything." It was an old habit, avoiding any mention of women to Judy.

"Oh, right. While we're married you chase everything in a skirt. But now that you're single, you're a monk." There came the slamming of pans, more water splashing.

"Can you leave the dishes for a minute?"

"I know when you're lying, Benjamin. Your voice goes up a half octave. It's your squeaky little liar's voice. So, no, I don't want to leave the dishes if you're going to feed me a load of horseshit."

Benjamin sighed. "I've had a few dates, if you must know."

"Dates? With the same woman, or different women?"

"Same."

"Who is she?"

"She's no one."

"What's her name?"

"Does it matter?"

"If it doesn't matter, then tell me."

He paused. "Her name is Audrey."

Judy said, "Didn't you know an Audrey in high school? Audrey so-and-so with the terrific ass."

"How do you remember that? That's really weird."

"What's weird is a married man going around for years talking about some high school girl's ass. I can't believe there are that many Audreys floating around. Jesus—is this the same one?"

Before he could respond, Judy uttered a noise of disgust—something between a bark and a cough. "What did you do? Call her the minute you left me? God, that's so pathetic."

He had forgotten how well she knew him. "It's *Aubrey*," he said.

"What?"

"The woman I'm dating. Her name is Aubrey. With a *b*."

"What kind of name is Aubrey?"

"Like the song. Her parents named her after the song. It was their wedding song."

"What song?"

"The song by Bread. Don't you remember?" He sang the verse for her: "*And Aubrey was her name. A not so very ordinary girl or name.* Et cetera."

"That song came out when, 1975?"

" 'Seventy-seven." In truth, he had no idea.

"So that makes her, what, thirty years old?"

"Twenty-nine," he said, trying to keep his voice low.

"You're dating a twenty-nine-year-old?"

"Not dating. We went out a few times." Somehow it always happened like this with Judy. He would tell one lie, then another, trying to get out of trouble but just ending up deeper, the whole thing a house of cards. "It's no big deal."

"Right," she said. "Let me decipher that for you. Let me tell you what you just told me. It means you're fucking this woman Aubrey and couldn't care less about her."

"Did I say that?"

"In so many words, yes, you did. Maybe she doesn't spoil you like I did. Maybe she doesn't drop to her knees every time you ask. Maybe now you can appreciate what I did for you—"

"Listen, Judy, I don't know how we got started on this—"

"We got started on this because you have the nerve to persecute me for moving on with my life. You're trying to suck me back in, in your own stupid way, and I'm not falling for it, okay? It would just turn out the same way. Besides, you don't want to come back, not really. You're just sick of living alone in Leonard's house and making yourself peanut butter sandwiches for dinner."

"That's not it at all." *Actually,* Benjamin thought, *that's pretty much it exactly.* Judy always knew when he was lying to her, to himself. Yes, he lied to her. But was there any other way to sustain a marriage? Wasn't lying to someone you loved sometimes the right thing to do? Who could bear to know the truth of what went on, day in, day out, in the other's mind? *You've gained weight. You say the same things over and over. You're looking older.* No, you didn't say those things. But Judy always knew, somehow, what he was hiding. Or maybe he gave her reason to know. He would lead her toward the place where she would find his secret. To enrage her, to punish her, but for what? Why had he always pushed her, prodded her, beat her with his own failings?

"Listen to me for two seconds, will you? I called to tell you that someone broke into the house last night."

"What?" she screeched. "Are you serious?"

"Yes, I'm serious."

"Did the cops catch him? What did he take? Wait. Start over. What happened?"

He told her. She didn't interrupt. She had always been a good listener, at least up until the last couple of years. "Franky DiLorenzo thinks it's some kid who moved into the neighborhood," he said. "The kid's been arrested before."

"Franky should know. He watches that neighborhood like a hawk. You should get an alarm system before Leonard comes home."

"I probably should." It felt good to be agreeing with her.

"Speaking of Leonard, did you call the Polish ladies?"

"Not yet."

"Typical. Always waiting until the last minute. You'll never change, Benjamin. But it's not my problem anymore."

She hung up, and Benjamin remained in bed. He didn't know what to do with himself. He tried the police department. He was transferred twice and put on hold for ten minutes before getting the tech guy, who said he'd be there at noon. Benjamin hung up and stared at the ceiling. It was a Friday morning, but because of the holiday, it felt like a Sunday. Sundays were for hanging around the bedroom, reading the *Times*. His lazy day. It was a tradition of Judy and his, since the early part of their marriage: Saturday night was hers—to choose a restaurant or movie or anything she wanted to do, or issue instructions for any servile tasks she could think up for him to do—and Sunday mornings were his. Judy used to bring him a tray in the bedroom—waffles, bacon, a glass of orange juice—and, yes, she would spoil him in bed, whatever he asked. That indulgence was gone too. Gone for good. That fact seemed inarguable now. For some reason their divorce had not felt definite to him, even after the meetings with lawyers, the negotiations, the signing of documents. But his wife fucking another man—now *that* was divorce.

THE TECH GUY was a civilian, dressed in a utility-type outfit, dark blue coveralls, same color as a police uniform, but no gun. He snapped on some latex gloves like a doctor and took photographs of the back door. Then he followed the route of the burglar through the house—kitchen, den, living room, Leonard's bedroom. He used a brush—like a woman's makeup brush, only larger—to paint a fine black powder, like soot, over small patches throughout the house—doorknobs, drawers, light switches. Each time he powdered an area, he would study the result with his head cocked at an angle, using a flashlight. As he moved through the house he jotted notes. "For my report," he explained to Benjamin.

All for nothing.

"He might have been wearing gloves," the guy explained. "But maybe not. It's not so easy to leave a latent. It takes a firm press without any slip. Doorknobs rarely leave a good print because the hand slips when turning the knob."

The tech took a few photos of the footprints in the backyard. "Sneakers. Looks like a size nine." He glanced up at the sky and exhaled deeply. "Nice working out here," he said. "A nice change of pace."

Benjamin followed him to his car. "Do we clean up now?"

The guy cleared his throat. "Oh, sure. I'm all done. If you have any problems with that powder, try Scrubbing Bubbles and 409."

It took Benjamin the rest of the day, battling the soot. He spent an hour in his dad's bedroom alone, trying to get a dark splotch out of the carpet. He nearly called the department to complain, but he figured the tech guy was just doing his job, even if he could have been a little neater.

That day and the next day, he expected the cop to get back to him, or Franky DiLorenzo to call, but he heard from no one.

By Sunday, he decided to put the incident out of his mind.

THAT DAY he found himself missing Audrey Martin. He hadn't seen her since the day before Thanksgiving. He left a couple of messages and texted her, without response. Finally, that evening, she got back to him. He could tell immediately that something was bothering her.

"It's good to hear your voice," he said, trying to sound cheery.

"Yeah," she said. "Sorry I've been out of touch. It's been a rough week-end."

"The holidays can be brutal."

"I'll say."

She was silent for a while, so he said, "Maybe a walk with the dog might help your mood. A real walk, that is. I've got an interesting story for you—"

"No, not tonight. I can't. Thanks for offering but—"

"I understand. It's getting late."

"It's not that. Just give me a couple more days," she said, and the line went dead.

He sat there for a while with the phone in his hand, his head lowered. Five days since he'd seen her, and she'd hung up on him. He felt morally wronged—his Italian soccer player expression, as Judy called it. He nearly called Audrey back to hash it out with her, but no. He wasn't supposed to pry, not after that meltdown of hers. What had she said that night? *Don't try to find out.*

He got on the Internet and did a search for "Audrey Martin." A series of newspaper articles came up—the *Hartford Courant, Greenwich Citizen, New Haven Register.* Even *The New York Times* had followed the story and its aftermath. He raced through the articles, switching from one to the next.

Daniel Martin-Murray, a seventeen-year-old senior at Greenwich High School, was driving home after school on a Wednesday in May 2006. He was alone in the car, a Toyota Celica, with his seat belt fastened, heading north on Wolf's Den Road in Cos Cob. The other driver, a landscaper operating his employer's truck, ran a stoplight at the Mulberry Avenue intersection and collided with the passenger door of the Celica. The impact of the crash hurled the Celica over the curb and against a brick retaining wall, causing the air bag to inflate and pushing the metal frame two feet into the driver's compartment. Emergency personnel were unable to free the victim from the wreckage until firefighters arrived with special equipment. The landscaper was not harmed in the accident. He admitted to police that he had been talking on his cell phone and had failed to keep a proper lookout, and he was issued a summons at the scene for reckless driving.

Police informed the boy's mother, Audrey Martin, that her son had been involved in an automobile accident and that he was en route to the hospital. At the emergency room, the duty nurse told her that her son had broken his left femur. When she saw her son, Audrey Martin reported that he was alert and communicative, but he complained of pain in his back.

Tests were ordered. At 5:22 P.M. X-ray technicians took images of Daniel's neck, chest, leg, pelvis, and abdomen. The patient was examined by the admitting physician, a trauma surgeon, and an orthopedist. A CT scan of his head was performed at 6:05.

At 7:18, the resident neurologist first examined the CT scan and was concerned with the image. He ordered an MRI, which showed extra-axial fluid collection in the fronto-parietal region.

At 7:25, the orthopedist, who had been waiting two hours to set the patient's broken leg, complained about the delay.

At 7:34, a neurosurgeon was summoned. Ms. Martin heard the call over the intercom and inquired what that meant. All this time, since her arrival at the ER, she had been sitting with her son and the duty nurse, Vera Kovalenko, chatting and laughing with him. He was worried that he would miss his summer tennis league. Suddenly, Daniel Martin-Murray complained of a terrible headache and blurry vision. He began gasping for air. He called his mother's name repeatedly. He heaved off the bed. Alarms sounded. Nurses and doctors ran in and out of the room, appearing frantic. The duty nurse tried to pull Ms. Martin away, but she refused to leave the room. "What's happening?" she asked. "What's wrong with him?"

The duty nurse answered: "Come with me. We will pray together."

Daniel Martin-Murray was pronounced dead at 8:54 from an epidural hematoma. In layman's terms, he'd bled inside his skull, crushing his brain and causing respiratory failure. Blunt injuries to the head often result from traffic accidents. Individuals who undergo immediate surgery to relieve the pressure inside the skull have a good chance of survival, but the chances decrease with each minute that the injury remains untreated or unnoticed.

Twelve months after the accident, Daniel Martin-Murray's family recovered an undisclosed settlement from the hospital for negligent treatment of their son. The state Department of Public Health ordered an investigation of the incident. A 105-page report was issued, identifying numerous protocol lapses at the hospital, most significantly, the failure to read CT scans in a timely fashion.

Andrew Murray stated publicly that the lawsuit filed on behalf of his deceased son was intended to make hospitals accountable and institute policy changes to prevent similar delays in reading and interpreting imaging scans. Audrey Martin was unable to speak to reporters about her son without sobbing. She revealed that she'd had trouble sleeping ever since that terrible day.

Sixteen months after the accident, the hospital posted a framed photograph of Daniel Martin-Murray in the emergency room waiting area. The hospital spokesman said that gesture was intended to make amends for its role in the Martin-Murray family loss. "It's healing for them," said the spokesman, "and it's healing for us." The Martin-Murray family did not attend the ceremony.

Benjamin turned off the computer.

AFTER A few minutes he picked up the phone and called his son.

"David?"

"Hey, Dad."

"I thought I'd get your voice mail, like usual."

"That's because you usually call when I'm in class."

Benjamin could hear background noise—some music and voices. "Where are you?"

"Student center."

"How was your flight back?"

"Fine. I just got in. What's up?"

"I just wanted to hear your voice."

"Did Grandpa die?"

"God, no. He's fine. He's better. He's coming home from the rehab center in a few days. Why did you think that?"

"Because you sound stressed. What's going on?"

Benjamin took a deep breath and wiped his eyes. "Listen, David, I'm sorry about everything. All those arguments with your mom. I'm sorry for screwing things up. It was my fault, all of it. Not your mom's. The whole thing was my fault." There was a silence on the other end. "You still there?"

"Yeah."

"I don't want to lose you. You and Sarah mean everything to me. You know that, right?"

"Dad, I'm eating a tuna sandwich."

"I'm serious. I want you to know, I love you, David. Whenever you need me, I'm here. I don't care what time—"

"Okay, Dad. I hear you." His son lowered his voice, the phone close to his mouth. "I'm sorry too. I can be a dick sometimes."

Benjamin laughed. "No, you're not. You're the best son anyone could have. I mean that."

"Listen, Dad. This is pretty weird."

"I know. Don't mind me."

"I should probably get back—"

"Your tuna sandwich, right. I'll give you a ring tomorrow."

"But I appreciate the call, Dad."

Benjamin recalled what Audrey had said that night. *I'm not over it. I'll never be over it.* Of course not. How could she get over the death of a child? How could she forget the last hours of his life, her sitting beside him, helplessly? He couldn't imagine the loss, a life without his son. The emptiness, so immense. Poor Audrey. How could he possibly help her? He couldn't even tell her he knew, since she'd asked him not to find out. How could he *un*know? How could he look at her now without this terrible knowledge showing in his eyes?

MONDAY WAS the big outing. Leonard Mandelbaum had been looking forward to it. It was about time he got out of this place, if only for the afternoon. But he didn't like this wheelchair business. He didn't like looking like an invalid. The doctors had told him to walk as much as possible, hadn't they? So why not let him use his own two feet?

"They have their rules, Len," said Terri Funkhouser. "Who knows why? Once we get outside, we can do as we please."

"*If* we get out."

Getting past the front desk was an ordeal. The nurse behind the counter where they kept the controls couldn't be reasoned with. He would approach her and say, "Excuse me, Nurse, I'd like to step outside for a breath of fresh air," and she would stare at him as if he'd babbled in Chinese. He had no rights in this place. But if Terri Funkhouser talked to her and signed her clipboard, then they would let him out; they'd press the buzzer and the front door would open. Thank God for Terri Funkhouser. Otherwise, Leonard was a prisoner.

Outside, he squinted into the sky, his hand blocking the sun. He wasn't used to such bright sunlight. Terri Funkhouser pushed his wheelchair down the front ramp and along the sidewalk.

"Upsy-daisy, Len," she said when they came to her car.

"Gladly," he said, throwing the blanket from his lap, rising stiffly. He stamped his right leg to get the blood going again.

"Stand back." She folded up his wheelchair and hoisted it like a man, stowing it in the trunk of her car. "I packed a picnic basket. Egg salad sandwiches and yogurt. We'll take a drive to the park. Get in."

"Is that allowed?"

"Of course it's allowed."

Her car, the Cutlass, smelled of cigarette smoke and gasoline. She must have a leak in the fuel line. Her perfume didn't bother him anymore; he barely noticed it, except when she arrived each day, that first aromatic blast.

"Put your seat belt on," she said, starting the motor.

The whole sedan shook, like one of those old-time hotel beds where you put in a quarter. No wonder Dickie wanted a new car for her. This one was ten years old, at least. It had engine knock. It needed a tune-up and bodywork; every panel looked dented.

"Knocking," said Leonard.

She wheeled out of the parking lot, hitting a pothole. A pair of sunglasses dropped from the dashboard into his lap.

"Who's there?"

He frowned. "The car's knocking."

"Okay." She turned to him, grinning. "The car, who?"

"This car. The car you're driving."

She laughed loudly, he didn't know why. "I'm playing fun, Len. You know, like 'Who's on first?'"

What was she talking about? "You got engine knock. You need a new car, is what you need."

"Don't get all worked up. I'm just ribbing you."

"Where are we going?"

"I already told you. Picnic in the park."

It sounded like a song: picnic in the park. "MacArthur Park" was Myra's favorite song. She would listen to the forty-five rpm over and over, playing it five times in a row. He would find her in the den, a drink in her hand, tears streaming down her cheeks, makeup ruined. That Irish actor, the drunkard. What was his name? Not Richard Burton, the other one, the redhead. He sang it. The song touched something deep inside her, some wanting unfulfilled, something Leonard couldn't reach. *What is it, Myra? What's wrong?* But she would turn on him, defiantly, her brown eyes aflame. *Go away! Just leave me alone!* A complicated woman, his Myra. He'd done his best to make her happy.

"Did you bring a cake?"

"I brought egg salad sandwiches, like I told you."

Someone left the cake out in the rain. Did that make sense? Why would anyone leave a cake outside? Because it was a picnic. Picnics were held outside.

"Is it raining?"

"No, Len. It's a beautiful day. Stop worrying so much. Terri's got everything under control."

"Who's Terri?"

"Jesus Christ, Len. What did they put in your cereal today?"

"I had eggs and biscuits."

She pulled into the park and directed the Cutlass over the rutted road. "Let's walk to the rose garden. It'll clear your head. See how nice it is? You're not cold, are you?"

"I'm fine. I'm fine."

"How's the leg?"

"Better."

The fresh afternoon air. He got out of the car and took a few deep breaths, opening his arms the way they'd taught him in the Navy.

"Look at you, Len, doing exercises. Pretty soon you'll be back in your house, back to normal. You won't need me anymore. You'll forget all about silly old Terri."

"They won't let me out. They got me locked up."

"Naw, Len, they're letting you out in a couple of days. Don't be so suspicious. This is America. They can't do anything bad to you. You have your civil liberties."

"That's what you think." She didn't know what they did when she wasn't around. They came into his room at night like it was Grand Central Station. They stuck him like a pincushion with needles and tubes. Benjamin said they were just doing their job; they had to give him medication, check his blood pressure. But in the middle of the night? What was the sense of waking a man to check his pulse?

"Look at the trees, Len. Aren't they beautiful?"

He shaded his eyes against the sun. What time of year was this? He didn't know. Well, he *knew*, but he couldn't think of it at the moment. They'd celebrated a milestone recently, a special meal. Terri Funkhouser had brought dinner and they'd eaten together in the lounge, turkey and gravy. *Turkey.* Of course, Thanksgiving, it was fall. The trees were bare, mostly. A few still had a shading of dry color. The fallen leaves were underfoot, crunching like peanut shells, as they crossed the wooden footbridge over the pond. Some ducks stood on the grass by the edge of the water. When he and Terri passed by, the ducks turned their heads in unison and looked the other way, as if insulted.

Terri Funkhouser clutched his arm, leading him down the gravel path through a series of vine-covered trestles. Up ahead, at the center of the rose garden, stood the wooden gazebo, the silver roof shimmering in the sunlight. Leonard exhaled heavily, feeling winded. The gazebo seemed far off.

"What's the matter, Len? Your leg hurt?"

"Looking at the trees."

"Aren't they pretty? Dick Senior loved fall. That's why he made us live in Connecticut all this time, why he wouldn't go to Florida like everyone else. He liked the change of seasons. *Fall is a time for reflection.* I can still hear his voice. He was like you, Len, always saying the same things over and over."

"I always liked Dick Senior."

"See what I mean? Whenever I mention Dick Senior, you say, *I always liked Dick Senior.*"

"He was a good man. I always liked him."

She cackled, startling him. That big laugh, you could hear it coming all the way up from her stomach. He'd say something, not expecting to be funny, and she would roar.

They ascended the wooden staircase to the center of the gazebo.

"Sit." She tapped the bench next to her. "I've got something to tell you."

Rosebushes, all around. Myra used to love coming here during the season. Red roses, they all looked the same to him. But Myra knew all the different names and where they came from. Climbers, tea roses, hybrid roses, big-headed English roses. She made them all grow. Her garden had been the envy of every woman in the neighborhood. Betty Amato, on the south side of the street, could manage only hostas and ferns. Stella Papadakis, next door, had a fenced-in garden, built on raised ground at the rear of her yard, but she grew only vegetables—tomatoes and cucumbers, beets and carrots—for her four children to gobble. A functional garden. But once her children grew and moved away, she gave it up; the patch lay abandoned, the fence broken in places, weeds growing three feet high. Not so with Myra. She'd made her garden every spring; even when she got sick, she had high school kids do the weeding and planting, giving orders from her lounge chair like a foreman.

"Len, I did it. I signed the house over to Dick Junior. What the hell, I figure. No use hanging on until the bitter end. I should've done it a long time ago."

"You changed your mind."

"It's a woman's prerogative, as they say. That Stefanie's not so bad. She seems to care for Dickie, and God knows he needs someone to look after him. The other day she asked for my kugel recipe. The woman is useless in the kitchen. I had to take her through step by step. Maybe she was just buttering me up."

"Don't sign any papers. I'll give Brendan McGowan a call. He'll draw something up for you."

"That's sweet of you, Len, but it's already done."

"Where will you go?"

"Oh, anywhere. I like those condos over by Stop & Shop. They got

a swimming pool and a CVS next door and a package store too. Everything a gal needs. One of my girlfriends lives there. Jenzie Boutilier."

"I thought she died."

"Bootsy died. Left her stocks and bonds worth millions."

"What about Florida?"

"Dickie and Stefanie want to go to Florida, not me. I never liked
Florida, not even to visit. Too many old people. Isn't it funny how you
get old but don't think of yourself as old? I look around and say, *When
did everybody get so old?* Not me, of course, everybody else. Where does
the time go, Leonard Mandelbaum? Answer me that."

"You look fine," he said.

"I don't know how it happened. I was always the young one. Dick Senior had twenty years on me. All of our friends too. *The baby*, they called
me. So that's how I saw myself. I believed them. What a fool I was. I let
my life go by. Now everyone's dead. For the last ten years I haven't been
able to put away my black dress. I got it hanging on the closet door, ready
for the next funeral."

"That'll be mine."

"Oh, Len, don't say such things!"

It was a sunny day, but it got cold quickly if you stayed still. The sun
passed behind a cloud for a few seconds and you nearly froze. Leonard
kicked his right leg up and down. It felt like it was asleep, just the right
leg, not the other. He would sit for a minute and lose all feeling, particularly at night, lying alone in his hospital bed.

"Your leg hurting?"

"I'm fine."

She leaned forward to massage him, digging in with those strong
hands of hers. He'd gotten used to her roughness.

"Feels good," he said.

"Yeah? Well, what are you going to do for me, buster?" she said, winking.

"You need a younger man."

"Why do you say that?" she asked, her hands stopping.

"You've got needs." He paused, lowering his voice even though there
was no one in sight. "Women's needs."

"For Christ's sake, Len. I haven't felt anything down there in years. I
just say that to be funny. Look at me. I'm a catastrophe."

"You're beautiful."

"And you're blind."

"You've always been beautiful. It's the way God made you."

Was it a betrayal to compliment another woman? Myra had always been jealous. She didn't like him paying attention to other women. Sophia Loren, now there was a beauty. He'd said so once, watching a movie on television, and Myra had kicked him in the shin, hard. *Is that the type of woman you want?* she'd yelled. *Well, go ahead. See if she'll have you.* She had stormed out of the room, deaf to his apologies. Didn't she know that she *was* that type of woman? Her eyes, just as lovely? Her olive skin?

"Oh, Leonard."

He turned, surprised to see Terri crying, tears bubbling from her eyes. She honked her nose, then fished for a handkerchief in her handbag, as big as a beach bag. What *didn't* she have in there?

"What's wrong?"

"No one's told me that in forever. I forgot what it feels like."

Told her what? He didn't ask. He let her cry; he could tell she liked a good cry. But she'd made a mistake signing papers. Didn't she know that? You can talk as much as you like, you can sing and dance if it makes you happy, but never sign your name to a piece of paper without forethought. You can't take it back once it's written in black and white. They got your signature, they got *you*. You can't say, *No, I didn't mean it, I made a mistake.*

"Bring me the papers. I'll call Brendan McGowan. Maybe he can do something."

"Don't be silly, Len. He's my son. I don't need a lawyer to give him my house."

"You don't want a condominium. Too much noise. They play their radios all hours."

"I'm not particular. I take a Valium and it's lights out."

"What about me?"

"You?" She patted his knee. "You're all better."

"They won't let me out."

"We already talked about this. You're going home soon." She clapped her hands together like a schoolteacher. "The doctor said to give you tests to check your memory. Here goes. Are you ready? Today is Monday. What comes after Monday?"

"Tuesday."

"Very good, Len. And after Tuesday?"

"Halloween."

"No, Len. Halloween is a holiday—" She glanced at him, but he couldn't keep a straight face. "Oh, be *serious*!"

He'd always liked teasing. Once he'd had Plimpton's Stationery Store print calling cards for him, saying, *The management kindly requests you to leave the premises immediately.* Whenever he saw a friend at Scoler's Restaurant or Dino's Italian Ristorante, he would ask the waitress to deliver one of the cards. The looks on their faces! The shock and embarrassment and indignation! Then he'd walk over, grinning, his hand extended.

"Wednesday," he said.

"Correct, and Thursday you go home, back to your very own house."

"You come too. Benjamin says I need someone."

"He'll have people to look after you. But I can visit if you like."

Leonard shook his head. Those nurses who came to care for Myra, she wasn't a person to them. They didn't listen to her; they picked her up like a sack of potatoes. She was *sick*, not stupid. He had fired three or four of them before the agency sent someone he liked, a Chinese woman. She could barely speak English, but she never missed the vein, like those others. Myra's thin and spotted arms, covered with welts. It had broken his heart to see her so bruised.

"You come," he said. "I don't want anyone else."

"You should talk to Benjamin about this."

"No, it's for the best," he said. "You got no house. You signed the papers."

"I'm not *homeless*, Len."

He got up. "I want a taco."

She rose, taking his arm. "Slow down there. Did you say *taco*?"

"Benjamin brings them home sometimes. You'll like it."

He had to stamp his right leg to get the blood flowing. It felt like dancing, that Irish dance. They called it a jig. It pleased him that he knew this word, *jig*.

"What now?"

"Dancing the jig," he said.

"You lost your marbles? Stop jumping up and down like that, you'll have a heart attack."

"I'm light on my feet."

"Leonard Mandelbaum. You're full of surprises today, aren't you?"

They started down the gravel path through the rows of roses. Were they going the right way? He didn't know. He couldn't remember. But she did, the woman he was with. She led him toward the vine-covered trestles in the distance, the sun blazing above like a halo, an entrance or an exit, he couldn't tell which, to some other place.

ON MONDAY NIGHT Benjamin returned from a busy day at the dealership and went through the house, checking all the doors and windows. He still felt shaken by the burglary, so he poured himself a scotch and drank it in the den, flipping channels. With his second drink in hand, he felt himself beginning to doze on the couch.

The doorbell roused him. He turned off the TV and checked the time: almost ten. Who could it be, so late? Audrey?

Through the window he could see a figure standing on the porch. It wasn't Audrey, he realized, feeling the excitement wash out of him. It was a girl wearing a hooded sweatshirt.

"Yes?" he said, opening the door.

She lowered the hood, revealing her face. "May I speak to the lady of the house?"

He took a closer look at her. He'd seen her only that one time, when she'd flipped him off in her driveway. But it was her, unmistakably. The dark hair, the Gypsy eyes. What was she doing on his front porch? "What's up? Selling Girl Scout cookies?"

"Not exactly," she said. "Do you know who I am?"

"I think so. You live in the farmhouse, right?"

She hesitated for a moment. "You won't tell my mother, will you?"

"Tell her what?"

"About this." She reached into her pocket and thrust her hand in front of his face. He peered into her open palm, his eyes narrowing. A ring. He took it from her and examined it under the light and then realized what it was: his mother's sapphire. He studied her face but couldn't read her expression.

"Come in," he said.

She stepped past him into the hallway. She smelled earthy, as if she hadn't washed in a week. In the hallway Yukon raised his head and sniffed at her as she passed.

Benjamin directed her to the kitchen table and pulled out a chair for her. He placed his drink and the ring on the table. He hadn't even known it had been taken. "This was my mother's twenty-fifth wedding anniversary present. She only wore it on special nights, to weddings and galas."

"It's beautiful."

"Would you care to tell me how you got it?"

"Can't you guess?"

"Did someone give it to you? A boy named Billy?"

Her eyes flared. "No," she said. "Try again."

"Emily. That's your name, right?"

"Yeah. What's yours?"

"Benjamin."

"How about I just call you Ben?"

She unzipped her sweatshirt and peeled it off, wrapping it around her waist. Beneath she wore a low-cut T-shirt, without a bra. She leaned forward, her breasts bulging. Benjamin sat back in his chair.

"You want me to believe you did it? Broke into my house?"

"Bingo."

"Why would you do that?"

"To pay you back for fucking my mother."

He felt the blood drain out of him. "That's crazy."

"Is it? I saw you. You and her together."

"I don't know what you saw—"

She reached for his glass and took a slug and set it back on the table. "Whiskey and ginger ale," she said. "Yum."

Benjamin felt a flash of panic. "I'm going to call your mother. I think she should hear this."

"Good idea. You call Audrey. I'll call my dad." She took her cell phone out of her jeans and offered it to him. "He's a lawyer. We'll get the whole family together."

He hesitated. "Look—"

"I didn't think so." She put the phone back in her pocket. "What do you want with her anyway? You could do a lot better."

"The only thing I've done with your mother is walk the dog."

"Is that what you call it? Sounds like something from the Kama Sutra." Her face was pale under the fluorescent light. "I don't blame her, though. You're hot. You're the hot older guy."

It dawned on Benjamin that she was probably drunk. Her words sounded slurred and she kept blinking, as if trying to focus.

She said, "Wouldn't you like someone younger? Me, for instance."

"Cut it out."

"What, you're denying it? I saw you checking out my ass that day. That's why I flipped you off. You're a horny old fucker, aren't you?"

He shook his head. "Your story doesn't make sense. You break into my house and trash the place. Now you bring back a ring worth thousands of dollars?"

"So?"

"So, why not keep it? Why not sell it?"

She shrugged. "I felt guilty."

"You could've just left it in the mailbox if you felt so bad."

"Didn't think of that."

"I don't believe you. You're covering up for your boyfriend, aren't you? He broke in, didn't he? That kid Billy." Though it still didn't make sense why she'd take the rap for him. But girls her age could be influenced by boys into doing stupid things.

"I took your fucking ring, okay? I steal things all the time. I took it and now I'm bringing it back. You should thank me instead of breaking my balls."

"Fine. Thank you. Now you should go."

She got up and strolled down the hallway toward the den. She kneeled beside Yukon and rubbed his stomach, and the dog turned over and put his legs in the air. "Would you mind if I warmed up in front of the fireplace?"

"Yes, I would mind."

"Chill out, Ben. Don't be so uptight. Go pour yourself another scotch. Get one for me too. I deserve a reward, don't you think?"

He got up. "Ah. So that's why you came to my house at this time of night. For money."

She shook her head. "Not money. Something better."

"Like what?"

"Like what you do to Audrey." She batted her eyes at him, looking like an actress in a soap opera. But he could see through the act. He didn't know why she was pretending to flirt with him, or what she wanted from him, but he'd had enough. He didn't like being played for a fool by a teenager. "That's enough," he said. "It's time to go." He took her elbow and led her toward the front door. Her skin was cold, surprisingly cold. At the door, she wheeled away from him with a sudden furious energy, swinging her arms and yelling, "Let go of me, motherfucker!"

And then she screamed—a scream so loud he would not have thought it possible. He waited for the sound to stop, unable to move. Yukon barked and jumped up to investigate. At that moment, she ran up the stairs and disappeared into his father's bedroom. Benjamin went after her. "Hey, come back here!" As he reached the doorway, he caught sight of her rushing into his father's bathroom, the door slamming behind her.

When he banged on the door, she called out, "You hurt my arm, asshole."

"I'm sorry."

She didn't answer.

He tried the handle but it was locked. "Are you okay?" He heard water running in the sink. After a while he called her name.

She didn't answer.

He sat on the edge of his father's bed. The way she had screamed—like a madwoman. His neighbors had probably heard. Why would she yell like that? He had gripped her arm, but not hard enough to hurt her. Why had she locked herself in the bathroom? He couldn't make sense of anything she was doing.

He knocked again. "Can you hear me?"

"Leave me alone," she called. "I've got cramps."

He couldn't decide what to do, so he just waited. After a while he seemed to lose track of time. He paced around the room. He hadn't done anything wrong, yet he felt sick with guilt. He should have called Audrey the moment the girl showed up. Why hadn't he? Should he call her now? Otherwise, what—knock down the door?

As he was getting ready to dial Audrey's number, the door swung open and Emily emerged. She'd put her sweatshirt back on, the hood around her head.

"If you tell my mother I was here . . ." The words came out heavy. "If you tell her any of this, I'll say you raped me."

"She won't believe you."

"Maybe not. But my father will."

She brushed past him and went out of the room. He followed her to the top of the stairs and watched her go out the front door. Yukon appeared and stood in the open doorway, looking after her.

"Stay, boy," he said, coming down the stairs.

This was the bill, he realized; this was the consequence for getting involved with a married woman: a visit from a deranged girl, threatening to accuse him of rape.

He looked out toward the street, but she was already gone from sight.

HE WENT INTO the den and turned on the TV. His hands, he noticed, were trembling. He felt jittery, unable to concentrate on the show. When he heard a car on the street he jumped up and went to the front window to look out. The car pulled into a driveway a few houses up. He needed to calm himself with a drink or, better yet, a joint. He realized he didn't want to stay in the house, so he jumped up and got his keys and drove into town.

He parked on the street outside Max Baxter's Fish Bar. Getting out he heard loud voices, and he turned to see a businessman, ranting into the pay phone on the corner. It was that kind of night, Benjamin figured. He went in and sat at the bar, ordering a scotch. It was a Monday, approaching 11:00 P.M., and the dining tables were empty, the kitchen closed. A group of waiters and dishwashers, dressed all in white, talked rowdily at a rear booth.

After the first scotch, Benjamin felt his nerves begin to loosen. *To pay you back for fucking my mother.* How could she know? Audrey, of course, would never tell her daughter something like that, but maybe the girl had overheard one of Audrey's phone calls and figured it out. But how would she know about *him,* specifically, where he lived? Had Audrey written something in a journal, which her daughter had discovered? In any case, he didn't believe that the girl had broken into his house. Her face had changed when he'd mentioned the boy's name. Maybe this kid Billy was behind the entire crazy stunt. But why? What did she—or they—hope to gain by confronting him like that? She said she didn't want money. And why had she given back the ring, the only valuable item they'd gotten away with?

The door opened and the businessman from the pay phone came in and sat at the other end of the bar, looking disheveled and red in the face.

He ordered a tequila but the bartender refused. Benjamin felt for the guy. Drunk as he looked, he seemed to need it at least as badly as Benjamin needed his second glass of scotch.

As he sipped, a waiter appeared next to him and ordered a draft beer. He stood watching the basketball game. After a few quick gulps, he hiccuped loudly. A moment later he hiccuped again, as if making a joke.

Benjamin turned to him.

"Sorry," the waiter said. "I can't get rid of them."

He was a young guy with curly blond hair. He reminded Benjamin of one of those guys back in college who could kick a Hacky Sack for five minutes without letting it fall. "How long have you had them?"

"Three days."

"You've had the hiccups for three days?"

The kid nodded. "I haven't slept more than a couple hours the whole time."

"Have you tried chewing a lemon?"

"I've tried everything you can think of. I even went to the hospital. The doctor yanked on my tongue and had me drink three seltzers—" A hiccup ripped through his body, causing him to wince. His voice was hoarse and dry. "Didn't help."

"That's all they did for you?"

"Yep."

Benjamin noticed the bags under his eyes but still couldn't help smiling when the kid burped and hiccuped at the same time. "That sounds awful."

"Everyone thinks it's funny. It's not. Feels like my chest is gonna bust open." The kid finished his beer and placed the glass on the bar. "Take it easy," he said, heading for the door.

A few minutes later the bartender passed Benjamin his bill. "We're closing soon," he said.

Benjamin finished his drink and left before they turned up the lights. Outside, Wintonbury Center was silent, the traffic lights flashing yellow, the streets deserted. He stood on the sidewalk, smoking a cigarette. He noticed the waiter, sitting at the bus stop near his car. The kid hiccuped, the loudest yet, like an otter's mating call.

"Good one," said Benjamin.

"Thanks, I guess. I just tried holding my breath for the hundredth time."

"How about getting high? You try that yet?"

The kid smiled. "It's funny you should mention that. I've been trying to get an angle on some weed ever since this started."

Benjamin dropped his cigarette and stamped it out. "I can help you out in that department."

"Seriously?"

Benjamin unlocked his car and signaled the kid to join him. The kid opened the passenger door and stuck his head inside. "You're not a narc, are you?"

Benjamin laughed. "I'm a fucking car salesman."

The kid climbed into the passenger seat and closed the door behind him.

Benjamin said, "Open the glove compartment. Look inside that yellow envelope."

The waiter reached in and produced the joint. *"Dude."*

"For medicinal purposes only."

"Seriously? You got a prescription?"

"Nah. I get it from a mechanic in my shop. Fire it up." Benjamin started the motor and turned on the heater. He fiddled with the radio, looking for music. The kid produced a Zippo and lit the joint, inhaling with a skilled ease, slow and deep.

"Yo," he said, passing it over. He hiccuped an enormous cloud of smoke.

They both laughed. Benjamin brought the joint to his lips and sucked in. Just what the doctor ordered.

They sat with the headlights off, passing the joint. A Motown song came on the radio. Benjamin felt high almost immediately, listening to Marvin Gaye—the old Marvin, before he got divorced and bitter, before he went celibate, before he beat his old man and shot him to death. Or did he have that mixed up? Did Marvin shoot his old man? Or had the old man shot Marvin?

He passed the joint, and the kid dragged on it, and hiccuped.

"That didn't work," said Benjamin.

"But still," said the kid. "A good try."

Benjamin took a final puff and stubbed the roach in the ashtray. "Good luck with those hiccups."

"Thanks, man," the kid said, getting out. "You gotta be the coolest car salesman ever."

"Yeah, let me know when you're in the market for a Cadillac."

What now? The thought of returning to the house brought on a rush of anxiety. He should tell Audrey about her daughter's visit, he decided. If he didn't, it meant he was guilty somehow. It meant he was hiding something. The girl might come back, break in, steal things, make accusations. He couldn't let that happen. Let Audrey deal with her crazy daughter. If he warned Audrey now, she could confront her daughter before she told her father. Contain the situation, as they said in the movies.

He reached for his cell phone—and realized he'd left it behind in his haste to get out of the house. What the heck, he figured, he'd go old school. He fished a few quarters out of the cup holder and walked to the pay phone on the corner.

He dialed her number and the line rang and rang. He realized it was late—nearly midnight. She must be asleep. Her husband must be asleep next to her. He expected voice mail to kick in, but at last she answered and mumbled a groggy "Hello?"

"Audrey?"

"Benjamin? Is that you?"

"Yes. I'm sorry to call so late."

"What time is it? Why are you—"

Before he could respond, he heard a clatter—and the line went dead. Had she hung up on him on purpose? Or a lost connection? He waited for a minute, giving her time to get out of bed, go into another room. He didn't want to cause any trouble for her. But this was important. He couldn't let it wait.

He slid two more quarters in the slot and dialed again. This time, she answered almost instantly, sounding much more awake.

"Hello?"

"It's me again."

"Benjamin?"

"Yes."

"What's going on?"

"I'm calling about your daughter. It's kind of an emergency."

"An emergency?"

"Maybe that's not the right word."

"Should I get her? She's packing for school. She's driving back first thing tomorrow morning."

What did she mean? Didn't the girl go to high school in town, a mile down the road?

He cleared his throat. "I'm not sure how to tell you this—"

"What's going on, Benjamin? You sound strange."

Something wasn't right. Her voice wasn't hers. In his stoned condition it took him a while to figure it out.

"Benjamin? What's wrong? What's the emergency?"

He had called the wrong number. By habit, he'd dialed his wife. He found himself laughing at his predicament. "There's no emergency. I just wanted to remind Sarah to check the oil. She always forgets."

Judy was silent for a while. "Are you sure you're okay?"

"Yes." He paused. "Well, not really. I don't know."

"Are you having an anxiety attack?"

"Something like that."

"Listen to me. There's nothing to worry about. Sarah's fine. David is too. He called and told me what you said to him. He said you creeped him out."

He sighed. "I tell him I love him and it creeps him out. That's priceless."

"Not like that," she said gently. "It was your tone. He said he never heard your voice like that before. He was worried."

"I'm fine."

"You don't sound fine. What's that noise? Is that the TV?"

"I'm at a pay phone in Wintonbury Center."

"A pay phone? Do those things still exist?"

"It's one of the last of its kind. Like a snow leopard." He took a deep breath. "I called because I was thinking how terrible it would be to lose him. Or Sarah. Or you."

She paused for a few moments. "I think you should come over," she said.

Her voice, so familiar. He felt some of the paranoia recede. He could picture her, sitting up in bed, wearing her blue sweatpants and his old Red Sox T-shirt. "Aren't you sleepy?"

"Not at all. I had a lousy night."

"Trouble with your divorce lawyer?"

"You could say that."

"Things went downhill that fast?"

"Crazy, isn't it? This dating thing. I don't know how people do it." She sighed. The Judy sigh. It had been her main manner of communication during the past few, difficult years. Once she started, nothing could change her mood. She would just get more and more irritated. But for once, he wasn't the cause of her discontent.

"Do you want to talk about it?"

"God, no. Thanks for asking. But no. I'd rather not waste any more breath on him."

"Do you really want me—"

He stopped himself. He was stoned. She hated when he got stoned, or when he came home drunk and reeking of cigarettes. A bad time to make any sort of overture. At the intersection, the light changed. A police car cruised by slowly, the cop studying him.

"What?" said Judy.

"Nothing."

"No," she insisted. "Tell me."

There was something different in her voice, a tone he hadn't heard in a long time. A softness. The impartiality gone. The voice of his old friend, his partner. She had been on his side all those years, waiting for him.

"Something's bothering you," she said. "What is it?"

He thought of Audrey Martin. What could he say to her anyway? What could he tell her about her daughter that she didn't already know?

He glanced at his watch. Late, but not too late. "Are you sure it's a good idea for me to come over?"

"What about you?" she asked. "What about your love life?"

"I have no love life."

"What about Aubrey?"

He emitted a dry laugh, almost against his will. "There is no Aubrey. I made the whole thing up."

"I knew it!" she screeched. "I knew you were lying."

"You were right."

"Why would you lie?"

"To make you jealous." *Here we go again,* he thought. *Lie upon lie, rising like a layer cake.*

"Well, it worked. *Aubrey.* That name drove me nuts. Leave it to you to come up with a name like that. I tried to find her on Google. How many Aubreys could there be in Wintonbury?"

"None," he said.

"I even downloaded the song. Which came out in 1972, by the way."

"Oops."

"You're a terrible liar. You just make it up as you go along."

A motorcycle went by, racing through its gears, drowning out all other sounds. "Wait a minute," he said. He lit up a cigarette and took a drag. The motorcycle finally faded into the distance.

He said, "I was pissed off about your divorce lawyer. I couldn't stop picturing him humping you with his hairy back."

"Your back is hairy too."

"Not like his. I pictured him like a baboon, thrusting and grinning."

"Gross. You see? This is what you do to me. You turn me into a crazy person. You get my head spinning, trying to figure out what's real and what's not, until I just about lose my mind."

"I'm sorry."

"Isn't it easier to just tell me the truth?"

"Yes. I suppose so."

"Don't do it anymore."

"What?"

"Lie to me."

"I won't."

"No," she insisted. "Promise me. I want you to think about it. I want you to understand the implications."

He pondered this for a moment. Could he simply tell Judy the truth? About everything? Always?

"I'm high," he blurted.

"I know. I knew that immediately. Your voice gets heavy."

What about Audrey Martin? Should he come clean about that too? If he and Judy were to get back together—and he suddenly found himself hoping they might—then somewhere down the line, today, tomorrow, a year from now, he would slip and it would come out, and Judy would know that he had lied to her two seconds after promising never to lie to her again. *Here goes,* he thought. "You were right the first time. It was her."

"Right about what?"

"Audrey Martin. The woman I dated."

"Audrey *Martin*!" she screeched. "Of course! How could I forget that name? *Audrey Martin had the finest ass in high school.* You said that same fucking thing for years. I can't believe you tracked her down as soon as you left me."

"I didn't leave. You kicked me out."

"You cheated on me. I still have that Holiday Inn receipt to remind me, in case I ever considered taking you back."

"Judy, I didn't cheat. I got drunk across the street and checked in to sober up."

"You're lying again."

"No. I'm not."

He could hear Judy pausing on the other end of the line, weighing his words, the tone of his voice. Then she sighed, like she'd made a decision. "Well, that *is* a surprise."

"You always think the worst of me."

"With good reason. And I'm supposed to believe that she called you. This Audrey Martin with the fine ass."

"I didn't have to call her. She moved onto Leonard's street. She and her husband bought the farmhouse on the corner."

"That old firetrap?"

"Yeah. And I . . . I kidnapped her dog."

"You did what?"

"Kidnapped her dog so I could meet her."

Judy snorted. "You broke into her house and took her dog? Are you insane?"

"No, the thing got out by itself. But I saw it and lured it onto my lawn with a turkey leg. And then she came to retrieve the dog."

"And one thing led to another."

"Yes."

She paused, then laughed. "Thank you. For telling the truth. Isn't that easier?"

"Yes," he admitted. "It is."

"Are you still seeing her?"

"No. That's over." As he said it, he realized it was true.

"Did you have sex with her?"

"Yes."

"How many times?"

He thought back over the past month—

"Just answer the question," she said.

"I'm trying to remember."

"How could you not remember?"

"There were multiple occasions."

"Now you sound like my divorce lawyer."

"How many times did you have sex with him?"

"Don't change the subject. Tell me. Five times?"

"More than that."

"Ten?"

"Closer to twenty, I'd say."

"Jesus, Benjamin. Twenty times in a month or so? You're such a pig."

"You asked!"

"Was it good?"

"It was good, yes. But different."

"Different how?"

"I felt—I don't know—distanced. Like a spectator."

"That means you didn't care about her. You were just fucking her for the fun of it."

"If you say so."

"Don't sound so proud of it. But maybe you finally got her out of your system, Audrey with the fine ass, and all the others too."

"Anyway, it's over. It sort of ended tonight, in fact. I haven't talked to her yet, but . . ." He hesitated. How much of this truth thing could he do? Judy had been his adviser all those years, she and Leonard. She had always known what to do whenever he got himself into a jam. "Her daughter—she has a seventeen-year-old daughter—"

"You didn't—"

"No. Of course not. Shut up and listen, will you? The daughter showed up at my front door tonight with Myra's sapphire and confessed to robbing me."

"She was the one?"

"She says she did it, but I don't believe her."

"Why not?"

"It's a long story."

"For goodness' sake, Benjamin. Come over. I want to hear this."

"Are you sure it's not too late?"

"It's not too late. I'll put on the porch light."

He hung up. He checked his watch:

11:58 P.M.
Monday
November 26, 2007

Part Two

THE MARTIN-MURRAYS

Audrey Martin

The third Saturday of October 2007

IT BEGAN on a Saturday, she recalled later, the day the electrician showed up at eight in the morning.

Audrey answered the door in her pajamas and slippers, barely out of bed. "Is this a bad time?" he said. He was alone, unannounced, and it seemed, hungover. He had a ponytail, a dented green toolbox, and he rceked of cigarettes. Audrey nearly said, *Of course it's a bad time.* But she needed him. Contractors were like blackmailers; they showed up when they pleased and they demanded however much they wanted. He was the last of the long line of workmen they'd hired that autumn to fix up the farmhouse, and she wanted to be done with them.

She let him in and showed him to the fuse box in the basement. The rest of that morning, she worked in the kitchen, trying to stay out of the man's way. The space was cramped, with only two short rows of cabinets. She unpacked box after box, trying to find a place for everything. A challenge, squeezing their possessions into this smaller house. What to do with all this crap? She'd been tossing out stuff for several weeks, ever since they started the move to Wintonbury, but it looked like she would have to do more. More plastic for the landfills, to float across the ocean, to fill the bellies of sharks. How had they gathered so many *things* in the first place?

Simplify, the self-help books said.

There was pleasure in divesting; they were right about that. But what would be left after she lugged the boxes of unneeded kitchenware to Goodwill, after she'd tossed away the moth-eaten and unworn clothes, after she'd dragged the old furniture and unused exercise equipment to the curb? And when to stop once you started? Why not give it all away, like the old men in India who one day opened the front door and simply walked down the road to nowhere, leaving it all behind—their homes, everything they owned—with only the clothes on their backs?

Midmorning, Andrew took his place at the kitchen table with the newspaper. "Are there any eggs?" he said.

This meant he wanted a cheddar omelet with green peppers (small squares, thinly sliced). Her husband had rules for everything—how to make the bed, how to clean the lettuce, how much sleep he needed—and any slight deviation could unsettle him. For a strong, athletic man, he could be extremely prissy. Years ago she'd found these foibles cute, like his habit of lifting one eyebrow.

Andrew was a fast talker, a fast thinker, a man who spent half his day barking into the phone. He thrived on argument, on being right; it was what made him good at his job. Law was a profession that rewarded an aggressive temperament, if you didn't burn out. Most of her friends who'd gone to law school had quit their jobs by now, had moved on to less stressful endeavors. Only the true devotees like Andrew kept at it. He *liked* the stress.

When he took the milk out of the refrigerator to add to his coffee, he brought the carton to his nose for a quick sniff, another of his habits. She knew why. She'd seen the old Tudor mansion in Longmeadow, Massachusetts, where he'd grown up. For a lovely woman, Andrew's mother had been a sloppy homemaker; she'd let food sit in the fridge and cupboards until rotten, until weevils burrowed in the rice and flour and moths flew out of the cupboards. Andrew would tell these tales at dinner parties to great effect, but Audrey knew the squalid kitchen was anything but funny to him—the filthy pantry, the unwashed dishes and soiled pans in the sink. So Andrew had gone the opposite way; he'd become a tidy, well-organized man. It made sense. So many things finally made sense when you visited someone's childhood home, when you met his parents and saw the rooms where he'd been raised.

"Will she be joining us?" he asked.

"I doubt it," said Audrey. She left the whisked eggs on the counter to settle for a minute and went down the hallway to Emily's room.

"Breakfast?" she said, poking her head inside.

"No, thanks." Emily was lying in bed with her enormous stuffed white bear. The room had been painted a fresh white, like the rest of the interior, the floors refinished. Her clothes were strewn everywhere. Her daughter didn't live in a room; she *destroyed* it; she turned the area into chaos. Hurricane Emily, her brother used to call her.

"Are you sure?"

"The smell of burning meat makes me sick."

"That's soy bacon, not meat."

"It's gross."

"Come and sit with us at least. You've been sleeping all day."

"I'm not sleeping."

"What are you doing?"

"Thinking."

The mattress rested directly on the floor, in the middle of the room. When she was five or six, Emily had pitched headlong out of her four-poster bed during a bad dream, knocking out a tooth, and ever since then she wouldn't use a bed frame or box spring. The walls were bare; she hadn't bothered to hang her framed art prints or photographs of her Denton pals.

"Are you ever going to clean this room?"

"I like it this way."

"I'll help you. We can do it together."

Emily rolled her eyes. "Would you please close the door?"

After breakfast Andrew got a phone call to play tennis with some new associate from the office. He raced around the house, gathering his gear. "Where's my racket?" he yelled from the bedroom, then appeared a moment later in the kitchen. "Where's my—?"

"What's the rush? You're making me nervous."

"Just tell me where—"

"In the garage. In the box marked—"

"Right. I remember."

A minute later he stuck his head in the doorway, manic-eyed, waving his Wilson. "I'll kick his ass and be back in time for dinner," he said, by way of good-bye.

"Go already."

After he raced out of the driveway, she destressed by cleaning the kitchen. She didn't mind the empty motions, the running of the water, the cleaning and scrubbing, the stacking of dishes, the separation of utensils. It wasn't much different from the mind-numbing process of grading undergraduate papers, once upon a time.

A leaf blower roared to life next door. This was just the start of the neighborhood racket, a cacophony of barking dogs and squawking crows, lawn mowers and chain saws that seemed to continue all afternoon. Once some irritant stopped, another would begin. Was there any place as noisy as the suburbs? The leaf blower operated at a deliriously high pitch, cutting through the other sounds. When the clamor died down somewhat, Audrey could actually hear a cardinal chirping methodically in the crab apple tree out front. But then another machine started a few streets over—a wood splitter, perhaps—making a crunching sound, like some giant monster chewing up rocks and gobbling them down, the whole earth vibrating under its feet.

SHE WAS from Vestal, a town in western New York that had the distinction of being one of the darkest places in the eastern United States, literally. Only a few other towns in the country, it was said, got less sunlight, and they were nearby—Syracuse, Utica. Her dad drove a truck for the phone company; her mom was a full-time housewife. Mom and Dad, Michael and Audrey. She was the youngest, the wild one, a star soccer player. In ninth grade, she left for Goodwin Academy on a scholarship, the first time she'd ventured away from home. When she was twenty-two, her parents retired to a condominium near Tampa, and her brother fled to the west, settling in San Francisco. After they sold the house in Vestal, Audrey had never had any reason to go back.

When her parents met Andrew, they called him a catch. "Finally," her mother said, "you bring home someone respectable. A Yale lawyer. Usually it's strays and misfits." In his crewneck sweater and wool pants, with his fine manners and lawyerly speech, he was all the things her mother wanted for her daughter—stature, security, class. Audrey liked him for a simpler reason: He listened to her. Unlike the poets and pseudo-intellectuals she'd dated, Andrew respected her for her mind, and sought her advice about matters of importance to his career. Later, after her parents had succumbed to long illnesses, their beach condo sold, their possessions scattered, Audrey wondered if she herself hadn't seen Andrew through their eyes too. Had the small-town girl she'd thought she'd left behind appraised him with a banker's eye, weighing costs and benefits? What else could explain her marrying Andrew, so unlike any other man she'd dated? Yes, they might have been misfits—artists, musicians, academics—but they were interesting misfits. Andrew was consistent, above all else. Consistent, thorough, predictable.

After she married, her sphere of acquaintances slowly diminished. All of Andrew's friends were lawyers, whether young and handsome or old and garrulous, and they all uttered variations on the same themes: money, expensive toys, envy, contempt. Andrew's clients were middle-aged white men, bald and potbellied, the management sector of corporate America. That was his job, protecting the bosses against their sexist and racist practices, shortcutting on taxes, cheating workers out of pay. Most of the time Andrew got them off the hook, at three hundred bucks an hour, the money their family had lived on for the past twenty years.

She had chosen this life freely, so why did she feel tricked? As an undergraduate at Wesleyan, when she was feeling mischievous or wanted to make her mark, she had a statement she used to write on bathroom walls and sidewalks: *To exist is to be spellbound.* She couldn't remember who'd said that, but she had always made an effort to live true to the dictum. During her junior year, she spent Christmas vacation in Middletown. She'd told her parents she had rehearsals for an Ibsen play. She didn't tell them that she was sleeping with her drama professor, a Harvard PhD who wore his hair in a ponytail halfway down his back. Every New Year's Eve he hosted a bacchanalia called the cannabis cup, where prizes were awarded to guests who brought the most uncommon contraptions to smoke marijuana—bongs and pipes, hookahs and other machines without names. Audrey had been one of the few undergraduates at the party, the recipient of inordinate faculty attention, and it had seemed correct to her then that she held that special honor. These days Audrey often castigated her daughter for her risk taking, yet how much like Emily she had been then, how willing to embrace everything that offered itself for her amusement or pleasure.

When she married Andrew, she hadn't intended to give up her career. But teaching composition on a 4/4 schedule for two years at Woodbridge

Junior College cured her of any enthusiasm for academia. When Andrew got his job at the firm in Stamford, making three times her salary, he said, "You should quit. Stay home. Have kids."

"Why don't you quit *your* job?" she shot back, bristling, her feminist streak fully engaged.

"You come home every night exhausted and irritated," he responded calmly. "I'm suggesting this for you. For your well-being."

She took a few days to think it over. He was right about her mood. She was smarter than anyone in her department, and they'd put her on the *parking committee*. She'd reached the point of disillusionment. She had intended to wait until she was thirty, but entrenched in Cos Cob, there seemed no reason to delay. Why not try something new, to deflect herself from the sameness of her surroundings? What were the suburbs for, if not raising children? She wasn't working on her doctorate; she wasn't doing much of anything but cooking and going to the gym and waiting for Andrew to come home and eat his dinner.

The children were born almost exactly a year apart. And suddenly the smallness of her life didn't concern her; she was too busy and too tired to notice. Daniel was a chess champion in the sixth grade, a tennis prodigy at fourteen, a rock climber during the fall season in high school. One afternoon she'd stood at the bottom of a sheer cliff, holding her breath, watching him climb with a sure-footed grace. The same night she and Andrew watched an evening performance of a play Emily had written and directed for her eighth-grade drama class, a comic retelling of the life of Sappho. These two lives she had created: Audrey couldn't help feeling proud of them, discussing their accomplishments with her husband. She volunteered at the library and women's shelter, and wrote a weekly column on culture for the local newspaper, but her children were her real work, her foremost achievement. She didn't like to admit this, but it was the truth, and she qualified it only by reminding herself that there would be time for herself *after*, when they didn't need her as desperately, when her motherly debt was mostly paid. It was a sacrifice, sure, but not that dire, as sacrifices go. She loved them helplessly and was happiest having them at the center of her world, but this did not keep her from wondering whose world *she* was the center of. Not Andrew's, certainly. He had always been the star of his own movie, and he considered her his *supporting* actress, at best.

As kids, Daniel and Emily were inseparable. They shared a bedroom until they were ten and eleven, because they wanted to. She would hear them late into the night, talking, scheming. They would sit side by side on the couch, reading the same Harry Potter book. They'd often seemed inscrutable and wondrous to her: They had the same dark eyes, the same smile. *Black Irish, the both of them,* Andrew had once said, *like your grand-mother Edna.* Audrey supposed she could see the resemblance in ancient photos, a girl posing in a large wicker chair, peering down through the generations, but Edna didn't have the same powerful beauty as Audrey's kids. Sometimes, at a glance, she'd mistake one for the other. Even as they entered high school they stayed as close as always. Coming home after school, the two would gather in the den or up in the attic, where they'd made a sort of parlor in one corner, and discuss their experiences of the day and do their homework together.

It had all gone along—the days and nights of her children, their triumphs and failures, the relentless wonder of watching them become who they were becoming—until that terrible day in May. The phone call from the Greenwich Police Department. The emergency room. A year and a half had passed, but she'd never really left that emergency room. The scene replayed itself, as vivid as morning: the endless waiting, Daniel's pallid face, those hectic last moments. This is the knowledge that consumed her: She had waited by his side those two hours, making small talk, *laughing,* while the whole time, he was bleeding inside his head, his life draining out of him; and she had done nothing. She should have forced them to look at the scans, to stop the blood before it crushed his brain, before he died gasping for breath. She shouldn't have just sat there, assuming they knew their jobs, assuming they would protect her son.

But she didn't know the danger. How could she have? But how could she not have *insisted,* anyway, that they move more quickly? What could she have done differently? Her mind returned, again and again, to that question. For a year after the accident she'd done nothing but cry. She'd wanted to be strong for Emily, but she was helpless against the grief, an illness without cure, a monster beyond reason, beyond mercy. The grief came in waves, sometimes so strong that she could not breathe, a thousand-pound weight atop her chest.

Of all days, that day Andrew had turned off his cell phone. She'd called him—his office line, his secretary—ten times at least from the emergency room, leaving messages, telling him what happened, telling him to come quickly. He rarely played golf, he disliked the game, but that day he'd gone off with some clients. Had he answered, it might have gone differently. Andrew was an impatient man. He would not have waited for two hours, chatting with nurses, as she had. He would have complained. Where's the doctor? Has he read the scan? He would have asked those questions, as he did later, in depositions and interrogatories, the same questions she'd failed to ask. He would have done what she had not: made them do their job and save her son.

She could never forgive Andrew for that day. For being absent the one time she'd needed him, the one time Daniel had needed him. Afterward he'd busied himself with arrangements for the funeral, the memorial, using a manic energy that bordered on psychotic. Later, with the same zeal, he'd filed a lawsuit, even though she'd argued against it. That was the last thing she'd wanted—to give affidavits and depositions, to corrobo-rate and testify, to be cross-examined. The events of that day were secured in her mind in real time, every moment. But he'd done it anyway. The money would go toward Emily's college education, he said, and it'll make the hospitals do better. That's what lawsuits are for: to make institutions change their practices. This was how her husband functioned, accord-ing to his own rules of logic. He'd *enjoyed* making money on their son's death, punishing someone. He had no real sense of regret or loss in him. She had grieved, for the most part, alone.

And the awful thing was, now, being around Emily made it worse. She had his Moorish eyes and thick dark eyebrows. Ever since the acci-dent, Audrey couldn't bear to look her daughter in the face. It pained her too much. Emily reminded her so strongly of Daniel: his expressions on her face, a ghostly reflection. She knew how much Emily was hurting, to have lost Daniel too, but she couldn't help it. Sometimes Audrey couldn't tolerate being in the same room with her, the resemblance was so strong. For months after his death, she would glance up and see *him*—sitting at the kitchen table, coming down the hallway, or lying on the couch—and then would follow the immediate, crushing rejoinder. The sight of Emily confounded her, tricked her, permitting a harrowingly quick moment of innocence. But: *It's not Daniel. Daniel is dead.* She knew he was dead. Of course she knew. That was how every day started, with Daniel being dead. And deep down she felt something dark and disjointed: Maybe she wanted it to be *him* who had survived; maybe she wanted it to be Daniel now sitting, whole and happy, in front of the TV, not Emily. And this thought, unbidden, made her despise herself.

She had to dull the pain, somehow. Wine in the afternoon, Valium at night. She couldn't escape its grasp, but sometimes she could distract the beast, she could make it look away. Now, eighteen months after the accident, that was the best she could do. Earn a small reprieve now and then.

AROUND NOON she heard the whine of the electrician's drill from the dining room. Then the crack of his hammer. His whistling. And finally, a short while later, the sound of his voice. Was he talking to himself? She peered down the hallway and saw her daughter leaning into the doorway, wearing only a long white T-shirt, barely covering her thighs.

"Best place I ever been is New Orleans," the man said. "You're talking a twenty-four-hour party, every day of the week. You can walk down the street with a bottle of beer in both hands. Perfectly legal."

Emily responded in a stagy voice: "Sounds like my kind of place."

"You should check it out. But who knows after the hurricane. Might be dangerous for a girl your age. How old are you anyway?"

"Old enough."

"Ha. Good answer."

"Emily," Audrey called, and her daughter pushed herself off the wall and came into the kitchen. "Put some clothes on," she said in a hushed voice.

"I am wearing clothes."

"Now."

Emily went lazily down the hall. After she passed the dining room, the electrician's head appeared in the hallway, following her movements. Didn't he know that it was inappropriate to stare at a girl half his age? As angry as she was, though, Audrey knew she couldn't really blame him, the way Emily had baited him. *Old enough.* Had she been trying to taunt the electrician or Audrey herself? That insolent slouch of hers. Men had started staring when she was only twelve or thirteen. Audrey knew how well Emily understood her own behavior, the effects it had on those around her. Even as a child, Emily had seemed to sense her reckless allure, the havoc she played with a toss of her hair, the narrowing of her big dark eyes. If someone looked back or said something, she would retreat into the embrace of Daniel, a child again. Without him to fall back on, she didn't seem to want protection anymore.

When the man went out to his truck, Audrey confronted her. "Stop flirting with the electrician."

"But he's cute."

"He's not cute. He's in his midthirties, at least. Men that age are not *cute.*"

"That one is."

"So was Ted Bundy."

"Who?"

"Do you think it's wise to prance naked in front of a stranger?"

"Prance?"

"You know what I mean. Do you act this way just to annoy me?"

Emily fiddled with her iPod, her head down. She placed the buds in her ears and looked at Audrey without expression. This was her daughter now, at seventeen, evasive and unfathomable. It was difficult even to *see* her anymore, the way she wore her hair, a long dark curtain in front of her face.

"What are you listening to?" said Audrey.

"You wouldn't know it."

Emily had always been restless and wild. As a child, she'd been a difficult sleeper, getting up at all hours, never allowing the day to end. Audrey had to watch her every minute, or she would wander off in the time it took to glance out the window. Audrey would never forget the summer when the children were in junior high school and the family had vacationed in Nova Scotia, driving from town to town along the coast. They stopped at Peggy's Cove, renowned for both the beauty of its rocky shoreline and its dangerous tide. Signs everywhere warned about the many who had drowned, swept off the rocks and out to sea by the unpredictable waves. Emily and Daniel went off alone, promising to stay away from the ocean. But they hadn't been gone for five minutes when Audrey began to feel uneasy. She left the inn and ventured down the path to the sea. Coming around the bend, she noticed Daniel standing on a precipice, alone, nearly obscured by the sun. When she reached him, out of breath, he raised his hand and pointed out to sea. There, twenty feet below, Emily stood on a jutting rock, waves crashing around her, her hands raised triumphantly. She'd somehow climbed down from rock to rock out into the sea, black and slick with the overrunning surf. *Come back*, yelled Audrey, her voice lost in the roar. Emily turned and waved to them, grinning, her face wet with sea spray. She started back, leaping from one rock to the next—a misstep would have sent her tumbling into the abyss, the sea churning between the rocks—until she finally reached the base of the precipice. *Mom*, she cried, all aglow, *did you see me!*

That was Emily, ready to assume any risk, seek out any thrill for the triumph of having done it. A wonderful but terrifying trait.

Finally, the electrician announced that he was finished. He stood in the front doorway, preparing his bill with a golf pencil. "I'll need you to sign this receipt," he said distracted, looking down the hallway for Emily. When he opened the door to leave, the dog rushed past him into the yard and raced away into the sunny afternoon.

That was how the dog got out, and how Audrey came to meet the car salesman.

BENJAMIN MANDELBAUM. The name meant nothing to her, but he remembered her from high school. He said he'd had a "serious crush" on her. She studied him more closely. He had a nicely worn face, a dusting of gray in his hair, and smile lines around his eyes. He moved with the bowlegged gait of an ex-athlete, like James Caan. He had a calm, seductive way of meeting her eyes. There were men like her husband, who encouraged you to play by the rules, and others who nudged you outside them. When he bent down by her side, she reached and touched the back of his neck, almost by reflex. He inclined his head, giving her permission to continue. She ran her fingers through his hair. It felt almost natural. The back of his neck was warm under the sun. He smelled slightly of BO and cologne, giving her a pheromone shock, summoning a backlog of sexual energy as sudden and powerful as a punch to the spine. This shocked her, the reaction of her own body. His long-standing crush for her—his blatant adoration—buoyed her, somehow, like filling her lungs with air. She felt almost well in that moment.

She didn't know then, and never would have foreseen, the enormity of what he would do for her.

Andrew Murray

The first day of work, fall 2007

A NEW JOB, a new house, a fresh start. It had made perfect sense to Andrew at the time. Later, looking back at those hectic few months, he would marvel at how quickly everything went wrong.

The house cost him his bonus in renovations and still wasn't finished by the day they moved in. "My shower doesn't work," his daughter complained. "Neither does mine," echoed Audrey from the master bedroom. His contractor, an Albanian who called himself Benny, wouldn't answer his phone over the weekend, leaving Andrew to contend with the new hot-water heater, which no one had bothered to hook up. By Monday morning he was relieved to get out of the house.

Carrington Farr was the second-largest law firm in Connecticut, with more than three hundred lawyers and offices in five cities. Andrew had been with the firm for fifteen years at its main office in Stamford. He'd made his reputation in the nineties, defending companies in employment discrimination and sexual harassment cases. Now, with this new promotion, he'd be leading the firm's employment litigation division, based out of Hartford.

He came from a family of lawyers. His father and grandfather had practiced out of a white cottage in East Longmeadow, Massachusetts, with a weather-beaten shingle on the front door: MURRAY AND MURRAY, GENERAL PRACTICE OF LAW. His father did real estate closings mainly, but every now and then he'd tried a case. In court, he would wear a dark blue suit with a bow tie and yellow suspenders. He had a shock of gray hair and wire-rim bifocals, which he would carefully take out of his jacket pocket, unfold, and place on the end of his nose to read some document. At home, he would fall asleep in the den with a glass of milk in his hand, a gurgling sound coming from his throat.

That first day in Hartford, Andrew called in his new team members one by one. They'd given him a corner office on the thirtieth floor, with floor-to-ceiling windows looking out over the northern Connecticut valley. He stood by the window, appreciating the spare modernity of his new surroundings, and watching the faraway cars and trucks inching up I-91 toward Springfield and beyond. Each time he gave his spiel he was pleased by the silence in the room, observing the serious and wary expressions of his employees. In closing each session, he said, "The bottom line is two thousand hours a year. That's what I bill, and that's what I expect from you."

As he delivered that line in his final meeting of the day, the man across from him yawned extravagantly. Johnny Sampson was a third-year associate out of Georgetown, but he looked like a college kid, with a smattering of freckles on his cheeks and longish blond hair that flopped across his forehead. He said, "Do you know what Rehnquist called associates in a law firm?"

Andrew eased back in his swivel chair. "No."

"Scrap metal."

"Is that so?"

"'A law firm treats the associate very much as a manufacturer would treat a purchaser of one hundred tons of scrap metal.'"

Sampson had an air of entitlement about him, with an articulate, almost British manner of speaking. An affectation, Andrew figured. Adding an extra slap of authority in his tone, he said, "Are you suggesting that two thousand hours is excessive?"

"Not at all. I billed twenty-two hundred last year."

"Then why are you quoting Rehnquist?"

"Because I've been here almost three years and haven't tried a case. I'm starting to think Rehnquist had it right."

"Tired of the stacks, are you?"

"That's putting it mildly." Sampson brushed the hair off his forehead.

"I understand that you and I have something in common. Is it true you played tennis at Amherst?"

Andrew nodded, surprised by the kid's insolent confidence.

"I was cocaptain at Williams," said Sampson.

"We crushed Williams all four years I was there," said Andrew. He said it automatically, not even bothering to recall if it were true or not.

"That was before my time," countered Sampson.

"Do you still play?"

"When I can find a decent partner."

Andrew sized him up. Sampson was a few inches taller, with long arms, a natural build for tennis. He would have a good serve, an excellent reach. Ten seconds passed, the two men staring at each other. This was something Andrew had learned long ago, in the courtroom, in negotiations: Let the other make the first offer; let him talk himself into a position. Let the silence do your negotiating for you. Sampson's eyes were pale blue, calm and expressionless. He smelled faintly of cologne.

Finally, Sampson said, "Would you like to play?"

Andrew almost smiled. "My backhand is tragic. That's what my high school coach said at least."

"Andover, right?"

Andrew regarded him with a raised eyebrow. "You don't get points for Googling me."

"I've done more than Google you. I've asked half the lawyers in town about you. I've read briefs you filed in the appeals court. Your argument in"—he named a case Andrew had tried in 1998—"on the whistle-blower's statute was particularly ingenious."

"You don't get points for brownnosing either."

"I'll try to remember that. As for tennis, Elizabeth Park has the best courts in the area. I like them better than Wintonbury Country Club, but we could go there if you prefer. You could be my guest." Sampson scribbled something on his business card and passed it over.

"I'll let you know," said Andrew in a formal tone, by way of dismissal.

Sampson went to the door. "I used to see Rehnquist around Georgetown. A stooped guy with a bad back, puffing on a cigarette. Did you know he dated Sandra Day O'Connor at Stanford?"

"You're making that up."

"If you say so."

After he left, Andrew did a quick Internet search. It was true; Rehnquist and Sandra Day had been law school sweethearts, just like Bill and Hillary. He took Sampson's personnel file from the stack on his desk and gave it another look. He was from Washington, D.C., the son of an ambassador. He'd gone to elementary school in London, which explained the accent. Graduated from St. Albans in 1994. Then Williams, summa cum laude. After that, Georgetown, editorial board of the law review. On his résumé he'd included among his hobbies: "the violin."

Andrew glanced at the business card: JOHNNY SAMPSON, ESQUIRE. On the back he'd written his cell number.

Andrew snorted. The pup. Did he think they were pals now?

AROUND 4:00 P.M., Jack Hannahan appeared at his door. Andrew put aside what he was doing and tried to look pleased. Hannahan, one of the senior partners, had been with the firm for forty years. He had a drinker's nose, fabulously red and pustuled.

"I come bearing gifts," he said, winking. He handed over a bottle of scotch, a limited-edition box of Cuban Cohibas, and a swipe key to the firm's skybox in the Hartford Civic Center. "Twenty-one years old, the Glenfiddich."

"You're going to spoil me, Jack."

"That's the point."

"Care for a sip?"

"Not at the moment. But they make a decent steak in the hotel bar downstairs, if you're free for dinner."

"I'll be finished here in an hour."

"Sounds perfect."

Hannahan had been one of the dealmakers for Carrington Farr in the Stamford office years ago when Andrew was fresh out of law school. He'd been a mentor then. They were both Amherst graduates, which meant a great deal to Hannahan. Every October they would drive up together to watch the homecoming game. *The Lord Jeffs have a strong backfield this year,* Hannahan liked to say; he'd been a fullback himself back in the first days of the plastic helmet. In Stamford, he'd been a fixture at a restaurant called Grandma Mimi's, where the local politicos gathered. He knew everyone, Republicans and Democrats, journalists and businessmen. Some said he'd had a hand in getting Ella Grasso elected in 1974. Now in Hartford, the old Irishman came into the office two or three times a week, mostly to make a nuisance of himself with his Dictaphone.

At 5:00 P.M. Andrew accompanied Hannahan down to the bar in the lobby. Only a few tables were occupied, all by men; they were a dreary-looking lot—insurance industry, judging by the drab brown and gray suits and pasty complexions: Hartford's standard-bearers. Each table held a glass vase with a long-stemmed rose. Hannahan gripped his arm, before heading off to the bathroom saying, "Never get old—damn prostate's as tight as a spring."

Andrew slid into a booth where he could watch the television mounted above the bar. As an associate, he'd spent many evenings placating the old guard, listening to their stories, fetching drinks. It was one of the many demeaning but obligatory tasks of the young associate, like photocopying. Andrew had paid those dues long ago; now he usually avoided the likes of Hannahan. But tonight he was in no hurry to get home. Audrey would be propped up in bed with her reading glasses on her nose, engrossed in some novel or watching an incomprehensible foreign movie. And Hannahan, for once, could be useful.

"I met with my new team this morning," said Andrew, once the food had been served.

The old Irishman looked up from his steak, fork in hand. "And?"

"One of them's a bit of a peacock."

"That would be Mr. Sampson."

Andrew nodded. "He yawned twice during a ten-minute meeting, didn't bother to cover his mouth. And get this, he offered to take me to the country club as his guest."

Hannahan cackled. "He's done impressive work. Bright. Ambitious. Brings in business too. His father had a summerhouse in Old Saybrook around the bend from Katie Hepburn, may she rest in peace. That's what brought him to Connecticut."

"Had?"

"A messy divorce. It was something of a D.C. scandal. The father and an eighteen-year-old girl, a runaway from Albuquerque if I recall correctly."

"The son tends the other way, was my impression."

"Ah." Hannahan swallowed a piece of steak and wiped his lips with the napkin. He leaned forward and said in a lowered voice, "The lad has certain proclivities. The firm had to have a word with him about looking elsewhere for his entertainment."

"Meaning?"

"Meaning he screwed half the secretarial pool. Male and female both."

"Did anyone sue?"

"No formal complaints, no. A fine softball player, they say, when he deigns to join."

"Tennis too, apparently."

"Is that so?"

"You say male *and* female?"

"That's the scuttlebutt, yes."

After the waitress cleared their plates Hannahan said, "Care for another?"

Andrew nodded, forcing himself not to glance at his watch. One more drink, then, before he could escape.

Again, Hannahan excused himself to the men's room. He was gone for five minutes, maybe longer. When the waitress delivered the scotches, Andrew poured half his glass into the rose vase, turning the water tan. One of the ice cubes plopped in.

At last Hannahan returned, his gray hair slicked back grotesquely, his face crimson. He cupped his glass. "Tell me about the home front. How's Emma?"

"Emily. She's up in arms. She hates the new house. Hates Wintonbury. Hates everything."

"A beauty, that one. How old is she now?"

"The worst age yet. Seventeen. Audrey's not adapting much better. Half our stuff is still in boxes. Even the dog's moping. She misses her old haunts, I suppose."

"You'll come through. You've been through worse."

"Yes."

"How long has it been?"

Andrew kept his eyes on the TV. "A year and a half."

Hannahan nodded. "A terrible day. I'll never forget it. Broke my heart."

In the silence that followed Hannahan picked up his scotch and took a slow sip. Andrew thought he saw the old man's eyes watering. The Irish and death: It was their great love; they never grew tired of mourning. Who else could have invented the wake? Sitting around the corpse, drinking and playing cards, dealing a hand for the dead man? Hannahan seemed to get more Irish as he aged, particularly when he drank. Pretty soon he'd be speaking in Gaelic.

At last Hannahan finished his drink and stood. "You're tired, Andy. Let's get going before the rose begins to wilt."

Andrew smiled. You couldn't count Hannahan out, no matter how many drinks, no matter how doddering he seemed. He didn't miss a thing.

"I can't keep up with you, Jack."

Hannahan winked. "Don't be daft. You're kind to keep an old bore company."

On the way out, Hannahan got his credit card back from the waitress. He'd already taken care of the bill.

A FEW WEEKS LATER, on a Saturday morning in October, Johnny Sampson rang the landline at his house, offering a match. "Well, sure, since you took the trouble to call information for my number. Where?"

Andrew followed his directions to Elizabeth Park. The sun shone directly overhead, a perfect day in New England. The wind barely rippled the tall pines behind the courts. A few men were watching one of the matches from the benches in front of the fence. Andrew went through the gates with his tennis bag and chose a free court on the far side. He got down on his back next to the net and raised his leg against the post, stretching his hamstrings, his weak spot; he'd tweaked both legs over the past decade, reaching for volleys or racing back to return lobs. After ten minutes of stretching, he did a few sets of crunches. If he didn't, his abs would cramp up during the match.

His game was rusty. He hadn't played for a while. He and his son used to play at least twice a week during the summer and almost as often in the off-season, indoors at the Greenwich Racquet Club. Daniel had been a marvelous athlete, excelling at nearly every sport although he hadn't liked winter sports, especially not skiing or skating. *I don't like having anything on my feet,* he would complain. He once ran the 440 on field day in bare feet, like a Kenyan. Tennis had been their father-son thing. Daniel had kept track of their matches in a log. *Dad and Dan,* he'd written in columns at the top of the page with the date and scores below. Andrew had found the log in his son's bedroom after the accident, among his school notebooks, ribbons from day camp, movie stubs, a stuffed animal he'd slept with as a toddler (Froggie, he called it, its green coat worn nearly white from being handled), the possessions of a child.

Andrew went around to the other side of the court to collect the balls, checking his watch. Johnny Sampson was fifteen minutes late. This irritated him. He didn't like waiting on anyone, particularly not a third-year associate. His own fault. He had agreed to the match because it was such a beautiful day, a gift of sorts, and because he wanted to beat Sampson. There was a smugness about him that annoyed Andrew. A know-it-all, with his Supreme Court trivia.

After gathering the practice balls, Andrew looked up to see Sampson hop out of a little black convertible. He jogged over with his tennis racket and a sweater draped around his neck, but nothing more—no gym bag, no water bottle, no tennis balls.

"You're late," said Andrew.

"My bad." Sampson explained that one of the partners had called as he was leaving his house and saddled him with some research for Monday morning.

Andrew nodded. "And that's your excuse? That's supposed to make me feel better?"

Sampson scratched his head.

"Do you think you should be doing research for someone besides me? Are you working on my team or someone else's? I got two files on my desk waiting for you. Litigation, not research. You'd be trying cases."

"I'd like that."

"Then one, don't take research from anyone else, and, two, don't keep me waiting."

"Understood."

"Now stretch out so we can get started."

"No need. I'm ready to go."

"You stretched at your place?"

"I don't stretch, particularly." Sampson pushed his hair to the side; his pale blue eyes gleamed brightly in the sun. There was something cloyingly feminine about the way he arranged his hair.

"Fine. Best of three," Andrew said. He popped open a fresh can of tennis balls.

"Loser buys dinner?"

"I wasn't planning on dinner," said Andrew, "but sure, why not."

"Good. I play better when there's money on the line."

Andrew snorted. "You're pretty cocky, aren't you?"

Sampson shrugged.

"Make it dinner and drinks, then. You serve."

Not a bad idea, Andrew figured. It would be nice to escape for a night. He couldn't chastise Audrey for her sadness, but the constant weight of it wore on him too. Did she not know that? Was she trying to bring him down as well? He felt just as bad as she did, every bit as bad. He didn't feel like getting up most mornings either. But he couldn't spend his days under the covers, weeping, could he? How could they continue otherwise? How could he afford to mourn like her, if no one went to work?

He played without conversation, not even speaking when switching sides. The games went fast. Sampson hit hard and deep. He had excellent form, a two-fisted backhand that was as strong as his forehand. He glided along the baseline with long strides, a beautiful thing to see, really. But many shots drifted long, and his placement was poor, usually smack down the middle. He served a handful of thunderous aces, but otherwise he had a low first-serve percentage. Andrew himself had a herky-jerky game, and his backhand, as anyone who played him quickly realized, was weak, but he hustled and rarely made mistakes. As his Amherst coach used to say, *Murray only does one thing right on the court, and that's win.* He moved Sampson from side to side, making him run. He took the first set easily.

Sampson proposed a water break. "Do you ever miss?"

"Not today."

The fountain outside the gate bubbled a lukewarm dribble. Andrew watched Sampson's Adam's apple bob as he drank.

Sampson wiped his lips. "Have you heard about the fruit loop?"

"The what?"

Johnny Sampson nodded toward the road that led to the tennis courts. It was a narrow one-way gravel path, about a quarter mile long, which circled a wooded area of the park. "When you drove in, did you notice the cars parked along the circle?"

"I guess so. What about it?"

"The hottest gay meeting place in Hartford. At night, all you have to do is flash your headlights and someone will come knocking on your window."

"You're kidding me."

"Weekdays at rush hour you can barely find a place to park. Mostly it's businessmen on their way home to their wives," Sampson added, turning an ineffable smile toward him.

"How'd you hear about this?"

Sampson shrugged. "It's common knowledge."

Andrew frowned. Why would Sampson impart this information to him? Did he think he'd be interested? Was this his way of coming on to him? He was his supervisor, for God's sake. Or did he come on to everyone this way, his flirty way of going through life, tempting boys and girls alike with his good looks and charm?

In the second set, Andrew lost his touch, making a slew of unforced errors. Sampson broke his serve and then held his own on four straight points. During the next game, while sprinting to net, Andrew felt his hamstring pinch. He dropped to a knee, rubbing the back of his thigh.

Sampson said, "Cramp?"

"Hamstring."

"Ouch. I hate to see that. Did you tear it?"

Andrew shook his head, grimacing. "I don't think so. Give me a minute, will you?"

He glanced at Johnny Sampson, almost twenty years younger. He didn't seem to be breathing hard, standing at midcourt, swatting his racket at butterflies.

"No worries," said Sampson. "Let's call it a day. We can pick up again when your leg feels better."

"No," said Andrew. "Let's finish it."

Andrew lost the second set in a tiebreaker. In the third set, as the sun began to lower in the sky and shadows claimed all but a patch of the court, Andrew moved stiffly back and forth along the baseline, squinting in pain, unable to catch up with Sampson's ground strokes.

"Are you sure you don't want to pack it in?"

"Stop asking me that."

During the next game, Andrew tried a lob, but the wind held up his shot and Sampson reared back and slammed the ball—a bunny—directly into the net. "Damn," he said, as if delivering a line. Andrew heard the false tone. He'd blown the shot on purpose, Andrew realized. Had Sampson been giving him points all along, trying to keep the match close, not wanting to embarrass him?

Andrew trudged back to the baseline, his T-shirt heavy with sweat. He hit the serve long, but Sampson played it anyway, returning a lollipop to Andrew's forehand. Andrew let the ball bounce past him.

"What's wrong?" said Sampson.

"My serve was out."

"I thought it caught the line."

"Not even close."

Sampson scratched his head. "Call it let, then."

Andrew bounced the ball on the baseline, staring across the net. "Are you ready to play?"

Sampson nodded.

Andrew served, and Sampson smacked a low backhand crisply down the line for a winner.

"Game," said Sampson.

DOWNTOWN they ate steaks at the hotel bar among the Saturday night revelers.

Women seemed to flock around Sampson. They slipped between him and Andrew at the bar, offered a quick smile while ordering their drinks.

"Do you have a girlfriend, Sampson?"

Sampson shrugged. "I like to bounce around." He took a handkerchief out of his pocket, delicately wiped the corners of his mouth, and sipped his glass of champagne. The bottle was Sampson's idea. He came from money, even if his family had lost it. He didn't seem shy about running up Andrew's bar tab.

Andrew checked his watch. His car was still parked at the tennis courts. "What time do they close the park?"

"No time."

"You sure? I don't want to get locked out."

"I'll drive you back after this round." Sampson refilled their glasses, finishing the bottle of champagne. "Meet the new boss," he toasted, "same as the old boss." He offered his self-satisfied smile. "Pete Townshend," answered Andrew. He had the urge to pour the champagne over Sampson's head. But in the face of such conceit, what could he do besides laugh it off?

Andrew excused himself to the men's room. In the mirror, his eyes were bloodshot, his hair wild, his sweatshirt stained down the middle. He tossed some water on his face, but it didn't help.

When he came out of the bathroom, he saw Sampson talking to two women who were wearing the same outfit—black miniskirts and clingy white tops. One of them leaned close to Sampson to whisper in his ear. This was a waste of time, Andrew decided. At a bar like this, he could squander the entire night, like a college kid. His time was more valuable than most people's: three hundred dollars per hour, to be exact. "To hell with it," he said under his breath. He'd already paid the tab, his debt satisfied, as much as it irked him to lose on a pulled hamstring. Time to go.

He went out to the lobby to flag a cab. As he stood on the sidewalk, Sampson appeared beside him. "Leaving so soon? It's still early."

"Not for me."

Sampson handed his ticket to the valet and poked Andrew in the arm. "Let us go then, you and I, when the evening is spread out against the sky . . ."

"What's that, more Townshend?"

"Something like that."

The car jockey pulled up and flipped the keys to Sampson, who snatched them nonchalantly out of the air. He drove with his left arm out the window. He pushed a CD into the player and classical music came from the speakers, something slow and mournful. Andrew remembered Sampson's résumé: "the violin." He pictured Sampson as a child: the spoiled little towhead toddling down the brick sidewalks of Georgetown with his violin case, pushing his stupid blond locks out of his eyes.

Andrew felt his head spinning and realized that he was drunk. He wasn't a big drinker by nature; he didn't like the feeling of losing control, or paying for it the next day with one of his killer hangovers. But tonight he didn't mind. It felt good to sit in the passenger seat, windows down in the Alfa Romeo, the night air rushing by.

Sampson turned in to the entrance to the park. There was a restaurant on the premises, well lit, with a row of cars lined up in front. Past the restaurant, Sampson turned onto the narrow, rutted lane that led to the tennis courts. *The fruit loop.* Who the hell came up with that? Andrew wondered. There were no streetlights, just tall trees lining the way, the branches overhanging like a canopy. Halfway around the circle, a car flashed its lights and jerked out into the middle of the road. There, the car idled, blocking the way.

"What's this?"

"The usual wanton and reckless conduct," said Sampson.

He turned onto the grass to steer around the car and continued to the tennis courts. Andrew's SUV was the only vehicle left in the dirt lot.

Andrew felt reluctant to get out of the car. "You won today, but you didn't beat me. There's a difference."

Sampson smiled. "If you say so."

"What's so funny?"

"Do you know the first thing everyone says about you?"

"What?"

"He doesn't like to lose."

"What else do they say?"

"That it's a mistake to get on your bad side."

Andrew nodded. "The inverse is true as well. You should know that."

"Like those two files on your desk, for instance."

"Precisely."

Andrew got out of the car. He fired up his SUV and wheeled out of the park. On the way home, he tried to keep it slow, not wanting to get pulled over after a half bottle of champagne, but he found himself juicing the gas, zipping around corners. He flipped to a seventies rock station and cranked the volume, singing along.

AT HOME, Sheba jumped up to greet him at the door. Andrew staggered around the furniture piled in the hallway, telling himself it would all be in its place soon. When he came into the bedroom, Audrey looked up from her book.

"Chicken's in the fridge, if you're hungry," she said.

"I already ate," he explained.

"Did you win?"

He shook his head. "Pulled a hamstring."

"Sorry."

He went into the bathroom and closed the door behind him. He fumbled for the light switch and knocked over the plastic cup that held their toothbrushes. "Shit," he muttered. The patter of piss seemed to go on for minutes. He was drunk, his bladder bloated.

He jumped into the shower for less than five minutes, but when he came out of the bathroom, the lights were off and Audrey was curled under the comforter. He went to his side of the bed, not bothering to put on his pajamas. Even on sober nights, he wasn't a good sleeper. He would try everything from counting aloud, which bothered Audrey, to pills, but the pills made him foggy the next day. He didn't count tonight; instead he thrashed about, shifting onto his back or stomach every few minutes.

Audrey was wearing a long white cotton T-shirt and hospital pants, her usual sleeping outfit; but she hadn't taken off her bra, as she usually did for bed, and his hand stopped when he reached it. "Hey," he said softly.

She groaned and turned away from him.

"Let me help you get this off." He reached under her T-shirt and un-clasped her bra and ran his hands over her breasts.

"Andrew."

"What?"

"It's late."

"It's not even eleven."

He pushed aside the comforter and eased down her scrubs.

"Cut it out." She pulled the comforter back over herself.

"I'll make it quick."

"No."

"Come on. It'll help me sleep."

"Go take a pill if you can't sleep."

"I'd rather do this."

She turned to him and said in a gentler tone, "I'm tired, okay? We can talk about this later."

"To hell with later."

"Jesus, Andrew. Why the sudden romance?"

"I want to, that's all."

"Well, I don't. Not at this hour."

He exhaled loudly. "Correction. You never want to."

"Keep your voice down."

"At least I make an effort. At least I want to have sex."

"You call that sex?"

"I call it the best I can expect."

"Go have another scotch, why don't you."

"That's not a bad idea."

He got up and went out to the kitchen. He opened the aspirin bottle and poured a glass of water. Then he went into the den and turned on the television.

ANDREW HAD MET his wife at Atticus Bookstore in New Haven about an hour before closing on a Friday night. He looked up from his bar exam guidebook to see her come through the door. When their eyes met she flashed him a smile and took a table in the café with her friends. They talked loudly, often all at once. When she got up and wandered to the fiction aisle, he followed, trying to think of something to say. She turned to him: "Law student?" She had dark blue eyes with copper speckles. "How did you know?" "Who else studies at ten o'clock on a Friday? Sorry we're so loud. It must be pretty hard to concentrate with all the noise." After they talked for a few minutes, she produced a felt-tip pen and wrote her phone number on the back of his hand. "Maybe I can buy you a beer sometime," she offered. At closing time, she left with her arm around a long-haired guy wearing a Superman T-shirt.

He left messages on her answering machine, but two weeks passed before she could find a moment for that beer. She was a master's student in English literature, specializing in postcolonial fiction. She dressed in silky skirts and embroidered tops, almost always earth tones. When she mentioned that she'd had a paper on V. S. Naipaul accepted for publication, he surprised her at her apartment with white roses and a card of congratulations. "No one's ever given me white roses before," she said. "Red red red. Always red. That must mean something."

"What?"

"I'll tell you when I figure it out."

He ran into her at all hours—lying on a blanket on the town green in the afternoon, coming out of Richter's at midnight. Once she called at 9:00 A.M. to rant, "What the hell is critical legal studies? Do you know anything about this? I mean, are they serious? Stanley Fish could knock these guys over with a pencil." Another time, she phoned a few minutes before the start of a Neil Young concert at the Palace, offering an extra ticket. He closed his books, although it was less than a week from the bar exam, and raced down Chapel Street, to find her—Audrey Martin, his gorgeous redhead—waiting out front with her arm around the Superman guy. Did he have no other shirts?

His name was Maximilian, Andrew learned that night. He was a poet. He'd published work in *The Paris Review*, she told him. He had a teaching job lined up at the university in Buffalo. "That's where we're going in the fall," she informed him. Andrew came home to his sweltering third-floor apartment on Chapel Street, above a Lebanese restaurant. Through open windows, he could hear the customers below, ordering sandwiches and salads, going in and out the front door, the bell chiming.

He wanted to forget her, but she kept calling. "We'll celebrate after the exam," she promised him. Mostly she complained about Maximilian, the way he dismissed her opinions about writers. "He called Kate Chopin *shite,* as if he were British. I hate the way he talks to me sometimes." It got to be more than Andrew could handle. "Look," he said at last, "I'm not one of your girlfriends. Don't complain to me about your love life. And I particularly don't want to hear any more about Maximilian, okay? You've got to be crazy to date a jerk like him anyway. It's not my problem. *You* are my problem, not him." A long silence followed. "Okay," she said, finally, in a serious tone. "I get it. I'm sorry."

Later she told him that this was the moment he went from friend to lover in her mind. For some reason, she hadn't thought of him as passionate—until he blurted his feelings for her. With some women, you had to take the risk. With Audrey, the risk had paid off.

The night he finished the bar exam, she met him and his friends at a basement bar. "Where have you been hiding her, Murray?" one of his pals asked. "Under his bed," she responded. They did shots of Jack Daniel's and danced until last call. At closing time he walked off with his arm around her. When they came to his building she said, "Are you ready to celebrate?" "I thought we just did." She reached up and wrapped her arms around his neck and kissed him on the lips. "Think again," she said. "Think bigger." In his room he could smell her sweat, her hot boozy breath. "I drank *everything,*" she said, taking off her skirt. "But I'm not drunk."

She left at dawn, and a week later she was gone, off to Buffalo with her asshole boyfriend. In September, Andrew began a job in Bridgeport, clerking for a federal magistrate. He received a card with her new address. *I miss you*, she wrote. The memory of her—her body, her scent, her voice—refused to fade. Her *drunk* self had made the right choice. But, after he'd had her for only one night, she'd disappeared, magnifying the hurt. When would he see her again? The answer, he realized as the weeks passed and she did not respond to his letters, was *never*.

Then she appeared at his door.

It was the afternoon of a rainy Sunday in October, two months after her departure. She stood in the foyer in blue jeans and high leather boots. "Here I am," she said, "if you still want me." She'd left Maximilian, she told him. He'd been fired from his job for plagiarism. The poems he'd published, they discovered, were lifted verbatim from early-twentieth-century German writers. Maximilian had translated the work of little-known poets and signed his own name. "He's a fraud," she said.

"I'll kick his ass, if you want," Andrew volunteered.

"I'd rather you kiss me," she said. "I thought about you a lot."

"Ditto as to you."

"Do you forgive me?"

"On one condition. That you never mention the name Maximilian again."

"Actually, that's not even his real name. He made that up too."

"I'm not going to say *I told you so*."

She smiled. "Thanks. And I figured out the white roses too."

"Tell me."

"Red is for romance. Everyone knows that. White roses represent unity and virtue, honor and reverence. I looked this up, if you're wondering. So you were telling me it wasn't just about romance, like a first date. You were telling me I was worth more than that. It means you think I'm special."

"I thought that was self-evident."

"Sorry," she said, resting her head on his shoulder. "Sometimes it takes me a while to get the easy ones."

Andrew, after his long quest, reveled in his luck. *Audrey Martin*, the woman he'd obsessed about those long months. In restaurants, at bars, in theaters, holding her hand, he was astounded that this brilliant creature was actually *his*, that she shared his bed, made his meals, cared about his little triumphs and discontents.

They were married the next June.

*   *   *

AFTER A FEW DAYS his hamstring felt back to normal. A series of fine fall days passed, perfect for tennis. He called Sampson into his office and handed over the files and suggested a rematch. Sampson made excuses, putting him off.

His insomnia returned, a bad case; he spent hours staring at the ceiling listening to the sound of his sleeping wife. He blamed some of this on Sampson; if he'd been able to get some exercise, he would sleep better.

At first light Audrey stirred and squinted at him with her myopic stare. "What's wrong?"

He checked the alarm clock. "Couldn't sleep." He ran his hand over his head—his hair was cowlicked, jutting upward.

"Is something bothering you?"

He exhaled heavily. "You were snoring."

"It never bothered you before."

"Of course it bothered me. It always bothers me. You sound like a teakettle."

"It's my allergies. I'm sorry."

"To hell with it," he said, jumping out of bed. He stood by his dresser, staring into the mirror. "Jesus. I look like a zombie."

"You probably slept without realizing it."

"I think I would know whether or not I slept. So don't placate me. Don't tell me I slept when I didn't."

"Could you lower your voice, please?"

"I've got a ten-hour day ahead of me, while you lie around the house doing whatever you do, which is nothing as far as I can tell. It would be nice if I didn't have to trip over boxes in the hallway."

"Would you like to tell me what's wrong?"

"Do you want me to go over it again? Do you want me to spell it out for you?"

He went into the bathroom and closed the door.

IN THE claw-foot tub he stood under the stream of hot water with his eyes closed. He shouldn't have yelled at her like that. True, she had snored during the night, often starting at the exact moment he'd felt himself drifting toward sleep. But all he had to do, all he ever had to do to quiet her, was nudge her, and she would flop over on her side, like an automaton. But he hadn't slept in the ensuing silence either. His mind returned to the tennis match. He'd had Sampson down a set and a break. Then he'd blown it, spraying the ball all over the court. Even before pulling his hamstring, he'd made all those unforced errors. And then Sampson had started giving him pity points.

Meet the new boss, same as the old boss.

He pondered Sampson's proclivities for men *and* women. Odd, that lack of preference. Andrew could understand being gay a lot easier than being bi. He'd never done anything sexual with men, unless you counted the dorm shenanigans at Andover. Back then, the guys on his hall some-times jacked off in a circle, seeing who could do it the fastest. All the guys did it. And there was that French kid, Claude from Quebec, who used to give blow jobs for five bucks a pop. *He* was a faggot, someone who sucked cock, someone who took it up the ass. Andrew had never used Claude's services, although a lot of his dorm mates had. It annoyed Andrew that he'd blown the match with Sampson. Winning would have established his natural male dominance over an upstart, a necessary act of authority. Because, once his position was secure, a guy like Sampson could be useful to him at the office.

But what pissed Andrew off, what ruined his sleep, was how Sampson had put off the rematch since then, making bullshit excuses. Particularly when there was money involved. You win a bet, you give the other guy a chance to get even. That was understood. That was the custom. You didn't avoid the issue. It was the lack of courtesy that annoyed him. The lack of deference.

Andrew stood before the mirror, toweling off. The shower had put some color in his cheeks and cleared the red from his eyes. He felt better, as he always did after a shower. He combed and gelled his hair. When wet, his hair looked thin, the scalp showing beneath. His hair, once as dark as his kids', was now gray around his ears. He needed a haircut, the best cure for a receding hairline. Maybe he'd shave his head entirely. He began to dress but couldn't find the proper shirt.

"Audrey."

His wife could sleep through any sort of disturbance—storms, bright lights, a blaring television. He shook her foot. When she rolled over, the pillow fell onto the floor and she yawned, suddenly childlike.

"I'm sorry about yelling. I get grumpy when I lose sleep."

"It's okay," she said.

"Which shirt, do you think?" he asked.

She squinted, nearly blind without her glasses.

"Olive suit," he told her.

"Your Ralph Lauren?" She reached for her eyeglasses on the night table, knocking a book onto the rug. She stacked the books five or six high, bookmarks in each; she read them at the same time, a practice he found mystifying. How could she concentrate on so many books at once? "Light blue shirt, black tie," she said. "It'll look great."

He got a shirt out of the closet, pulling off the dry cleaner's plastic. When he tucked the shirttails into his pants and buckled his belt, his stomach bulged uncomfortably. He sucked in his gut. "I've got to work out more often. I've been trying to set up another tennis game, but the guy I played with last week won't set a date."

"The guy from your office?"

"Yeah. Johnny Sampson."

"*Johnny?* Is he a grown man?"

"Allegedly."

"I thought you liked him."

"Who said that?"

"I just got that sense. You've mentioned him a few times now."

Andrew shrugged. "He's a third-year associate. His job is to impress me, not the other way around. After I pinched my hamstring, he started giving me points. Hitting shots into the net on purpose."

"I know. You told me about it already. He was just trying to suck up to you, obviously."

"I don't need that kind of charity. That's him thinking he's better than me. I was ranked in New England." Andrew pulled on his suit jacket. "How's this?"

"I'd go with black shoes. Are you going to court?"

"Just a couple of depos. Why?"

"You never wear that suit to work."

"Don't I?"

He went into the bathroom and splashed some cologne on his neck. He hesitated in the doorway. "Audrey, I really am sorry."

"I know. Do you want some breakfast?"

"I'll grab a coffee on the way. You stay in bed. Sleep."

He grabbed his gym bag and tennis racket out of the closet, just in case. He went out the kitchen door in his overcoat, holding the racket in its vinyl cover over his head against the rain.

ON THE DRIVE to the office he flipped open his cell and pressed Sampson's number. It rang five times before going to voice mail. Andrew hung up and dialed again, and this time Sampson answered, his voice heavy.

"Attorney Murray. How's that hamstring?"

"I'll risk it."

"I've been swamped, thanks to you."

"Yes, thanks to me. How about tonight? There must be some indoor courts around here." Andrew thought he detected a voice in the background. He pressed the phone closer to his ear but couldn't hear over the road noise and the slapping of the windshield wipers. "Well?"

"Sure, I know a place. I'll call for a reservation."

"Do that."

"What time is it anyway?"

"Time to get up. I got some ideas on that employee privacy case. I'll come by your office in the afternoon."

Andrew shut the phone, then checked the time: a few minutes before seven. He hadn't realized it was so early.

AFTER HIS final deposition of the day Andrew picked up his tennis racket and went down the hall to Sampson's office. He stood outside the door, holding his breath. Sampson was talking on the phone, his voice low and confident: "When did he say that?" and then, "No, I don't know that guy," and, "Perfect, that's perfect." After a minute Andrew stepped into the doorway, posing with the tennis racket as if about to hit a forehand. Sampson waved him in, his feet up on the desk. He gestured with his hand like a duck quacking. Finally he replaced the phone. "Sorry about that."

"Who was it?"

"Insurance adjuster."

"This time of day?"

"He's West Coast."

"Which case?"

"Not one of yours. Hey, let me see that."

Andrew passed over the tennis racket, and Sampson took off the vinyl cover and felt the grip. "You've got big hands." He picked at the twine, straightening the strings.

"Did you reserve the court?"

Sampson handed back the tennis racket. "Bad news. I can't do it tonight."

"Seriously?"

Sampson shrugged. "Sorry."

"You should have told me earlier. I would have made other plans."

Sampson adjusted his glasses. "This came up at the last minute. An old buddy of mine is coming into town for the night. I have to pick him up at the airport."

"That's no excuse."

"I'll make it up to you. How about this weekend? Dinner on me this time."

"Maybe. I'll get back to you."

Andrew went back to his office but found it difficult to concentrate on his work. After a half hour he walked down the hall and knocked on Hannahan's door. When no one answered, he pushed open the door. The old man was leaning back in his chair, snoring quietly. Andrew rapped his knuckles on the door, and Hannahan's eyes came open. He cleared his throat and wiped his lips. "Caught me napping," he said.

"I had a glass of that single malt last night," Andrew lied. "Smooth stuff."

"Glad you liked it." Hannahan opened the bottom drawer of his desk and pulled out a bottle. "Care for a nip now? It's the same year."

"Glasses?"

"Right behind you."

Andrew glanced at the framed photograph on the bookshelf. There was Hannahan in black and white, twenty-five years younger, smiling confidently alongside four cohorts. Andrew could summon the name of only one, the tall man in the center. William Oshry. All four were dead. He remembered their shiny faces, their banter and quips, their sturdy handshakes. They used to gather at the center table at the University Club in Greenwich. They would drink and blather. After each round they would throw dice to see who would sign the chit for the drinks. The club was gone now, which was fine with Andrew. Those stifling summer nights. The heavy red leather seats in the drawing room. The cigar haze. The air conditioner always seemed to go wrong. The club hadn't admitted women until the late eighties. He'd often had to pinch himself to stay awake, listening to the old men ramble on. Oshry had been the worst bore, the oldest of the lot. In his prime he'd represented the railroad, and he talked about little else. One evening Andrew had noticed that the old man's complexion was a shocking orange. He'd nearly said something to him. But it wouldn't have mattered anyway. Oshry was dead within the month—liver cancer—and the others in the picture followed soon after with no great loss to humanity or the gross national product. Next came the wrecking ball to knock down their precious University Club. They were all gone, that world was gone, all but Hannahan, the last man standing.

Andrew passed the glasses across the desk, noticing that Hannahan looked slightly orange himself today. He usually had that nice rosiness, the pustules around his nose aflame. Perhaps cancer was in play here as well, eating away at Hannahan's lungs or spleen, some other vulnerable organ. Perhaps Hannahan knew it. If so, he would never tell anyone, the old phlegmatic bastard.

"How are you feeling, Jack?"

Hannahan poured the scotch with a trembling hand. "Never better."

Perhaps Hannahan was dying. If so, Andrew asked himself whether he felt anything remotely like sympathy for him, and he decided that he did not. Hannahan was what, seventy-nine? Eighty? He'd had his run. It was the natural order of things that he should expire. He had been Andrew's mentor, sure, but not out of any great kindness. With all that work, he'd needed someone to carry the load. Hannahan had picked him as his prize mule, had brought him along, and Andrew had done well for him. That was the natural order. You passed it down, just as Andrew would pass it down to Johnny Sampson.

"How's your protégé?" said Hannahan, as if reading Andrew's thoughts. "The young Mr. Sampson."

"In my bad books at the moment. I invited him for tennis tonight and he canceled on me at the last minute."

"I always preferred golf."

"Off to the airport to meet a buddy, he said."

"You don't believe him?"

"Not for a minute."

Hannahan shrugged. "Maybe he's up to his old tricks with the secretaries. A handsome boy, you can't blame him for taking advantage. Even if it's not a particularly smart career move. We had to issue a formal reprimand."

"You told me. But I trust you were exaggerating about the number of his conquests."

"Not at all."

"Which secretaries? Anyone in my department?"

Hannahan rubbed his chin. "There was a Hispanic fellow who has since left the firm, a paralegal."

"What was his name?"

The old man squinted. "Pedro, I believe. There were others."

"Well, he's a faggot. You know what they're like."

"Now, now, Andy. Tell me what he did to earn your ire."

"We played tennis last week. I had him down a set before my hamstring gave out."

"Aah." Hannahan laughed. "You never liked to lose."

"So they say." Andrew took a sip of the scotch. That sudden warmth filled his mouth, his nostrils, his chest. With the warmth came a flickering of affection for Hannahan. He was the last of his kind, like a bison or buffalo, some near-extinct North American mammal that once roamed the plains in herds of thousands. "Your skin looks bad, Jack. Have you had a checkup lately?"

Hannahan waved him off. "I'm Irish. Of course my skin looks bad." He leaned back in his chair. "You know, I'm only half-joking, calling him your protégé. There's a lot of potential there."

Andrew nodded. "I'm willing to give him a chance."

"You don't sound convinced."

"He's smart, that's for certain. But I'm not sure whether he wants it badly enough."

"That'll become clear once you put him to the test." The old man sipped the scotch with his thin lips. "We had a sergeant in Korea, a Swede by the name of Pederson. Toughest SOB you'd ever want to meet. Arms like concrete blocks. He lived on cigarettes and coffee, as far as I could tell. The first time we saw combat, he turned and ran like a schoolgirl.

They found him cowering in a ditch two miles behind the lines. They had to ship him stateside. You never can tell until that first shot how someone will react."

Andrew sensed more Korea to come, so he finished the drink and set down the glass. "Well, I gave Sampson a couple of choice cases, so I hope he's up to the task."

"Care for another? It's Friday, after all."

Andrew got up, offering a deferential smile. "I should head home. Thanks for the drink."

"Of course, my boy. Give my best to Audrey and Emma."

As Andrew left, he saw the old man refill his glass.

ANDREW PACKED his briefcase and took the elevator down to the ground floor. The bar in the lobby was crowded and brightly lit. Andrew ducked inside and had two quick tequilas. A drink he hadn't had for years, maybe since law school.

The fellow on the next stool introduced himself as a heavy machinery salesman from Des Moines, Iowa. A large man with liver-spotted hands. He nodded toward a table of office workers. "There's something sad about a fat woman wearing a party dress. All gussied up like that." He squinted at Andrew, looking him up and down. "Well, that's a coincidence."

"What?"

The man pointed at his suit jacket. "We're both wearing olive suits and blue shirts."

"Is that a Polo?" said Andrew.

"My suit? It's Big and Tall Man Shop." He offered to buy Andrew a drink. "Since we seem to appreciate the same color schemes in men's fashion."

"Thanks, but this is my last one."

The salesman nodded. "A wise choice. In my experience, happy hour is neither happy nor does it last an hour."

It was a sodden night, the wind and rain coming in sweeps. Andrew turned up his windshield wipers. Without really thinking, he turned in to Elizabeth Park and drove slowly around the loop. The road was unlit and rutted with potholes, with cars parked haphazardly on either side. Some were idling with brake lights on; most were dark.

At the end of the loop, he parked in the dirt lot in front of the tennis courts. He told himself he was taking a breather, a moment for himself. The lot was empty. The courts were leaf-strewn and covered with pine needles. Yet bright outdoor lights illuminated the courts, shining from the tops of telephone poles around the perimeter. A few stray tennis balls lay near the fence. When the wind rose, wet leaves flapped on the courts like injured birds.

Andrew turned off the motor. The outdoor lights gave off a hive-like buzz, which he found strangely relaxing. After some time, the car grew cold. When his cell phone rang he glanced at the caller identification—Audrey—and turned off the phone. He'd promised always to answer his phone, ever since that day. But he couldn't talk to her at the moment. He tried to put her out of his mind. He tried to think of nothing. As if turning off his phone were some crime. As if she hadn't sat on her hands for— No, he wouldn't. It did no good. None of it had done any good. The lawsuit. The memorial. What had he expected? *Nothing*, he told himself. Think of nothing. He imagined walking down the center of an empty street in an abandoned city . . .

At precisely 8:00 P.M. the outdoor lights went off with a metallic clang, and a deeper silence followed. A few minutes later a car pulled up next to him—a beat-up Toyota Corolla with electrical tape covering the rear window.

The car door slammed. Then came a tapping at his window. Andrew lowered his window a few inches. "What's up?"

The young man was very thin, wearing jeans and a tight black T-shirt, his shoulders bunched against the rain. His head was shaved perfectly clean. "Can I get in?" He spoke with an accent, Russian or Polish, it sounded like.

"How old are you?"

"Twenty-one years," he said.

He looked eighteen at the most. Andrew said, "Sorry, no."

"Come on, open door. You think I hurt you?" He grinned and flexed his biceps: The muscle barely moved. He weighed no more than 135 pounds.

"What do you want?"

"Want? I want nothing. What you want?"

Andrew realized he wanted information. He said, "Do you know a guy who comes around here? He drives a little black convertible. You ever see anyone like that?"

"Yes."

"What does he look like?"

"Good looks. He is very good-looking. Can I get in now?" He shivered, his bare arms trembling.

"You know him?"

"Yes, I know him."

Andrew pressed the unlock button and nodded toward the passenger door. The boy passed in front of the car and climbed in, filling the interior with the smell of cigarettes. He rubbed his hands together and breathed on them. His shaved head was startlingly white, like an egg.

Andrew said, "So you know this guy?"

The boy nodded.

"When did you last see him?" Andrew spoke slowly, articulating the words. The boy stared back with cloudy blue eyes, his expression blank. His arms seemed to be made of bone only, they were so thin. "Was he here tonight?"

"Yes."

"He was in the park?"

"Yes."

"When did you see him?"

"I see him now."

"What do you mean?"

"You are him, yes?"

"What?"

"You want me to say yes, yes?"

Andrew rubbed his brow. "No. This isn't a game. I'm asking you—"

The boy placed his hand on Andrew's thigh and began rubbing him. Andrew pressed his legs together. "No, no. I'm asking about my friend."

"Let me, please. I see you are hard. I like very much."

The boy leaned over and undid Andrew's pants and used his mouth. The egg-like head, dipping and rising. Andrew looked over the steering wheel, staring at the tennis courts and the dark woods beyond. When he came, he heard the boy's breath quicken.

A moment later the boy got out.

The rain picked up, a sudden slap on the windshield, like a sheet of glass falling. The car beside him clattered to a start, then backed out of the parking lot, its lights illuminating the tennis courts for a moment, then sweeping across the woods.

Andrew reached into the backseat, grabbed the container of antibacterial wipes, and cleaned himself. As he buttoned his pants, he realized his wallet was missing. He checked his suit coat, his overcoat, the seat, the floor.

Nothing, of course.

"Stupid," Andrew said aloud. He used more of the wipes, soaking his groin. "Stupid. Stupid. Stupid."

He started the car and drove off.

BACK DOWNTOWN, he had the security guard cut him a new swipe key. He went up to his office and got his personal file out of his desk. He kept photocopies of the entire contents of his wallet, the front and back of each item, and the telephone numbers of his credit card carriers. In twenty minutes he'd canceled the credit cards and ordered replacements. Then he telephoned the three national credit-reporting organizations and placed a fraud alert on his name and social security number. Next he notified the Federal Trade Commission on their website. He didn't keep a copy of his social security card in his wallet, so he wasn't particularly concerned about identity theft, but he found it calming to go through these procedures. The Russian boy would get nothing—a few twenties, no more.

Only one more call to make: the cops. If somehow the Russian boy did manage to break into his accounts, Andrew would need a police report for insurance purposes. Plus, he knew, Audrey would ask, *Did you call the cops?*

He took the elevator down to the lobby and went into the bar, nearly empty now. He recognized the bartender, the same man who'd been on duty earlier.

"I lost my wallet," said Andrew, "when I was here earlier."

"You sure it happened here?"

"I had it when I came in. I gave you a twenty for the drinks. I was sitting next to a guy who said he was a salesman from Iowa. Maybe he was a pickpocket. Who knows?"

"Yeah, I remember that guy. Well, no one turned in any wallet to me. But let me check with the manager."

Andrew watched the bartender out of the corner of his eye as he went into the dining area and conversed with a man in a blue blazer. He came back, shaking his head. "Tequila, right?" the bartender said. "How about one on the house?"

"Actually, a Heineken would be great. And a steak if you're still serving. Medium rare."

The cop showed up an hour later. Andrew went through the same rigmarole, again mentioning the salesman from Iowa. What had he said? That they shared the same color scheme in men's fashion? Andrew wondered now if that were some kind of come-on. Had the salesman been trying to pick him up? Jesus, he thought. Was he giving off some kind of vibe?

The cop closed his notepad. "I'll let you know if anything turns up."

"I'll need a copy of that report for my insurer."

"Call the station tomorrow. I'll have it ready for you."

"I'd appreciate that," said Andrew.

His tasks complete, he enjoyed the last of his steak and ordered a piece of blueberry pie for dessert, feeling strangely satisfied.

AS SOON AS he walked into the living room, Audrey jumped up from the couch and barked, "Where have you been? I've been calling you all night."

He set down his briefcase and took off his raincoat. "Battery must be dead. What's up?"

"Emily hasn't come home."

He checked his watch. "It's eleven o'clock. What's her curfew?"

"What happened to you? You look awful."

"Someone stole my wallet at the hotel bar after work. I took a client there for a drink—"

"I'm worried about her. She's supposed to be home by ten."

He wanted only to ease into the tub and let the hot water rise around him. "She goes out every night. She probably just lost track."

Audrey picked up the phone. "Here. You try. I've called her twenty times already."

"Are you saying you haven't talked to her at all today?"

"She left a message this afternoon saying she would get a ride home after school. After that, nothing."

"If she's not home by the time I finish my bath, we'll call the police. Okay?"

"They won't do anything," she said. "You have to wait twenty-four hours to file a missing person report."

"No. That's just something you hear on television. You can file a report on a juvenile anytime. The sooner the better, in fact."

"Then let's call now."

"You're that worried?"

"Why are you arguing with me?"

She was on the verge of tears, her hands clenched. Andrew found it doubtful that anything had happened to Emily. She'd missed curfews and disobeyed them many times before. He was confident she would be home any minute with some excuse. Emily was an excellent liar.

He sat at the kitchen table and dialed the police station on the regular business number, asking for the officer on duty.

A half hour later a policeman arrived at the house, a suburban cop, wide around the middle, with a receding hairline.

"Tell me what happened," he said.

He smelled like coffee and fast food. He stood in the front hallway with a black clipboard, scribbling onto a report form. Every so often he touched the radio microphone attached to his right shoulder and spoke into it.

"Okay," he said, after Audrey finished. "So you last saw her when you dropped her off at school this morning?"

"Yes."

"What was she wearing?"

"Blue jeans," said Audrey. "Black cardigan over a frilly black undershirt. Black leather boots."

"Does she take any medication? Anything she can't go without, like insulin?"

"Just some antidepressants," said Andrew.

"Is she depressed?"

"Who isn't."

"How about boyfriends? Anybody new?"

"I couldn't tell you," said Andrew. "We just moved into town two months ago, so all her friends would be pretty recent."

The cop asked for a picture of Emily. Audrey came out of the bedroom with the eight-by-ten frame they kept on the dresser: Emily and Daniel in the backyard at Cos Cob with their arms around each other.

"Is this her boyfriend?"

"That's her brother."

"Could she be with him?"

"No."

Andrew smelled chewing tobacco on the man, a scent he recognized from his dorm room days. Had they interrupted his nightly routine, sitting alone in his patrol car with his tin of tobacco? Would the policeman do anything to investigate, or would he just return to his cruiser?

He handed Andrew his card. "I'll put out a radio broadcast on the missing person. If you hear from her, give dispatch a call. I'll be in touch if I learn anything. Otherwise the detective will contact you tomorrow morning to follow up, as soon as he comes on duty."

Andrew thanked the man and showed him out.

During the hours of waiting that followed, he and Audrey sat in the den, the TV playing. The rain plinked against the windows and roof. Every time a car passed on the street, Audrey would rise in response to the sweeping sound, like a wave coming to shore.

"Relax," he said. "We would have heard something by now if anything happened."

"I can't relax."

"You know Emily. She can be reckless."

"That's why I'm worried."

A dark dawn. When the cab pulled into the driveway, Andrew pulled back the curtain and watched from the window as his daughter got out and walked up the path with her head bent against the rain.

He shook Audrey, who had fallen asleep on the couch.

"She's home."

Emily came through the kitchen door. Her hair was tangled. She looked sleepy and childlike.

Audrey met her in the hall. Andrew expected hysterics, but his wife's exhausted voice came out calm and sad: "Why are you doing this to me?"

HE GOT UP after a few restless hours in bed. He tried to fall back to sleep but his body refused to comply, attuned as it was to getting up at 7:00 A.M. After a while he dressed and had breakfast and wandered from room to room in the silent house, trying to find something to occupy his attention: the newspaper, the sports channels, a book Audrey had left on the couch: *Eat Pray Love: One Woman's Search for Everything Across Italy, India and Indonesia*. His wife and daughter remained in their beds, neither making a sound.

His phone rang around eleven. It was Sampson, offering a rematch.

"What about your pal from the airport?"

"Long gone. Well? Do we have a game?"

Well, indeed. Andrew felt sluggish from lack of sleep and slightly hungover. But some exercise might clear his head. Better than loafing around the house in his slippers, he figured. He looked out the window: The weather had cleared.

"Same place?" he asked.

"Yes," said Sampson. "Dinner and drinks are on me this time."

"Absolutely not. We'll play for it, like before."

"If you insist."

"I do."

"Although I'm thinking of a different bet."

"For what?"

"I'll tell you later," said Sampson. "Meet you at the courts in an hour."

Andrew slipped into the bedroom and got into his tennis clothes. From the bathroom he took a bottle of Advil and a tube of menthol cream. Audrey snored softly, a lump under the comforter.

In the den he massaged the gel into his upper thighs to warm the tendons, all the way to his butt and down to the backs of his knees. He popped two capsules. No way would he pull up lame again, not today. He'd felt that same thrill before a college match, when he'd played number one, and the same certainty that he could not be beaten.

This time, he did his stretching exercises before leaving the house, concentrating on his hamstrings and Achilles tendon. He didn't want Sampson to see him going through these old-man labors, on his back, his legs in the air. Let Sampson wait on him for a change.

As he began his sit-up routine, Emily wandered into the room. "Oh," she said, nearly stepping on him. She rubbed her eyes.

"Rough night?" he asked.

"Understatement." She stepped around him and went to the kitchen for a glass of water. She chugged a full glass then refilled it. As she passed him on her way back, he grabbed her foot. "You could have phoned. Your mother was—"

"Let me guess. Worried sick."

"I was going to say concerned. But your version is probably more accurate."

"I doubt it."

He raised an eyebrow. "She called the police. They put out a missing person report."

"Seriously?"

"Yes, seriously. The cop left his business card on the kitchen table if you want to see it."

She groaned. "How embarrassing. Is my name up on some billboard?"

"What do you think?"

She sighed and sat on the couch in front of him. She took a slow sip of the water. "Actually I couldn't," she said. "Call."

"Come on, Emily. Make an effort. Keep your phone charged."

"That wasn't exactly the problem."

He continued with his sit-ups. "Try a little harder next time, okay?"

She grabbed his feet and held them. "You're supposed to stay flat. And don't wrap your hands behind your head like that. You're doing a 1980s sit-up. Calisthenics have evolved since then. Hold your arms out in front of you instead."

"The eighties were my heyday," he said, exhaling heavily. "You're right. It's harder this way."

"Feel the burn," she said. "What's with the early abs?"

He grunted instead of answering, lunging toward her. He didn't want to say "tennis" because the word would summon Daniel—the marathon weekend matches they used to play in Cos Cob, first to win five sets. They would play for three or four hours, if no one was waiting for the court. Sometimes Audrey and Emily would come along on their bikes to watch for a while. Emily would play ball girl, crouching by the net and chasing after errant serves, while Audrey would sit on the bench with her straw hat covering her face, reading a paperback. Both of them rooting for Daniel.

"I've got a match," he said, finally, not wanting to lie to her. He watched her faint smile fade. Was it disloyal to return to tennis, now that he was gone? She seemed to think so. She released his feet and picked up her glass.

"Have fun," she said, getting up.

"Do you want to come along? Get some fresh air? You can take my car back if you get bored. I can catch a ride—"

"Stop," she said. "I'm going back to sleep."

He got to his feet and filled a couple of water bottles in the kitchen, one with electrolyte water, the other with a sports drink. It was a summerlike Saturday, absurdly warm for the last weekend of October, but he took along a fleece pullover, knowing it would turn cool later in the day.

At the park, he wheeled around the fruit loop, empty at this time of day. He pulled up next to Sampson's convertible. His rival was alone on the far court with his shirt off, practicing his serve in the sun. His chest, Andrew noticed as he approached, was hairless, his skin a pale pink. All he'd brought, again, was his racket, Andrew noticed. His service motion was effortless, almost lazy, textbook in its perfection—front foot angled diagonally toward the court, back foot parallel with the baseline, the ball rising from his fingers without spin, seemingly floating on the air, awaiting the racket.

After his follow-through, Sampson glanced up and offered an easy smile, and at that moment, Andrew knew the strategy he would use and, indeed, how the match would play out. He would prolong the match into the late-afternoon hours, when the sun would dip low onto the horizon and the wind would rise and Sampson would grow tight-muscled and chilly in his thin T-shirt. Andrew would draw out rallies, moving Sampson from side to side, using drop shots and lobs, even if it meant losing a few points. He would extend their warm-up session, even— anything to wear down Sampson, to get him into that fifth set, where Andrew's will would carry the game and Sampson's effortless grace would break down with exhaustion and lack of proper hydration and his perfect strokes would drift long in the wind.

"Best of five?" Andrew proposed, popping open a can of tennis balls, the compressed air releasing with a satisfying fizzle.

"Are you sure your hamstring will hold up?"

"You let me worry about that."

Sampson pushed his hair out of his eyes. "Best of five, then."

HE TOOK THE fifth set six–love. After the last point, Sampson collapsed at the fence and lay on his back for nearly five minutes. Andrew gathered the balls and stood over him.

"Hotel bar again?" said Sampson, shading his eyes against the late sun.

Andrew wanted to put some distance between himself and the firm. "Why don't we try Wintonbury Center this time."

"Good idea," said Sampson. "I heard about a good Afghan place there. Hop in. We can come back for your car."

Andrew shrugged, as if undecided, although he had been about to propose the same arrangement. He locked his gym bag in his SUV and climbed into the little convertible.

Over dinner Sampson asked, "What was your favorite case in law school?"

"My favorite case? Well, let me think on it. That was a long time ago."

"Don't think. Just tell me the first one that comes to mind."

"What is this, a psychological test? There's the cabin boy case."

"*Dudley and Stephens.* A grisly tale on the high seas. You've got a cinematic imagination."

"Whatever that means."

"My criminal law professor told us that it was quite common back then, in case of shipwreck and privation, to eat the cabin boy."

"So much for drawing lots."

"Any others?" asked Sampson.

"Did you remember the sleepwalking case?"

"Remind me."

"I can't recall the name of the case. It involved the issue of criminal intent. Mother and father were sleeping soundly in bed one night. Mother had a bad dream. She dreamed that North Koreans were attacking her house, so she went out to the shed and got an ax and came back inside and barged into her daughter's bedroom and split the girl's head open. All while sleepwalking, she said."

Sampson cackled. "How did I miss this?"

"'I think I hurt Pattie,' she told her husband, with bloody ax in hand."

"What was the ruling?"

"Not guilty for lack of mens rea."

"North Koreans?"

"This was back in 1951."

"Ah." Sampson took a forkful of rice and pumpkin puree and slipped it between his lips. After swallowing, he dabbed at his mouth with his cloth napkin. "Maybe you could shed some light on that employee privacy issue—"

Andrew raised his hand, cutting him off. "I'd rather not talk about that."

"No?"

"We're off the clock." He leaned back in his seat and took a sip of red wine. "Tell me about that bet you had in mind."

"You expect me to reveal the bet, now that I've lost?"

"Of course. Gentlemen's honor."

Sampson paused. "Are we truly off the clock?"

"I just said so, didn't I?"

"Because it's been my experience," he said, sounding more British than usual, "that sex and law don't mix."

"Sex? How did we get onto sex?"

"The bet. It has a somewhat sexual element to it."

"*Somewhat* sexual?"

"Basically sexual."

"I see." Andrew felt himself stirring. He finished his glass in a long draw, trying to appear nonchalant. "Should we get another red?"

"Why not? I'm buying."

Andrew caught the waitress's attention, looking past Sampson but aware of the other's gaze fixed on him, and signaled for another bottle. "Do you think you're telling me something I don't know? I heard all about your indiscretions my first day in Hartford."

"Is that so?"

"Yes. And I couldn't care less."

Sampson pursed his lips. "Frankly, I didn't appreciate the lecture. I don't need a morality lesson from homophobic seventy-year-olds. I intend to make my displeasure on that issue known at some point."

"Well, that was none of my doing. I'm the new boss, remember? So, yes, we're off the clock. In fact, the clock was never on today."

Sampson smiled. "Agreed."

"So, the bet?"

Sampson leaned forward. "Winner gets a blow job," he said. He shrugged. "I wasn't planning on losing. You surprised me. You're good. Damn good."

"You fell into my trap."

"Did I? What was it?"

"You expect me to reveal my strategy?"

"Your strategy was obvious," said Sampson. "Your strategy was to run me around like a headless chicken. And you succeeded. I'll be sore for a week."

"And you didn't even have to give me points this time."

"Touché," said Sampson.

"You're a little bit too sure of yourself."

"It's been said before."

"For instance, what makes you think I'd be interested in your bet?"

Sampson smiled. "Who wouldn't be? Shish kebab and a blow job: two of the great pleasures in life."

"Yes, but—"

This time Sampson cut him off. "If you haven't tried something, don't be so quick to dismiss it."

"Everything in moderation?"

"Yes, including moderation."

The waitress came with the bottle and filled their glasses. "Boys' night out?" she asked.

"You could say that," said Sampson.

BACK AT the tennis courts, dark and deserted now after 8:00 P.M., Sampson turned off the motor. Andrew fished in his pockets for his keys, making a show of it. He didn't want to appear anxious or foolish. He didn't even know if the "bet" was a gag, another of Sampson's ploys.

"Do you know what else they say about you?" asked Sampson.

"What's that?"

"That you've got a huge cock."

Andrew snorted. "Who told you that?"

"I'm right, aren't I? Your racket grip." Sampson didn't smile. His eyes were avid.

Andrew had a bottle of wine under his belt, enough that he didn't care. It felt almost natural, unzipping his pants. "Time to pay the piper," he said.

Sampson took a long look. "Right again," he said. He had that superior tone again, Mister Know-it-all. "Do you mind if I—"

Sampson reached across the seat. He had a firm grip, soft hands, except for a spot on his thumb—a tennis callus—which excited and irritated the head of his penis.

Andrew reared up in the seat, to allow Sampson access. Sampson leaned over and took him in his mouth. He started slowly, just the head.

"Jesus."

Sampson took his time, drawing it out. Every now and then he would push the hair out of his eyes and glance up. "You like it, don't you?"

At last, Andrew released.

Sampson straightened in his seat and wiped his mouth. His pale blue eyes were bloodshot, but otherwise he looked fresh and clean, as always.

"Not bad," said Andrew, his breath catching in his throat. "I've had better."

"Liar," said Sampson. "You came like a fountain."

AROUND NINE Andrew returned to a silent home. Audrey was sitting at the kitchen table with a wine bottle, a glass in hand. She was wearing her robe, her hair still damp from the shower. Her book lay on the table. She was upset, he could tell at a glance—the usual sadness, but some annoyance on top of that.

"Did you have dinner?" he asked, trying to sound cheerful.

"I made chicken. And tofu for Emily."

"Did she actually eat something?"

"She's seventeen, Andrew. Do you remember what it was like, being seventeen?"

"I didn't spend quite so much time in my room alone."

"That's because you were a fairly well-adjusted male."

He put down his gym bag and sat at the table. "Fine. But if you catch her throwing up again," he said, "I think we should consider sending her to a treatment facility."

"You'd do that to Emily?"

"It's not something I would *do* to her. It's something that we'd have to consider, for her own good."

"Come off it. You'd do it because it's easier for you that way, to have someone else deal with her." She got up and hit the reheat button on the microwave, igniting the radioactive whirl of light and sound.

"You didn't answer my question," he said.

"She took her plate into her room. I'm not going to check up on her."

"She could at least sit down with us once in a while, hungry or not."

"What's with the parenting all of a sudden?"

He shrugged. "She seemed depressed this morning."

"Well, tonight's probably not the best night to lay down any new rules."

"Why not?"

"We had an argument," she said. "I'm thinking of grounding her."

"Grounding her? Where did you get that idea?"

"Thought I'd try something new." Audrey turned off the microwave and slid his plate onto the table. Thai chicken with rice and broccoli, her default dish.

He was about to tell her he'd already eaten, but he realized he was hungry again. The Afghan place had served small portions, just one skewer of chicken and vegetables, and he'd burned off some major calories during the five sets with Sampson. The tiredness struck him all at once. He'd been running on adrenaline most of the match, willing himself through rallies. Now, he felt spent.

"What did you fight about? Her staying out last night?"

Audrey shook her head. "I found a stash of pills in her closet, hidden in a box of tampons." She sipped from her wineglass. "Vicodin, Oxy-Contin. Enough to put a horse to sleep."

"Really?"

"Yes, Andrew. Really."

He cursed. "You've got to give her points for ingenuity. I never would have looked in a tampon box. That's just plain devious."

"She takes after you in that regard."

He picked up his fork. "What did you do?"

"What do you think? I flushed the pills down the toilet."

"Where does a teenager get OxyContin?"

"Go ask her. She's not talking to me."

He chewed the chicken without tasting anything. "Did you run out of peanut sauce?"

"Peanut sauce?"

"Some kind of sauce? Tastes bland."

"Maybe that's because it was sitting in the microwave for two hours."

He found it difficult to lose his temper, even in the midst of his physical exhaustion and sleep deficit. Sampson was correct about one thing. A good blow job was indeed one of the great pleasures, a tonic for anyone's mood. "Well," he said, sampling the broccoli, "at least I know where to go if my sciatica acts up."

"I'm glad you find this funny."

"This is your department, not mine."

"My department? Emily is a department?"

"As you said, I'm a fairly well-adjusted male. These kinds of issues are completely beyond me."

"You don't need to be a therapist to spend some time with your daughter."

"You know what I mean. I *do* spend time with her—but I can't advise her on eating disorders or body dysmorphia or whatever else they call that sort of hysteria these days."

"So what does that leave you? What's your department?"

He gestured outward in a circular motion—the lawn, the driveway, all that lay beyond the boundaries of their property. "Everything else."

"And I'm the little homemaker, doing the cooking and—"

He tried to change the subject, unwilling to spoil his mood. "How's your book? Any good? You've been reading that one for a while."

She took a sip of wine. "I haven't really been focusing on it."

He studied the back cover as he ate. He grinned. "How about this for a title. *Eat Ass Regret.* How's that?"

She didn't respond.

"Subtitle: *A Straight Man's Search for Everything in Another Man's Underpants.* How's that? Is that funny?"

She glared at him above her bifocals. "If you're a homophobic frat boy, it is."

"I never joined a frat."

"To my undying surprise."

"I rowed crew—"

"Yes, Andrew, I know. Crew in the fall, tennis in the spring. You've told me of your physical exploits. Ad nauseam."

"*Eat Ass Shame.* Is that better? Shame is always more interesting than regret."

She let out an exasperated sigh. "It's like talking to a child. I'm going to bed," she announced, getting up.

Andrew pushed aside the book. He didn't want to eat anyone's ass or suck cock or engage in any such gay exercise. He wanted to treat Sampson like a woman. It made sense. Sampson was nearly as pretty as a woman anyway, with his blue eyes and blond hair. He wanted to see Sampson on his knees, with Andrew's cock in his mouth. He wanted to fill his mouth with come. Again.

The new boss.

DURING THE WEEK he ran into Sampson a few times in the hallway and coffee room. He detected no discernible difference in the other's affect, no awkwardness or superiority, nothing to indicate that anything of any import had occurred between them. They scheduled a tiebreaker for the weekend ("More like a jawbreaker if I lose again," said Sampson under his breath), but the weather did not comply. It rained on Saturday and Sunday, and Andrew couldn't reserve a court at the indoor club in Glastonbury ("Booked up for a month," the woman told him).

Instead, they agreed on dinner in Wintonbury Center after work on Monday.

There was a fifty-minute wait at the Italian joint they'd picked, so they walked together to a place called Max Baxter's Fish Bar—apparently the local pickup spot for the middle-aged crowd. At the bar, smartly dressed men and women crowded together, practically yelling at each other. Three bartenders were working hard to fill orders. As Sampson caught the attention of a waitress, a woman in a leopard dress smiled at Andrew from her barstool, just a few inches away, her lips painted a startling pink. "I like your suit," she said. "It takes a real man to wear olive."

He smiled at her and retreated from the crowd. They took a table in the rear. Sampson removed some pages from his briefcase—Lexis research, he said—and summarized his findings.

"Most of the cases are fairly recent, trial-level stuff," said Sampson.

Beyond him, Andrew noticed some local Lothario in a black turtleneck approach the lady in the leopard dress, flashing a smoker's browntoothed grin. A bad dream, this place. He could hardly imagine anything as dreary as sitting on one of those padded red barstools with a martini, waiting to chat up some wanton divorcée.

The waitress arrived, a lithe Asian wearing a black miniskirt. She set down two glasses of scotch. "Our aperitifs have arrived," said Sampson in his British tones, pushing aside his papers. Not cocktails, not scotches, *aperitifs.*

"Cheers," said Andrew.

They ordered steaks and the waitress disappeared.

Andrew said, "I gave you these files for a reason. Internet monitoring, employee privacy—that's the cutting edge. That's what employers want to know about these days. Can we monitor employee email? What about employer-provided phones? Can we read their texts? Can we listen to their voice mail? Can we fire them for something they post on a social media site? They've got clowns spending half their day locked in their offices, jerking around on YouTube and every porno site you can name. Drunkensluts dot com. Hairyasses dot com. These are actual sites, I'm not making it up."

Sampson laughed, a phony, breathy exhalation. Like giving him points in tennis.

"I had a case last year," Andrew continued. "An in-house insurance attorney called and told me that two FBI agents had just walked into his office, asking for consent to monitor a VP's company computer. They say he's accessing child pornography. *What should I do?* the guy asks me. He's got no idea, and frankly neither do I. Why? Because there's no precedent. New technology, new law. You can make your name on a case like that. Take it up to the appellate court."

"I appreciate the chance."

"Better than scrap metal, wouldn't you say?"

"Much."

When the waitress appeared with their steaks, Johnny Sampson offered one of his easy smiles, calling her "darling," and when it was time for the check, she stood by his chair for a minute, flirting.

"Come on," said Andrew. "This place is giving me a headache. I know somewhere better."

"Fine by me," said Sampson.

They drove together in Andrew's car. Andrew turned off his cell phone and stowed it in the glove compartment. On the way downtown, he had a luxurious feeling of being unaccountable. They passed from the suburbs into the outer limits of the city: strip malls and gas stations, run-down tenements and abandoned factory buildings. He drove through the deserted north end of the city, past the landfill, the main police station, and the car dealerships with their football-field parking lots, the vehicles lined up in neat rows. The streetlights and stoplights reflected off the windshield, blurring from white to red to green, to all the neon colors of the night.

"Where are we going?" said Sampson, looking uncertain for once.

"Never been down here before?"

Sampson shook his head.

"You'll see in a minute."

Andrew turned down a darkened side street, past a mattress factory, and pulled into the parking lot of a large windowless, one-story building as big as a warehouse. ECSTATIC, said the sign in fluorescent pink. In smaller letters on the marquee: CONNECTICUT'S PREMIER GENTLEMEN'S LOUNGE.

"A strip joint?"

"Only the best."

Inside, the music was deafening. A lone dancer strutted the raised runway that ran nearly the length of the room. All this noise, but only five or six patrons sat at the stage, a few seats apart from each other, studying the dancer with humorless concentration.

At the bar, Andrew ordered tequila shots and beer chasers. The girls came on one at a time, dancing for the length of a song, wearing G-strings, their breasts bare. Most were skinny with bad implants, their arms and lower backs tattooed. They followed the same general choreography—first dancing languidly, then swinging around the pole, then simply lying spread-eagled in front of one of the patrons in the first row. One girl liked to slap her ass in the viewer's face, which signified she was done with him—she'd earned her dollar—before moving on to the next glazy-eyed slob. Andrew liked watching her, a tall blonde on four-inch platforms, strutting back and forth, her enormous saline breasts bobbing.

Tequila, just like the night of the Russian kid. Salt, liquor, lime. Andrew adopted the same mind-set as that night, absolving himself of responsibility. This bar, like the park after hours, was a place of no consequence. The people around him led squalid, reckless lives—strippers and drunks, bouncers and men not gainfully employed. This was not his life. But there was an excitement in mingling among the lowly and dragging Johnny Sampson into the same wretched mire.

He put his arm around Sampson. "Do you like her?"

"Who?"

"Blonde."

"I wouldn't call her a natural beauty."

"Have another shot. She'll grow on you. Or should I request an Asian? You seemed to like our waitress, did you not?"

"If you say so."

The room seemed engulfed in a thick haze, although no one was smoking. Andrew signaled the bartender again—tequila with chasers. Their second round, third. He lost track. He felt himself losing control. The parade of cheap harlots circled in endless repetition. Heavy metal music, a constant roar. He glanced over at Johnny Sampson, whose face had taken on a sphinxlike inscrutability. Daintily, he raised his glass of beer. His cheeks were flushed. He was watching the stage with the disinterested countenance of a judge.

"Don't sip like that," yelled Andrew.

Sampson leaned forward, touching him on the forearm. His fingers were chilled from gripping the beer, providing an icy sensation. "Say again."

"You drink like a lightweight."

"Fuck you."

"Johnny Lightweight. You should put that on your business card."

"I repeat: Fuck you."

He toasted Sampson and drank the rest of the beer. "Your round," he said, then spun off the barstool.

In the men's room he pissed for what seemed like minutes, whistling, growing bored with pissing, directing the stream into the urinal cake. On the way out the door, he noticed the VIP area in the rear, cordoned off by a red velvet rope. A squat black man sat at the entranceway, texting on his cell phone in the dim light. He looked up with expressionless brown eyes. Andrew explained what he wanted. As they negotiated, Sampson appeared beside him, his hair slicked back. Andrew passed the bouncer the cash, and the man unsnapped the rope and let them pass, saying, "Number six."

The room was at the end of the hallway, with a black curtain in place of a door. They pushed aside the curtain and went in, their feet sinking into a thick carpet. An enormous fish tank extended the length of the far wall; inside, two giant koi—one gold, one white—floated in the blue-lit water, dumbly opening and closing their mouths. There were two cushioned chairs without armrests in the center of the room. There was a wet bar with mirror backing. A disco ball hung from the ceiling, speckling their faces with psychedelic hues.

Andrew took one of the chairs and Sampson slid onto the other, facing each other like actors in an avant-garde play.

"Have you ever been to Montreal, Sampson?"

"Of course." He pulled out his cell phone and began checking messages.

"Put that away. One of the partners in Stamford, an old-timer, had a fetish for strippers. That's how I know about this place. He took us here once. All he talked about was sex, but in the most proper terms, if that makes sense. 'I appreciate a pudendum that protrudes like a pitcher's mound,' he would tell you. Things like that. He preferred foreign girls. He used to organize trips, up and back on the late train to Montreal. They called it the disco train, I think. We'd hit the places on St. Catherine Street. The French girls were beautiful, like fashion models, perfectly naked. You didn't hear a word of English, all night long, *Oui oui,* like doves cooing. Inexpensive too, considering the exchange rate. I went only once; I can't say I enjoyed it. But it was necessary for the advancement of one's career. Put that thing away, will you?"

Sampson glanced up, the light from the phone display, reflecting in his eyes. "I'm listening," he said. "Strippers cooing like doves."

"It was necessary, I was saying, to perform certain duties which you might not otherwise enjoy."

"I don't find this unenjoyable."

"Look at you, sitting there like the Sphinx. Employing double negatives."

The curtain was pushed aside, and the blonde came into the room with a hard, awkward walk, as if falling forward with each step. She was wearing her pink G-string, nothing else, her skin bronzed with a salon tan. Her perfume instantly filled the room. She had a name tattooed across her shoulder blades in large cursive letters: ROMANO. She was not young, not by a long shot. Her rear end was square and flat, the tops of her thighs rippled with cellulite.

"Who's Romano?" asked Andrew.

"A mistake."

"Want to make another?"

She emitted a raspy laugh, all whiskey and cigarettes. "Story of my life. What do you have in mind?"

"The usual."

She laughed. "You cops?"

"On the contrary," said Sampson. "We're lawyers."

"I love lawyers. Always straight to the point."

Andrew handed her the roll of bills and she tucked them into her tiny pink purse and went to the bar. "Drink?"

"Whatever you're having," said Andrew.

"Jack and Coke," she said, pouring. "My specialty."

Andrew took the glass from her and finished it with a few quick sips. He pulled her close and squeezed her breasts with both hands, making the areolas bulge grotesquely. She kissed him on the mouth, tasting of lip gloss.

"So, Counselors," she said, looking over his shoulder to Sampson. "Who goes first?"

"Neither," said Andrew. "That is, both."

"You mean, at the same time?"

"Exactly."

"Oh, dear. I'll get lockjaw."

"You can manage, I'm sure," said Andrew, opening his zipper.

OUTSIDE, the gray November night. Andrew took a deep breath, clearing his lungs. He started the car, feeling sublimely drunk and yet unimpaired. He checked the dashboard clock: a little before 11:00 P.M. It seemed later than that. They drove along the deserted streets toward the office buildings in the distance. Andrew felt content with their silence, as if he and Sampson had come to an agreement. In the lounge, with the disco ball coloring their faces, he had watched the girl on her knees, her shiny lips, her dark purple tongue. Sampson's cock was long and thin, the head bulbous, pink. Pencil dick, they used to call a guy like that back in high school.

Andrew turned in to the parking garage in Wintonbury Center, where they'd left Sampson's car, and navigated the narrow, circular passage down to the underground level. He pulled up next to Sampson's convertible, the only vehicle in sight. When he turned off the motor, a sudden quiet emerged. Overhead, the garage lights burned brightly, making a fluorescent racket. Somewhere on the upper floors of the parking garage, tires squeaked, like an animal bleating.

"What's your schedule for the rest of this week?"

Sampson stared straight ahead. "Full. And I'm heading down to D.C. for the weekend."

"When will I see you?"

Sampson shrugged. "Whenever."

"Whenever?"

"Yes, whenever."

"Whenever means *fuck you*. Is that what you're telling me? To go fuck myself?"

Sampson glanced at him. "If you say so."

"What about Monday? Can you get back to town by then?"

Sampson nodded.

"Fine. Next Monday. Indoor tennis after work and a late dinner. Put it in your book."

"Fine."

Andrew smiled. Yes, Sampson had come to understand the arrangement, it seemed. The know-it-all was subdued, at last. "You liked that back there, didn't you? Is that what you did with Pedro? Suck him off?"

Sampson blinked a few times, but otherwise his face revealed nothing. He looked as fresh as always in his V-neck sweater, a few strands of blond hair falling across his forehead. "Which means what, exactly?"

"Which means what it sounded like."

"Sounds like you're jealous."

"Jealous? I don't give a shit about some paralegal—"

"He's a law student." Sampson got his cell phone out of his pocket and flipped it open.

"For Christ's sake, you're like a high school kid with that thing. Give it a rest when I'm talking to you."

"Shut up for a second." Sampson pointed the phone at him and clicked a photo. He examined the image, nodding. "Not bad," he said, holding it toward Andrew.

He squinted. There was his face on the tiny screen, serious and pale against the pitch-black background. "What's that for?"

"I want a picture of you."

"Why?"

"You're the smart guy. You figure it out."

Then Sampson leaned in and kissed him full on the lips, a long and lingering kiss. This was a surprise, an admission of sorts. It was the first time they'd kissed.

Sampson pulled away, opening the door to get out, and Andrew nearly blurted: *Wait*. But he caught himself, and Sampson left without saying more.

THE WEEK PASSED. Andrew saw Sampson only once, in the hallway on Friday afternoon, and his protégé strolled by without speaking, offering instead a salute and a whimsical grin.

On Monday morning, when he called Sampson to confirm their tennis date, he got voice mail. He walked down the hall at lunchtime and found Sampson's office door closed. His secretary told him that he'd called in sick that morning. Andrew left three or four messages, without getting a response. He was tired of talking to a recorded voice. He vowed to tell Sampson the next time he saw him: Answer my calls or don't expect to try any more cases.

On Tuesday morning, Sampson's secretary gave him the same news: "He called in sick."

"What's wrong with him? Is he in the hospital or something?"

"That's all I know," the woman said.

"He didn't say?"

She shook her head. "I didn't talk to him. He left a voice mail before I got in."

All week he got the same response. On Friday morning, when he appeared at her desk, she simply shrugged and said, "Sorry."

"Nothing?"

"Same message. 'I won't be coming in.'"

Andrew had dinner with Audrey and Emily every night that week and worked on his laptop in his home office, writing a brief that was due in appellate court the next month. The household was quiet, good for concentrating. His daughter rarely came out of her room, still "grounded." Audrey went out every night after dinner, taking the dog on walks or running errands in town. The weekend came and went.

On Monday he found a message from Sampson's secretary on his office line. "He's still got the flu, Mr. Murray," she said. "He says he'll need someone to cover for his deposition Tuesday."

That was all.

* * *

THEY HAD Thanksgiving at home—Andrew, Audrey, and Emily. Their second Thanksgiving without Daniel. No one mentioned this fact, but they did not have to. Audrey set a place for their absent son, and they bowed their heads before the meal. Andrew recited a prayer, over Emily's objections. An atheist, his daughter.

He'd invited his parents to come down from East Longmeadow, but his mother said that his father was "out of sorts." His ulcer, apparently. The old man disliked going to doctors, like most men of his generation.

The next day Andrew wandered the house, unable to sit still for more than a few minutes. He called Johnny Sampson to see how he was feeling, but his voice mail box was filled. In the afternoon the postman delivered some correspondence from a law firm, registered mail, but Andrew couldn't bring himself to open the envelope. For once he didn't feel like working; he'd finished his appellate brief already, two weeks before it was due, and needed a break from legal matters. All that long weekend his daughter locked herself in her room, disdaining family meals, instead coming out for the occasional snack—nothing more than cheese sticks, as far as Andrew could tell.

"This is getting worse," he told Audrey after Sunday dinner.

Audrey occupied herself with her book and red wine, curled on the couch. "She won't talk to me. What do you expect me to do about it?"

"I expect you to discuss it."

"Why are you obsessing about her diet? She eats. She just doesn't do it in front of us."

"And you call that normal?"

"Her weight is fine, Andrew."

"How can you tell?"

Audrey sighed. "They weigh her at school and at the doctor's office. She had a checkup this summer. And her weight has been the same, every time, for the past year, give or take a few pounds. Okay?"

"Why didn't you tell me that the last time we spoke?"

"Because you didn't ask."

"She's been missing a lot of school lately," he said.

"I know that, Andrew. I've got doctors' appointments scheduled next week. I'm worried it might be Lyme."

"Lyme," he murmured.

Audrey had gotten the disease herself in her thirties and was vigilant about ticks ever since.

Sheba appeared at his side. He rubbed her along her flank and the dog panted. "Aren't you going to take the dog out?" he asked. "You haven't left the house in three days."

"You do it. I'm on a break."

On Monday morning he went into the office early, anxious to get back to work. Thanksgiving, as always, had thrown him out of whack; it wasn't long enough for a real vacation, but too long for a weekend, and it just made him conscious of all the work waiting for him. The floor was nearly deserted so early, not yet 8:00 A.M. Whenever the elevator dinged, he perked up, noticing the lawyers and secretaries as they marched by his office with their coffee cups and muffins. A few peered in, offered greetings. He realized he knew only about half of them by name. Fuck them, he decided. It wasn't his job to learn their names like some grade-school teacher.

By nine the place had filled up, but he hadn't seen Sampson go past. He went down the hall and knocked on Sampson's door, but it was locked. His secretary was not at her station. He posted a sticky note on the door: *Come see me.* For Christ's sake, was he still sick? Or playing possum? Andrew tried his cell phone again; there was no answer and his mailbox was full. Where was Sampson? And why the hell hadn't he gotten back to him, the prick?

Around noon Hannahan appeared in his doorway. "Got a minute?"

Hannahan, the last thing he needed. "Actually, Jack," he said, trying to sound cheerful, "I'm playing catch-up today."

"Just a word." He gestured for Andrew to follow.

Andrew rose, annoyed. Couldn't Hannahan take a hint? And why not just sit down in Andrew's office? Because the scotch was in Hannahan's desk. Drinkers didn't like to drink alone; it would be an admission of sorts, to sit alone behind a closed door in the afternoon with a bottle, like a disgraced priest.

Hannahan shut the door behind him and pulled out the Glenfiddich from the bottom drawer. "Join me?"

Not a bad idea, Andrew decided. "Sure. What's on your mind, Jack?"

"A delicate matter." Hannahan poured the booze and took a slow sip, letting the words hang in the air.

Andrew waited for him to continue. But the old man couldn't be rushed. Drunk or sober, in or out of the courtroom, Hannahan picked his words carefully, releasing them like pigeons. A good habit for a lawyer, of course. He never gave anything away, never offered his opponent an advantage. But today Andrew didn't have the patience for the act. He scratched behind his ear.

"I've just come from a meeting with the partners—" Hannahan offered at last.

"I didn't know one was scheduled."

"An emergency session."

A glaring sun splashed against the floor-to-ceiling window. Outside, he could see only blue air, a cloudless sky thirty stories high. "Well, fill me in."

"There's been a complaint from within the firm. It involves you, I'm afraid."

"Oh, Christ. Whose feelings have I hurt now?" Andrew had a gruff management style, he knew. Over the past fifteen years, three or four secretaries had complained about him, had asked for a new assignment. One of them had called him *a bully*—as if this were a school yard, not a place of business. Did he have to say *pretty please* every time he wanted a photocopy or a cup of coffee? Apparently so, or you risked putting someone's panties in a bunch. "Which secretary is it?"

"It's no secretary. It's John Sampson. He resigned from the firm last Friday and filed a sexual harassment complaint with the superior court the same day."

Andrew felt a lurching sensation, like the earth falling away beneath him. His voice came out hollow-sounding. "Against whom?"

"Against you individually and the law firm as principal. I'm surprised you haven't received the complaint."

Andrew recalled the registered letter he'd received over the weekend, unopened at home. "Let me see it."

"I don't have the document in front of me," said Hannahan.

"Well, ask your sec——"

"Let's take a minute, Andy, before we talk to the partnership. I wanted to have a word with you as a friend, first and foremost, to figure out the best way to address this thing."

"The partnership."

"We'll be meeting again at one-thirty."

"Jack, this is absurd."

"I have no doubt of that. But we have to treat it seriously. He's alleging sexual misconduct against the head of our employment litigation division. You can anticipate how that might attract attention."

"Consider the source. You yourself said he'd been reprimanded for improprieties with coemployees in the past."

Hannahan nodded. "And that's fully documented in his personnel file."

I don't need a morality lesson from homophobic seventy-year-olds. I intend to make my displeasure known at some point. Andrew said, "This is retaliatory. This is about him getting even with the firm."

"We've considered that motive." Hannahan leaned forward, bringing his hands together. "What I'm asking you now is to weigh our exposure. Does he possess anything that could compromise our position?"

"Of course not," Andrew said.

"Think on it for a moment. Anything at all."

"As I said, Jack, it's frivolous. He's after a quick buck. It's outrageous. After all I've done for him."

Hannahan nodded slowly. "He purports to have photographic and video exhibits."

"That's impossible."

"It's alleged in his complaint. So, of course, we have the right to production of those exhibits."

Andrew heard it in Hannahan's voice, what he didn't want to say aloud. And he realized with a shock, suddenly and irrevocably, that the whole thing had already been decided. The partners had met, deliberated, voted, adjourned for lunch. They'd wiped their hands of him. Now he and Hannahan were merely going through the motions. Hannahan was the messenger, delivering the grim news.

"What are you saying, Jack?"

"Look, Andy. You came to Hartford for a change of pace. But maybe you need more than that. Maybe this is a chance to take some time for yourself. After all you've been through, no one could think poorly of you for doing so."

Did that mean he'd already *seen* the exhibits? *Photographic and video exhibits.* Andrew recalled all the times Sampson had pulled out his cell phone. Jesus Christ. A camera phone, of course. He'd recorded every-thing. They hadn't even offered camera or video phones when Andrew bought his mobile a few years earlier. Leave it to a guy like Sampson to keep up with the latest technology. *You're the smart guy*, he had told him. *You figure it out.* How had he not realized until now?

"Let's say, for the sake of argument, that there were something. What then?"

"That would complicate the matter, of course," said Hannahan.

Complicate. Andrew grimaced. He saw fully how it would play out. There could be no halfway, no leave of absence. The firm would have to cut its ties, and quickly. That was what Hannahan was telling him now with his severe silences. There was no way they could let this suit go to trial. They couldn't risk it. They couldn't have the name of Carrington Farr on the news, his picture splashed in the newspaper, the sordid al-legations of homosexual acts in the park, in a strip joint. It might take a year or longer to settle the suit, but the decision had been made. He was out. Andrew saw it all in an instant. His resigning, packing boxes, hand-ing over his key card, taking the elevator down to the parking garage. And the aftermath too. What firm would take a chance on him with this indiscretion in his past? He'd have to seek out clients anew, at forty-six. All those years of accomplishment, falling away like pebbles down a mountainside.

"You're telling me the firm wants to settle. Avoid complications."

"There was discussion toward that end." Hannahan cleared his throat. "And your resignation as well."

"I wouldn't disagree. I'd advise the same."

"They'll want a covenant not to compete. A guarantee that you won't take clients with you."

"The file will be sealed, I take it."

Hannahan nodded. "That could be part of the settlement terms."

Andrew got up. His legs felt unsteady.

"Wait a minute now. This is all hypothetical. I have some ideas we can present to the partnership. Buyout terms. You should keep a percent-age—"

"Not now." Andrew emptied the glass and set it on the desk.

Hannahan raised an eyebrow. "I'm sorry, Andy. I did everything I could."

"You don't have to apologize. It's the only choice you had."

"It's a damn shame."

In the hallway Andrew was suddenly aware of gawkers, the heads looking up as he passed their offices and cubicles. The word had already spread. He'd been doing this walk of shame all day and hadn't even known it.

Worse, Sampson had played him from the start. He'd seen an opportunity and he'd taken it. Now he would move on to some other firm, maybe some other city, a hundred grand or more in his pocket. From the very beginning there had been only calculation and forethought. All of it, a ploy.

Odd, he didn't even know where Sampson lived. Before leaving that afternoon, he logged on the company network and looked up Sampson's home address.

HE SHOULD HAVE gone home, destroyed the registered letter, figured out what he was going to tell Audrey, but instead he spent most of the day at the hotel bar in the lobby. Tequila, again. He nursed a slow rage at Sampson and at himself for his own stupidity. At 5:00 P.M., he got into his car and drove to a package store and bought a twelve-pack of Anchor Steam. He wheeled past Sampson's house, the fruit loop, the restaurants where they'd dined, but found no sign of Sampson or his convertible. He stopped at a few bars, drinking until he felt a numbness coming on.

At ten o'clock, he parked on the street across from Sampson's house and sat, waiting. Sampson lived in the far west end of Hartford, a half block from the park, only a hundred yards from the Wintonbury town line. The house was a three-story Victorian with a sloped turret and a wraparound porch. A dim light shone from a second-floor room, but otherwise the windows were dark, the driveway unlit. Andrew could hear traffic a mile away on Farmington Avenue, one of the main arteries into the city, but this side of the west end was quiet, most of the houses locked down for the night.

Where was the little shit?

Well, wherever he was, he had to come home sometime, and Andrew would be waiting. He squinted up at the turret on the third floor. That would be Sampson's den, he imagined, where he could look down upon his fiefdom, the little prince. Perhaps he practiced his violin with the window open, letting the music drift out toward lucky passersby.

Andrew grabbed a bottle out of the backseat. The beer was warm. After he took a sip, the suds bubbled onto his lap. He drank the beer quickly, because it tasted better that way, then clinked the bottle atop the pile scattered on the floor behind the passenger seat. He was wasting his time, he told himself. He should go home and get some sleep. But there was no reason to sleep, no reason to get up at 7:00 A.M. He was fucked. He didn't want to face Audrey, didn't want to make up some bullshit story to tell her. His house was only three or four miles to the northwest, but it felt like a different country.

After a few minutes he had to piss. He considered driving down to the gas station on the corner, but that would have required too much effort. He got out of the car and veered drunkenly across the street. He went up the stone path and stepped onto Sampson's porch. Two skinny cats jumped off the railing, startling him. They came toward him in tandem, tails raised high. He shooed them away, and one of the cats hissed at him.

Andrew peered through a darkened first-floor window, cupping his hands against the glass. Inside, in the large empty room, there appeared to be only a single piece of furniture, a couch angled against the far wall. A few boxes were piled on top of each other with balls of newspaper scattered across the floor.

He crept along the porch to the next window, nearly halfway around the house, but the blinds were drawn. In the darkness he tripped against a potted plant, nearly falling. It was a rubber plant, the large broad leaves glazed with cold. He unzipped and pissed into the base of the plant, the urine puddling noisily.

Did Sampson live alone in this enormous house or did he rent the upper floors? It appeared to be a single-family dwelling, with only one mailbox. Did Sampson own the house? Did he have roommates? Andrew realized how little he knew about Sampson, how little he had revealed about himself. He had never invited Andrew to his home, had never volunteered any information about his past. The few facts Andrew knew, he'd learned from Sampson's résumé. And where was he now, on this late Monday night? Had he remained in Washington, D.C.? Had he even *gone* to D.C.? Had he ever been sick? There was no telling. The prick had lied to him from the start. Andrew had known it on some level too. The way he'd given him points in tennis. His sycophantic laugh. His rapt attention when Andrew spoke. All of it bullshit, but Andrew had allowed himself to be taken in. He'd wanted to be taken in.

He recalled something his father had taught him when he was young, something every kid knew: *There's nothing worse than a stool pigeon.*

Somewhere nearby a door slammed. Farther off, a few streets away, a motorcycle roared, briefly obscuring all other sounds. Andrew walked back to his car and got inside. In the silence that followed, he became aware of the low, rhythmic hum of an unseen generator. It lulled him, and he caught himself dozing once, then again, his head falling back against the headrest.

Sometime later he woke with a shiver. The car windows were fogged, blanketing his view of the night. He blinked a few times and realized that his phone was ringing. He dug into his pocket and checked the display. Well, there he was.

"Murray?"

"Yeah." Andrew glanced at his watch. He'd slept only twenty minutes, but he felt cold and hungover. His voice was hoarse.

"How are you, buddy? I heard you had a rough day."

"Tell me something. Did you plan to screw me from the start? Or did the idea come to you as you went along?"

"Oh, come on. Don't be a spoilsport."

"A *spoilsport?*"

"All's fair in love and war, right?"

"I'm serious. When did it occur to you to ruin my career? My livelihood?"

"Look on the bright side, Murray. If you stay at that place, you'll end up like Hannahan. Do you want that? To be like Jack? Hell, you're halfway there already. Now you got a chance to change trajectory."

"Fuck you, Sampson."

"Honestly, I did you a favor. Someday you'll thank me."

"Where are you? Are you in D.C.? Scared to answer your phone?"

"That's the reason I'm calling, actually. You have to cut down on the drunk dialing. You're filling my mailbox."

"Fuck your mailbox. Where are you?"

"Does it matter?"

"Well, buddy, you've got to come home sometime and guess where I am? Right across the street. Hell, I might even pull into your driveway."

"You probably should. There's no street parking after midnight."

"And guess what I got in the backseat? Not that I need it to kick your ass, but—it's a bat. Not regulation size. It's a mini-bat, they give them out for free at Fenway. I got it right here, to break your fucking teeth."

"That's a collector's item. You should put that on eBay."

Andrew rubbed the condensation off the window and squinted across the street. On the third floor, he thought he saw the outline of a man in the turret window. But, no. There was no one there. Just a shadow from a tree's top branches. And, in fact, the house now appeared wholly deserted, the bushes overgrown, the potted plant left out in the cold.

"You moved out, didn't you? You don't even live here anymore, do you?"

"Seriously, Murray. Go home. Go home to your wife."

"Answer my question. When did you decide to wreck my career?"

"It was either you or me, pal. They were never going to make me partner at that place. They pretty much told me so. You were the only one there willing to let me try a couple of dog-shit cases, and I had to suck your cock to get that, even. I had to get out of there some way, didn't I?"

"So you came up with this trumped-up lawsuit?"

"You'll get over it. You'll move on. You'll have bigger and better adventures."

Andrew shook his head, feeling the anger beginning to turn into something else, something more painful. "After all I did for you, this is how you pay me back. I had your career in mind."

"Bullshit."

"I'm serious. I was grooming you."

"Grooming, like a dog? That sort of grooming?"

Andrew tried to summon the words for what was welling up in him. "Tell me where you are. Let's talk this over in person. If it's money you want, we can talk about money. Just drop this stupid suit. We can work it out."

"That's blackmail, Murray. No thanks."

"I'm serious, Sampson. I can—"

"There's nothing more to talk about. We had a few laughs in the park. Maybe we can play again someday."

"It was more than that and you know it."

"Look, Murray, I gotta go."

"Don't hang up." He heard his voice crack, and he felt a wave of emotion coming on him, self-pity and hopelessness and drunken longing.

The line went dead.

In a rage, he twisted and ripped apart the phone and threw it into the backseat, the pieces scattering. His crappy old flip phone.

HE DROVE TO Wintonbury Center. He couldn't go home, not yet. He was way too angry, too drunk, to let Audrey see him like this. He parked outside the restaurant where he and Sampson had dined—Max Baxter's Fish Bar. A drink to calm his nerves. Getting out of the car, he noticed a pay phone on the corner and headed for it, nearly tripping on the curb. Sampson didn't answer. The little prick, he'd sniffed him out. Andrew vented into his voice mail. *I'm going to do everything I can to fuck up your career* was the gist of it. "I know every litigator worth a damn in the entire Northeast and I'm going to call every one of them personally and give them the scoop. You didn't think that far ahead, did you? Sure, you might get your pissant settlement, big deal. Then what? You think anyone will want to hire a backstabbing piece of shit like you? Who sues his own firm? They'll see you coming a mile away. You'll be lucky to get a job as a paralegal—" He went on until the mailbox filled.

Inside the restaurant there was only one other customer—a middle-aged guy sipping a scotch at the bar—and some waiters at a table in the rear, eating a late dinner.

"Tequila," he told the bartender.

"How about a beer?"

He looked up. "Didn't you hear me?"

"Your eyes look a little red," the bartender explained.

"Fine, then. A beer. You wouldn't want to risk a lawsuit."

He sat at the bar, watching the waiters at the rear table. One of them had the hiccups. The others found this humorous; they laughed every time he erupted. Andrew studied his beer, running foggily through explanations he might present to Audrey, trying to make them turn out in his favor. When the lights came up, as sudden and shocking as a camera flash, Andrew downed the rest of his beer and went out to his car.

He sat in the driver's seat, staring at the empty street. He checked his watch.

11:58 P.M.
Monday
November 26, 2007

He didn't want to go home before midnight. He wanted to be sure Audrey was asleep before he got there. He grabbed another beer out of the backseat and slowly sipped, gathering his resolve. When he finished the beer, he checked his watch again and said aloud, "To hell with it."

He started the car and pulled away from the curb. On the next corner was a gas station. He parked and got out and went inside to pour himself a cup of coffee. He was hungry, he realized; he hadn't eaten all day. He picked a premade grinder out of the refrigerator and paid the attendant. He drank the coffee in the front seat of his car and gobbled half the grinder, which was stale and dry.

On the drive home he passed a police car at an intersection without incident. Pulling into his driveway, he noticed every light in the house was on. What the hell was going on? From the outside it looked like they were throwing some kind of party.

In the kitchen he called his wife and daughter, then went from room to room, even checking the basement—but no one answered, only the dog, who followed him, whining and sniffing: despite the lights, no one was home.

Where were they? Had she opened the legal letter and read the numbered points of the lawsuit, the narrative of his disgrace? Had she left so quickly, without even waiting for an explanation, without wanting to hear his side of the story?

He tried Audrey's cell phone—only to have it go to voice mail.

THE NEXT MORNING he woke on the couch, hungover in his soiled suit, still wearing his shoes. He opened his eyes to see Audrey standing above him. She looked terrible. Her eyes were bloodshot, her face puffy.

"Where were you last night?" she asked.

"Where was I? Where were you? Aren't *you* the one who stayed out all night?"

"Didn't you get my messages?"

"No."

"Check your phone."

"My phone is broken," he said.

She turned to leave, but he called after her. "Hey. Talk to me. What's going on?" He realized that something else had happened, something unrelated to him; she knew nothing about the lawsuit. "Where have you been?"

"I've been with Emily."

"Emily?" He paused. "Isn't she in school?"

She stood in the doorway and in a calm, expressionless tone told him what had happened the night before; he didn't interrupt or ask any questions—and when she was done, as she was turning to go, she uttered two final words—words, he realized, that he'd been expecting for a long time and that, later, much later, living in a different state with a different woman, he would come to recognize as a blessing:

"Please leave," she said.

Emily Martin-Murray

The first day of school, 2007

WHEN HER PARENTS announced their plan to move to the suburbs outside Hartford, Emily couldn't believe it. *Move?* They were kidding, right? Move from her own house, where she and Daniel had grown up, the place she loved the most? How could they do this to her—and right before her senior year, to make it worse? The feeling of disbelief would remain with her for weeks afterward. She'd never even heard of the town—Wintonbury—or the public school she was forced to attend, Wall High School. A fitting name, Wall: The place was like a prison, with its high, pseudomodern concrete walls and thin horizontal windows.

On her first day of school she got sick twice due to nerves—once before leaving home, then again halfway through morning assembly. She sat in the back row of the auditorium, terrified that the principal might ask her to stand and introduce herself. The new girl. She slipped out of her seat and went directly to the bathroom, barely reaching the stall before letting it out. At the sink a blonde painting her lips with gloss turned and said, "Can you close the door when you do that, please?" At lunch period, this same blonde pointed at Emily and mouthed something to her companions, who all turned to gawk. Emily ate quickly, alone, then fled the building.

She wandered toward the rear courtyard, hearing music from a boom box. A group of boys were standing around a giant metal sculpture that looked like an anchor. She considered going over to bum a cigarette. But

203

the bell rang, and the boys came loping back toward the building. One of them approached her and whistled between his teeth. "Yo, what up?" he said.

She was wearing her tightest jeans and a fitted tee, her hair straightened—not her style, generally, but for the first day she figured she should try to fit in, to get a sense of the scene. He was tall and incredibly hot, with dreads to his shoulders. He looked Hispanic, at least in part. He had a tattoo of a snake crawling out from under his collar. "B-Ray," he said. She stared up at him and raised an eyebrow. In her nervousness she somehow didn't understand that this was his name, that he was introducing himself, so finally she just blinked and looked away.

"You deaf, new girl?"

"You rude?"

"So what's your name?"

"You just said it. New girl."

He laughed. "That's easy to remember. That's what I'm gonna call you."

Classes were ridiculous. Her Spanish teacher talked about his supposedly favorite novel, *Love and Death in the Time of Cholera*, and no one even bothered to correct him. In American history, the teacher mispronounced the word Hessians. This same teacher called her by name and asked her to read from her paper, apparently due that day, about her summer reading assignment.

"I can't," said Emily, her voice filling the hushed classroom.

"And why not?"

"I didn't get the assignment."

The teacher shook her head. "Everyone got the assignment."

Emily couldn't stop her voice from shaking. "I'm new."

"New?"

"I'm a transfer."

"Well, why didn't you say so? Welcome to Wall. Now, let's hear from someone else."

She vowed not to speak in class again. In the hallway, among the throng, she looked for the tall boy with the dreads. *B-Ray.* He would be easy to notice; he towered over the crowd. She caught a glimpse of him standing by a locker, but she panicked and turned the other way.

At last, the final bell. She waited in the parking lot for Audrey, cursing that she didn't have a car of her own: her parents wouldn't even let her get her license. A yellow bus pulled away from the curb and roared off, everyone inside yelling. Kids peeled off down the street, honking horns. From the playing fields came screams and a whistle.

Someone came up beside her. She gave a quick glance: a jock in a varsity jacket, his friends lurking behind him. After a moment he said, "So how was your first day?" She smiled, relieved that she'd been noticed, but she could sense something mocking in his expression, in the expectant face of the boys behind.

"Fuck off," she said and walked to the other end of the lot.

Her mother was fifteen minutes late.

"What the hell, Audrey?" She got in, dropping her backpack at her feet. They'd given her mammoth textbooks for nearly every class.

"I'm sorry, honey. I haven't figured out these back streets yet. How did it go?"

Emily shook her head.

"Not good?"

"Abysmal, Mother." Her eyes were filling with tears; she turned toward the passenger window, looking out at nothing.

"It can't be *that* bad."

"It's worse."

Her mother sighed. "None of this was my idea."

WEEKS PASSED, autumn turned everything earth-toned. School sucked, worse than she'd even imagined. She didn't make a single friend. She went through the halls alone, her books clenched to her chest. At the start, she'd tried to decipher the hierarchy, deciding who she should talk to, who she should avoid. It was a large school, more than two hundred in the senior class, and the social order was not immediately apparent. The pack of mall blondes were popular, but they didn't want her, and the feeling was mutual. They were Spackle girls, caked in makeup, dressed atrociously, probably none of them had even been to New York. But there was a part of her that wanted their attention anyway, wanted them to want to know her. It didn't make sense. At Denton she'd ascended to the top of the social structure with no effort. Here, she was invisible, irrelevant, shunned. When they didn't come to her, she decided not to care. At lunch she sat by herself, looking out the window at B-Ray and his pals in the rear courtyard, wanting to know them, because bad boys would be good for her reputation; with their drugs and tattoos, they offered a certain level of cover. Mainly she wanted out; she couldn't wait to graduate. A few weeks into the semester someone broke into the school at night and smashed up the trophy cases and administrative offices. It was a building that *should* be trashed, all bad karma and tears and wasted time. But as long as she was stuck here, at this miserable place, she wanted to be known, talked about, envied.

Saturday mornings felt like a reprieve; she didn't have to get up, dress, confront the masses. She stayed in bed, listening to music on her iPod, texting and emailing friends from the city. She would open her calculus textbook and doodle in the margins: designs for dresses, skirts, purses. Above these figures she wrote in an elaborate script: *Fashions by Emily Ricci*. Her designer name, borrowed from her favorite actress. She opened an issue of *Vogue* and copied some of the evening gowns, then colored them with a red marker. Disembodied gowns. Sometimes she'd add a single arm or leg to the drawing.

One Saturday in October, a blue-collar dude banged around the house all morning, putting in new light switches and fixtures. Her mother hissed at her for flirting with the guy, but she wasn't flirting; she was playing him. When he went outside to get a tool, she followed him to bum a cigarette. They smoked leaning against his truck. Most workmen had drugs on them, she'd learned, but when she asked if she could buy any, he teased her and called her jailbait.

"You're not worth the risk," he said.

"Jerk," she said, tossing the cigarette at him.

In the afternoon her mother barged into her bedroom to announce that Sheba had escaped.

"How?"

"The electrician—" said Audrey impatiently. "Just come help."

Emily pulled a sweater over her tank top, a floppy V-neck with moth holes in the sleeves, and buttoned on a skirt. This—rather than the false polish of her school outfits—was her usual look: mismatched layers over long skirts. The sweater had come from one of the first boys she'd ever dated, a senior, during her freshman year. Daniel had met him and hated him, of course. ("Phony," he'd called him, "wanna-be," which was a pretty good summation.) It had lasted only a month anyway. But he was her first older boy, and she liked it. Boys her own age didn't interest her; they didn't know anything; they hyperventilated when they kissed her, and they had none of the things she liked.

"I can't believe you lost my dog."

"Hurry. Put your sneakers on."

Emily grabbed an elastic hair tie from the dresser and followed her mother into the bright afternoon.

"Sheba," her mother called. *"Sheeeeba, come!"*

A lawn guy, clipping hedges next door, glanced over. Emily saw him take in the spectacle of Audrey, screaming at the top of her lungs. *Embarra-Mom.*

"You don't have to yell like that," she said.

"How else will the dog hear me?"

"You can yell less hysterically. Dogs have very good hearing."

"Please, Emily."

"You sound like a disturbed person."

"I am disturbed. You are disturbing me."

Geese flew overhead, honking and flapping furiously, the V formation moving over the hill.

"Go down toward the grammar school. I'll go up the street."

"Good thinking, Mom. That way we'll double our search capacity. Why didn't I think of that?"

"Thanks for the sarcasm, Em. That's a big help."

Her mother started up the hill, pumping her arms like an Olympic race walker. Emily pitied her, how ridiculous she looked. When her mother tied her hair back, her nose looked enormous, the same awful nose she'd inflicted on Emily, the only feature they shared. Two years ago Emily had asked her parents for a nose job. Many of her friends had gotten them, and summer was the time to do it, when no one would know. Her parents refused. There was nothing wrong with her nose, they said, couldn't she see that? She was a beautiful girl, her face was lovely. Everyone tells you how beautiful you are, do you think they're all lying? Do you think it's a conspiracy? Why would she want to change her nose? "Because it's long and bloated at the end," she told them. "I have a penis nose, and so do you, Mother." Her father sent her to her room for that one. But how was she supposed to feel? *Beautiful?* She could barely look at herself in the mirror. Her nose, too big. And her chin was sort of dented, like Willem Dafoe's. On a man like him, with his wide face and acne scars, the chin worked. On her face, a disaster. She wanted to fix her nose, her chin, and she wanted a tattoo on her wrist, a lowercase *d* in the font of an old typewriter followed by a period: *d* for Daniel. No, said her parents. No to the nose job, no to the chin job, no to the tattoo. No to everything.

It hadn't always been this way; they used to be much cooler. When she was thirteen, she'd read about Denton, an alternative private high school on the Upper East Side that allowed students to design their own curriculum. She showed her parents the website and they talked it over with her like an adult, and they agreed to let her go there instead of Greenwich High, even though it cost thirty thousand dollars a year and meant taking the train into the city. Each morning her mom or dad dropped her at Metro-North in Greenwich—a ninth grader climbing the platform alongside the business suits, the train roaring toward her: This was being alive. The city was a secret she carried with her back to Connecticut every night: the crowded subway, the street musicians playing Bach on violins and cellos, the homeless men who called to her as she passed, the lights of downtown, beyond anything she could have imagined. It seemed unbelievable that this life existed, just an hour from Cos Cob.

Denton was another revelation. The kids were nothing like her classmates in junior high. They knew movie directors and famous chefs, and they'd been to places like Madeira, Hong Kong, Johannesburg. They didn't treat her like a freak because she had her own style. Some of her classmates were related to famous writers. Harold Bloom came to school one afternoon to lecture about Shakespeare, his belly jiggling as he paced before the chalkboard. Another day, after school, a movie star drove up in a Porsche convertible to pick up his sister, and he winked comically at Emily, the same expression she'd seen him make on-screen.

At Denton she made friends with the kinds of people who didn't seem to exist in Cos Cob: mixed-race boys, gay boys, drug dealer boys. Her best friend, Leo, lived in Chelsea with his father and his father's boyfriend, a fashion designer. Emily stayed over at their loft a few times a month, gorging on sushi or foie gras, while the boyfriend showed her sketches of clothes he'd created for YSL.

Another friend, Douglas, a scholarship student from Camden, taught her how to punch—how to make a fist, how to turn her body. She would stand outside the front gates of Denton, punching his biceps. "Harder," he would say, no matter how hard she hit him, "I can't feel it." She would throw lefts and rights until her hands were sore. And then he would half-hit her if she asked for it, once on her arm, as heavy as a sledgehammer. How wonderful, that feeling of deadness and the bruise that would blossom later, the deep purple flower, and the sensation that lingered. She and Douglas didn't get together, they only punched each other; but the feeling was just as satisfying as sex, maybe more so.

Numbness was what she wanted. After the accident, she didn't want to feel, think, exist. She sought out oblivion. Her prescription for pain: more pain. It somehow brought her closer to Daniel, to wherever he was. At times he seemed so close, she could hear his voice. He could not be dead, not really. He was somewhere else, she just had to figure out where. She went with boys to their parents' apartments, unoccupied in midafternoon. She did not feel used afterward. Just the opposite. It had felt good and she had pleased the boy; he'd held her close and wanted her, she could see the need in his eyes. That was the main pleasure, the feeling of being desired, of being beautiful, of being at the center of someone's world. The act didn't last long; a few minutes, and it was done. How could she tell them that they were too gentle? That she wanted that sensation of numbness, like when Douglas punched her? She wanted them to know this, but the boys, even the bad boys and drug dealer boys, the ones who gave her coke and X, even they never seemed to figure it out. And of course saying it was impossible, it would defeat the point. None of them knew how she felt, the emptiness without Daniel. Even Douglas, even Leo, who said they could only imagine, who said they would do anything to help—even they seemed to retreat from her. She didn't blame them, not really. Of course it was too much for them. It was too much for *her.*

Now, though, all that was over. Her father had transferred to Hartford. Her parents forced her to leave Denton before her senior year, even though she'd asked them if she could stay with Leo and his dad in the city—it was fine with them. But, no. Instead they'd moved to this creaky old house in the middle of nowhere, hours from the city, and she had to be the new kid, all over again.

She crossed the intersection and headed down the hill toward the grammar school. The sunny afternoon had drawn the suburbanites out to their driveways and yards, washing cars and raking leaves. *Have you seen a malamute?* she wanted to ask. But she couldn't do it—that moment of approach, the collision of strangers: The expectation was too great, like when you had to tell the waiter your order; always, at that instant, she could barely speak. So she passed by, glancing about for Sheba. There were dogs in nearly every yard—Labs and golden retrievers, boxers and German shepherds—and all of them barked at her, but no Sheba.

Then, out of nowhere, Emily found herself worried, sickeningly so. What if Sheba had gotten run over? What if she was lying by the side of the road, broken and bleeding? She closed her eyes, driving away the image, and did what she always did when a dark feeling smothered her: She spoke to Daniel.

Do you think she's okay?

And his voice, from somewhere inside her, wiped away the anxiety, as it always did.

She's fine, Em. Don't worry.

Where is she?

She's having fun. She's playing.

She allowed herself a private smile. Daniel had always wanted a malamute. They'd seen some movie when they were little about a wild pack of dogs, all malamutes, living in Canada, and Daniel had never gotten over it. Her parents had finally caved on his fourteenth birthday, taking him to a breeder. *That one with the black muzzle,* he'd said, picking Sheba out of the litter. *She's the one.*

Up ahead, Emily noticed a boy leaning against a Jeep, staring at her. There was a pickup truck in the driveway. Through the open garage door she saw an assortment of junk: old furniture, metal pipes, big rubber tires.

"Hey," he said as she came near.

"Hey."

He was shirtless, smoking a cigarette in the sun. He had tattoos on his chest and arms. She recognized him—one of the boys from school who hung around the rear courtyard anchor at lunchtime, listening to rap.

"You're in my history class," he said.

She nodded.

"I'm Billy."

"I know."

"What's your name?"

Emily kicked a pebble. "Why should I tell you?"

"You don't have to. It's Emily Martin-Murray. With a hyphen. All you stuck-up girls have hyphens."

"Don't you mean hymens?"

He snorted. "That too."

She looked down, pleased with herself. As foreign as she felt talking to boys, she somehow didn't show it. Some actress part of herself took over, at ease, good at teasing. Not her, really. Her representative. The girl they wanted to see.

He exhaled a long line of smoke. "You live around here?"

"Two streets that way. We moved here a few months ago."

"Lucky you."

"I'm looking for a dog. A malamute. You happen to notice one?"

He shook his head. "I hate dogs. You see this?" He pointed to the side of his face. She took a step closer. A scar on his cheek, shaped like a half-moon. "A hundred and fifty stitches," he said. "Rottweiler got me when I was eight. Wouldn't let go. My dad came out of the house and cracked it with a baseball bat."

"I like scars. I wish I had one like that."

Up close she could better see the tattoos. Words in Spanish on his neck. LA VIDA LOCA. On his biceps, the face of Jesus. And bunny ears on his pecs.

"I got plenty of scars." He stuck out his right leg and raised his jeans, revealing a patch of mottled skin on his calf. "Motorcycle burn," he said. He showed her a few more on his hands and upper back.

"I've only got one," she said.

"Show me."

She nearly did. The cross on her inner thigh, she'd cut it into herself with an X-Acto knife. The skin had peeled away so cleanly, revealing the pure layer of white, the blood bubbling out. "Can't."

He shrugged. "What's a malamute look like?"

"Like a husky."

"Haven't seen one of those." It was clear from his tone that he was done with the conversation.

She turned and headed back the way she'd come.

"Hope you find him," he called.

"Her."

"Whatever."

She knew he was watching. She tried not to hurry. Why had she worn her ugliest skirt, the plaid one her mother had given her last Christmas? Her ass looked huge in it. When she reached the end of the street she glanced back, and he was still there, staring.

"Hey," he called. "What's your number?"

HE CALLED that evening and they talked for a couple of awkward minutes, and the next day they hooked up after school at his house. Afterward, she lay on his bed in purple panties and a toe ring, watching him fiddle with the joystick. Her jeans, shirt, and sweater lay on the floor next to her black motorcycle boots. She could never understand the male fascinations: video games, heavy metal, comic books. Each boy had his own particular obsession, which he would explain to her in excruciating detail. The "genius" of some band or movie: *South Park. The Big Lebowski.* "Check it out," the boy would say, wrapping the headphones over her ears or sliding the DVD into the player. "Awesome, right?"

Billy Stacks was no different. Sex on his twin bed had taken two minutes. But his GameCube captivated him so thoroughly that, even after an hour of wrestling with the joystick, he couldn't avert his attention for a moment to answer her question. He sat at his desk with his feet up, staring at the television, his eyes darting.

She asked again. "Do you have any pills?"

The walls of his room were covered with posters of swimsuit models and rap artists. His little brother's twin bed had a comforter decorated with horses. The room smelled like sweat socks and stale food, along with the lingering scent of her own sex.

"Check this out," he said.

She glanced at the screen. In the game, a U.S. Army soldier moved through an underground passageway while the bass thumped out of the subwoofer like a crazed heartbeat. Suddenly, from around a corner, a villain wearing a turban appeared, raising a machine gun. Billy thumbed the joystick and the villain's head exploded; three torrents of red sprayed out of the carcass.

"What is it?"

"*Spider Hole II,*" he said. "I live for this shit."

"It's really stupid. You know that, right?"

Emily picked a Victoria's Secret catalog off the night table; there was a whole stack of them, going back for years. It was an old issue, with Gisele on the cover. Flipping through the pages, looking at the smooth hip bones and perfect thighs, she felt fat and envious.

"Turn that down," a woman screeched.

Billy paused the game, and Emily grabbed her sweater off the floor.

"Dammit, Billy, I can hear it from across the street. And how many times have I told you not to lock your door?"

"Chill, Mom. You're acting totally uncool."

"Does your friend want dinner? I've got fried chicken and potatoes."

Emily said, as loudly and politely as she could, "No thank you."

"What about you, Billy?"

"No. Can you stop standing outside the door like a narc?"

"You're supposed to be studying, not playing video games. And I want this door unlocked. Now."

Emily heard her steps moving down the hallway. Billy shook his head. "Ever since my dad took off she's been acting like supermom. Baking brownies and shit."

"My mother hasn't made cookies in forever." She set the catalog back on his night table and picked up a framed photograph: Billy, a few years younger, with long curly hair, standing next to a man dressed in Army greens on a tarmac, in front of a helicopter. It was a sunny day; both were wearing aviator sunglasses.

"Is this your dad?"

"Yeah. They got divorced last year."

"Is he in the Army?"

"Marines."

"Where is he now?"

"Deployed."

"You mean Iraq?"

"Afghanistan."

She put the picture back on his night table. "Do you miss him?"

He shrugged. "He emails almost every week."

"Is he coming back soon?"

"Dunno. They never tell you that kind of thing."

"Are you worried about him?"

"My dad? No way. He can take care of himself. And that's putting it lightly." Billy had small, mean-looking brown eyes, and he was always puffing out his chest. He wasn't more than an inch taller than Emily.

His cell phone began vibrating on the desktop. He picked it up and glanced at the display, then grinned and texted something back. It was the fifth text, at least, since she'd arrived at his house.

"Who's that?"

"No one."

"Is it your girlfriend? Because I don't care, if you want to know the truth."

"Actually, it's none of your business, bitch." He turned back to the game, unpaused, and turned down the volume so his mother wouldn't hear.

"Fuck off, asshole." She grabbed her boots and bent to put them on. She was struggling with the second boot when he bear-hugged her from behind.

"Hey, don't get all freaky. I'm just goofing around."

He had small, sharp muscles, and she liked the feel of him squeezing her. She went limp under his grip. "Don't call me a bitch. Ever."

"Okay."

"Got it? I can't stand that word."

"I got it." He let her go. "And there isn't any girlfriend. It's B-Ray, that's all."

"You know him?"

"Course. He's my boy."

"I have English with him," she said. "He's hot. Seriously hot."

"Yeah, all the bitches say that."

She opened her mouth in astonishment. "Oh my god. What did I just say?"

"I didn't call you a bitch," he protested. "I said *all the bitches.*"

She sighed. "What does he want?"

He shrugged.

"Tell me," she demanded, "or I'm leaving right now."

"It's no big deal. I texted him, you and I were hanging out and he started writing back like every three minutes."

"Why?"

"Wants details."

"About me?"

"Who else?"

She tried to keep herself from blushing. "What did you tell him?"

"That's between bros—hey!"

She grabbed the phone and saw the words *big titties* on the screen before he wrestled it back from her.

"Seriously? *Big titties?*"

He stashed the phone in his jeans pocket. "That's a compliment. You got great tits. Most girls would be happy to hear that."

"I'd be happier if you weren't texting about it."

"I was just answering a question."

"What question?"

He sighed. "B-Ray wanted to know, nice ass, nice boobs, or what. Guy stuff."

She rolled her eyes. "Tell me about him."

"Like what?"

"Like everything."

B-Ray, he said, was the first friend he'd made at Wall High. Billy Stacks had moved here from Dallas a year earlier, after his father left. As a military kid he'd switched schools enough to know not to make friends with anyone the first couple of days. But he and B-Ray—there was no doubt. They had everything in common. They both sat in the last row in homeroom, wore the same kinds of clothes, had the same music on their iPods.

"And you text each other every time some girl sleeps with you."

"Just the rich bitches."

She reached to smack him, but he grabbed her around the waist and lifted her in the air. She shrieked in surprise, then covered her mouth. He carried her to the chair in front of the TV, setting her on his lap, bouncing her up and down like a carnival ride.

"Okay, okay," she said, laughing. "I'm getting dizzy."

"What kind of drugs you want, chica?"

"I already told you."

"You some kind of junkie?"

"Does that mean yes?"

"It means, I can get anything you want, anytime you want."

"Do you have a dealer?"

"I don't need no dealer. I get what I want, right out there." He gestured toward the window. "They all got their little medicine cabinets."

"You mean break into houses?"

"Damn straight. You down for that?"

"I bet I've stolen more than you."

He laughed. "Yeah, right."

"Not from houses. From stores. You don't believe me? Let's go to the mall, I'll show you."

"You crazy, girl."

The video game recaptured his attention. He picked up the joystick and fiddled with the controls. The figure on the screen switched from a man to a woman, with her name blazoned across her chest in red letters, MISS DESTRUCTION. A curvaceous blonde dressed in skintight Army greens, cradling a rifle. "That's you," he said.

"I like me."

"This is your directional, the toggle. The red button is your weapon. Double-click for rapid fire. You ready?"

"Double-click?"

"Never mind. You'll get the hang of it." He pressed the button. "Okay. Go."

Within a few seconds, before she even got off a single shot, the bad guys cut off her head with a machete. Then they danced on top of her corpse and dragged her through the streets, shouting in Arabic.

"You got wasted," he said.

THAT WEEK they hung out every day after school at his place. He kept offering her hits off his joints until he finally got the message that she liked pills, not pot. Okay, he said, we'll get some tonight.

"Really?"

"Yes, really," he said.

Back at her house that evening, a Thursday, Emily endured her parents' obligatory late-night rituals—her dad flipping between Leno and CNN in the den, her mom appearing at her door, face smeared with cream, *Everything okay, honey?*—until at last, at midnight, they settled down to their unquiet slumbers. She killed some time on her laptop and texting Leo and a few other friends in the city, who never slept anyway, waiting for 2:00 A.M. At last, she dialed Billy's cell. "Are you ready?"

He sounded groggy. "Who's this?"

"Wake up, jackass. It's time to go."

He coughed. "Oh, right. We doing this?"

"Yes, we're doing this. I'll be at your house in five minutes."

She listened for any sound from her parents' bedroom; the house was so cramped, you could hear everything. Except for the ticking of the hall clock, all seemed perfectly quiet. She pulled on a black fleece jacket and her black yoga pants. She tiptoed down the hall, carrying her sneakers, pausing when the kitchen door creaked and Sheba raised her head to study her for a moment before collapsing back on her cushion.

Outside, the wind gusted. She considered going back for her winter coat, but decided against it. Too risky. How could she explain taking a stroll at 2:00 A.M. on the coldest night in October? She hurried across the intersection, not a car in sight. She clutched the neck of her jacket to keep the wind from getting in. As she passed a driveway, a bright light came on, startling her, but it was just a motion sensor. Most of the houses were wholly dark except for the stray porch or kitchen light, everyone snug in their beds, the wind howling. No one was looking out the window, no one could see her shivering in the street.

Her heart was racing, that same thrill. She'd started shoplifting when she was eleven or twelve. The first time had been an accident; she'd been standing in the checkout line at the grocery store with her mother, reading *Seventeen*; only when she got to the car did she realize she hadn't paid for the magazine. Just like that, that simple. She told Daniel what she'd done, and he said it was stupid. He didn't get the thrill of it, the way she did. In junior high, she would hit the mall after school with her friends, picking their stores. At first, it was little things, things she could fit into her pocket: a tube of lipstick, fake pearl earrings. She started carrying an oversize bag. She would pay for a toothbrush at CVS, smiling angelically, making conversation with the cashier, her bag loaded with mascara and nail polishes, lotions and makeup. The sensors at the door did nothing. Then, she started on clothes. She would go into dressing rooms and slip on whatever she wanted under her coat. It was easy. In department stores she would pick out a nice pair of shoes—Coach heels, BCBG flats—and put them on, stuff her own shoes into her bag. She told Billy Stacks about it, how she'd carried a jackknife to cut the security tags off expensive dresses or purses. She had two Chanel bags, a closet filled with designer clothes, price tags still hanging from the sleeves. She'd never gotten caught.

"That's cause they're not watching little rich white girls like you," said Billy.

It was true, she didn't need money. She could simply ask her father, and if he said no, which was rare, it didn't matter; he and her mother left their wallets around the house. She would take a couple of twenties whenever she wanted, and they never noticed. She stole for the rush, not the money. She and Billy made a deal: He could keep whatever they got except for the pharmaceuticals.

Pharmies were her department.

She kept stashes in her closet and school locker. Douglas, her pal from Denton, sent her pills in ancient cassette cases every couple of weeks. Billy Stacks smoked weed all the time, but she didn't like the mellow, hazy way it made her feel. She liked coke and scripts: painkillers and tranquillizers. She could go the day, sometimes, without opening one of her bottles, but she couldn't fathom the notion of *not* having some medication on hand. When her stash got low, she became panicky. How did people do without? Pills to get going, pills to fall asleep, pills to ward off bad thoughts. At friends' houses, she raided parental medicine cabinets: Ambien, Vicodin, Xanax, even Viagra (which all the fathers seemed to have), which she would trade or sell. One time, a few years back in Greenwich, she'd cleaned out the bathroom cabinet of some friend of her dad, after her parents had dragged her and Daniel to a law firm Christmas party, with about fifty guests. She'd disappeared upstairs and found at least twenty brown bottles, the best haul ever, a zillion Xanax, the two-milligram kind. Take one of those and you entered the outskirts of heaven.

Billy Stacks appeared in his driveway wearing a dark tracksuit, carrying a backpack. "Fucking cold," he said.

"Why didn't you wear a coat?"

He shrugged. "Come on."

They went back the way she had come, crossing the street by her house. She glanced at her parents' darkened bedroom window and pictured them sleeping with their backs to each other, illuminated by the green night-light from the bathroom, like an Edward Hopper painting. Her father snoring, her mother lying on her side, clutching a pillow in front of her face. Thinking of her parents—so helpless, so pitiful—could make her cry. Being in their presence infuriated her; only when she was away from them could she feel any sort of affection.

Billy turned up Juniper Lane, the street parallel to hers. "It's a private road," he said. She raised the sleeve of her sweater and wiped her nose, which had begun to run in the night air. "You see or hear anything, you whistle. Got it?"

"Yeah."

"You know how to whistle, right?"

"Yeah," she said. "I just put my lips together and blow."

He went up the driveway of the corner lot, slightly crouched. A station wagon was parked in front of the garage. She watched as he opened the passenger door—the inside dome flashed on—and got in the car. No movement came from the house. Water trickled down the sewer in the middle of the street. She waited. Finally he appeared, creeping toward her with that catwalk of his, and she began to giggle.

"What?"

"This is fun."

"I got a wallet from the glove compartment," he said, holding it up. "And some shades." He put on the sunglasses, oversize pink ones, for an old lady. He slipped the loot into his backpack and zipped it up. "Come on."

The minivan in the next driveway was locked. But the SUV beside it opened and he disappeared inside. She no longer noticed the cold. The night was overcast, a long blanket of gray, obscuring the stars. The wind didn't bother her. She liked when it gusted because the sound drowned out their footsteps and the opening and closing of car doors. He joined her at the end of the driveway, jiggling the pack. "Bunch of CDs," he said.

It was easy. Half the cars were unlocked. Twice he disappeared through garage doors. Each time she waited silently for him to emerge, watching his flashlight beam streaking across the darkened windows.

When they reached the house at the top of the street, a cul-de-sac, he said, "Your turn."

"Really?"

"Go for it, Little Miss Klepto," he said, handing her the backpack.

The driveway was long, curved, and steep. She glanced up at the house, toward the dark third-floor windows. The car was an old Mercedes convertible, unlocked. She opened the driver's door and slipped in. The interior smelled like pine air freshener. She opened the glove compartment and the little bulb went on: CDs, owner's manual, a ten-dollar bill, a scattershot of business cards, a pack of cigarettes, a pile of coins. She swept it all into the backpack. In the backseat, she saw a *Vogue* and a red teddy bear holding a heart that said I LOVE YOU, and grabbed them too. Suddenly a face appeared against the window—she nearly screamed—but it was only Billy, making a goofy smile. "You almost gave me a heart attack," she said, getting out of the car.

"Come on," he said. "We can get in through the basement."

She eased the car door shut, barely making a sound. "Are you kidding? They're *home*, dipshit. You can't just—"

"Suit yourself," he said.

He went around the back of the house. She waited, staring after him. Was he really going to break in? He was probably just screwing with her again. In a second he would jump out from behind the bushes and scare the crap out of her. She squinted after him into the darkness, holding her breath.

Then came a shrieking—an enormous horn bellowing. The sound was shocking, incapacitating. A moment later she saw Billy scrambling down the lawn, waving for her to follow. She ran after him across the backyard. They vaulted over a wooden fence and disappeared into some woods, she falling behind, branches whipping her face. In the distance the alarm continued to roar, and unseen dogs joined in, howling and barking. Her sneakers slipped on the grass and she nearly fell. Ahead, Billy jumped over a low stone wall. She followed, scraping her hand on a rock and kicking over an empty planter. They ran along the dark side of a house and finally emerged into the street.

"Come on!"

He grabbed her hand and they ran downhill. They were making so much noise, their sneakers slapping against the asphalt, the rattling of his backpack. At the bottom of the street—*her street,* she realized with a shock; they were outside her own house—they crossed the intersection and kept running all the way to his house. He led her to a toolshed in the backyard and they collapsed onto the floor.

"Who taught you to run?"

"Fuck off," she said, gasping for breath. She rolled onto her back, her chest heaving. There were bags of fertilizer, wood chips, and soil piled against the wall, smelling like cow shit. Faint moonlight streamed through the cracked window above the door.

A car came along the street, its engine rumbling loudly. He said, "Shhh." They looked at each other, eyes wide, as the noise of the car came closer, then very near, then slowly faded into the distance.

"Cop," he said.

"How can you tell?"

He shrugged. "You cold?"

"Not anymore."

"Check it out." He unzipped the backpack and dumped the contents onto the wooden floor. A silver flask fell out, along with all the rest. He unscrewed the top and took a sip. "Whiskey," he said, wiping his lips.

"The pink sunglasses are mine."

"I'm keeping the wallet," he said.

"What happened back there?"

"Fucking ADT, is what happened. I kicked in the door and two seconds later, screech."

"My heart's still racing." She placed his hand on her chest. "Feel."

"Feels good." He ran his hands under her sweater and pushed her tits together.

She pushed him away. "Your hands are fucking cold."

"Rest of me's warm," he said, rolling on top of her.

Outside the wind whined. Miles away, trucks hummed along the interstate, like a far-off surf. All those people going places in the middle of the night. It was just a few hours before dawn, and so perfectly dark. She heard the wind rattling the windowpane and her own voice, whispering the words guys liked to hear.

AT DAWN the skies opened and rain clattered on the rooftop. Back in her bed, Emily drifted in and out of dreams, knowing she was oversleeping but not caring. So what if she were late for school? Besides, it wasn't her fault. Her mother woke her every morning precisely an hour before school. Then she would usually return a few more times to cajole and yell at her to get up. But this morning the door didn't open, her mother didn't appear.

Finally Emily roused herself, went down the hallway, and peered into her mother's bedroom. She was curled under the comforter, a pillow over her head. "Mom," she called softly, then louder, and at last Audrey turned toward her, blinking. "Mom? Are you sick?"

"What time is it, honey?"

Emily went to the bed and slipped under the comforter. "Ten."

Audrey blinked. "How did that happen?" She moved to get up, but

Emily draped her arm over her. She felt like a girl again, like when they were little and she and Daniel used to snuggle with Audrey after her dad went to work.

"Chill, Mom."

"You have to get to school."

"I don't have class till eleven." A lie, but her mother wouldn't question her. Emily lied to her all the time—about where she went, what she did, what she ate—but her mother wouldn't want to know the truth about those things anyway.

"Don't you have to be in study hall or something like that?"

"You can fill out a pink card."

"I've filled out too many of those pink cards already."

"Just one more hour, Mother. Then you can drive me to school." She pulled her close, stealing her warmth. She was so tiny. Emily felt huge beside her. Why couldn't she have gotten her mom's body? Boys liked short curvy girls. Instead she'd inherited her father's big arms and broad, Scottish ass.

"Am I a terrible mother for letting you sleep in?"

"Like I'm going to miss anything. That school isn't exactly challenging. Denton was ten times harder. Besides, I've got all As and nearly perfect SAT scores, remember?"

"How did you manage that anyway? The best I could do was twelve eighty."

"I can't believe you remember your SAT scores."

"Does that make me a nerd?"

"A *nerd*, Mom?"

"Whatever the word is these days."

"The word is the same. It's using it that's problematic. Why are you so warm?"

Audrey turned toward her. "Honey, are you planning to shower before school?"

"Why?"

"You smell a little."

"Mother!" Emily sniffed her underarm. "You're right. I reek." All that running around last night; then later in the shack, fucking on top of a bag of wood chips. She still had on the same clothes. She hoped she didn't smell like sex.

Audrey yawned. "Your father couldn't sleep. He woke me up early today. Still, I don't know why I'm so tired."

"You're always tired when it rains. You and Sheba both."

"Thirty more minutes, sweetie. Then we get going."

"You said an hour."

"No, *you* said an hour."

"Fine, thirty minutes."

Her mother was asleep again almost immediately, her mouth falling open. Emily watched the comforter rise and fall above her. Every so often a sound came from Audrey's mouth, like a distant seagull squawking. The rain on the roof was a drumming of hooves, a hundred horses running. All that rain, where did it go? Water in the gutters, funneling into sewer pipes, seeping underground. A soggy earth, sliding away underneath her.

WHEN HER mother dropped her off in front of school, Emily dashed toward the door, carrying her backpack, getting soaked in only a few seconds. It was mid-period, the hallway empty but still stinky with the student smell. The overhead fluorescent lights hissed like summer insects. She wiped the rain from her face.

"You're late."

She jumped. She hadn't seen him, standing beside the lockers: *B-Ray*. He towered over her, eight inches taller, maybe more, his long, thick dreads pulled straight back.

"Who elected you hall monitor?"

He brought his mouth close to her ear, so close she could feel his breath, his hands buried in his pockets. "I heard you were looking for something for your nose."

"Who told you that?"

"B. Stack."

"What else did he tell you?"

He smirked. "You really want to know?"

"Sure."

"He says you give good head."

"What is this, junior high? I'd have told you the same thing if you asked."

She walked away, knowing he would follow, and he did, falling in step beside her. He played on the basketball team, she knew, although she never went to any of the games, not football, not basketball, none of that rah-rah crap. She'd heard other stuff about him too: that he was a rapper in a group that had played at the school dance last spring; that he'd been suspended for a week for having a knife in his locker; that he'd gotten into a fistfight in the gym and knocked some kid's tooth out. In English, he sat in the back row and spent most of the time looking out the window. But she often caught him staring at her. She'd decided she would sleep with him a couple of weeks earlier when he'd stood up in class to read a poem, as they were all required to do that semester; he'd recited the lyrics to one of his own songs, which had a refrain she'd found herself repeating later in her head, remembering the musical way he'd said it. *Because it is what it is what it is.* He had expressive hands, forming the shape of the words as he spoke them.

He said, "Every girl says that. *I give good head.* That's just talk."

"You be the judge, then."

She stopped outside the girls' bathroom. He scratched his neck, sizing her up. "All right. Show me what you got."

"Whenever you want."

"What about today, after school?"

"What about that something for my nose? Or is that *just talk*?"

"That depends how much you want to spend."

She shook her head. "I don't pay for drugs. People give them to me." She batted her eyelashes, her mall girl routine. "Don't you want to give me something?"

He scoffed. "All right then. Parking lot after last period," he said, without looking back. His jeans were bunched below his hips, black briefs visible, boots untied, the laces dragging.

She waited until he turned the corner, then slipped into the bathroom, her heart pounding. Looking in the mirror, she raised her eyebrows, the same expression she'd used on B-Ray. Leo's dad's boyfriend—the YSL designer—once told her that she had "perfect eyebrows." They were okay, she guessed. Her eyes were good overall, maybe a bit large; she often looked startled. She dabbed some makeup on her nose, trying to tone it down. She had giant features—the long nose, the dark eyebrows, the wide mouth. Boys told her she was *hot.* But few kissed her during sex, and never afterward; they stared past her with that distant expression. She wondered what B-Ray would be like, what sounds he would make, how rough he would be, and she felt a surge of blood or adrenaline, something between fear and desire. She couldn't believe she was meeting him after school. She'd thought about him so much, ever since that first day. Now she would be with him.

A girl came into the bathroom, glanced at Emily, then went into a stall. A moment later came the sound of the toilet flushing—two, three times—to cover the sound of retching, Emily figured. She would do the same thing if someone were standing at the sinks. When the girl came out, Emily said, "Hey." She took the pill bottle out of her bag and swallowed a Xanax. "Want one?"

The girl shook her head and hurried to the door.

"Puke girl," said Emily under her breath.

At the end of the day, when the last bell rang and everyone swarmed toward the exits, she ducked into the bathroom. She took off her bra, stuffed it into her bag, and popped a Vicodin. She didn't want to feel anything quite so vividly right now. She left her mom a voice mail, telling her she was getting a ride with some friends, she'd be home before ten. When she approached B-Ray in the parking lot, he turned without saying a word and got into his car. He drove an old station wagon, the back end raised high. The black vinyl seats squeaked beneath her jeans. There were fuzzy dice hanging from the rearview mirror—a parody of a car her parents might have driven in the seventies. When he gunned the engine, the car gurgled like an outboard motor.

"My cousin's got everything you want," he said. "He got his own place in the city. Man make you dizzy with his crossover."

He continued talking, but she zoned out. She couldn't make him the person she wanted him to be if he kept saying stupid things. Finally he cranked the music to a deafening volume. He turned to her once during the drive, lowering the volume to ask, "You like it?"

She nodded—easier than trying to speak. The bass seemed to be reverberating through her, beating like another heart inside her. "Who is it?"

"Me. My group."

She recognized the refrain: *Because it is what it is what it is.*

Everything seemed to be moving slowly, a pleasant sensation, this Vicodin haze, a little deeper than normal. Had she taken more than usual? She tried to remember. A couple of Xanax in the morning, a Vicodin at lunch, another in the bathroom before leaving school. Keeping her eyes open took a profound effort; her eyelids seemed as heavy as the rain.

Daniel, I feel weird.
Open your eyes, dummy.
I can't.
Sure you can. Don't be a wuss.
I think I might pass out.
Or, you could observe the passing scenery. It's a rainy day in New England, blustery for this time of year. Rain expected until tomorrow morning. Remember to bring your umbrellas, kids!
Why are you so chipper?
Because you're drowsy and the music is way too loud.
And that makes you happy?
I'm trying to cheer you up, silly.

B-Ray parked the car, the music suddenly gone, a jarring silence. He got out, and she followed, nearly falling backward while climbing the tenement stairs. They went up to the third floor. B-Ray knocked and a guy appeared. The cousin. He had a huge smile. An enormous TV flashed sports highlights. In the kitchen they drank vodka out of plastic NY Yankees cups, which tasted like nothing. She embraced the feeling of letting go, of being here but not being here. The luxury of blacking out. Of not being able to remember what she was about to do. Of being close to Daniel in that silent place.

Later, she would remember asking for orange juice. The ding-dong doorbell ring tone from B-Ray's cell. The sound of cheering from the television. She surfaced twice, once with the cousin standing over her, the second time on the bed, on her stomach, someone fucking her from behind.

WHEN SHE came out of the haze, the room was dark. She found her bag by the bed and checked the time on her cell phone. It was a few minutes after ten o'clock. Past her curfew. Shit.

She found her clothes and followed the light down the hallway. B-Ray lay on the couch in the den, his face illuminated by flashes from the television.

"Yo," he said, not to her.

"Just in time, girl," said a bald guy. He was wearing long gym shorts and white tube socks, without a shirt. His chest was perfectly hairless, like his head, shaved clean. It came back to her. The cousin.

"I got to go," she said. "Can you give me a ride?"

B-Ray switched channels with the remote. "What's the rush?"

"Curfew," she said. She got a head rush, making it difficult to stand. "Whoa." She wavered, then sat on the rug, landing heavily on her ass. The room seemed to shake, and the boys laughed.

The cousin crouched next to her. "Check this out." He held out a hand mirror and razored a couple of lines. "This'll wake you up."

She took the rolled-up dollar bill and snorted both lines. That same charge as the first time she'd done it.

"More," she said.

SHE TOOK a cab home—late, really late, the sun coming up. Her parents were waiting for her in the den. They looked miserable and dead tired. They didn't bother to yell. "Why are you doing this to me?" her mother asked, a rhetorical question, apparently, because she didn't wait for a response. Everyone went to sleep.

The confrontation came the next afternoon, after her father went to play a "match." He'd even asked her to come along, as if she could sit there and watch, as if she could even look at a tennis ball without crying. Daniel used to juggle them for her, always bouncing the last one off his nose like a trained seal.

Around noon she took a book out to the backyard and sat on a lounge chair in the sun, with Sheba on the ground beside her. She couldn't read for long without dozing, her head foggy. She didn't remember much about the night before, and what she did remember she pushed away. When she went inside to get an Adderall for her head, her mother called her into the bathroom.

"Look," she said, standing over the bowl, and there were her pills, a hodgepodge of colors, like Froot Loops, floating in the toilet water. Before Emily could react, Audrey flushed, and Emily watched them swirl and disappear—a hundred pills, maybe more, at least five hundred dollars' worth. There would be some happy fish and frogs and baby alligators in the sewers tonight.

She tried to keep her pulse steady, tried not to think about her whole stash, gone. "I can't believe you went through my closet," said Emily, as evenly as she could.

"Where did you get those?"

"Why don't you read my journal while you're at it?"

"If it would help me understand why a perfectly healthy girl would take prescription drugs, maybe I should."

Her entire stash. This was a catastrophe. She had no backup supply. She had a few Adderall in her bag, but nothing for sleep or to slow the motions of her mind.

"I asked you a question."

"I'm not talking to you," said Emily.

She went into her room and locked the door. Her mother ranted outside, but Emily didn't respond. She vowed not to speak to her mother for a very long time. She called Douglas in New York and left a voice mail. It took him two hours to get back to her. No, he said, he had nothing. Things were dry.

Try back later, he told her.

WHEN THE sun went down she headed over to Billy's place with her homework, lugging her book bag, just to get out of the house. He and his mom were finishing dinner, hamburgers and French fries. The place smelled like burnt meat. She spotted the pan on the stove, greasy and black. Disgusting. His mom offered her some, but she told Mrs. Stacks she'd already eaten.

In his bedroom, she told Billy what had happened to her stash.

He nodded. "Okay. Lemme see what I got."

He disappeared for a few minutes and came back with an aspirin bottle, which he tossed to her. She opened it to make sure: BAYER ASPIRIN.

"Seriously?"

"My mom's. Don't make it look like you took any."

"It's aspirin, you idiot."

"You take it with a Coke. That's supposed to get you high, right?"

She tossed the bottle back to him. "Very funny."

He raised his leg and farted. "Cheeseburger, cheeseburger," he said.

"You are so gross."

"I just ate, it's not my fault."

"Why do you always do the wrong thing?"

Billy fussed with his phone; it was like a pacifier for him, that thing. It never left his hands. After ten minutes, just as she was getting into her schoolwork, he looked up and said, "What did you do last night?"

"Nothing. You?"

He shook his head.

Didn't he know? She'd assumed B-Ray would have filled him in already, the way those two gossiped. Wasn't he texting him right now, as they spoke?

"I called a few times," he said.

"I didn't get any calls."

"Did you check?"

"Of course I checked. What did you want?"

"I thought we might go out."

"Out?"

"A movie or something."

"Like a date? Why are you acting so weird?"

"What's weird? I thought we could go out, that's all."

"Let's go tonight."

He shook his head, his eyes on the phone, working with his thumbs. "I don't feel like it tonight. My stomach hurts." He scrunched his face and farted again.

"Aren't you going to say 'Cheeseburger, cheeseburger'?"

"It doesn't smell," he said.

Actually, it did. It smelled awful. She pulled her turtleneck over her nose. "Once more," she said, "and I'm leaving."

As she did her schoolwork, she was aware of him staring at her. He stared for a full minute, longer—until, finally, she lowered the book and said, "What?"

"So where did you go last night?"

"Why are you obsessing about last night?"

"I'm just asking."

"Shut up. I don't want to talk about it."

"Why not? Something happen?"

She ignored him.

"Because I heard you gangbanged B-Ray and his cousin."

She felt her skin go cold. "Did he tell you that?"

"Not exactly. I mean, he wasn't the first."

"What does that mean?"

He laughed. "Everybody knows, you moron."

"You're a fucking liar."

"And you're a major slut. Take a look." He held out the phone. She could see her profile. She was lying facedown on the bed, her ass bright white, most of the picture darkness and shadows, a lamp glowing yellow in the corner.

"How did you—"

"Check out this one."

She looked at the picture—and turned away immediately. She stuffed the book into her bag and went out the back door. By the side of the house she bent and threw up on the grass. She felt dizzy, her mouth filling again with bile. She would scratch his eyes out when she saw him. But, no. She wouldn't see him, she wouldn't go back to school, she couldn't go back to school, she would never go there again.

His voice came out of the darkness.

Em.

What do you want?

If number two pencils are the most popular, why are they still number two?

Seriously? You're telling jokes?

Yep.

Not funny. Not funny at all.

Okay. How about this one? What did the green grape say to the red grape? Breathe. Funny, right?

No.

Come on, admit it. You smiled.

I don't like jokes. You know that.

That's because you can't remember them. Even the ones I just told you. You probably forgot them already. You're the amnesia victim of joke telling.

Can you believe anyone would do that? I mean, what is the point?

Boys are creeps.

Trust me, I know.

Not all, though. Some of us are okay.

Yeah, the dead ones.

Ouch. You really know how to hurt a guy.

Sorry.

And besides, I'm not dead. I'm incognito.

You're in a casket buried in Fairhaven Cemetery.

Says you.

An oak casket that cost six thousand dollars. I saw the bill.

Wow. Somebody overpaid. Mom and Dad should have shopped around, gotten a few estimates. Maybe a secondhand one.

She wiped her eyes. *Okay. That was almost funny.*

Better than my one-liners?

Much.

The rain started, drenching her all at once. She hurried toward home with her arms wrapped around herself. At the intersection up ahead, she saw her mother walking with Sheba. She called out, but Audrey kept striding up the street and tugging Sheba's leash, not letting her sniff or pee or do the things she liked to do on a walk. "Mom!" she called, her voice cracking, the tears starting to fall. "Mom, wait!" She expected her mother to turn and notice her, but she didn't. Emily hurried after her, squinting against the rain, lugging her book bag. She was about to call out again, louder this time, when her mother turned up someone's driveway. A moment later the front door opened and she disappeared inside the house with the dog.

Emily reached the end of the driveway. What was going on? Her mother had no friends in this town; she had no social life whatsoever. All she did was read novels and burn through Netflix, the unlimited plan, piling up stacks of red envelopes for the mailman. Who did she know in that house? What was she doing in there? Borrowing a cup of sugar?

The house was dark except for a first-floor room around the side. After a few minutes, Emily crept across the lawn, staying in the shadows. In the yard, she maneuvered around some bushes and stood on her tiptoes, looking into the lighted window. The curtains were half-open. Inside, in the den, the fireplace was blazing. Audrey was standing in front of the fire, talking to a middle-aged guy with curly salt and pepper hair. He turned his back to Audrey and stared out the window with a blank look on his face. Emily froze. He seemed to be looking directly at her, but after a moment she realized he was not seeing her; she was invisible in the darkness beyond the window. Behind him, Audrey slipped out of her clothes and stood naked in a pair of fuck-me panties. She bent and put on black high heels. The guy turned around and embraced her, kissing her and reaching around to fondle her butt.

Emily felt like banging on the window and screaming, *What the fuck,*

Audrey? Soon her mother was pulling at the guy's pants, the both of them sliding to the floor. Emily found her way out of the bushes, wiping her face, the snot and tears. She ran home and waited in the den. She stared at the dark TV screen, registering nothing.

An hour and a half later Audrey returned, subdued, the dog hyper. Emily looked up from the couch. "Your face is red," she said.

"Does this mean you're talking to me again?"

"I'm making an observation about your face."

"Would you like some dinner? I made tofu earlier."

"Where did you go?"

"For a walk."

"You were gone a long time."

"Have you finished your homework?"

"You know what, Mother? I think I prefer not talking to you."

She went into the kitchen and found the plate of tufu and rice and took it into her room. A minute later came the sound of the shower from Audrey's bedroom. Washing off the sweat. Scrubbing away the dried semen.

This is un-fucking-believable. Can you even begin to believe this?

Poor Mom.

Poor Mom! Daniel, are you joking? First she flushes my stash, then she sneaks out for a quickie with the neighbor?

Maybe they were just making out.

Sure.

She's lonely, Em.

Is that what you call it? I can think of another word.

You know how Dad is. He takes her for granted.

He's an asshole, is what you mean.

No. He cares about us.

Seriously, Daniel. Since you went away, he's changed. He doesn't care about anyone. And now she's, like, Mrs. Robinson.

That doesn't even make sense.

You know what I mean.

Down the hall, the sound of the shower ceased.

THE NEXT DAY her mother pronounced that she was grounded for a month: She wasn't allowed to leave the house except for school. Emily glared at her but didn't respond. "And if I catch you sneaking out, because that's what you'll do, then it'll be another month. Understand?"

Was she joking? *Grounded?* The concept was a little anachronistic, like sock hops and the hula hoop, wasn't it? Emily found it humorous, almost. Humorous except that Audrey wouldn't drive her to the mall, wouldn't drop her at Starbucks or let her walk around at night in the town center, wouldn't let her do squat. How much time could she spend on MySpace without losing her marbles? She checked about ten times that day to see if anyone mentioned those pictures. So far, nothing.

Hypocrite, she nearly responded. *Adulteress.*

By Monday morning she couldn't stand being trapped in the house with Audrey anymore. Besides, she had to see Billy and get his phone and delete those pictures. B-Ray too. She hoped Billy had lied about *everyone* knowing. Maybe he was just jealous, trying to get back at her for going off with B-Ray. B-Ray was a total asshole to take those pictures. She couldn't believe how stupid she'd been—to have a crush on him all those weeks, without even knowing anything about him. He was a macho creep. How had she not known that? Talk about stupid—she'd stayed up all night doing coke with him and his jerk-off cousin *after* they'd already snapped those pictures of her, while she was passed out. Still, B-Ray wouldn't tell or show anyone besides Billy, would he? As for the cousin, he didn't even know her name, so who could he tell? No, it was probably just B-Ray and Billy, texting back and forth, their usual junior high bullshit. Maybe they were the only ones who'd seen the pictures. She decided to risk school.

She got dressed and went out to the car. While waiting for Audrey to unlock the door, Emily glanced up to see *him*, the boyfriend, cruising down the street in his wannabe Hummer. He was staring straight at her. *Gawking.* Emily raised her hand and flipped him off. He stared back, openmouthed, dumbfounded, which pleased her.

Fuck you, old man. Go fuck someone else's mother.

As soon as her mother dropped her at school, she went to the courtyard to find Billy Stacks, who was standing around the anchor with the usual crowd, shivering in place, blasting hip-hop. No sign of B-Ray. She beckoned to Billy with one finger, and after a while he came over, dragging his feet, his laces undone. He was wearing bright yellow basketball sneakers with black socks. He said, "What's up, gangbang?"

"Don't call me that."

"Why not?"

She tried to play it off. "Because two guys isn't a gangbang, dumb-ass."

"You should know."

"And if you call me that again, you won't be getting laid for a long time." She paused. "Nice socks, by the way."

"Nice reputation."

She ignored this only because she needed to get to the point. "Where's B-Ray?"

He shrugged. "He's your boyfriend. Go find him yourself."

"He's not my boyfriend. He's an asshole."

"Whatever."

"Can I see your phone?"

"What for?"

"Cause I left mine at home."

He shuffled his feet, looking down. "Not my problem."

"Don't be a jerk. I forgot to tell my mother something. I have to call her. It's important. I'll give it right back."

"One minute," he said. "I want it back in one minute."

"Fine," she said.

He passed it over. She checked to make sure it was unlocked. When he turned to rejoin his reject friends, she bolted. She ran into the building without looking back and went up to the second-floor music wing. At the end of that hallway, past the band room, were the individual practice rooms, which were soundproof. You could lock the door from the inside. She liked them for the sound-insulated quiet, a good place to chill away from the masses. In one of the rooms, a kid was honking on a saxophone; in the next, a guy was beating the drums. She tried a few doors and found the last one open. She slipped inside the tiny room without turning on the lights. She closed the door behind her and sat on a wooden bench in front of an upright piano.

She opened his phone and clicked on his in-box—*98% filled*, according to the meter. She scrolled down, snooping through texts, but mainly looking for anything from B-Ray. She found them, finally, two texts from last Saturday. There was a photo attached to the first text, and four more photos attached to the next. He hadn't CCed anyone on either text. The pics went to Billy alone, she was relieved to see.

She forced herself to click on the photos. One was a close-up of her tits. Another was a shot of her crotch, her legs spread open. Pale flesh, it could be anyone. But in the other three you could see and recognize her face. The worst one—she nearly got sick looking at it again—was the shot of her face with her eyes half-open, zombielike, and one of their dicks lying across her cheek, poking into the side of her mouth.

The first text said:

This is B Ray, yall. U get my leftovers Stack, to bad for U.

The second text said:

Yo, tell me this bitch deserves this!!!!! U see how big har hole is! Its from me!

From the nearby rooms, the muffled instruments seemed to get louder, a nonsensical collision of tom-toms and fast sax lines—two of the geeks from the jazz band practicing their parts. *Har hole.* Was that a misspelling? Or had he typed it that way on purpose? Was this some new slang—*har* meaning whore, like *ho*? Or was he just clumsy with his thumbs, as well as being a scumbag?

She deleted the photos one by one.

She checked Billy's sent mail to be sure he hadn't forwarded any of the photos, and went into My Pictures in case he'd saved them. He hadn't. There was one picture of her—he'd taken it in his bedroom that first afternoon—but she was clothed (black cardigan, blue and white tube skirt). She double-checked, looking for hidden folders. Pictures of his mom and dad, little brother, friends, a few other kids she recognized from school, his cat—that was it.

In his sent box there was a text to B-Ray from last weekend, in response to the first picture:

WTF? Is that real?

The next text said:

Not cool at all, B-Ray. Totaly uncool even for you.

That seemed to be his final text to B-Ray. She scrolled, looking for more—

First bell went off, startling her. She nearly dropped the phone. In the next room, the drummer stopped, and a moment later she heard the door open and the guy walk off. The sax player kept it up, honking scales now.

She had to get going. She had Spanish in five minutes.

She went to New Messages and pressed B-Ray from Billy's list of contacts. She wrote:

Yo, B. Heads up. Better delete those photos you sent me. You could get arrested if they find that on yr phone.

She read it over. Right message, wrong style. She deleted and tried again . . . *Yo, B-Hole. Heads up . . .*

Billy's phone dinged, a new text. *Anders.* She recognized the name. A creep from her chemistry class. He spent half the lab staring at her ass. She'd never said a word to him. The text said:

Isn't this your GF? Doesn't look like your dick, bro!

Attached were the five pictures.

Her mind seemed to shut down. She smashed the phone on the piano to make it stop. The phone exploded and the battery flew across the room.

She needed to find Billy. Ask him what the fuck was going on. She bolted. Running headlong down the stairs, she almost crashed into some kids coming up from below. They stopped and gawked. The mall blondes, she saw through her tears and tunnel-vision rage.

"Watch out, Taylor," one of them said, stepping aside, "you don't want to catch anything."

"You're all such bitches!" Emily screamed, rushing past them, and the name they called back echoed down the stairwell and in her ears all the way on her long run home.

Slut.

SHE COULDN'T SLEEP. She hadn't slept the previous night or the night before that. She hadn't slept properly since her mother flushed her stash. Without Xanax or Ambien, her thoughts would swirl in endless repetitions. It was almost as bad as Daniel going away—the feeling that everything was over. All the things she'd done in her life, all her studying and effort and everything she'd built and wanted to do, and this was all she was now. *Slut. Gangbang.* The zombie-eyed girl with the dick shoved in her mouth. *U see how big har hole is!* She didn't even know who took the pictures, B-Ray or his cousin. She didn't even know whose dick it was or which one to curse to hell, but it didn't matter. They were both scumbags, rapists, lower than dirt.

Her life was ruined.

* * *

FOR DAYS she went without sleep. When she turned off the lamp at night, her heart would pound and she would suffer a simultaneous dread of falling asleep and *not* falling asleep. If she managed to doze off for an hour or two, she would wake gasping in the darkness. The house was deathly still. Around 4:00 A.M. the paperboy would pull into their driveway in his rumbly piece-of-shit car and toss the *Times* on the front porch with a thud. Around five, in the blue-dark of coming dawn, a big plane would pass overhead; it felt like she'd waited the entire night just to hear that phantom passing, a thirty-second displacement of air and space that erased all other sounds, like the coming of the end. She didn't dream, not when she slept. But in the daytime she would wander the house in a daze, seeing shapes in front of her that were sometimes people—Daniel, friends from the city—and then watch these dream people, daytime ghosts, vanish into nothingness. In her exhaustion, she felt like she was about to fall forward, as if her head were too heavy, and she moved hesitantly, planting one foot ahead of the other. It seemed like the only time she could sleep was when she shouldn't—at the dinner table, in the bathtub. She called Douglas to see what was happening, but he said he had nothing, no change, dry.

She told her mother she was sick. She had no energy. She couldn't get out of bed. Which was all true. It felt like an illness, a disease, something that would never go away. She deleted her Facebook and MySpace profiles, ignoring the postings. She got three or four prank calls, clearly from the mall blondes, who pretended her line was an escort service—before she stopped listening to her voice mail. She turned off her ringer.

After a week or maybe longer—she lost track of the days—her mother suggested she get tested for mono. Sure, fine. Whatever, Mom.

Stuck in the house, she had little to do but observe Audrey. There was primping, excessive makeup, furtive cell phone calls taken in the next room. At first Emily eavesdropped on the conversations; then she tried to avoid them. Didn't the neighbor have anything better to do than phone-sex her mother twice a day? Emily had overheard Audrey, plotting wheres and whens. Emily followed her to his house once, but she didn't go around to the den window. She didn't want to witness that scene again, or anything worse. Even the thought of it—her mother having sex—made her stomach turn. The one thing a kid should never have to see is her mother getting laid. He also had a dog, a husky; she'd seen him walking it on weekend afternoons. He lived alone, as far as Emily could detect. No wife, no kids. Just good old Salt and Pepper zipping into his driveway after work, leaving the porch light on for Audrey. Otherwise, his house was as dark as a tomb; he never left any lights on. Every night after dinner Audrey would disappear with Sheba. Once Emily grabbed her sneakers, saying, "I'll come too." Her mother stiffened and fumbled and told her no, she was grounded, and besides she was ill, wasn't she? She should try to catch up on all the schoolwork she was missing. Sure, Mom. And off she went to see her suburban suitor, who was probably so jacked up on Viagra or Cialis or some other cock stiffener to keep that up every night that he must be seeing double.

Her father, meanwhile, didn't notice a thing. He hardly said a word to anyone. He had disappeared into the abyss of *work* in a huge way. Every night he'd return with his leather briefcase, tie loosened, cocktail-breathed. Dad, après work. To her: "Hi, honey. Good day? Feeling any better? I had mono too, when I was in college. I lost an entire semester and had to make it up over the summer. . . ."

She spent most of her time in bed, the comforter pulled over her head.

A FEW NIGHTS before Thanksgiving, she lay on her mattress, not feeling even remotely tired. The longer she lay in the darkness, the more alert she became. After a while she stopped trying to sleep. At 5:00 A.M. the big plane displaced the quiet, then was gone. When the first glow of predawn light appeared outside her window, she heard a noise. She looked up, and Daniel was sitting on the beanbag chair in the corner. His hair was long and curly, his face tanned.

How long have you been there?

Not long.

I can't sleep.

That's nothing new. When you were little you used to wake me up in the middle of the night and say you were bored. "Let's do something fun," you would say. Remember? We'd sneak downstairs and watch TV.

With the volume turned low so no one would hear.

Right. And I would be so tired the next day that Dad would have to drag me out of bed by my feet. But you would be raring to go. You had that pink backpack with the monster on the side—

Tasmanian Devil.

And you'd stand at the bottom of our street, waiting for the bus, swinging that bag and twirling around.

I liked spinning because after you stopped the ground would come rushing up toward you.

The world's always spinning, you just don't feel it.

You're not really here.

Then who are you talking to?

Nobody.

I'm not nobody.

You're me.

And I'm you. That'll never change.

What does that mean?

It means I'm here, I'm always here. You just have to find me.

He turned to vapors and drifted up through the ceiling. "Don't go," she said aloud. But his presence had calmed her, and sometime around dawn she fell asleep for a few hours.

This was her secret. She'd never told anyone, and she never would. Daniel hadn't really died that day. He was just waiting for her someplace else.

ON THE DAY before Thanksgiving, she got up at noon. She was safe, for now. But her mother had scheduled doctors' appointments for her the next week. "It's just mono," Emily complained. "There's nothing they can do for that anyway." But Audrey had been insistent. She'd lined up an internist and a specialist in Lyme, since she'd had the disease herself when she was younger and she said Emily's symptoms sounded the same. If she only knew. But that was one good thing, Emily guessed: Her parents didn't know. For all the people who'd seen those pictures, her parents hadn't.

Not yet, at least.

She needed to erase that possibility from her mind. She went to the kitchen for a Red Bull and added a few ounces of her father's Grey Goose. She heard music from her mom's room: Neil Young. Her mother had a nice voice. They used to sing together, back when Emily was a kid. Neil Young, Carole King, the Carpenters. Daniel would strum along on his acoustic guitar, good at that, like everything else he did. She and Audrey hadn't done a sing-along in ages . . .

She could tell her mother, it occurred to her. She'd *wanted* to tell her, on some level, ever since it happened. She didn't want Audrey to find out, and she never wanted Andrew to know—that was inconceivable, her father seeing those pictures. But it seemed possible, at this moment, to explain it to Audrey, to reveal the nightmare of the last few weeks and somehow lessen it.

Her hand went to the doorknob. She nearly turned it. But she heard her mother talking in a low murmur.

Jesus.

Him again.

She put her ear to the door. "I'll be cooking all day," she heard Audrey say. That was a lie. She bought half the stuff premade at Whole Foods. Was she trying to seduce him with her cooking prowess? God, it was so pathetic—

Then: "Really? At your ex's? That sounds interesting. At least you'll get to see your kids . . ."

Emily went to her room and turned her phone on. The idea came to her fully formed; she knew what she wanted to do.

His voice-mail greeting annoyed her, as usual. *Yo, it's Billy. Tell me something good.*

She said, "Call me when you get this. I need to talk to you. It's important."

HE GOT BACK to her that night. "What up? Where you been?"

"Mono," she said.

"Does that mean I'm gonna get it?"

"What? No, of course not. I'm not contagious and I haven't seen you in forever anyway."

"I had a cold a few days ago."

"Listen. You got any drugs?"

"For mono?"

"No, dumb-ass. For me."

"I got weed."

"I need pharmies."

"Weed's all I got. Take it or leave it."

"Well, let's go get some then." She paused. "I'll make it worth your while."

He was silent. She could practically see him, mouth open, brain working. "What's wrong with weed?" he said finally.

"You said you could get pills anytime. Or was that just bullshit?"

"You know what that means, right? You up for that?"

"I'm up for anything."

He scoffed. "Listen to you, big gangsta girl. You practically pissed your pants last time and that wasn't nothing."

"We're going inside this time."

"Fine with me. Just say when."

"I say tomorrow night."

"Why not tonight?"

"Tomorrow," she said. "I know the perfect place."

"Where?"

"I'll show you."

He said, "You sure I won't get sick from you?"

"I already told you. I'm not contagious."

"Cause that mono shit is nasty, I heard."

"You're fine. Don't be so paranoid." She paused. "How's school?" She wanted to ask what was happening—what they were saying about her, the pictures—everything.

"Same old bullshit."

God, he was stupid. "What are they say——"

"Hey," he said, interrupting. "You owe me two hundred bucks, bitch. I almost forgot. I called you ten times. What, you didn't get my voice mails? What the fuck? Bring it or I'm not doing anything with you."

"What are you talking about?"

"My phone. Someone turned it in to lost and found, all fucked up. I had to put a new one on my mom's credit card—not to mention my whole life was on that phone. What the fuck—"

"Fine. I'll give you the money."

"You admit it? You trashed my phone? Shit, I'm like the only one who stood up for you. And you fuck up my phone for no reason? What the fuck is that?"

"Stood up for me? How, exactly? By calling me *Gangbang*? Does that ring a bell? Yeah, my hero."

"I'm supposed to be happy I find out you're out fucking my best friend?"

"I didn't *fuck*—"

"Whatever. I don't care. Old news. Just bring my money."

God, he was annoying. "Fine, I'll bring it. Tomorrow night, eight o'clock. Don't forget."

"Yeah, yeah."

She hung up.

WHEN SHE FINALLY got out of bed late in the morning on Thanksgiving, her mother instructed her to change clothes for dinner. Her father got out his camera and snapped a few pictures for the family album. Emily stared into the lens without expression. She hated eating so early in the day.

"Let's join hands," her father said. He was sitting at the head of the table, the turkey in front of him giving off greasy vapors. He put his hands out toward Emily and her mother. They'd set a place for Daniel.

"Are you serious, Andrew?"

"Yes, I'm serious. I want to say grace. I want to say a prayer for your brother."

"He didn't believe in that stuff and neither do I."

"Well, I do. So humor me, will you?"

She glanced at her mother, who mechanically extended her hand.

"He wouldn't want this," said Emily. But she did it anyway, and they joined hands: Andrew's moist palm, her mother's thin fingers. Emily held them limply, staring at the butchered animal, all buttery brown burnt skin.

Andrew intoned grace, and she tuned him out. Words of blessings, useful for inducing drowsiness but not much else. During the annual graces, Daniel used to whisper under his breath, trying to make her laugh, and he would always follow his father's blessing with one of his own: "And let us not forget Her Majesty Queen of England, Defender of the Faith, Empress of India." This was something their Great-Aunt Ethel had once blurted during a holiday dinner years ago, to their wonderment. *Everyone blessed the Queen in Nova Scotia when I was a child*, she insisted.

Her father finished his prayer and pronounced his *Amen*.

A silent passing of dishes ensued, the clanking of porcelain. Her mother's good china, for special occasions only. How absurd it seemed, the ritualized feast. With Daniel by her side, the familial gatherings had held an ironic pleasure; they would roll their eyes at each other, suppressing laughter, while Grandma Mabel dribbled cranberry sauce onto her white ruffled blouse and decrepit Ethel invoked the Queen. But the elderly were now dead or interred in nursing homes, and Daniel was gone. So what was the point? Why maintain the pretense, sitting with joined hands to break bread, their sorry threesome, dressed in their Sunday finery, uttering banalities?

"Turkey?" Her father offered the serving plate.

"Have you just met me, Andrew?"

"Give it a try. Your mother slaved all day."

"I didn't slave. I cooked," Audrey said, taking the plate from him and setting it upwind, out from under Emily's nose. She offered tofu and green beans instead, and Emily spooned some onto her plate.

"You have to get your protein somehow."

"Leave her alone, Andrew."

Emily scooped some mashed potatoes and slopped them next to two white onions, awash in heavy cream.

Her dad started in on college applications, his favorite topic of late. "So what's it going to be? Ivy League's a good place to start. Then there's the Little Three, which is even better in some ways. You could try Wesleyan like Mom, or Amherst like dear old Dad. And there's always Williams, that is, if you want to stoop that low."

"I wouldn't apply to Amherst if my life depended on it."

"Why not?"

"And major in what, prefascism?"

"I'm not sure that was on the curriculum in my day," said Andrew.

Emily took a bite of the yams. "If you must know, there are only two places I would even consider: RISD or Wesleyan."

"That's a pretty short list," said her father. "You should have some backups."

"Berkeley, then."

"That's a little far away, isn't it?"

"Far from where?"

"From Mom and Dad," he said cheerfully, sawing a leg off the turkey.

"Are you drunk, Andrew? Why are you acting so pleasant?"

"That holiday feeling, I suppose."

She glared at him, ready to let out her exasperation. She didn't even want to go to college, not now anyway. She'd seen a website for an Outward Bound program on the eastern coast of Australia, hundreds of miles from anywhere, where you hiked thirty miles a day in a wilderness so uninhabited that they dropped your food from helicopters in prearranged spots, which you had to find or go hungry. A year in the middle of nowhere, on the other side of the world: That was what she wanted now.

But something in her father's expression stopped her. His smile looked forced. She wondered why he'd wear that phony smile. For whose benefit? Why perform if the courtroom were empty? Did he do it from habit? She lowered her fork.

"What now?" said her father.

"Nothing," said Emily, feeling the weight of obligation. "I'm not very hungry."

"Berkeley's top ten," said Andrew, peeling the skin off his turkey leg. "But Harvard and Yale are better, and we've got them in our own backyard. It seems extravagant to go all that way. Plus, you have to think about some real backups—"

"Andrew, really. She doesn't want to talk about this right now. She's not feeling well."

"I know, but applications are due soon. We can do some day trips if you like. The stuffing, please."

"It's from a box," said Audrey, passing the plate. "You won't like it."

"Of course I will. I *love* box stuffing."

That same joviality, not Andrew, but *dear old Dad*. It was for her, of course, the cooking and serving, the dressing up and picture taking. To help them all forget who wasn't in the picture. Left to themselves, her mother and father fought or ignored each other. And it wasn't just the holiday meal, but the rest of it too, she realized with a sickening feeling; they did it all for her, like actors in an after-school special. The shopping and cleaning, the keeping of appointments, their busy little lives. Without her, it wouldn't continue; *they* wouldn't continue. Daniel's absence had revealed the entrance to the abyss, in plain sight all along; she just hadn't noticed it before. Emily was the sole doorkeeper now, like that dog in Greek mythology who guarded the gates of Hell. But she couldn't remember if the dog prevented people from breaking in or the damned from getting out. Who'd want to break into Hell?

Lots of people, she decided.

"What, honey?"

She'd spoken aloud. Sometimes that happened when she hadn't slept for days; words would escape, sometimes even in public, and everyone around her would turn and stare. Lots of people would like to break into Hell, wouldn't they? But you had to be dead first. You couldn't just take the grand tour, like Dante. So the snarling dog has to guard the door, like the muscle-bound bouncers at nightclubs in Manhattan. *You, you, and you,* they'd say, pointing out the lucky ones and shaking their heads at the unchosen. Emily, going from club to club with her friends and her fake ID, had always been chosen. *You, girl. Come join us.* She'd accepted the invitation, always. There was so much to see, so many flames to fan.

"Stuffing's excellent," said her father.

"These yams are pretty good too," she said, making an effort.

Audrey smiled. "Thanks, honey."

After a reasonable interval, Emily excused herself, skipping dessert. "What, no Jell-O mold?" said Andrew, looking wounded. She felt like crying, but she couldn't make herself sit with them any longer. It was way too boring, too annoying, too sad, too everything. Maybe if she'd had a Xanax, maybe then she could stick it out and watch the rest of the performance.

The holiday feast done, Emily escaped to her room.

AROUND 8:00 P.M. she changed into her cat-burglar outfit: black leggings, black sweater, black fleece jacket. Her mom went to bed early, after polishing off three or four glasses of wine. She would be down for the night. Her father, comatose in front of the TV, would never realize she was gone. She stuck a few pillows under the comforter, like in some bad prison movie, just in case he looked in on her.

Outside, she breathed deeply, her first taste of fresh air all day, and got out her phone. Billy answered on the third ring.

"I'm on my way," she told him.

"Did you get my money?"

"Yes, I've got your money. Can you stop obsessing about that for a minute and concentrate?"

"Just bring it."

He was waiting for her in his driveway, wearing a dark knit cap and a long overcoat. His yellow basketball sneakers poked out underneath, only the tips visible.

"Nice coat," she said. "You could fit me in there with you." She handed over the wad of bills.

"Don't wanna freeze my ass off this time." He counted out the bills one by one, his mouth moving.

"Come on," said Emily. "Let's go."

"Wait—"

Mouth breather, she thought, trying not to lose her patience. If he closed his trap, he might fall down from lack of oxygen.

Finally he stuffed the money in his pockets. "Where to?"

"You sure you don't want to count it again? Make sure it's all there?"

"Very funny."

It was a clear night. A half-moon gleamed in a corner of the sky. On Apple Hill Road cars were parked on the street, the windshields cloudy with moisture. Piles of moldering leaves dotted the roadside, stinking of apple rot. Smoke rose from chimneys, wafting into the starry air. Through a picture window, she could see a man slumped in an armchair in front of an enormous television. A dog barked inside the house as they passed. They were doing nothing wrong, she told herself, just walking up the street. One family was still having Thanksgiving dinner—she could see them through the kitchen window—sitting around the table, drinking wine, an American postcard.

Halfway up the street, they came to his house, dark as always. No lights, no car in the driveway. He'd gone to his ex-wife's house for the holiday, just as she'd overheard from his conversation with Audrey. She wondered if the dog would be there; she hoped he took it with him. She'd brought along a pocketful of Sheba's dog bones, just in case.

"This one," she said, "with all the lights out."

"Why?"

"Because I know the guy lives here and I happen to know he's not home tonight. And he's a real shithead."

"What did he ever do to you?"

"He exists. Come on."

She started around the side of the house, and Billy followed, his long coat billowing out behind him. She nearly slipped on the grass, which glistened with a silvery glow.

"You sure there's no one in there?"

"Don't talk so loud."

The den window was dark. She got on her tiptoes and peered in. A moment later she moved to another window, dissolving into a deeper darkness. She glanced next door at a house obscured by tall trees. Even if someone were looking out the window, he wouldn't be able to see them in the darkness.

"Let's do it," Billy said, his breath visible.

"Better check the garage first. See if his car's there. Just to be sure."

He disappeared around the side of the house. She had a sudden, almost uncontrollable desire to pee. Were they really going to break in? Cars were one thing, but what if he *was* in there, already back from a meal somewhere, sleeping soundly? Or what if his dog was lying in wait, jaws ready to snap? A car passed on the street like a rush of wind. Then, in the silence that followed, she became aware of the commonplace riot of the creatures of the night, unseen in the grass and woods around her, what sounded like a single giant insect, scratching its back. From up in the trees, every ten seconds or so, came a *clack clack clack*, the sound of a marble falling down wooden steps. Her sneakers were wet from the grass. She wondered what was taking him so long. Billy was mostly talk, like all boys; he would rather lie than admit he didn't know what he was doing.

Finally he appeared beside her. "Garage is empty," he said.

They crept across the lawn to the back door. He turned the handle, and when it didn't open, he reached inside his coat pocket and produced a long screwdriver, showing it to her like some sort of prize.

"Wait," she whispered. "Check under the mat."

He bent and pushed aside the mat, revealing the glint of a silver key.

"See? It's the suburbs, stupid."

She thought he would smile, but he didn't. He put the key into the lock and turned the handle; the door opened an inch or two, then caught on a latch. He put his shoulder to the door, and it gave way with a splintering of wood, an impossibly loud crack. They both froze.

"Come on," he said.

They entered a dark corridor. She grabbed the back of his overcoat, unable to see in the darkness. She could make out a few jackets hanging on wall pegs and boots lining a low shelf. There was a smell in the house, unnameable, the scent of strangers, their sweat and shed skin, all the exhaled breath of a lifetime.

He took a flashlight out of his coat pocket and directed it around the kitchen: a bright yellow linoleum floor, pale green countertops. It looked like the house of someone's grandfather. She could see the remnants of breakfast on the kitchen table, a plate, a coffee mug, a spread-out newspaper. On the far wall the digital clock above the oven emitted the time in neon blue: 8:35 P.M.

He went to the refrigerator, releasing a shaft of light, and pulled out a bottle of Corona. He snapped off the cap and drank two giant swigs, then set the bottle on the counter. "You just gonna stand there?"

The first step, crossing the threshold into the kitchen, was the hard part. Once she got her feet to move, she found she could breathe again.

They didn't turn on any lights. They went by the beam of his flashlight: dining room, living room, den. An unseen clock ticked noisily. There was the low rumble in the basement of the boiler, pumping heat. Otherwise it was a quiet house, their footsteps cushioned by a thick white carpet. Only the den looked lived in, two remote controls lying on the couch next to a *TV Guide*, pillows askew. Billy's flashlight darted around the room: a painting on the wall, framed photos on the tabletops, grandfather clock in the corner.

"Hold this." He pulled out a duffel bag and knelt in front of the home entertainment center. He took handfuls of DVDs from the shelf, pushing aside books and glass figurines. "*Matrix* trilogy," he said. "Someone's got good taste." In the dining room, he rifled through the drawers of a hutch with glass doors. She knew they were alone, but her body still expected someone from upstairs to call out at any moment: *Who's down there?*

"You're making way too much noise," she hissed.

"Chill."

He opened a velvet-lined silverware box and studied the contents, as if he knew anything about silver, then overturned the box into the duffel bag—spoons, forks, and knives—all landing with a clang, the bag growing heavy in her hands.

"What are you going to do with this stuff?"

"Pawnshop."

"Are you joking? Have you even been to a pawnshop?"

"They got 'em on every street corner in my old neighborhood in Dallas. I bought my first laptop there for forty bucks." He took the duffel from her and slung it over his back. "Upstairs."

"You first," she whispered.

She waited on the landing as he ascended the stairs, the bag clinking against his back. He disappeared down the hallway in the dark. She expected a scream, a commotion, the bark of an angry dog, but he reappeared a few moments later saying, "All clear."

After that, after she was truly certain they were alone, it was easy, it was scary-fun. She checked the bathroom at the top of the stairs, but found only the usual guy crap—toothpaste, razor blades, the same stinky soap on a rope she'd given her father for his last two birthdays.

In the big bedroom at the end of the hall, Billy rifled through bureaus and closets, opening and closing drawers. There was a king-size bed, neatly made, with a floral comforter. Did Salt and Pepper sleep here? The room smelled of old people. For a moment she was uncertain: Had she made a mistake? Had she broken into the wrong house? But no. That was impossible. She scoped out the place like a professional burglar. She'd cased the joint. There was no mistake.

"Bingo," said Billy, taking something down from the top shelf of the closet.

A jewelry box. He dumped the contents onto the bed and spread the jumble of silver and gold with his hands. Rings, necklaces—old-lady stuff. There was a brooch shaped like a peacock with a spray of emeralds for feathers.

"They won't give you anything for that. They'll know it's stolen."

"They don't give a shit."

Why was she trying to talk him out of taking the jewelry? This had been her idea, not his. But she'd wanted to mess with Salt and Pepper, not some old lady. Was this his mother's jewelry? His grandmother's? On the bedspread, a sapphire ring caught her attention, glimmering cornflower blue. She held it up to a strip of light from the window. The stone was square-cut and encircled with small diamonds, set in white gold. She put it in her jacket pocket and zipped the pocket shut. In all likelihood she was robbing a dead lady, or someone cooped up in a nursing home. That must be some kind of sin. A *venial sin*, perhaps. The phrase popped into her head, unbidden.

As Billy fumbled in the closet, she stepped into the master bathroom and closed the door behind her. There were no windows, no one to see what she was doing. She turned the wall switch and there came a flickering like lightning, then a stunning fluorescence. She blinked into the brightness until her eyes adjusted.

She pulled open the mirrored cabinet. Unlike in the other bathroom, these shelves were crammed with prescription bottles. She checked the labels, her eyes widening. Valium, Ativan, Percodan, Vicodin. *Jackpot.* A fucking junkie's cabinet. She couldn't have hoped for anything better. On the lower shelf there was a stack of thin prescription boxes, at least ten of them. She read the label: morphine sulfate suppositories. *For insertion into back passage.* Morphine, just one step below heroin, something she had never tried. The morphine tablets were a year out of date, but that wouldn't matter. *Side effects*, said the label, *include euphoria.*

Euphoria, she thought. *What an excellent concept.*

She stuffed a couple of the boxes into her pocket and was reaching for more when Billy yelled her name. The noise made her heart skip. She froze. Then the door opened and he grabbed her hand.

"Move!" he screamed.

"What? What happened?"

They bolted, flashlight zigzagging crazily across the ceiling and walls— all *Blair Witch* and out of focus—down the stairs, feet thumping on the rug. "Run run run," he was saying. At the bottom of the stairs, he hesitated for a split second, then bolted toward the kitchen. She ran blindly, following him in the darkness. A garage door rumbled. Someone was parking the car. In the kitchen, she tripped on a dog bowl, which went clattering and splashing across the floor. He pushed open the door they'd broken into and they ran into the backyard. He stopped at the fence at the rear of the yard and cursed, his breath steaming.

"What?"

"I left it."

"Left what?" *The duffel bag*, she realized before he could respond. Could they trace it to them? Did they leave anything else behind in their panic? "Forget it. You can't go back."

He hesitated for a moment. "Shit," he hissed, giving in, and they vaulted over the fence and raced away into the night.

* * *

THE NEXT DAY was vacation—the day shoppers mauled each other for marked-down kitchen appliances—and then the weekend came and went, and then—*back to school.*

"No way," she told her mother. The prospect gave her shivers, if she weren't in the proper state of mind.

For four days now, ever since raiding Salt and Pepper's medicine cabinet, she had been absent, a spectator at her own death. That was what morphine felt like—being dead but awake for it. Most of the time she was floating on the ceiling looking down at her body, observing herself but also inside herself. It felt exquisite to be so still, to be without pain, without movement. How pleasant to be dead, to be nowhere. She'd spent an hour, or what felt like an hour—perhaps it was half the day—contemplating lifting her arm, then deciding no, she would not lift her arm. She'd been unaware of the passing minutes and hours. There was only the eternal present, she nodding in and out, on the border between real and unreal. The label prescribed one capsule for every twenty-four-hour period. She'd doubled, then tripled that dosage, inserting a suppository whenever she felt the fade. *After 24 hours,* said the pharmacist's label, *expel from rectum as if moving bowels.*

Gross.

The requirements of the body were so gross. There was *her* and there was this *thing* she had to carry around. Feed it and bathe it, make it go to the bathroom, suffer its illnesses, endure its discontents. It was blissful to exist outside the body, above it, her real self looking down.

Sometime that evening she felt the high dissolving. She reached for the packet of morphine and found it empty. All gone, just empty plastic receptacles. She checked the clock: It was 9:42 P.M., Monday night. This was now, the time of the living. All the triviality suddenly returned, like geese splashing down in a pond. She felt a panic descending, a four-day backlog of anxiety, striking all at once. What had she forgotten? What had she done?

She got up, feeling suddenly light-headed, and steadied herself with a hand on the dresser. The world was spinning and she with it. She grabbed her fleece jacket and went through the pockets: There it was, what she'd forgotten.

The sapphire.

Her face stared back blankly from the dresser-top mirror. Her skin seemed paler, her lips, darker, almost goth. She practiced a smile, observing the results. Curious, this mask. How strange that people considered it *Emily*. She had been outside her body for four days. Shamans, she'd once read, could free their spirits, could hover above themselves the way she had. They did it through trance and a lifetime of training. She wanted to get back there a whole lot faster. She combed her hair and changed into her low-cut jeans and a belly shirt, a suitably slutty look.

The sound of the TV came from the den, voices speaking in French. Audrey, the Netflix addict, sat on the couch. Emily tiptoed down the hall—her father still at work—and stopped in the kitchen for a belt from his Black Label, a super-long shot, slugging directly from the bottle.

She grabbed her sweatshirt from the closet, stepping around the dog. Sheba whined and got to her feet, but Emily shushed her. "Stay," she whispered. She closed the door behind her and went out into a cold night, her first breath of fresh air in a long time. Immediately, she felt shivery and light-headed, but light-headedness was part of the shaman program, was it not? For four days she had holed up in her bedroom with almost no food—a few handfuls of baby carrots and cheese sticks—peeling away the excess layers, eradicating all but the essential. Her bedroom was her sweat lodge, morphine her peyote.

Above, a plane passed over the crest of the mountain. She could imagine the scene from the cockpit: all the little houses, lined up like cereal boxes on a shelf. They all looked the same, probably *were* the same design, inside and out, built by the same hand sometime in the black-and-white 1950s.

She approached his driveway. Inside, the bluish light of the television glowed from the first-floor den. She rang the bell, and a few moments later the porch light came on. He appeared in the doorway, stubble on his cheeks, a curious expression. "Yes?"

"May I speak to the lady of the house?" she asked. A bizarre question, but she was winging it, letting her actress-self take over.

He had a glass in his hand. Whiskey, it looked like. She felt drunk just sniffing the alcohol. But she knew how to cover herself; no one ever knew how wasted she was, right up until the moment of blackout.

"What's up? Selling Girl Scout cookies?"

"Not exactly."

He studied her, his eyes narrowing in recognition.

"Do you know who I am?"

"I think so," he replied. "You live in the farmhouse, right?"

That surprised her. She hadn't counted on that. As far as she knew, he'd seen her only that one time, when he'd given her a pervy stare from the driver's seat and she'd responded with the finger. She suffered a moment of hesitation, contemplating the consequences. Fuck it. She didn't want to think about consequences. She'd come this far. Stupid to back out now. "You won't tell my mother, will you?"

"Tell her what?"

"About this." She dug into her pocket and produced the sapphire. He leaned forward to study her open palm. His face changed, and then he picked the ring out of her hand and said, "Come in."

In the hallway, the dog raised its snout as she went by. The house smell reminded her of that night, but the rooms seemed benign now, absent the manic zigzagging flashlight in the darkness. He passed the den, his seducer's lair, with the fireplace burning in the background. She could hear the wood crackling and hissing, and she decided it wouldn't be so bad if she were to fuck him. Like mother, like daughter. That would be a victory of sorts, to get his pants down, his cock inside her. But he directed her into the kitchen and pulled out a chair for her.

"This was my mother's twenty-fifth wedding anniversary present," he said, placing the sapphire on the table. "She only wore it on special nights, to weddings and galas."

"It's beautiful."

"Would you care to tell me how you got it?"

"Can't you guess?"

"Did someone give it to you? A boy named Billy?"

Emily blinked, trying to focus. How could he know about Billy? Had he found out, somehow? Had Billy gotten caught? She hadn't even seen him or talked to him since that night. Did this man know about the raided medicine cabinet, the missing morphine? Would he call the cops now? A gauze filter seemed to cover her brain. Everything seemed loud and echoing—the drip of the faucet, the rasp of the oven clock, his breathing. "No," she said. "Try again."

"Emily. That's your name, right?"

"Yeah. What's yours?"

"Benjamin."

"How about I just call you Ben?" She leaned back to take off her sweatshirt, and her head felt loose on her neck. She tied the sweatshirt around her waist, offering him a view of her breasts.

"You want me to believe you did it? Broke into my house?"

"Bingo."

"Why would you do that?"

"To pay you back for fucking my mother."

"That's crazy."

"Is it? I saw you. You and her together."

"I don't know what you saw—"

She reached for his glass and took a sip. The cough-liquid boozy vapors made her head swim. "Whiskey and ginger ale," she said. "Yum." This was the preblackout stage, the part she wouldn't remember later, just flashes of this and that, the part she liked the best because she wasn't responsible, there would be no memory, nothing to cringe over or be embarrassed about.

"I'm going to call your mother. I think she should hear this."

"Good idea. You call Audrey. I'll call my dad." She took her cell phone out of her jeans and handed it toward him. "He's a lawyer. We'll get the whole family together."

He paused. "Look—"

"I didn't think so." She put the phone back in her pocket and smiled. He wouldn't call anyone. She could mess with him all she wanted. She needed to get upstairs, that was all that mattered; she would say she had to use the bathroom. "What do you want with her anyway? You could do a lot better."

"The only thing I've done with your mother is walk the dog."

"Is that what you call it? Sounds like something from the Kama Sutra. I don't blame her, though. You're hot. You're the hot older guy." She batted her eyes at him, her mall-girl act again. "Wouldn't you like someone younger? Me, for instance."

"Cut it out."

"What, you're denying it? I saw you checking out my ass that day. That's why I flipped you off. You're a horny old fucker, aren't you?"

He shook his head. "Your story doesn't make sense. You break into my house and trash the place. Now you bring back a ring worth thousands of dollars?"

"So?"

"So, why not keep it? Why not sell it?"

"I felt guilty."

"You could've just left it in the mailbox if you felt so bad."

"Didn't think of that."

"I don't believe you. You're covering up for your boyfriend, aren't you? He broke in, didn't he? That kid Billy."

It pissed her off, him thinking that she couldn't rob his house by herself—even if she hadn't. "I took your fucking ring, okay? I steal things all the time. I took it and now I'm bringing it back. You should thank me instead of breaking my balls."

He sighed, looking at her with his puppy dog eyes. Her mother had fallen for that gaze. "Fine. Thank you. Now you should go."

She got up and went down the hall and knelt next to the dog, rubbing its belly. "Would you mind if I warmed up in front of the fireplace?"

"Yes, I would mind," he said.

"Chill out, Ben. Don't be so uptight. Go pour yourself another scotch. Get one for me too. I deserve a reward, don't you think?"

"Ah. So that's why you came to my house at this time of night. For money."

"Not money. Something better."

"Like what?"

"Like what you do to Audrey."

"That's enough," he said. "It's time to go." He grabbed her elbow and pulled her toward the front door. She was surprised at his strength, how easily he was dragging her along, and she felt weightless and unable to resist. No, this couldn't be happening, she couldn't leave without raiding the cabinet. She gathered herself and wheeled away from him, swinging her arms, yelling, "Let go of me, motherfucker!"

She screamed—as loud as she could. When he dropped her arm, she ran up the stairs, clutching the banister for support. Everything was moving so slowly. It seemed to take an unusual effort to move her arms and legs. She heard his voice, close behind her.

"Hey, come back here!"

At the top of the stairs she ran into the bedroom and ducked into the bathroom and locked the door behind her. In the mirror, the sudden appearance of her face startled her, pale and wide-eyed, her lips bluish.

He pounded on the door.

"You hurt my arm, asshole."

"I'm sorry."

She opened the medicine cabinet. There it was: the stash. All those brown bottles—more than she'd remembered—and the cardboard packets of morphine, stacked on the bottom shelf, right where she'd left them. *Ativan*, she decided. Ativan had that nice mellowness, just what she needed to dissolve the stress of first-degree larceny or whatever crime she was committing. She fumbled with the childproof cap, giddy with the effort. How to line up the lines. Turning, twisting, like her dad's old Rubik's Cube, looking for the groove. Finally, the happy click.

Ta-da.

There were only five pills in the bottle. She dumped them into her hand and bent under the faucet for a mouthful of water. She popped all five, like Tic Tacs.

Good-bye, anxiety.

She went to work on the cabinet, taking off the caps and dumping the pills into her pockets. She didn't need the bottles; she knew the pills by sight. Halcion were the tiny round blue ones. Ambien, the cylindrical white ones. OxyContin, perfect yellow circles. The jumble of reds, whites, and blues, the colors of America. And what was more American than modern pharmacology? God bless Pfizer and Merck. If only they didn't torture and kill dogs, the fuckers.

When he banged on the door, she froze. For a moment she'd almost forgotten where she was. "Leave me alone," she told him. "I've got cramps." The magic words; they never failed to scare off teachers, horny guys, anyone who wanted you to do something you didn't. She filled her pockets, enough to last a year, longer. And she would hide them well this time, where her mother wouldn't find them. She returned the empty bottles to the cabinet, lining up the labels.

Done.

She pulled on her sweatshirt and raised the hood. When she opened the door, he was standing directly in front of her, a worried expression on his face—worry and something else too. *Fear.* She saw it in his eyes. He was frightened of her. This exhilarated her, made her want to go further.

"If you tell my mother I was here . . ." The words felt heavy in her mouth. She started again: "If you tell her any of this, I'll say you raped me."

"She won't believe you."

"Maybe not. But my father will."

She pushed past him and scrambled down the stairs and out the front door. She broke into a run, the pavement rising to meet her, the pills shifting in her pockets like handfuls of sand. She ran all the way to her house and slipped open the kitchen door. From her parents' bathroom came the sound of a running faucet.

She closed her bedroom door behind her and collapsed onto her mattress. She removed one of the packets of morphine from her pocket, spilling some pills onto the floor, and tore open the box. She pinched one of the capsules out of the foil. Down went her jeans, in went the bullet. After a few moments, the pill seemed to expand as it warmed to her body, then softly explode. She pulled up her jeans and rolled onto her back.

Mission complete, she said to herself.

She waited for the euphoria. She stared at the white stucco ceiling, and after a while the ceiling seemed to multiply and morph like a screen saver. She blinked, watching the cosmic vision, the kaleidoscopic patterns, but it soon made her feel sick. A dizziness overtook her. She tried to blink it away, but it got worse. This wasn't blackout. This was something different. Something scary.

She tried to get up, but the force against her was too strong. Then the void came all at once, like a roller-coaster drop. She disappeared for a moment. Where was she? Had she passed out? Her arms felt numb. The muscles in her legs started twitching. An alarm sounded in her ears, nearly too much to contain. This was wrong, this was not like before. She tried to call out for her mother, but no sound came forth. It took a great effort to conjure the word and get her voice:

"Mom!"

Then she fell into the void, downward, toward a deeper darkness.

The display, unseen on her cell phone, read:

11:58 P.M.
Monday
November 26, 2007

Mother and Daughter

Two hours earlier

LATER, AUDREY would remember the silence, the first sign that something was wrong. She looked up from the TV, realizing that she hadn't heard a peep from Emily for a while—no blow-dryer, no music, no opening and closing of closet doors, none of the usual sounds her daughter produced.

"Honey?" she called.

She didn't expect an answer. Her daughter hadn't really spoken to her for weeks. She knocked on her daughter's bedroom door. "Is everything okay?" Getting no response, she cracked the door and looked in. The bed was unoccupied, the blankets askew. Audrey checked the bathroom, then turned out the lights in the room and searched for her daughter—kitchen, living room, basement, garage. Nothing. Emily wasn't home. Ten o'clock at night and her daughter had snuck out. So much for trying to ground her. She wondered if Emily was even sick. Or had she just been feigning illness all along? Audrey didn't think so. Her daughter hadn't looked well for a couple of weeks, and it would be unlike Emily to want to stay home, away from all the excitement of the world. Maybe sneaking out meant she was finally feeling better. Maybe that was a good sign. With Emily, nothing was clear.

What now?

Audrey got her jacket and went outside. Andrew, as usual, was no help. He hadn't come home from work yet. Audrey didn't bother calling him. Emily had probably gone to meet a boy. He would have arrived at the appointed hour, some suburban badass driving his father's Mercedes. She would be wearing her black cardigan, buttoned too low. He would honk the horn, or maybe she'd told him not to so her parents wouldn't hear, and she would jump in—and disappear until dawn again.

In the distance an animal howled—a coyote, it sounded like—from somewhere on the mountain. Audrey listened, holding her breath, and the coyote pealed again, a sort of laughing now, trailing away. She suddenly felt foolish, standing watch like some chaperone: *Mom the bummer*. She didn't want to play that part anymore. Emily didn't listen to her anyway. Tell her to stay away from the ocean and she would swim out to the jetty. That was her nature, to test the limits. Audrey just happened to be the one setting those limits. She'd been silly to think she could ground her daughter. So Emily had snuck out. That was to be expected. Audrey was surprised it hadn't happened sooner. Maybe it had; maybe she just hadn't noticed. There was no need to call the cops or wait up all night, as she had done the last time. No need to worry. Emily would return when she was ready, as always. Adolescence was a form of insanity under the best circumstances—the body changing, desires bulging, insecurities howling. How could she make her daughter understand that this was only temporary?

Audrey went back into the house and began the ritual ablutions of day's end: creams and cleansers, scrubbing and brushing, nose blowing and bladder emptying. When had it become such an enormous effort just to go to sleep? Fifteen minutes later she emerged from the bathroom, lathered with lotions, and slipped into bed.

She reached into the bottom drawer of her night table and opened the compact case, where she kept her Valium, where Emily wouldn't find them. She took two. This was how she slept without dreams, without grief rousing her at 3 A.M.—the only way she could sleep, now. The holiday had made it worse, as always. She turned out the light and stretched, a luxury to have the bed to herself. Almost immediately, she fell asleep.

Later, she would wonder how she heard the sound, so faint, like a faraway bird. Her head felt clogged, her body heavy. The sound persisted until it drew her to the surface. Her cell phone, she realized. She cursed. She didn't want to open her eyes and get out of bed—the floor was cold, she was exhausted—but she found herself rising and shuffling to the dresser, drawn by some maternal force. It might be Emily; she might be in trouble. She flipped open the phone and said hello.

"Audrey?"

"Benjamin? Is that you?"

"Yes. I'm sorry to call so late."

"What time is it? Why are you—" She held the phone out to check the display and dropped it. It knocked against the night table and fell behind the bed. She cursed, reaching to turn on the lamp. When she retrieved the phone, the call was lost. Why would he call at this hour? He'd never done that before. She dialed him back, but the phone rang a few times and then went to voice mail. She hung up without leaving a message. Without her glasses, she squinted at the screen. She didn't recognize the number; it was not his usual phone.

The last time they spoke, she'd told him she would get in touch after the holiday. He hadn't waited. Instead he'd woken her from a dead sleep. Did he not respect her at all, to call at this hour? She checked for a message; there was none. She returned the phone to the dresser and climbed back into bed. Rude of him, she thought. What could he want from her at this hour, other than the obvious? Booty-calling, like some college kid. She remembered that night at Starbucks. He'd gone to his car before her, leaving his coffee cup on the table. She had brought it to the garbage and tossed it in with a splash. Cleaning up after him, just like she did with Andrew. That was the way of men, leaving their messes behind. She felt a surge of disdain for him. It angered her, enough to shake off the effect of the Valium, enough to keep her from returning immediately to sleep.

A moment later she heard the faint cry:

"Mom."

She sat up in bed and turned on the light. What now? Had she heard her daughter's voice or imagined it? She got up and shuffled down the hallway in her slippers. There was a light coming from beneath Emily's door.

Thank God, she's home.

She knocked. "Emily? Do you need something?" There was no answer. She would not lecture; she wouldn't even mention her little escape. She just wanted her daughter to say something kind to her—to wish her good night, a spoken word, any word. They'd gone too long without speaking.

"I just want to say good night—" Audrey said, opening the door.

Emily was lying on the mattress, her hair spread out around her like a shawl. All the lights were burning in the room, like a crime scene. There was something strange about her face. Her lips were bright blue. Audrey wondered why Emily would put on such strange lipstick. Then she realized it was not lipstick, but her lips, somehow turned that unnatural color, as if she'd been frostbitten.

"Emily?"

When she didn't open her eyes or stir, Audrey went to her, stepping on something—tiny pills; *prescription pills*—scattered all around her bed.

"Emily, wake up." Audrey knelt beside her and touched her daughter's cheek; her skin was cold and clammy. Her breath came in rasps.

"Emily, what did you do? Can you hear me?"

She grabbed her daughter's arm, squeezed her, jostled her, slapped her across the face. But Emily did not open her eyes, did not show any response at all, except for that terrible raspy breathing. She needed to call an ambulance. But she seemed unable to move. She did not want to leave Emily alone. It took all her will to get up and run to the kitchen.

AT LAST the sirens sounded.

Audrey rushed outside, wearing only her T-shirt and hospital pants. Soon a fire engine roared to a stop, lights flashing. Why would they send a fire engine? The big rig stopped on the street and an ambulance turned in to the driveway. Two EMTs got out, a man and a woman.

Time altered, a herky-jerky acceleration. The EMTs clambered down the hallway in their blue uniforms, their two-way radios emitting human voices and squelching sounds. Their boots were open, the laces dragging behind. Emily lay on the floor, the EMTs working over her. Audrey stood behind them, looking over their shoulders.

"Whose pills are these?" asked the male EMT. He gathered the pills off the rug and examined them one by one.

"I don't know."

"Has she ever done anything like this before?"

"I found some pills in her closet a while back and threw them away. I don't know how she gets them."

"What sort of pills?"

"I don't know. Vicodin. Please help her. She's freezing cold."

"We're trying, ma'am," said the female EMT, without glancing up.

A fireman appeared in the doorway, standing quiet and motionless.

Sheba padded into the room; the fireman took her by the collar, and Sheba sat by his side, watching and whining. A stretcher was unfolded and Emily was lifted onto it and strapped down with Velcro wraps. They carried her to the ambulance, and Audrey climbed in after her. As the vehicle began to move, Emily's head flopped to the side. Her lips, that terrible shade of frostbite blue, a shade Audrey would never forget.

THEY TOLD HER to wait in the curtained cubicle. Waiting, she called Andrew. There was no answer. Just like before, absent, unavailable. She left a message, telling him to come to St. Francis Hospital, now. A minute later she tried again. Voice mail, again.

She sat with her head in her hands, half-listening to the muffled humdrum: nurses chatting at their station in the center of the ER; the beeping and buzzing and whirring of a thousand different machines; the sudden yelp of the intercom; an amplified voice; the creaking wheels of stretchers rolling past; doors and curtains opening; squeaky-soled shoes; a janitor's mop swishing along the tiles; the orderlies talking in Spanish; the sudden complaint of a drunken man; the low groan of the building itself. She couldn't say how much time passed. It might have been twenty minutes. It might have been hours.

She had been here before. This was a replay of the worst hours of her life. It seemed impossible that this could be happening again. She felt her mind reeling and breaking, unable to differentiate between now and then. She was back in the ER, everything in between then and now leading to this same place. What had she done to deserve this? What could she have done to avoid this? She had failed her daughter. That was clear. She had refused to look her in the eyes. She had wished her daughter dead in place of Daniel, and this, this now, was her punishment.

AT LAST the ER doctor entered the cubicle. He told her that they were giving Emily a drug to offset the narcotics. It was a matter of getting the poison out of her system. The problem was, there was no antidote for some of the pills she had taken. She had to excrete the toxins through her urinary tract, so they were hydrating her through multiple IVs to assist that process. These fluids would keep up her blood pressure, said the doctor. When she started breathing normally again, they would take her off the respirator, but not until then.

"In simple terms, she has to wake up," the doctor told her.

"Will she?"

The doctor squeezed her arm and left the cubicle.

EMILY WAS BACK at their house in Cos Cob. All the furniture had been taken away and the walls were painted a fresh coat of white, the wooden floors polished. In the living room a gust of wind blew the curtain away from the window, and bright sunlight filled the empty rooms.

A deer was standing perfectly still in the center of the room, its head lowered, as if its antlers were too heavy. She approached the animal and touched its velvet fur. The deer raised its head, observing her with its large kind eyes.

Follow me, said the deer.

The animal moved toward the kitchen, its hooves clacking and echoing on the wood floor. She hurried to keep up, passing through the kitchen and then up the narrow rear staircase to the third floor. She lost sight of the deer but heard its steps, directly above her. On the third-floor landing, she pulled down the attic ladder and stepped up, one rung after another.

The attic seemed bigger than she remembered, a long, deep cavern. All the junk they'd piled up there—their discarded furniture, summer-camp trunks, old toys—was gone. In the far corner, behind cobwebs, she noticed a tiny door in the baseboard, no bigger than a postcard. She bent down and pulled open the door and peered inside, and there came a sudden expansion, the doorway widening to reveal the secret room.

It was a sunny room with sloped walls. There was a large bay window where she could sit and look out over the backyard. Down in the grassy yard below, two children were playing with a beach ball. A boy and a girl, four or five years old. It was she and Daniel, she realized with a thrill. He caught the beach ball against his chest, and she ran after him, calling his name. She couldn't catch him, he was so fast, running in circles.

Look, Daniel! It's us!

I know.

Is this where you've been? All this time?

Yes.

I didn't know. I should have known. All along, I knew you were somewhere. I just never thought to look in the attic.

It's a secret.

Outside, in the backyard, he threw the ball high in the air. She shaded her eyes as the ball climbed into the sky—so bright, so blue. The ball soared, and she waited for it to come down, her arms stretched wide open.

I'm so sorry, Daniel. I should have found you.

You're not supposed to be here.

It's beautiful. You can see everything from here. And you must be lonely.

No.

I am. Without you.

High above, the beach ball hovered in front of the sun, becoming the sun, exploding in brightness. A fearsome light emerged, ripping apart the sky. Something terrible was coming forth.

Daniel, I'm scared.

You can't stay.

I can't leave without you.

Yes, you can.

But I want to stay.

No, Emily. You have to go back.

Do I have to?

Yes. You have to go. Go now!

SHE EMERGED into brightness. The effort of waking was wrenching. She couldn't speak, couldn't cry out. Something was on her face, suffocating her. An interminable time passed on the cusp of consciousness, trying to surface. She fought to open her eyes, gasping and choking. She could see only the brightness, blinding her. At last, she could see beyond the light.

They were all around her.

A face appeared above her. He had no eyes, no mouth. Not a man but some devil. His voice came from elsewhere, the sounds guttural. Someone sliced her arm, opening her. She tried to scream, but the words turned to mush. She felt herself falling. Down, deep down, back into the sludge. Nothing here but blackness. Not water. Not air. Not anything.

She fought back to the surface. There was something in her mouth. She pulled the thing out and it kept coming, from all the way down her throat, deep down inside her, making her vomit. She spat a black sludge, the taste of death. The thing emerged, something foreign. A plastic tube.

She kept pulling until it was out and threw it or tried to, her hands were so weak, she could barely move.

She could hear them, understand them. But she couldn't speak to them. Bile came spilling out of her, black and thick. She fought to stay conscious even as she vomited. She wavered, falling back. It was impossible to come awake. She couldn't do it. It was an enormous stone on top of her. To struggle against it was pointless.

Wake up, said the voice. *Open your eyes.*

I can't.

Of course you can.

And somehow she did.

LATER she would remember nothing, or almost nothing, of that night. Glimpses, that was all, like images seen while flipping television channels. She pushed it out of her mind, she did not want to recall what she'd done. She was too ashamed to remember; she would tell no one of her visit to the man's house, not even her mother.

All of that night, as hazy as a dream—all except the attic. *That* she remembered clearly, every detail—the sloped, soft-yellow walls, the bay-window seat looking out to the backyard. She not only remembered it but *felt* it—the sunlight, his presence—a feeling of pure goodness. It stayed with her, a gift she carried wherever she went. She told no one—not the hospital doctors or the therapists who pressed her during her seventy-two-hour stay in the psych ward, not the shrink she met Wednesday afternoons for six months after that, even though she liked the woman and didn't mind sharing her every other secret with her. She told no one of the attic. That was hers alone, a constant, a feeling undimmed for years afterward—but never as strong as that next morning, waking in the hospital room at dawn with no idea where she was, and her mother sitting beside her. She told no one except her mother—the only person she could ever tell, the only person in the world who could understand.

She opened her eyes and looked around, registering the exhaustion in her body, the tiredness that comes after giving everything. It was like starting blank. *Where am I? How did I get here?* She felt the IV attached to her wrist, and she turned to see her mother, holding her hand.

"Mom," she said, "I saw him. I saw Daniel." She rushed to get the words out, but her voice was hoarse, no louder than a whisper.

"Emily?" Her mother's hand was warm against her skin. "Are you okay? Can you hear me?"

"Of course I can hear you."

"Emily, I'm so sorry."

"What are you sorry about?"

"Everything, honey. I'm sorry about everything." Audrey was weeping, the tears running down her cheeks. Her face was pale and drawn. "You've been sick and I didn't do anything to help. Will you forgive me?"

"Oh, Mom. You look awful."

Audrey laughed and wiped her eyes. "I forgot to put on makeup."

"Did you hear what I said? About Daniel?"

"Yes."

"You can't tell anyone. Not even Dad."

"How are you feeling? Do you need anything?"

Emily pushed herself up in bed. "Mom, you're not listening to me." Outside the window, the sun was a red blob, rising over a line of trees. They were somewhere on the fifth or sixth floor, high above the city. "He's here. He's with us."

She told her mother what she had seen. The attic room, how she had opened the tiny door to find him, the warmth and sunlight, like no other place. Heaven. It could only be heaven. "Do you believe me?"

Her mother nodded. She brushed her hair away from her face. "I see him every time I look at you."

"You do?"

"Yes."

That morning: It was like starting blank. She let the past refill her, choosing what to admit and what to banish. It would become her story to tell. Later, she would look back and say that when she was seventeen, she tried to commit suicide but ended up killing only the parts of herself she no longer wanted.

EIGHT YEARS LATER, she will arrive in Berkeley, California, to attend graduate school. It is a late-summer day. She walks through town, seeing it all for the first time, this place she will come to know so well. In People's

Park, she finds a place to sit on the warm grass. She watches and admires the activity going on around her—boys playing basketball, students tossing Frisbees, homeless men sleeping in the sun, hippies smoking pot and strumming guitars. All this, she thinks, she could have missed.

A tall young man comes strolling across the grass, like an actor out of a play. He is dressed in a tuxedo coat with tails, wearing a purple top hat. He looks so elegant, so tall, so magical. As if on cue, as if he knows she is watching, the man in the purple top hat takes a few quick steps and throws himself onto his hands and cartwheels—three, four, five cartwheels in a row, a blur of arms and legs, with the top hat somehow staying in place—

Are you seeing this?

I am.

Is this amazing or what?

It is.

He lands on his feet, bows deeply, and doffs his hat in her direction. The kids with the Frisbees hoot and applaud, and she stands and claps with the others for the sheer grace and beauty of what he has done, so happy to be a part of it, this crazy park, this beautiful life.

Epilogue

The first day of winter, 2007

ON THE TWENTY-SECOND of December a heavy snow fell. Benjamin Mandelbaum closed down the business early to give his employees a chance to make it home safely. He was one of the last to leave. On the drive home the roads were clogged. On the interstate a few cars slipped out of control, smashing against the guardrails or other vehicles.

His cell phone chimed.

"Where are you?" asked Judy.

"Halfway home."

"I need you to stop at Whole Foods in Wintonbury Center."

"Give me a break, Judy. It's like the demolition derby out here."

"It's for your daughter."

He squinted at the swirling snow, riding the brake, barely moving. "Why didn't you go to the store earlier?"

"Because she didn't tell me earlier."

He took a deep breath. "All right, fine. What do you need?"

She gave him a list. His daughter had gone gluten-free over the past semester; she needed items that Benjamin had never even heard of: amaranth, quinoa, arrowroot.

"And don't forget the brown rice pasta."

His children would arrive that weekend on Christmas break. His family would be together for the holidays, despite all, unbroken.

"Right," he said. "Got it."

"Say it back to me."

"Don't bust my balls, Judy."

"And as long as you're in Wintonbury, drop off those presents at your dad's house. Hanukkah's over and you haven't even given him a card yet," she reminded him. "I know that doesn't mean much to you, but for Leonard it's a big deal."

"Anything else?"

"Yeah. Don't wreck the car."

He inched along with the traffic, the windshield wipers slapping away the snow. After he passed through Hartford, the lanes opened up. He exited in Wintonbury and made his way along the unplowed roads to the food store.

As he pushed the shopping cart down the narrow aisles, he noted two distinct types: the wild-haired bohemians who worked there and the middle-aged yuppies who shopped there. Organic food was healthy, yes? So how to explain the unsightly appearance of the patrons—their sallow complexions, their thin and frizzled hair, their shuffling gaits? Many looked like recent victims of accident or disease, limping and wheezing, loading their carts with every sort of vitamin known to the natural world. In Benjamin's opinion they would do better getting a steak and some frozen peas at the Stop & Shop down the street. How much granola and broccoli could one tolerate? Hitler was a vegetarian, he'd learned on the History Channel, and a compulsive farter.

He took his two bags from the cashier and was heading to the door when he felt a tap on his shoulder. He turned to see Audrey Martin standing before him. "Oh, hey, it's you," he said, startled, stumbling on his words. "Wow, what a surprise. I've been meaning—"

To his astonishment, she wrapped her arms around him. She held him tightly, her head pressed against his chest.

"Thank you," she said. "Thank you so much."

She held him like that, and after a few moments he returned the embrace. They stood in the front of the food store, people passing by them, holding each other.

He would never know what he did for her. Emily had gotten to the hospital in the nick of time, the doctor had told her. A matter of minutes, and it might have been too late. Audrey had replayed the events of that night in her mind countless times since it happened, and it all came down to the phone call. Benjamin's call. That had made the difference. Otherwise she wouldn't have been awake to hear her daughter's faint cry for help. She had taken her Valium and gone to sleep, oblivious. Emily could have died in the next room, not thirty feet away, with Audrey snoring in her bed. But he had called and let the phone ring—and ring—until she woke. He'd called her in the middle of the night, seeking what? Companionship? Sex? Someone to say good night to? It didn't matter why, only that he had done so. Nothing else mattered but for the enormity of this simple act. He had called at midnight and he had saved her daughter, and Audrey too.

"Thank you," she said again, finally releasing him, and before he could respond, she hurried off.

THE SNOW was falling harder, the temperature dropping. It took Benjamin a half hour to travel the two miles across town.

On Apple Hill Road, the houses seemed lifeless at this unsettling time of day, too early to turn on the lights but not yet dark. Bamboo reindeer and plastic Santas stood on lawns, like ghostly sentinels, brushed white by the storm.

In his father's driveway he found Franky DiLorenzo, wearing a furry-hooded parka, shoveling three inches of fresh snow off the asphalt.

"Let me help you with that," said Benjamin, getting out of the car.

Franky looked up, breathing smoky-cold air, and shook his head. "I'm retired, remember. This gives me something to do."

"You should at least let my father pay you."

He waved away the notion. "I'm happy to lend a hand. Your dad would do the same for me."

Benjamin nodded. His father would indeed. That was Leonard's primary impulse, to help out his family and friends where he could. It came naturally to him, that sort of generosity. Benjamin knew that he'd failed to live up to his father's ideal. He'd always taken care of himself above others.

"How's it going back at your old place?" asked Franky DiLorenzo.

"Ups and downs, to tell you the truth," said Benjamin. The night before, during an after-dinner argument, Judy had yelled, *You're acting like a selfish jerk, Benjamin. Haven't you learned anything? When are you going to grow up?* Yes, Benjamin figured, he would have to try harder, or at least pretend to. He would have to learn to please or placate Judy, if he didn't want to get kicked out of his house again.

Franky leaned on the shovel and stared into the down-falling snow. "I almost got married once, but it didn't work out. I figure it's better for my blood pressure in the long run, to stay single."

"You're right about that. Without a doubt."

Franky DiLorenzo leaned in close. "Did you hear about that Stacks kid?"

Benjamin frowned. "No."

Franky grinned. "I don't mean to pat myself on the back or anything. But I was right all along about that kid. Last week the cops nabbed him, red-handed. They got him breaking into Jimmie's Pizza Palace at two in the morning wheeling a jukebox into the back alley. Seventeen years old. That's the least of his crimes, I bet. You should follow up with the cops, see if they can nail him on your break-in too."

Benjamin shook his head. "Doesn't really seem worth the trouble."

"I suppose not," said Franky, although Benjamin could tell he didn't agree with him.

Franky gestured toward the bottom of the street. "Did you see the sign outside the farmhouse?"

"What sign?"

"The place is back on the market."

"Really? When did that happen?"

"Couple of days ago. I just got back from three weeks in Boca, so I've been out of the loop. But from what I've heard, it's a bit of a mystery. The guy who lives in the house across from them saw an ambulance pull into their driveway late one night, a few weeks back. A fire engine too. But since that night, they've pretty much disappeared. No one's home, as far as I can tell. Not a peep. And yesterday the posthole diggers showed up and planted that sign."

"Was there a fire?"

"No. They always call out the fire department as first responders. I'm guessing a domestic."

"A what?"

"Some kind of marital incident." Franky DiLorenzo wiped his nose, his black eyes flashing. "You're friends with her, right?"

Benjamin shrugged. "Not that close. I didn't even know they'd moved out."

He didn't tell Franky about seeing her in the food store a half hour earlier, her long and warm embrace. He didn't know what to make of that. He was surprised that she would even say hello to him, the way he'd dumped her without a word and ducked her phone calls until they stopped coming. But she had hugged him like a loved one, and thanked him with true sincerity. For what, he had no idea.

Franky pursed his lips. "I was hoping you could clear up the mystery."

"No idea."

"The house is listed at nearly the same price they paid for it," said Franky. "That's after all that money they put into renovations. I'm guessing they split up and are trying to get rid of the place, fast."

"You could be right." Benjamin pondered whether any of this might have something to do with him. Had the husband found out about their affair? Was that why Audrey had thanked him, for giving her a reason to get divorced? The way she'd described her husband, he was a man accustomed to getting his way. If he found out that Audrey was screwing around on him, he wouldn't take the news well. Sure, that could lead to some yelling, a call to the cops—a "domestic." Although Audrey hadn't looked hurt or upset. She'd looked as lovely as ever, so much so that he still felt a faint longing from seeing her. So maybe something else entirely had caused their departure. Maybe it had nothing to do with him.

"Well," said Franky DiLorenzo. "I guess it's a mystery."

"I guess so."

Franky raised his shovel toward the darkening sky, a low cover of gray. "I better finish up while it's still light."

IN THE KITCHEN Benjamin shrugged out of his overcoat and checked the hallway thermostat: eighty-six degrees. He felt woozy, coming in from the cold to the hot, airless kitchen. Why did old people like to be so warm?

"Is anyone home?"

He went down the hallway and checked the den. Leonard was asleep on the couch, an afghan tucked around his legs. Next to him, Terri Funkhouser lay sprawled in the recliner chair, knitting needles crossed on her lap, her head back. His father wheezed, she snored, a sort of conversation going back and forth. The Weather Channel played on the TV with the sound off. The floorboard radiators hissed softly. Outside a tree branch scratched against the window like a cat.

The two seemed innocent in their slumber, as if they'd been married for fifty years. Benjamin felt a mixture of emotions—sadness and love, too jumbled to clarify. Terri Funkhouser was a godsend, he knew. For the last couple of weeks, ever since Leonard came home from the rehab center and she moved into the spare bedroom, she did everything for his father. Fed him, bathed him, cooked for him. Leonard seemed almost childlike in his need for her; he became anxious when she was not near, the same way he used to act with Myra, and Benjamin wondered whether his father, in his reduced state, truly understood the difference between the two women. Did he realize that she was not Myra, not his wife?

Benjamin backed out of the room, careful not to wake them. He left the gifts on his father's desk and softly closed the door behind him.

Outside, he brushed the fresh coat of snow from his windshield. At the bottom of the street he stopped and rolled down the window to look at the farmhouse, shuttered and snowbound, the driveway and lawn untrodden. He noticed the Realtor's signpost near the stone well, the FOR SALE board swaying soundlessly in the wind. The windows were dark, the chimney cold. It looked eerily familiar, like a vision from his own unlived future, and he shivered and closed the window against the storm and drove away.

Acknowledgments

TOWARD THE creation of this book I would like to recognize the assistance of the Connecticut Commission on Culture and Tourism, the Greater Hartford Arts Council, the Millay Colony for the Arts, my editor at Simon & Schuster, Millicent Bennett, who provided invaluable guidance through multiple drafts; and the following individuals, in alphabetical order: Samantha Atzeni, Luke Blanchard, Kim Brooks, Ethan Canin, Brian Clemments, Rand Richards Cooper, Kevin Dowd, Elizabeth Ferris, Laura Fish, Katie Rose Guest, Jennifer Haigh, Esmond Harmsworth, Deborah Hornblow, Sara Lewis, Andrea Lipsky-Karasz, Rinku Patel, Darryl and Dede and Doris Pope, Shelby Smith, Don Snyder, Sally Stamos, Brian Thiem, Jennifer Vanderbes, and finally, Lynn Wilcox.

About the Author

DAN POPE has published short stories in *Crazyhorse, Harvard Review, The Gettysburg Review, The Iowa Review,* and many other literary journals. He graduated in 2002 from the Iowa Writers' Workshop. His first novel, *In the Cherry Tree,* was published by Picador USA. He lives in West Hartford, Connecticut.